I0760867

Hades

The PROMGEN files

OPERATION: LATENSIFICATION

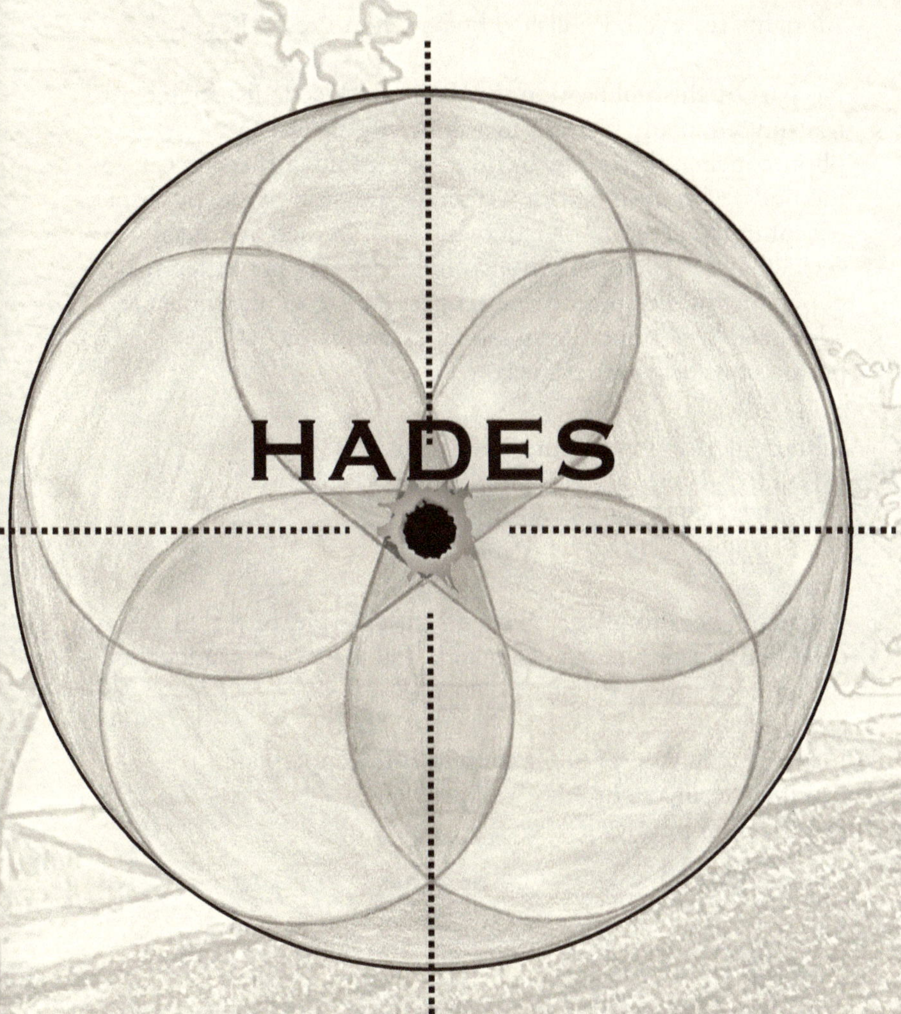

HADES

Aly Kay Tibbitts

BATTALION PRESS

FARMINGTON, UTAH

Library of Congress Control Number: **2022916110**
ISBN: **978-1-955192-05-7** (Hardcover)
978-1-955192-06-4 (Ebook)
978-1-955192-07-1 (Paperback)

The text type was set in Garamond and Copperplate.
Front cover image by Alyx Tibbitts.
Book design by Alyx Tibbitts.

Published by Battalion Press.

First Edition, Dec. 2022

To My Mom and Dad

Thank you for always being my greatest support, and for buying me A LOT of books.

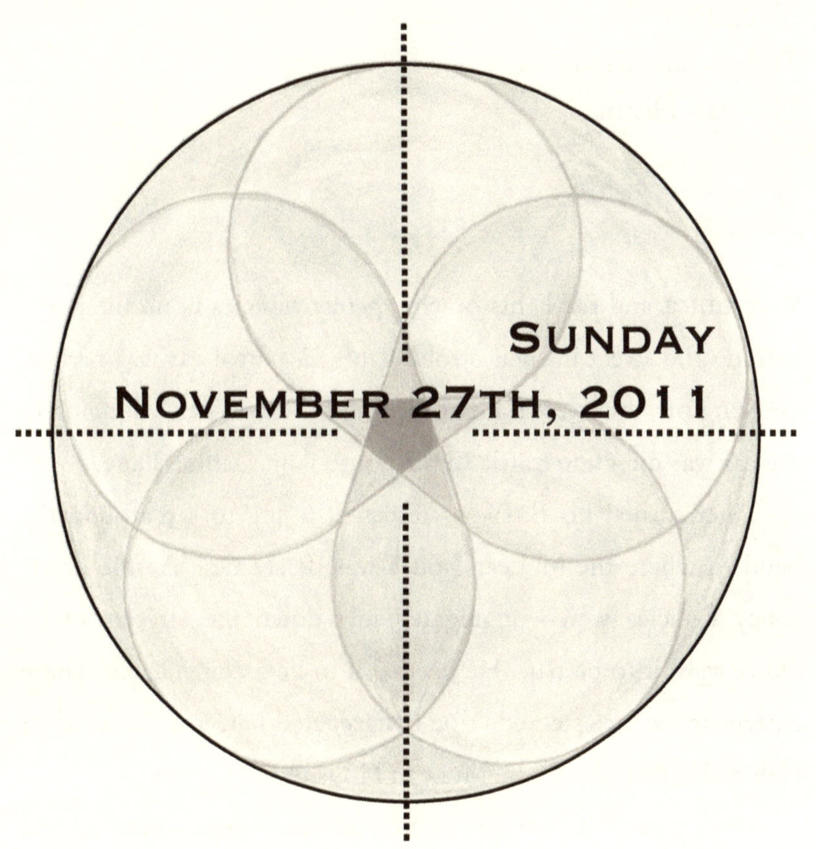

Sunday
November 27th, 2011

22:22 PST
Tracy, California
McLean Home

THE BLUE and red lights of emergency vehicles lit up the night, bathing the street in their strobe lights. A patrol car was parked, blocking off the street right at the bend. The officer belonging to the car was directing traffic to turn onto Ann Gabriel Lane.

Peter turned his BMW as directed, trying to see around the bend to where the McLean house was. It seemed like the emergency vehicles were congregated just down the street, but he didn't want it to be true. He needed it to be a coincidence. These emergency vehicles couldn't be congregated here for the incident Hall had called him to the McLean House for. If it was…

Peter parked his car just down the street from where he had been forced to turn, pulling his phone out of his pocket to try to call Alyx again while walking back down the street toward her house. He swore as he got her voicemail box again. He hung up. It had only been a few minutes since Hall had called him, and leaving voicemail number five seemed like a bad idea. He could leave it at four.

Nothing stopped him from dialing her again.

The cop on the corner was too focused on turning cars away from the street. He didn't pay any attention to the pedestrian that walked around the corner, getting past his blockade.

Past the lone officer, and around the bend, the scene could only be described as organized chaos. There were two fire trucks and an ambulance. It looked like half of Tracy's police department were present with several patrol cars parked on the street. All of their lights were on, bathing the area in a dizzying blur of blood red and blue that could barely be distinguished by each other on the houses.

Everything was almost glowing purple.

Peter hung up as he got Alyx' voicemail yet again, letting himself take a refreshing breath when he saw that Tracy's emergency officials were focused on the single story house next door to the McLeans'. He watched as a gurney was rolled out of the house carrying a black body bag that was loaded into the ambulance.

Like a moth drawn to a flame, Peter left the sidewalk, crossing the street diagonally towards the house he had been in more times than he could count any more. He may have been allowing himself to hope Alyx was fine for the first time since he'd received the phone call from her uncle, finally explaining her not answering her phone with reasonable things, instead of his fears.

"Sir!" One of the police officers called. "I am going to have to ask you to return to your house."

Peter glanced at the officer, but kept walking. "I'm just trying to get to my girlfriend's house." He replied.

"Not through here," the officer insisted, sticking his arm out to stop Peter.

Peter pointed at the house that felt more like home than his own. "It's just right there. She just got home from Virginia. I told her I'd come by."

As the officer saw where Peter was pointing, his eyes told Peter everything he needed to know. "I'm sorry. I can't let you into an active crime scene."

The officer pushed him back towards the sidewalk he'd come off of. He was saying something more to him, but he didn't hear any of it. All he could hear was the echo of two words. *Crime Scene.* Two words was all it took to knock the air out of him worse than any tackle he'd survived in Football. Two words hurt more than every punch he had taken in the name of training.

The only time he'd felt a pain like the one he felt now had been when his mom had left him with his dad, and had stopped accepting his phone calls.

That day, he'd promised himself he would never let himself feel that pain again. That day had been the reason he had never let himself get close to anyone else. He didn't want to be hurt when they left.

The officer had succeeded in pushing him back to the sidewalk. "Where did you live. I can get someone to take you home."

Peter didn't answer. He was focused on where his real home was. FBI jackets were walking in and out of the McLeans' House. He had been so focused on the local emergency vehicles, he hadn't noticed the black SUVs that were evidence of the heavy FBI presence. He recognized some of the agents walking in and out of the house. They worked with Neil.

Determined, Peter stepped off of the sidewalk again, shaking off the arm of the police officer who had still been standing in front of him. "Special Agent," he called. "I want to talk to Special Agent Neil McLean. This is his house. Where is he?"

One of the Agents broke away from the others, sticking his hand up. The police officer that had still been trying to grab Peter, stepped back, returning to what he had been doing before a persistent teenage boy had intruded on their crime scene.

Peter recognized the agent walking towards him as the agent Alyx had given her statement to after she had rescued him and the others from the house Hall had used to hold them, but he hadn't paid enough attention at the time to know his name. He had been focused on Alyx. Had he known that paying attention to his name then would help him get information about Alyx now, he may have made more of an effort.

"I'm sorry I didn't catch your name last time. I need to speak to Agent McLean." Peter said, oozing a confidence and authority he had no reason to. If his training was good for anything, it better be good for this.

"You are the boyfriend." The agent said. "Peter Carlyle."

Peter nodded his head. "Yes."

The agent stuck his hand out. "I'm Agent Carter. McLean is busy right now, but I can help you."

"Is Alyx ok? I just want to see her. I don't have to go inside, I just need to know she is ok. Maybe if she can come out for just a minute…"

Agent Carter nodded his head. "Alyx is fine. She is giving her statement right now, but if you stick around a bit, she can come out. Agent McLean mentioned something about having you take her to an uncle's for the night."

Peter nodded as he took a deep breath, not realizing he had been depriving himself of oxygen.

"Actually, he will be heading in with me."

Peter turned toward the voice, seeing Dylan Hall walking up towards the FBI agents. His voice was commanding, but Peter could still see the hesitation exuding from both the police officers and the FBI agents.

Hall stuck his hand out towards Agent Carter. "Deputy Director Dylan Hall. I believe Neil let you know I was coming."

"Of course." Agent Carter shook Hall's hand. "If you don't mind me asking, why is the CIA interested?"

Hall smiled. "For one, my sister is married to Neil, and I am the uncle Alyx will be staying with tonight. Second, Neil's father is my boss. We want to make sure this wasn't to get to him, especially since they just got back from visiting them. And I'm sure you remember Peter from the training mission."

Carter chuckled. "I don't think he's here for official reasons."

Hall shrugged. "Never said he was." Hall gestured for Peter to walk into the house, and the two of them passed by Carter and the other agents congregated out front to cross the threshold.

22:28 PST
Tracy, California
McLean Home

THE INSIDE of the McLean's house was defined by a cacophony of noise, the combinations of several conversations happening all at once. Despite all the voices, Peter could hear Alyx, her voice telling the version of events she witnessed. Peter wanted to turn right, and follow the sound of her voice until he found her. Hall stopped him with a firm grasp on his arm.

"Before you go check on her, Neil and I need you for a moment." Hall told him, motioning for him to follow him up the stairs.

Peter had never been upstairs before. Going upstairs had always seemed like an invasion of privacy. Yes, he felt at home in the house. He knew where they kept their dishes. He would volunteer to set the table for dinner. He would get himself water. On occasion, he had even helped Alyx cook or empty the dishwasher. He had watched movies with the McLean family. The week before they had gone to Virginia, he had even gone to the downstairs guest bedroom to get a blanket for Alyx to use while they cuddled on the couch to watch a movie. But going upstairs felt like something entirely different. Upstairs wasn't a shared space. It was where their private spaces were.

Not to mention Neil had made things abundantly clear on the rules of his house, and how he expected Peter to behave while he in this house. He had also been clear on how he expected Peter to treat his daughter. What Peter had gotten from the conversation was that Alyx' parents expected him to respect Alyx, her choices, and their rules. In return, he would have their respect and love.

Going upstairs felt like a breach of that respect.

Once he and Hall had reached the top of the stairs, Peter looked around, and knew immediately that Alyx had been the target. The door at the very top of the stairs was open, and led to a large room which was clearly the master bedroom. There weren't any FBI agents there. To the left, there was a hallway with three doors: two on one side, one across from them. The second door down the hallway was open, and the light was on. As he and Hall walked down the hall, four FBI jackets came out of the room, each of them carrying evidence bags. Hall moved to the right to let them pass, so Peter did the same, looking in the clear bags they carried. His eyes followed the bag the last agent carried, unable to look away from the small pink teddy bear, and the stuffing exploding from the bullet hole in its head.

Peter tore his attention away from the bear as the agent carrying it went around the corner and headed down the stairs. He turned back just in time to watch as Hall walked into the room the FBI agents had come from. Peter followed. Once he reached the door, he stopped at the threshold, unable to continue. Instead, he glanced around the room, taking it all in.

It was amazing how much he could learn about the girl he loved by seeing her room. It was mostly as expected. She kept a small bookcase next to her desk with her textbooks and other reading books on it. Missing from that shelf was the French book the two of them had been using to study. That little piece of information would have made him smile, knowing she took it with her to Virginia, but the circumstances stopped him. She had her bed in the corner opposite the window, the head of the bed on the same wall as the door so she could wake up with the sun shining through the window onto her.

"They have finished processing the room, so we have it to ourselves for a couple of minutes." Peter heard Neil tell Hall. "I also made a call to Emily's captain. He wasn't sure why, but he let me borrow her for this case. She's on her way."

"It's about time she use her talents to help." Hall scoffed.

"Be nice." Sarah said from the door behind Peter. He turned to see Sarah with Emily.

Emily gave Peter a sad smile as she went around him to get into the room. As she walked across the room to inspect the holes in the window, Sarah stayed next to Peter, putting a comforting hand on his back the way a mother would.

"I'm pretty sure Neil called you for your computer expertise." Hall criticized. "We could use your help trying to track the call Alyx received just before the shooting, not analyzing ballistics."

Emily straightened, looking her older brother in the eyes. "He called me because it's my niece, who I have helped raise. And I can be useful for a number of purposes. Not only do I have a degree in Computer Science, as well as training in forensics, but I also have training in taking this kind of shot."

"I warned him." Sarah whispered to Peter. "But no one ever listens to the older sister. How would I know anything? It's not like I've been through it before or anything."

"How long has it been since you've shot your rifle?" Dylan asked. "Remind me, I forgot."

"You assume I don't spend my fair share of time at a range practicing with all of my weapons." Emily shot back. "It has most definitely been since you. And don't forget that I've worked hard for every promotion I've gotten, unlike you. How is the new office, Deputy Director?"

"See, I'm willing to admit I'm rusty. That's why I called Carlyle." Dylan replied.

Emily laughed. "No, you invited *Carlyle* here because you thought you could use this as a training opportunity. You also knew seeing his girlfriend's room with bullet holes, you could convince him to go along with whatever protection detail we develop, because Alyx will hate it otherwise." She shrugged. "But fine, I'll play." She turned to Peter. "What do you see?"

The room went silent as all eyes settled on him. Peter took a deep breath, stepping further into the room. Looking at the window, he could see two distinct bullet holes. He knew from the evidence bags that had been carried from the room, one of those bullets had gone through the teddy bear. His first impressions of Alyx' room screamed maturity; the teddy bear didn't fit with everything else he had seen.

Peter scoured the room looking for any hint as to where the teddy bear had been, and to figure out where the second bullet went. He glanced at the bed, noticing that the blankets looked like the bed had been made, but the pillows were askew, and there was a hole in the wall with score marks from where the evidence techs had dug the bullet out. So the teddy bear had come from the bed.

His eyes returned to the window, trying to mentally calculate where the second bullet had gone. He turned around, seeing a second hole in the door frame. "Where was Alyx when the shooting happened?" He asked quietly.

He already knew the answer, but he hoped he was wrong.

"In the doorway." Neil replied.

Peter closed his eyes, giving himself a moment to compose himself before sharing what he saw.

"It was symbolic." He said beneath his breath. He turned around to look at the others. "From the neighbor's roof, the shooter would have had a clear shot at everything in this room."

Peter took a deep breath. The shooter had only hit what he wanted to, and everyone in this room knew it.

"He chose his targets very carefully. First, he shot the doorframe. It was probably close enough that Alyx felt the heat of it as it flew past her. The second shot was meant to show that he missed intentionally. It didn't matter what it was, as long as it showed his skill. He chose the teddy bear out of symbolism. They killed her innocence. That's why he missed. They are playing a psychological game."

Peter watched as the adults looked at him. They were seeing all the same evidence he was, but they didn't seem to believe that what he had said was true. Then again, he had different experiences that shaped how he interpreted what they were all seeing.

"I've spent most of my life battling an egotistical psychologist. I know what it looks like when someone is trying to break you." He added.

"And who said he missed?"

Peter spun as he heard Alyx' voice. He wanted nothing more than to just envelop her in a giant hug. His relief was overwhelming. He may have been told that she was alive, and he may have heard her voice when he walked into the house, but finally seeing her eliminated any doubts he had that she was alive.

But he heard something in her tone he hadn't heard from her before: fear. As he looked at her, searching her face for what she wasn't saying, he saw that same fear in her eyes mixed with pain. He slowly let his eyes drop, seeing the bandage on her left arm.

Who said he missed.

Peter's heart clenched, realizing what she was saying. His observation still rang true. It was symbolic to shoot the teddy bear. It told everyone that they had been deliberate in their attack. But they weren't afraid to hurt Alyx while they were at it.

That terrified Peter more than he wanted to admit.

He couldn't move his eyes from her arm. They were glued to the horizontal line of blood that had seeped through the gauze of the bandage. Staring at the dark color, he wished he could take her pain. Just the thought of her suffering made it hard for him to breath.

Sarah walked over to her daughter. "Let's check your bandage, then send you to Thane and Chelsi's to get some sleep." She led her daughter back out of the room, towards the master bedroom just at the top of the stairs.

Peter couldn't help but watch her leave.

"We got this." Emily said, causing Peter to turn and look at her. "Someone should be with her. Sarah might be her mother, and her bedside manner is descent, but it's always nice to have someone there to comfort you."

Peter nodded. He didn't wait for another invitation to leave, immediately following where he had seen Sarah taking Alyx.

He paused in the doorway of the master bedroom, watching

as Sarah came out of the attached bathroom with medical supplies in hand. She nodded her head toward Alyx on the bed, which Peter took as an invitation. He quickly entered the room, sitting down on the bed on her right side, sliding his fingers through hers.

Alyx closed her eyes as she mom worked, her medical training taking over as she effortlessly took care of her daughter's wound. He felt Alyx tense any time what her mom did hurt. Occasionally, she would squeeze the hand that he was holding. Peter didn't say anything. He didn't voice his suspicion that Sarah had chosen nursing when she left the CIA for exactly this eventuality. He didn't make Alyx promises that it would be ok, because he didn't know if it would be. Alyx didn't need words or promises right now. She just needed him. She just needed support. And Peter knew that. So he sat there. He let her squeeze his hand, even when she squoze too hard and it hurt. When she closed her eyes tighter than she ever had, and she desperately tried not to tense her entire body or jump away from her mom in pain, he leaned his head in close to hers, ran his free hand through her hair, and gave her a kiss on the top of her head to give her something else to focus on.

Meanwhile, he focused on how he would keep her safe from something like this happening to her again.

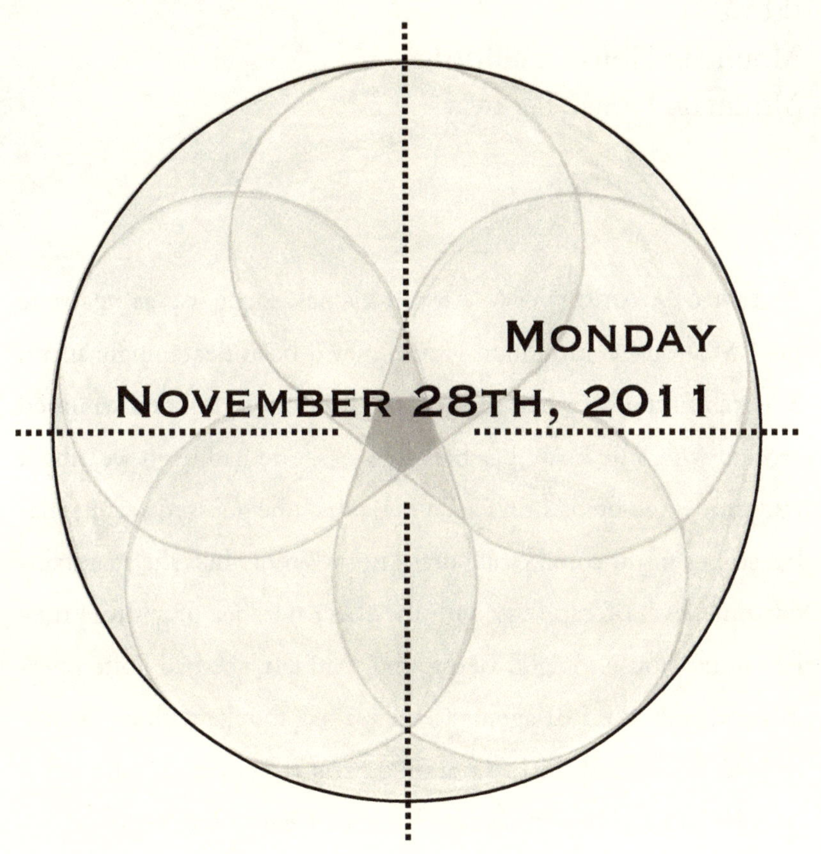

Monday November 28th, 2011

0:15 PST
Mountain House, California
Mountain House Parkway

PETER GLANCED over to Alyx in his passenger seat as he drove his BMW out to Mountain House. She'd been deafeningly silent. She was sitting with her head on the window, right hand wrapped around where he knew her bandage was. She had been wearing a tank top when he had first seen her, which he guessed was probably so her mom could easily dress her wound while she maintained some level of modesty with the sheer number of visitors they had in the house tonight. Before they had left, she had gotten permission from the FBI agents to pack a bag to take with her to her cousin's house, and she had put on a sweat shirt over the tank top.

She had grabbed the Senior hoodie he gave her.

Peter wasn't taking any chances. Everyone was pretty sure that the sniper had taken off, and that Jackson didn't have anyone stationed around the house, but Peter didn't want to take the risk. It was late, but he had aimlessly driven around Tracy for an hour, ensuring he didn't have a tail. Even so, he decided it would be best to take the long way to Mountain House where her cousins lived. With the back roads he was taking, he was glad as he found an extended period of time he didn't have to shift the car's manual transmission. Not only did it finally give him a chance to relax his left foot, but he could reach his right hand across the car and intertwine his hand with Alyx'.

She shifted her head against the window, looking down at their joined hands and tightened her grip on his.

This had been what he was trying to prevent when he decided to give the files to Hall. This is what he feared would happen if he didn't give Hall what he wanted. When Hall had told him Alyx had thwarted his plans, he had wanted nothing more to scream at her the next time he saw her. He wanted her to understand what was at risk. In the end, he didn't. He was too glad that she had forgiven him, and come to rescue him. Besides, Hall ended up with access to the files.

No one had wanted to admit this moment was inevitable. It was never *if* the Circle of Fifths found Alyx. It was always *when.*

Peter briefly wondered if Alyx was thinking about the same thing. Maybe she regretted not letting everyone make the sacrifices they wanted to in the name of her safety. But Peter knew Alyx better than that. Having thoughts like that were more selfish than Alyx could ever be.

"I might have to fight Thane for it, but I am going to drive you to school tomorrow." Peter told her.

"I'm not going to school tomorrow." Alyx replied, her words almost quiet enough Peter couldn't hear them over the engine.

Peter's first instinct was to tell her he would stay with her then. If she wasn't going to school, he wasn't either. He wanted to be wherever she was right now. But he knew the school wouldn't like that. Besides, he knew her parents and her uncle. She would probably be smothered in agents from two agencies. "OK, well, I will come by and see how you're doing after school then. I will take in your assignments tomorrow, and bring you home your new ones. If you feel up to it, we can study French—"

Alyx sat up, removing her head from the window. "Michael is sending his jet for me. My parents will arrange something with the school so I can keep up with my assignments."

Peter tried to control the sadness he felt hearing her say those words. Sending her to London made sense. He himself had told her to go to London when he was waiting for Hall to kidnap him. Staying with her uncle Michael meant she was surrounded by a full-time security detail. From what he knew, the grounds of Feilds Palace were large enough Jackson couldn't reach her with his sniper from outside the grounds, and there was enough security that breaching the grounds was impossible. "That's a good idea." Peter commented. "That's probably the safest place for you."

"I don't exactly have a say." Alyx complained. She put her head back on the window, turning to face away from Peter again while she pulled her hand from his and folded it across her body.

"I should have known you would take my parents side."

Peter sighed, but let her comment return them to silence. As much as it hurt to have her yank her hand away, he needed his hand to down shift as he approached Mountain House. He turned on his signal, slowing the car to make the left hand turn to enter the development. He wound through the streets until he reached the Hall's driveway, where he pulled in and parked.

Alyx hit the button on her door to unlock the car, but Peter just locked it again with the key fob. If she tried to use the button in the car again, it would set off the alarm. Alyx turned to Peter, anger flaring in her eyes.

"Let. Me. Out."

"I'm not taking your parents side." Peter told Alyx. "If I'm honest, the selfish part of me doesn't want you to go. Going means I don't get to see you. I just made a trip to Virginia and stayed with the father who hates me just so I didn't have to go a week without seeing you. No matter what I try, I can't follow you to London." Peter paused. "But you don't know what it felt like as I walked up to your house tonight. You weren't answering your phone, and the cops were using words like *crime scene* and all I could think was that you were dead, and—" Peter took a deep breath. "If you going to London means you are safer than you are here, I will make that sacrifice. Hopefully you can return to school soon. I want to stand next to you at graduation, and many other times in the years to come. I don't want to stand alone at your funeral."

Having said his piece, Peter unlocked the car. As Alyx opened her door, Peter opened his. He walked around to the trunk, opening it to retrieve the bag she had packed, and the small backpack he kept there as well before closing it.

He followed Alyx up to the porch, his eyes on her while hers were on the door, waiting for it to open. He reached up with his free hand, brushing the bandage on her arm through the jacket. “I know you would probably hate me a little for this, but part of me wants nothing more than to take your pain away.” Peter admitted. He looked up from her arm to her eyes as she turned to him. He knew she was acting strong, but there was just enough moisture in her eyes that he could tell she was still in a fair amount of pain.

“As long as you didn’t have to feel it, I might let you.” Alyx quietly confided.

Peter set her bag down on the ground, then enveloped her in a hug for the first time tonight. Alyx nestled into his shoulder, as she wrapped her arms around him too. Peter could feel his shirt becoming wet where her face was, telling him she was letting the tears fall. He just held her. He wasn’t scared for her safety while she was in his arms.

They hadn’t knocked on the door, but the Halls were expecting them, so it wasn’t long before Peter heard someone unlock the door. Peter leaned his head into Alyx’ hair, giving her a kiss on her head before she pulled away as they heard the door open.

Alyx turned away from Peter, looking at Thane who stood just inside the now open door. She picked up her bag from the ground where Peter had set it. "Where am I sleeping?" Alyx asked.

"Chelsi's room." Thane answered, letting Alyx in the door.

"Really?" She said as she walked in.

"It's the safest place for you. No one can get to you in there."

Alyx rolled her eyes. "Yeah, because I won't survive the night. I barely survived the last time." She complained.

Thane shrugged. "You don't have many options."

Alyx glanced back at Peter, their conversation from the car coming to mind. Even with the brief eye contact, he could see how much she hated the entire situation. "I don't have *any* options," she mumbled under her breath, walking into the house and up the stairs, clearly knowing where she was going.

Thane glanced back out the door, his job of safely letting Alyx into the house complete. His eyes went to the black back-pack strap he could see coming over Peter's shoulder, and he knew. He opened the door wider, letting Peter come in, before closing the door behind him.

"You know you can't stay with her." Thane said.

Peter nodded. "I have to be close tonight though. If something else happens..."

Thane sighed. "You can stay in my room. Is the floor ok?"

"Perfect." Peter replied, following Thane up the stairs.

6:02 PST
Mountain House, California
Hall Residence

THE HALL'S dining room was oddly silent, considering the sheer number of people sitting around the table. Thane was sitting in his chair, glowering into his bowl of milk, using his spoon to push around the granulated remnants of his long gone cereal. Chelsi sat next to him, picking at the bagel in front of her, occasionally popping pieces in her mouth. Sarah finished her bowl of oatmeal, standing up to rinse it in the kitchen sink while Neil stirred his granola into his yogurt. With Sarah at the sink, Addy Hall put a comforting hand on her sister-in-law's shoulder as she walked past her on her way to the counter where there were several slices of bread lined up so she and Dylan could make lunches quickly by treating it like an assembly line.

Peter couldn't help but look at the empty chair they had left for Alyx as he ate a breakfast sandwich, wishing he had some caffeine to help fuel him today. He hadn't gotten much sleep last night. He had woken up anytime he heard the slightest noise, getting up to make sure the house was still secure and check on Alyx. After his restless night, and having to get up early to discuss the plan for today, it was the kind of morning where Peter usually indulged himself with a cup of coffee. As he glanced around the kitchen at all the people who he knew had also not slept well last night—if at all—he wondered, yet again, how they were all able to operate without coffee.

Dylan glanced at the microwave clock to check the time. "Thane, Chelsi, you should get going soon." He reminded them.

Thane got up. He had finally finished the milk in his cereal, but he left his bowl as he stormed off. Before breakfast, they had all discussed the plan for today. Every one had a very specific role to play, and Thane was less than thrilled with his.

Michael had contacted the Tracy Municipal Airport and requested the necessary permissions to have his pilot land there. Dylan and Addy would secure the airport, and once the plane landed, they would ensure it remained secure as well. To minimize the risk of the airplane becoming compromised, it would only be on the ground long enough to refuel. They also didn't want Alyx exposed any longer than necessary, so the refueling time had been calculated down to the minute, and the travel time to the airport had been subtracted from the refueling time. As soon as the plane landed and they started to refuel the plane, Dylan would contact Sarah, who would start the countdown. When she gave the signal, they would leave. She, Neil, and Peter would each drive their own cars, taking one of three predetermined routes. Before they left, they would draw straws to see who Alyx would ride with, and she would hide in the backseat.

While everyone else had an active plan in the safety protocols to get Alyx to the plane and out of the country, Thane and Chelsi had been relegated to diversion. Their part, if enacted properly, would convince anyone watching that they had Alyx with them, at least until Alyx was already on the plane. It was important, and Thane knew that, but he couldn't help but feel as though he was doing nothing. He went about his day *business as usual* while his mom, dad, aunt, and uncle risked their lives to get Alyx out of the country. Even Peter—the *boyfriend*—got to help, while Thane had to pretend everything was fine, and his cousin hadn't been shot at the night before. He had to look at her empty desk in the classes they had together and lie to his teachers and friends about why she wasn't there. He would have to say *I don't know* because it wasn't his place to tell anyone.

Thane wasn't mad because his part was unimportant. He was mad because he wanted any other job than the one he had: pretending everything was fine when it wasn't.

Chelsi stood up, popping the last bite of bagel in her mouth as she picked up her plate and carried it to the sink.

"Chels, will you do me a favor and make sure Alyx is ready?" Sarah asked, to which Chelsi nodded in reply.

6:10 PST
Mountain House, California
Hall Residence

CHELSI STEPPED through the doorway to her room, causing Alyx to glance up at her before rolling her eyes and turning away.

"Your mom sent me up to check and see if you were almost ready." Chelsi said.

She watched Alyx, hoping she would respond, but she didn't. She kept her back to Chelsi, as if ignoring her would make all her problems go away.

"We're both ready, even if Alyx doesn't want to admit it."

Chelsi turned her body towards where the voice came from, watching as Lynn slipped Peter's senior hoodie on. She looked her cousin up and down. With the danger the Circle of Fifths posed to Alyx, Lynn had insisted she come to California to help protect her. She had arrived mere hours before Alyx and her parents had returned from Virginia, and had been picked up by Addy and Chelsi. She was supposed to go the McLean's house once they got home, but before she had a chance to get a ride over, the Circle of Fifths had struck.

Having Lynn here provided them with an excellent opportunity. While Lynn wouldn't pass scrutiny close up, she looks enough like Alyx that from a distance, it might trick people. And Peter's jacket was a nice touch. More often than not, Alyx grabbed that hoodie to wear at school, especially if she was stressed. If the Circle of Fifths had been watching Alyx, as suspected, they would be expecting her to wear that jacket. Seeing Lynn in the car with Thane and Chelsi would divert any attention watching for Alyx to them while her parents and boyfriend snuck her to the airport.

"You don't look enough like me for this to work." Alyx criticized. "I don't understand why you have to take Peter's jacket for a plan that is bound to fail."

Chelsi rolled her eyes, looking at Lynn. "Don't listen to her. No one will get close enough to tell a difference until we get into Seminary, which is all the plan is. She's just going through withdrawals. I swear she hasn't been away from Peter more than a couple days since they started dating."

Alyx huffed, pushing past Chelsi to leave the room. She left behind both the suitcase she had packed for London, as well as her school backpack, which Lynn was meant to take any way.

"This is a good plan." Chelsi told Lynn. "If Alyx wasn't so mad about being made to go to London, she'd see that."

Lynn shrugged. "This was my mum's plan. If Alyx hadn't figured out that I was the target last summer, not Kate, I would have switched places with her. I was hidden so I could be a decoy." Lynn picked up the backpack. "I just wish I could have gotten here sooner. Maybe she wouldn't have gotten hurt."

Chelsi shook her head. This morning she had heard too many *if only* from everyone. Her dad. Alyx's mom and dad. Peter. Thane. Now Lynn. They all thought that if they had done something different, they could have protected Alyx. Maybe they were right. But it didn't matter now. It was too late. They couldn't go back in time and try anything else. All they could do was do their best to protect her going forward.

And try to convince Alyx to let them.

6:13 PST
Mountain House, California
Brett Avenue

BANTHUP WATCHED the Hall's house from his post down the street and around a corner. As expected, chaos had resulted from Kalen McKenzie's shots at McLean the night before. Unfortunately, in the chaos, Banthup had lost McLean. There had been cars coming and leaving the area all night. When he watched Dylan Hall, Sarah McLean, and Special Agent Neil McLean all leave the house, none of them with Alyx, he realized she must have left with someone else.

Unfortunately, they took separate cars. He could only follow one of them, and Sarah was extremely good at detecting and evading tales. Once he found his way out of the neighborhood in Livermore she'd lost him in, he had come here. It was a wild guess, but it was one he hoped would pay off. When he had started working for Hall, he had seen the work he had put into the house where he held the captured agents to make it secure, both from external breach, as well from an escape. He'd heard whispers from other agents about the Hall family's ability to secure a house. Their skills had become a legend at the agency. One of his instructors at the Farm had joked that the best way to protect an asset was to throw a bag over their head and hand them to a Hall. Supposedly they had a network of safe houses across the world. Even if you knew where they all were (and no one did), half of them were rumored to be impossible to get to. If you did get to one, you wouldn't be able to get in.

Banthup still hadn't decided if Alyx got lucky when she rescued the captured agents, if she was that good, or if her heritage made it so she knew exactly how the house had been secured.

The street was oddly void of any of the cars he would expect to be here, but if they were trying to avoid drawing attention, it should look normal. Banthup had only ever been here once before, and that had been when McLean had tricked him into following Hall's daughter who had been driving McLean's car. McLean's car had been the only car in front of the house that day, but he had seen the entire Hall family, suggesting they typically parked in the garage. If they wanted everything to appear normal, this morning should be no different.

He was betting on too many *ifs*.

Banthup ducked in his seat, watching as Derek Stevens drove past the Hall house, turned around at the end of the street, then parked in front of the house.

What was Stevens doing here?

Banthup watched him closely. If Stevens had been called here, it was most likely for good reason. Stevens hadn't trained at the Farm. He had just been a Computer Science student from the local community college Hall had hired to help him navigate Social Media. After McLean rescued the captured agents, and the mission concluded, Stevens should have signed a Non-Disclosure Agreement and returned to civilian life. Instead, he had been made a permanent part of Hall's team. Apparently he was in the Reserve Officer Training Corps (ROTC for short) at his community college, and Hall thought he was helpful enough to contact his program administrator. Instead of continuing with ROTC, Hall hired Stevens as a CIA Intern.

As Hall's Intern, Stevens should have been the one giving the Promising Generation Training Program orders. Instead, in a pathetic attempt to repair a friendship with Peter Carlyle, he often dropped everything to help him. So when Banthup saw Stevens pull out his phone and call a number in his speed dial, he had a pretty good guess who Stevens was calling.

Banthup had been right. Alyx had been brought to the Hall's house. If Stevens was here, it likely meant they were about to move her and wanted some extra protection. Everyone seemed ready to protect Alyx like she was some sort of last hope. He wouldn't put it past them to protect her using similar methods to the Secret Service protecting the President of the United States.

Then again, this was the Halls. If the legends were true, they had probably improved on the Secret Service methods.

Stevens hung up his phone. From where Banthup was watching, he could see him set the phone down somewhere in the center of the car before his eyes searched his surroundings, his hands on the steering wheel. If he had received even a fraction of the training Banthup had, Stevens should have identified Banthup's sedan down the street.

Stevens still had so much to learn.

Thane Hall's black Honda Civic pulled out of the driveway. He looked like he was just going about his day. His sister was in his passenger seat. They looked tired, but it seemed as if this was just another morning for them.

Stevens pulled out behind them, following the car down the street toward Banthup. If they were leaving the neighborhood like Banthup anticipated they were, they would turn before they reached the street Banthup was hiding on, which is why he had chosen the spot he had, but the fact that Stevens was following Thane intrigued Banthup. He watched closely as the car came towards him. Finally, as the car made the right hand turn onto the street that would take them out of the neighborhood Banthup saw her: Alyx McLean.

She was on the driver's side of the car, wearing the same jacket he had seen her wear almost constantly since telling the school she was dating Peter Carlyle. The hood was up, hiding her face, but her right hand was crossed over her body, still gripping the arm he knew Kalen was supposed to shoot.

It seemed Jackson's plan to instill fear in everyone around McLean was working. Once the shock of the attack wore off, she would be stuck in the suffocating net the people who claimed to love her put her in, and her only way out would be by joining Jackson.

Banthup pulled out, following the other two cars at a safe distance. He would play his part in Jackson's plan to perfection.

6:37 PST
Mountain House, California
Hall Residence

PETER LOCKED his phone after his phone call with Derek Stevens. Hall and Neil looked at him expectantly for the answers they all had hoped the call would give them.

"Where is Alyx?" Peter asked the other two.

Neil nodded his head to the north. "Sarah took her through the secret passage to the house next door. She's changing the dressing on her wound again."

Peter took a deep breath, pushing down the feeling he should be with her to hold her hand through the pain. Keeping her alive was more important at the moment. That was what he was doing.

He looked at Hall. "You were right. It looks like Banthup is working for Jackson. He followed Thane and Derek."

Hall rubbed his head with his eyes closed. It wasn't hard to guess what he was thinking. They had all had similar thoughts over the course of the last several hours. Their fear was feeding their self-loathing and their self-loathing was feeding their fear.

He was blaming himself for Jackson finding Alyx. He was blaming himself for hiring a double agent.

"Does he know it wasn't Alyx yet?" Neil asked.

Peter shook his head. "No. He's being careful. He parked his car in a cul-de-sac down the street. He didn't see Lynn head into the building, and even if he did, he wasn't close enough to make out that it wasn't her."

"Good. That buys us more time." Neil said. He turned to Hall. "Dylan, what do you want to do about Banthup?"

"I don't know." Hall admitted. "We are sending Alyx to London, so I'm tempted to not do anything yet. We don't know what Jackson's plan is yet. If we let Banthup think he has us fooled, we can watch him. Maybe he is the key to figuring out, and stopping Jackson."

Peter nodded. "Alyx out smarted him. There are more of us. Even if we aren't as good as Alyx, we are better than he thinks we are, and there are more of us."

"Let's not tell Alyx," Neil said. "She's not acting afraid right now, but it's only a matter of time. I don't want her taking Jackson's offer because she feels like he has her surrounded."

Peter opened his mouth, but before he could share his opinion, Hall spoke. "I agree. It's safer for her not to know." He paused for a moment, checking the time. "I am going to head to the airport to join Addy. I'll see you both in a bit."

Hall walked through the door that led to the garage.

"Come on." Neil told Peter. "Let's get over to the others."

Peter followed him into the pantry, watching as he moved boxes of pasta out of the way, then grabbed a clear container with lentils in it, and pulled it forward. Peter heard a small click, so he turned to the shelves on his right. The tiles on the floor under that shelf slid out of the way, revealing a ladder leading down.

"After you." Neil said, gesturing to the hole now in the floor of the pantry as he moved the boxes back in front of the apparent switch. Clearly the Halls never ate lentils.

As Peter climbed down the ladder into the secret passage, he couldn't help but think about Alyx' response to it. She had been beyond angry the last time she discovered her parents were keeping secrets from her, and that anger still hadn't died out yet. Her anger at them for keeping secrets had fueled her anger about being sent to London, even though he could tell the shooter had rattled her, and she was scared of staying.

The last thing her parents needed to be doing right now was keeping more secrets from Alyx. *When*—not if—she found out Banthup was working for Jackson, and everyone but her knew about it, she would be *livid.*

6:38 PST
Mountain House, California
Waterlogs Safehouse

ALYX CLOSED her eyes, trying not to wince as her mom used a syringe to create a high pressure stream of saline as she methodically irrigated the wound.

Alyx liked to think she had a pretty high pain tolerance, but it felt like her mom was testing to see how much she could really take. If her mom didn't stop soon, Alyx just might take Jackson up on his offer. Maybe he would have medical professionals that wouldn't torture her in the name of saving her life. Would it really kill her mom to use a local anesthetic?

Forget the drugs; where was Peter? He had been the only one who could be dragged away from the *investigation* last night to sit with her while her mom cleaned her wound for the second time in a matter of hours. It may not have been a medication for which a doctor could write a prescription, but being able to hold his hand while her mom tortured her almost made her forget about the pain being inflicted on her. And when he ran his fingers through her hair, placing soft kisses on top of her head—who needed prescription anesthesia?

Alyx hadn't even left for London yet, and she was already missing Peter.

Joining Jackson would be a very bad idea for one very important reason: she needed Peter, and he absolutely would not forgive her if she joined him. Once reason returned, pushing out the fear and pain, she knew why her momentary contemplation of Jackson's offer was complete insanity. There was no promise Jackson wouldn't hurt her again if she joined him. It could be a ploy to kill her. Jackson was a sadistic sociopath that enjoyed inflicting pain on others. Lynn was a testament to that.

Ally was a testament to that.

Alyx glanced at her mom as she thoroughly cleaned the wound on her arm. Sarah had done nothing but show patience and care while she made sure the graze on Alyx' arm didn't have any foreign particulates left in it. She had cleaned it, dressed it, and covered it multiple times. There was no ill intent. She was simply providing for her daughter's health the best way she could. She hadn't shown Alyx her fear, even though Alyx knew it had to be there. Jackson had taken her sister from her, and now he was trying to take her daughter... her last daughter.

Alyx watched at her mom wrapped her arm in gauze once more, realizing as she finished that just thinking of Peter had distracted her from the pain enough that she hadn't felt her finish.

Lynn and Chelsi really had no idea how much she needed Peter's jacket to get through the next few days.

"When you get to London, you will have to clean the wound again. Michael said he will have supplies ready for you, and since you likely can't do it yourself, he says he has someone who can take care of it for you." Sarah told Alyx.

Alyx nodded. "Probably Stephan. He started taking emergency medicine courses after the summer I talked Kate into repelling down into the garden from my balcony."

Sarah shook her head. At least something positive had come from that summer. Alyx had a horrible habit of getting in trouble when she was bored, which happened often when she was in London. Unfortunately, most of the trouble she caused in London was often *international* in nature. The Firework Incident when she was thirteen had, thankfully, been the last one, since it had sparked Michael giving her something to do, and had turned her summers into working summers since then.

Before then, she had caused some sort of drama every summer she was there once she ran out of things to do. There had been the summer she had helped Kate and the French President's daughter ditch their security so they could go out in the garden and play tag. Not only had it caused panic among the security teams, but the search for them had lasted for so long, it had disrupted the meeting Michael and said President were having, and the authorities had been called. Words like *kidnapping* had been tossed around before they were found.

There was also, of course, the incident Alyx referenced. She was conveniently forgetting that it wasn't just Kate she had taught how to repel that day. She had also taught Prince James. Once again, she had helped them escape their security detail, as though she hadn't learned her lesson about doing so after the incident with the daughter of the French President. When their detail had found them, they were hiding in a bathroom, an open medical kit on the sink, and Kate was using a suturing needle to sew closed a wound on Alyx' arm while the prince watched.

Sarah had wondered several times if teaching Alyx emergency medical care had been a bad idea. She had done it so Alyx would have the skills to stay alive if she was attacked and was somewhere she couldn't seek medical care, but with the way she sought out trouble, she often just used it to try and treat herself so she wouldn't get in trouble.

"If Stephan needs help, FaceTime me, ok?" Sarah told her daughter.

Alyx just gave a small nod as a reply.

Sarah started cleaning up the mess at the table. She placed the needle she had been using to irrigate Alyx' wound into a sharps container. She had a small bag next to her that she used to dispose of the no longer sterile gauze, either because it had blood on it, saline that had dripped down Alyx' arm, or just because it was the spare piece from the small pack Sarah had opened.

Alyx looked away from her mom taking the gloves she'd been wearing off, and placing it in the same disposal bag as she heard the pantry door open. Watching as Peter stepped out of the room that held a secret passage, she could feel herself relax even more than she had just thinking about him. Seeing him almost made her forget about her anger surrounding being forced to go to London, or the anger the existence of a secret passage had caused.

Almost.

Her dad walked out of the pantry behind Peter. "Dylan just left for the airport."

"Well, he better hurry." Sarah replied, tying the bag she had tossed the used gauze in. "Addy has already called. The plane arrived early."

"How long do we have?" Neil asked.

Sarah checked her watch. "We need to be in the cars in five minutes."

"Then we better pick straws." Neil commented. He went to the cupboard, pulling out the pieces of broken toothpicks that they would use when trying to divide up chores. The three lengths of wood once symbolized the camaraderie Alyx shared with her parents. Looking at the broken toothpicks, all she could see was yet another lie. Her parents made her move from this house that she loved...for what?

Broken toothpicks. Broken trust.

Neil turned his back to the others, mixing up the three sticks, and making sure to line them up in his hand so you couldn't tell which one was which length before turning back around.

"Same rules as always. Whoever has the short straw will hide Alyx in the back of the car." Neil explained, then offered his hand sporting the three tips of the toothpicks to Peter.

Peter took a toothpick, not entirely familiar with the concept of drawing straws. He had lived alone for longer than he should have at his age, and tasks in the Generation were assigned based on merit, not randomly assigned by the arbitrary choice of a small piece of wood.

Sarah took a toothpick as well, then held hers up, comparing it to the toothpick Neil still had. Neil's was shorter, so he turned to Peter, holding his out.

Peter had drawn the short straw.

Sarah turned to Alyx as Neil collected the straws, putting them back in the cupboard. She pulled her daughter into a hug. "We likely won't see you at the airport," Sarah said, holding her daughter tight. She already had a tendency to hold her daughter tighter than most mothers, having lost two children, but having almost lost her…

Neil came over, hugging both his wife and his daughter. Their growing family had quickly shrunk eleven years ago. The last thing he wanted to do was let go of their small family.

He couldn't.

He would protect his daughter by any means necessary.

With one last kiss on Alyx' forehead, he let go, allowing Sarah to do the same. "Addy took your bags with her, so they are already being loaded on the plane. Your mother and I will try to come visit for Christmas, but we have to make sure we're not followed, and we aren't jeopardizing your safety, so we'll let you know, ok?"

Alyx nodded. She didn't feel *safe* at the moment. She was feeling discarded. She felt like her voice didn't matter, even though they were discussing her life.

It was really annoying.

6:55 PST
Tracy, California
Tracy Municipal Airport

PETER PARKED his car on the tarmac next to the private plane he identified as belonging to Michael Feilds based on the tail number. Peter didn't want to know how much money had been offered to the airport to close down this runway for the couple of hours they needed it, but it had been enough that he was let onto the runway, no questions asked.

Alyx' safety was important, and clearly worth everything to her family.

Peter got out of his car, subtly doing a visual sweep of the area before pulling the lever that allowed him to tilt his seat and move it forward. He offered his hand to Alyx, who was curled up in what he knew had to be an uncomfortable position in his back seat. Alyx accepted it. He pulled her out of his back seat, wrapping his arm around her in a protective way as he led her to the plane. As they reached the stairs to board, Hall appeared at the top.

"The plane is clear. You can take her aboard." Hall reported, running down the stairs.

Peter nodded, relaxing his arm around Alyx, shifting it so he had a gentle hand resting on the small of her back, encouraging her to climb the stairs. He followed her to the top, and stepped into the plane behind her. As he followed behind her, Alyx turned to him, a hopeful look in his eye that crushed him because he knew he was going to let her down.

"Are you coming with me?"

He couldn't bring himself to vocalize his response, so he just shook his head. "I would have to be excused from school, which means reading my parents in, and it's best if they don't know." He added, "I really wish I were."

Alyx threw herself at him, wrapping her arms around his neck in a hug that he returned. They didn't know how long it would be before they saw each other, so Peter would take it while he could.

"You were right," Alyx said, her voice barely audible as it was muffled by Peter's shoulder. "Last night," she expounded, "when you said it was the beginning of a psychological war."

Peter sighed. He wished more than anything he could be wrong about that. Protecting her from physical attacks was doable. But psychological attacks were harder to protect her from. Locking her up in a palace would protect her from kidnapping and snipers, but it couldn't protect from attacks to her mind. There were so many different ways the Circle of Fifths could play with her psyche. They could call her. They could email her. They could send her messages through the news. And if the people protecting her weren't careful, their efforts to reduce their manipulations would only add to the manipulations. It was a tactical nightmare. And already, her parents had opted to keep secrets, which he knew would backfire in the worst way.

"Jackson called me last night before his sniper took the shot. When I told him I wouldn't work for him, he said *we'll see*." Alyx added. "I don't know what he's planning, but I'm terrified I'm not prepared to withstand his attacks." She confessed.

Peter rubbed Alyx' back, not backing out of the hug. Alyx would be the one to end the hug, not him. "You are always surprising us with your strength." He comforted. "If anyone is strong enough to withstand the Circle of Fifths techniques, it's you."

Alyx shook her head. "I was shot at less than 12 hours ago, and I have already seriously considered joining him more times than I'm willing to count." She admitted. "The only thing that stopped me from calling him back and accepting his offer was the thought of you."

"Then think of me often." He joked, trying to get her to smile, to laugh. They both needed some levity at the moment.

"That's going to be hard to do without your jacket." She grumbled.

Peter placed a soft kiss on the top of her head. "I'm sorry. I will make sure to get it back to you as soon as possible." He promised. "Until then, I have something else to give you."

Alyx backed away, looking up at Peter. "You do?" She asked.

Peter nodded. He moved his right hand from her waist where his hands had fallen when she backed out of the hug, but left his left hand. He reached into his pocket, pulling a keychain out of his pocket. It looked like one of those souvenirs you could pick up in the airport gift shop, with a miniature license plate attached to a chain and key ring.

"I saw this in the airport as I was flying back, and it reminded me of our date, so I bought it." Peter told her as he placed it in her hand. "My plan was to originally give it to you when I saw you at school today, but since that's not happening…"

Alyx stared down at the keychain Peter had handed her while he placed his hand back on her hip, keeping the two of them close. It was a miniature Virginia license plate with the state's tourism slogan where the number would be on a real one: Virginia is for Lovers. Next to the slogan was a red heart.

"The best part is I got two. I put mine on my backpack so I will have it with me everyday." Peter told her. "Whenever you need to, hopefully you can look at this and remember that we are fighting for our future."

"Our future is Virginia?" Alyx teased.

Peter smiled, glad that Alyx was in a mood to tease him. "No. Virginia is where we planned our future."

Alyx smiled contently, wrapping her arms around Peter's neck, the key chain tightly gripped in her hand. "Remind me what this future looks like."

"Well first, we are going to graduate from high school on your birthday." Peter said. Thinking about their future would be a good distraction from the trauma Alyx clearly didn't want to remember at the moment. "We are going to take a gap year together. You are going to apply to Oxford in September, interview in December, and get your acceptance in January."

"And then?" Alyx asked.

Peter smiled. "You start your fancy degree at Oxford. I come visit you on breaks. On one of the trips, I surprise you with a ring. We graduate. We get married. And we figure it out from there."

Dylan stepped into the plane. "Plane is fueled." He announced to the them, before stepping through to the cockpit.

Peter took a deep breath, kissing her on her forehead. "I love you so much."

Alyx stood up on her toes, bringing her lips to his. She gave Peter a soft, slow kiss. "I love you too," she whispered.

Peter placed another kiss on her forehead. "Stay safe for me."

Alyx nodded, dropping her arms from Peter's neck.

Peter tucked Alyx' hair behind her ear, giving her one last quick kiss. He started walking away, turning to look back at Alyx as he reached the door. Dylan came out of the cockpit, placing a hand on Peter's back, letting him know it was time to leave.

Alyx watched as they disembarked, Michael's stewardess closed the door, and a member of the ground crew rolled the staircase away. "We will be taking off momentarily," the stewardess told Alyx. She recognized it for what it was: a barely disguised request for Alyx to sit down and buckle her seatbelt. So Alyx did just that.

Not like she had much of a choice anyway.

7:50 PST
Tracy, California
John C. Kimball High School

Banthup stopped his car in the school parking lot a few rows over from Thane Hall's car. For a group of people who were agency legends, and were supposed to be the best at protecting people, it had been too easy to follow them.

He watched as the passengers exited the car. Thane and Chelsi exited the front seat, moving around to the trunk to retrieve their bags, leaving Banthup to watch the back seat door on the driver's side. As it opened, and the girl in Carlyle's jacket got out, however, he understood why it had been so easy to follow the CIA director's son. When she got out, he realized why it was never a good idea to underestimate the Halls.

Because the girl in the back seat, wearing Carlyle's jacket, was not Alyx McLean.

Worse, he didn't know who it was, where she had come from, and when she had arrived.

The possibility of the Halls being prepared for a situation just like this was looking more and more likely. If they were prepared for an attack on Alyx already, now that the attack had happened meant they would be all the more prepared.

Maybe Jackson wasn't as unpredictable as he though he was.

Banthup pulled out his phone, snapping a couple of photos of the girl getting out of the car. She had a familial resemblance to Alyx, but wasn't a family member he had seen thus far while studying Alyx. If there were more players in this game, Jackson needed to know.

Banthup waited until the three people entered the campus, then turned his car out of the parking lot.

8:02 PST
Tracy, California
Circle of Fifths Safehouse

FROM THE street, the flurry of activity in the Circle of Fifths safe house on Young Court was well hidden. Kalen McKenzie had occupied the house since his uncle Phillip Jackson had bought the house a couple of months earlier. Nosy neighbors watching the new owners only saw the coming and going of two young men: Kalen McKenzie and Timothy Banthup.

As Banthup stepped into the house, dodging a man in grey fatigues who was carrying a box, he couldn't help but think about what the neighbors would think now. When he had pulled up, there wasn't any indication that anything had changed. Despite the facade of nothing new from the street, the inside felt completely different.

Banthup stopped in the kitchen as he watched Kalen come walking out of a hallway, using a towel to dab the sweat off of his face. Banthup smiled at Kalen as he moved out of the way of another agent.

"I see you aren't alone anymore." Banthup snarked.

"Now that McLean has been found, it's all hands on deck until we break her and convince her to join us." Phillip Jackson said, stepping around Banthup towards Kalen. He gave his nephew a pat on the shoulder. "You better have an update for me." Jackson said, turning to face Banthup. "Where is McLean now?"

Banthup took a deep breath. "I don't know. At 06:15, Thane Hall left his house in his car. His sister was in the passenger seat, and who I thought was Alyx McLean was in the back seat. Stevens was called over. He was the follow car. I followed them to the church, where they go every morning for some boring extra curricular class, and then to the school."

"She went to school?" Kalen asked incredulously. "She's either braver than I thought, or stupid."

Jackson narrowed his eyes. "I take it the Halls didn't make it so easy for you."

Banthup shook his head. "Even though Sarah lost me in Livermore last night when I tried to follow her to where they were keeping her daughter, they used a decoy. When they parked at the school and I saw them get out of the car, this girl climbed out of the backseat." Banthup pulled up the picture he had taken on his phone and showed it to Jackson.

"Aw, yes. Lynn Feilds. She is the daughter of Ally Hall. The cousin of Alyx and the other two children in the car. She has been a decoy since birth. I see she has recovered from our encounter enough to return to work." Jackson commented. "I will admit, I didn't anticipate Lynn would be a player again so soon. I underestimated her." Jackson took a deep breath. "Do you know where Alyx is?"

"No. I don't know if Alyx was in the car when she left the Hall's house and she switched with her cousin at the Church, or if it was her cousin the entire time. If she switched at the church, then I know where she was last night, but after Sarah lost me, I had to guess as to where they would take her, so I don't even know if I was watching the right spot." Banthup admitted.

"And they haven't contacted you to read you in on her security detail?" Jackson asked.

"No. With Stevens being called over to be the follow car, my guess is Carlyle will insist on being with her. He is the best trained member of the Promising Generation." Banthup reported.

Jackson nodded. "I'll keep that in mind as I am making plans." He looked at Kalen who was still just leaning against a countertop. "Shouldn't you be getting ready?"

"I thought you would want me here in case Banthup's update meant you had an assignment for me." Kalen replied.

"Someone is jealous." Banthup quipped.

Kalen shot Banthup a dangerous look.

"Banthup, you are dismissed." Jackson said.

Banthup nodded and left, leaving Jackson and Kalen alone. The rest of Jackson's operatives cleared the room without being asked, his tone when dismissing Banthup enough to cease the nonstop stream of operatives that had been swarming in and out of the kitchen all morning.

"I gave you an assignment. Or did you forget?" Jackson asked with a demeaning tone.

"You asked me to enroll at Kimball. But that was before your double agent lost Hall's trust." Kalen pointed at where Banthup had disappeared. "He had one mission, and that was to keep an eye on McLean after I shot her, which he failed. Banthup was already undercover at the school. Punish him with that boring assignment. I'm more use to you here, following when needed, and training for the next time you need me to take a shot at McLean."

"There won't be any more shooting at McLean." Jackson said. "We need her alive."

Kalen stepped closer to his uncle. "I thought the plan was to make her unsafe. Cause her to become mentally unstable. Fragile. How are you supposed to do that if you won't let me shoot at her. Isn't that the reason you bought a house that borders on the school? To tell her *I can get to you here too*?"

"If you think you can do a better job of leading this mission than me, by all means, lead it." Jackson growled.

"You're the one that raised me. I'm just applying the skills you taught me." Kalen said.

"You remind me of your mother." Jackson mumbled.

Kalen's face darkened. "Don't compare me to her."

Jackson got in Kalen's face. "Then stop acting like her." Jackson stood up, backing away from Kalen. "I need you imbedded at Kimball for a reason. She can connect you to me. No one else can. She might not like Banthup, but she doesn't know he is working for me. She knows you are the one that shot at her. You destroyed her sense of security in her own home. What do you think it will do to her when she sees you eating lunch with her friends?"

"I understand." Kalen conceded.

"Good. If she shows up at school, I want you to keep your distance, at least for now. Today, I want you to identify which of her friends you are going to get close to. Which of her friends will let you in? What angle will allow you to successfully infiltrate?"

"Yes sir." Kalen said before leaving the room, recognizing his dismissal.

Jackson nodded, waiting until Kalen was out of the room to let his façade fall, and the frown appear. Kalen reminded him more and more of his sister the older he got. He too often showed his emotions, and doubted his orders too often. Ultimately, his sister had given herself over to remorse, and had used that remorse to betray not only her family, but the Circle of Fifths. If she hadn't betrayed them, she wouldn't have had to make the sacrifice she did.

Jackson shook it off and left the room himself. His sister had deserved exactly what she had received, and her son was better off for it. Kalen wouldn't make his mother's mistakes.

8:13 PST
Tracy, California
John C. Kimball High School

THANE MADE eye contact with Peter from across the cafeteria as he walked in. He was part of the security detail taking Alyx to the airport, so his being here should have meant she had made it safely. Still, Thane was asking the question he couldn't out loud with the eye contact.

Peter gave the almost imperceptible nod in response.

Alyx made it to the plane, and the plane had safely taken off.

"I wonder if Peter knows where Alyx is. She hasn't replied to any of my texts." Carlie commented. "He was with her in Virginia, so if he's back, that means their flight wasn't cancelled."

"How cute is that?" Savannah asked. "How do you find someone like him? I mean flying out to Virginia because you are going to be in Virginia."

"He was in DC, visiting his dad." Thane corrected.

Lynn rolled her eyes. "Don't be daft. DC is so close to Virginia it's not even funny."

Carlie smiled at Lynn. "I knew I would like you."

Lynn just shrugged. She wasn't here to be liked by Alyx' friends, but it wouldn't hurt.

"Did you hear that he took her for a walk through a park near her grandparents' house, and they had a picnic?" Savannah added. "That boy has some serious game. No wonder Alyx fell in love with him. I'd choose him over a prince too?"

"Prince?" Lynn asked. "You don't mean James do you?"

Savannah nodded. "Yeah! Do you know him too?"

"Well, yeah." Lynn replied. "He accompanies his dad on business on occasion. He's getting old enough he usually stays with his dad in my dad's office as they talk, but sometimes he comes and spends some time with Kate and I. I didn't know Alyx chose Peter over James."

"Didn't you see the tabloids?" Savannah asked.

"Some of them." Lynn laughed. "You don't take what they say seriously do you?"

"It's less what the tabloids said, and more what Alyx had to say about them." Kaden interjected.

"What did she say about them?" Lynn asked, curious to see how her cousin had diffused the media crisis they had been trying to mitigate back at home.

"She said that she was friends with James, but they both liked different people." Savannah told Lynn.

Lynn narrowed her eyes. "I didn't know he liked anyone. But

Alyx said he did? Did she say who. Does she know who?"

"She implied she did." Kaden reported. "Never told us who."

"I'm going to go talk to Peter." Carlie interrupted, standing up abruptly.

Carlie skirted around the cafeteria tables, heading towards where Peter was sulking. "Hey Peter, do you know where Alyx is? Thane said she's not going to make it to school today, but she's not replying to any of my texts."

"Something happened last night. She won't be at school for a little bit." Peter replied vaguely.

"Oh my! Is she ok?"

Peter took a deep breath. "She's fine, just shaken up."

"What happened?"

"You know, you should really ask Alyx. It's not my place to say." Peter replied.

"But she's not replying to my texts." Carlie complained.

Peter shook his head, grabbing his backpack and standing up. "I'm sorry. Just give her some time. I'm sure she will reply once she feels like she can talk about it."

Peter walked away, leaving Carlie standing there awkwardly at the table with his friends.

"Is he usually like that?" She asked a group of kids she had never hoped to associate with.

"Nope." One of the cheerleaders replied. "The last time he was like this was when he was fighting with Alyx right before he was kidnapped."

Carlie nodded. She remembered the fight. Alyx had told them they were dating when that fight started. She had been pretty mad at him. She never told Carlie why. But if the last time he had acted like he was now was when he thought he might lose Alyx…

How bad was this thing Alyx had been through? And why wouldn't she tell Carlie about it?

9:18 PST
Tracy, California
John C. Kimball High School

KALEN PULLED a notebook out of his backpack, setting it on his desk before pulling out a pen. He flipped to the back of his notebook, finding the page with the name *Thane Hayes* at the top. He started a list on the paper:

THANE HAYES

THANE HAYES IS THE SAME THANE THAT WORKED WITH BANTHUP
- DYLAN HALL'S SON

- PRO: IF I CAN GET HIM ON MY SIDE, HE WOULD BE INVALUABLE
- CON: HIS LOYALTYES LIE WITH HIS FATHER AND FAMILY
  - WOULD BE HARD TO TURN HIM
  - HIS LOYALTY TO MCLEAN MIGHT SUPERSEDE ANY CONNECTION I MAKE

Kalen stared at the small list he'd made about the first of Mc-Lean's friends. After observing Thane before school, it was clear he was a loyal person once you broke through to his inner friend group. The person he was in class was much different than the person he was with his friends. None of his classmates had broken through to be gifted with his loyalty. If Kalen could do it, it would make him the strongest ally he could possibly have out of all of McLean's friends. Unfortunately, gaining entrance to her friend group didn't seem plausible.

Kalen glanced over as a dirty-blond young man sat down next to him and began pulling his things out. He had fuzzy memories of a boy he played with when he was little. He shrugged it off, focusing on the binder the young man had pulled out. Slid into the clear plastic cover was a picture of McLean in the uniform Kalen recognized as for the tennis team from the research that had led him to Tracy in the first place.

As the young man placed his backpack on the ground, he noticed a Virginia keychain on one of the zipper pulls. It was the only splash of color on the otherwise black backpack.

"You been to Virginia?" Kalen asked, pointing at the souvenir.

The young man looked up at Kalen. "I have. Just got back. I went to visit my dad in DC for Thanksgiving, so I made the trip to see my girlfriend, who was staying with her family for the week."

"I just moved here from Virginia." Kalen admitted. "I'm kind of missing the snow, and the beautiful fall colors."

The young man nodded. "The fall colors were gorgeous. I took a picture of my girlfriend using the trees in the area as the back drop. I can't wait to have it printed, so I can add it to my binder."

"Is that your girlfriend?" Kalen asked.

He nodded. "She plays tennis here."

Kalen schooled his features just like his uncle had taught him to, not letting his face betray his excitement. Banthup had talked a lot about some guy named Carlyle that was dating McLean. If he could get close to him, he would be much closer to annihilating the security detail around McLean.

"What part of Virginia did you visit?"

"McLean. I didn't explore very much, I must admit." Carlyle paused. "I'm Peter, by the way."

"Kalen," he replied.

10:05 PST
Tracy, California
John C. Kimball High School

KALEN WALKED across campus towards his next class with a smile on his face. He didn't think using Peter to get to McLean was going to be any more plausible than using Thane, but Peter had opened up to him, if only just a bit. He suspected Peter's loyalties lied with McLean, more than even their training program, if what Banthup had reported was true. Depending on the timeline his uncle had set for Kalen to infiltrate McLean's friend group, he wouldn't have enough time to try to gain Peter's trust, but if he found someone easier to manipulate, Peter would make a good ally among her friends.

With his evaluation made on the two spies who were in Alyx' inner circle, he felt pretty good about finding someone easier to manipulate.

Kalen walked into the next class on his schedule: Intro to Psychology. It was the same class that McLean's friend Carlie Udall was in. Even if she wasn't useful to him, he had a feeling the class would be. Jackson was playing a psychological battle against McLean, and Kalen didn't understand half of the moves. Maybe this class would help him understand.

Kalen lined up at the back with the rest of the students, waiting for the teacher to tell them where they were sitting for the next unit. He knew where he was going to sit, because Jackson had one of his computer hackers manipulate the seating charts to make sure Kalen was next to the person he needed to be to fulfill his mission, but he played by the rules, waiting to see who was going to sit to the left of him.

When the teacher called Carlie's name, Kalen watched as a girl with straightener-straight mid-length black hair with bleached blond highlights walked up to take her seat. As Kalen's name was read, he too made his way up to sit next to Carlie. He looked over at her, which she saw and greeted with a large smile. "My name is Carlie," she said.

"I'm Kalen," he replied. He tried to return her smile, momentarily lost in her hazel-colored eyes, that stood out sitting against her caramel colored skin.

"You're new right? Where did you move from?" She asked.

"Virginia," Kalen answered. "I'm missing the snow."

"Yeah, we don't have much of that here." She laughed.

Carlie's laugh was infectious. Kalen had only been talking to her for a few seconds, but already he could tell that she was a happy, bubbly person. You couldn't be around her and *not* be happy.

How could she be friends with someone as awful as McLean?

"What lunch do you have?" Carlie asked.

"I believe my councilor told me I have first." Kalen lied. Just like the seating charts, his classes had been carefully orchestrated to make sure he had the same lunch as Alyx and her friends.

Carlie smiled. "So do I! If you would like, and don't have anyone else to sit with, you can come sit with me and my friends."

Kalen returned the smile. Maybe it would be easier than anticipated to work his way into Alyx' friend group. It was only third period, and already he had an invitation to join them at lunch. "I would love to, but I will have to take a rain check. Because of the move, I'm a bit behind in some of my classes, and my teacher offered to let me come in at lunch to fill in the gaps. Maybe the offer will still be open when I'm caught up?" Kalen asked.

Carlie nodded. "Always." She turned toward the board as the teacher turned the projector on and gave the class a warm-up, asking for a summary of the sleep tracker they had kept over the break. As the teacher walked toward him to give him a modified assignment, he knew this would be his favorite class.

14:45 PST
Tracy, California
Circle of Fifths Safehouse

Banthup stomped through the house to the garage where Kalen kept his in-home gym equipment. He walked straight past the weights and treadmill, heading for the punching bag. He threw one, two, three punches, not caring that his hands weren't wrapped. He threw another quick succession of punches, feeling some of his frustration leave through his fists. All he needed was an hour session with the bag, and the pain in his fists would make him forget why he was angry.

Kalen walked in behind him, throwing a roll of wrap at Banthup's head. "At least wrap your hands. I don't want to clean your blood off the bag."

"I want to kill her. I swear, if it takes too long to break her, I might try." Banthup muttered.

Kalen smiled. "It's harder than it looks. Trust me. I've tried."

"You were alone with her for what, like five minutes?" Banthup argued, starting to wrap his left hand.

Kalen folded his arms, leaning against the wall. "In those five minutes, she fought me, beat me, knocked me out, and left me for dead. I have been fighting to get back in my uncle's good graces since."

"Well, she not only attacked me, breaking my nose and leaving me in the doorway while she saved her boyfriend, but she tricked me. And now I have to *protect* her. They won't tell me where she is, or when they are bringing her back from *wherever*, but they are assigning me to take some of her classes. Have you seen her class schedule?"

"You're not the only one undercover at the high school." Kalen rolled his eyes.

Banthup scoffed. "You mean your assignment to take all of the easiest classes that her friends are in? I have to take Statistics, Calculus, and AP US History. When they said it was all the classes no one was in, I should have known it was the hardest ones. Oh, and here is the real kicker. I have to start the classes before she even gets back," he ranted.

"You think McLean is annoying, but you haven't met her friends," Kalen commented. "Thane is antisocial and off-putting, but that is expected considering who his father is. Peter is—"

"Smug and condescending," Banthup finished as he tucked in the loose ends of the wrap so they wouldn't come undone.

"I was going to say not awful, but sure. You've spent more time with him. Kaden is eccentric, and way too much for me to even understand. Not to mention his name is so close to mine, people are already confusing the two of us. And Savannah talks a lot. She's useful for gossip, but not much else. Also, if Peter is smug and condescending, Savannah is extremely artsy and knows it. Half the class I spent with her, she told me everything I was doing wrong. By the end I wanted to strangle her."

"McLean has another friend too. Carlie, I believe was her name…" Banthup commented, starting to wrap his right hand.

"Carlie is—" Kalen started, but cut off as Jackson entered the garage.

"Progress report," he demanded. "Kalen, you first."

Kalen sighed. "Any of her friends would provide adequate access to McLean. They all eat lunch together. Befriending Peter would be the most beneficial, with a friendship with Thane being close behind. Unfortunately both of them are spies, and are by definition less trusting. Working to gain their trust and loyalty, especially loyalty that trumps their loyalty to McLean would take time that I'm not sure you would give. Her other friends are all much more welcoming, and quick to give their friendship. It would take minimal effort to gain their loyalty, and it seems like she kept her relationship with Peter a secret from Savannah and Kaden. They found out when a rumor about it spread are around the school, hinting at a strain in their friendship and trust. With her ties to Savannah and Kaden being so weak right now, it might be best to focus my energy on befriending Carlie. She seems to be someone whose presence radiates joy. From what I can tell, she is quick to forgive, so losing her as a friend would be quite the blow to McLean."

"Noted. Begin to build a connection with Carlie, but don't make it known to McLean yet. If she kept a relationship secret from her friends last semester, see if you can't convince Carlie to do the same, or at least make it appear to be secret." Jackson ordered. Banthup's phone beeped, drawing attention to him. "And Banthup."

Banthup locked his phone after reading the message that had come in. "Good news and bad news." Banthup started as he finished wrapping his right hand. "Good news, I've been asked to be part of McLean's security detail at school. I will be in all but one of her classes. Carlyle is in charge of her detail, and has ordered an airtight detail. I don't know who else will be in class with her. Bad news," Banthup held up his phone, "McLean is gone, supposedly hiding out at some safe house. They won't tell me where, but they just told me she will be gone at least until after Christmas."

Jackson nodded. "Try and see if you can't get her location from someone. If she is stuck in a safe house, my plan might still work, but I would prefer to know where she is. Once you are part of her detail, report any time she tries to ditch you, especially any time she succeeds, to Carlyle. If they want an airtight security detail, let's give it to them. We need to systematically find the ways she feels free, and convince the people she loves and trusts to take those freedoms away."

Banthup nodded. "Yes sir."

If Jackson knew teenagers—and he had studied their psychology—he knew teenagers who felt boxed in were more likely to rebel. McLean would be no different. She had long felt trusted by her parents, and that trust, paired with the freedoms she had been given, meant she had easily followed the rules her parents had given her. Banthup had suggested that after the kidnapping, there seemed to be some tension between her and her parents, yet she had been extremely definitive in her decision not to join him.

He needed to break down her resolve.

McLean may not have had very much trust with her parents at the moment, but she still believed they were good people. While the tight security detail would eventually make her feel suffocated, he needed to convince McLean that her parents weren't the saints she believed them to be. The other play would be to convince McLean she had already done something unforgivable. If he couldn't convince McLean that her parents were bad people, he would convince her she was.

He already had an idea of how he might be able to do that.

"Banthup, I have another assignment for you."

Banthup turned to Jackson, straightening his posture. "Sir?"

"I need a file from the Promising Generation files. Since you are on the inside, start trying to get it for me, whether by legitimate means, or by conniving, I don't care. As long as you don't get caught."

"What file?" Banthup asked.

"*Icarus.*"

Banthup gave him a nod. Jackson eyed the two young men he had working for him before turning and leaving the room. Banthup returned to the punching bag, working out his anger while trying to come up with a plan to get Jackson the file he needed.

Kalen rolled his eyes, pulling out his phone, wishing he had asked for Carlie's phone number. This morning, it probably would have annoyed him that his uncle had given Banthup so many assignments, and hadn't given him very many. Instead, he spun his phone in his hand and left the garage, deciding to work on his homework instead. He wasn't likely to do very much of it, but he would do his psychology homework, and only partially because he wanted to learn more about the things his uncle was trying to do to break McLean.

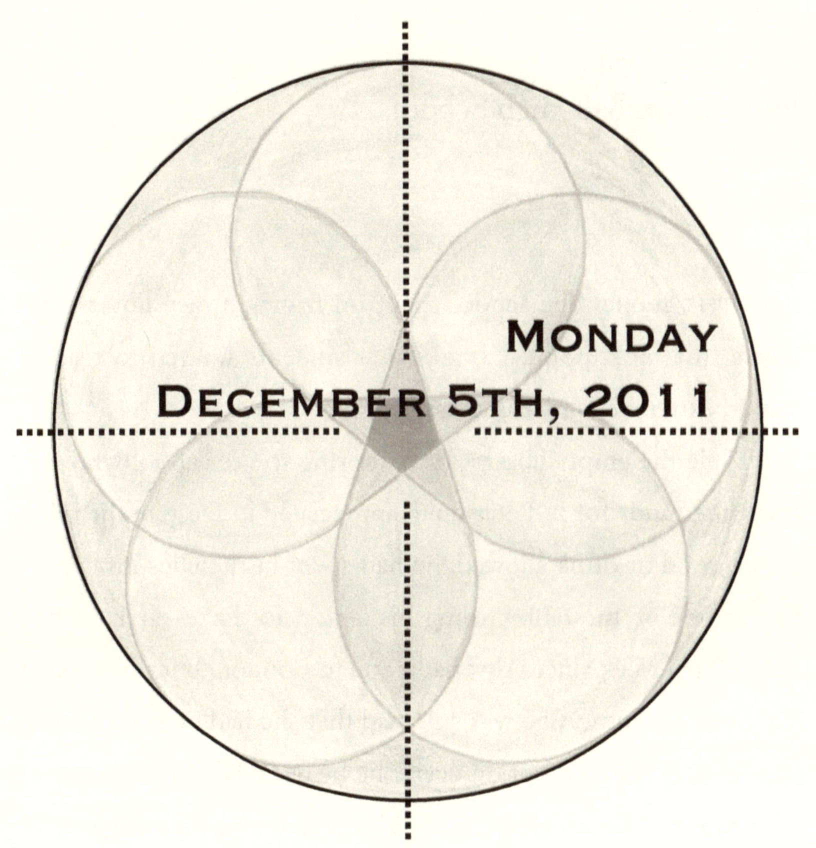

Monday
December 5th, 2011

11:01 PST
Tracy, California
John C. Kimball High School

FOR THE money the school spent on having a nice library, and buying the most popular books that students wanted to read, it was an extremely underused asset.

While the empty library was annoying to the school who had spent the funds for it, Peter quite appreciated it. Despite there being no food or drink allowed, he had spent his lunches inside, sitting at one of the tables, using his laptop to do research. It had only been a week since Alyx had gone to London, but it felt like it had been a lifetime. She was still mad that she had been sent away, and she was taking it out on everyone by not talking to anyone.

Carlie still hadn't heard from Alyx, and he was running out of excuses to give her.

Just add another reason why he was hiding in the library for his lunches.

He didn't know when the last time was he had eaten lunch.

Peter pulled up a risk assessment. The McLean's were trying

to decide if it was better to find a new house and fortify it before bringing Alyx home, or if they should fortify the home they currently lived in. If Alyx was going back to school at Kimball, which she would insist on because she was months away from graduation, it wouldn't matter if they found a new house to live in, because unless everyone took extreme countersurveillance measures, the new home would be found and compromised.

So far, he had yet to find a solution that guaranteed her safety more than her staying in Feilds Palace. That was where she was going to stay until they either found a safer option, or staying was no longer an option. Peter was hoping to bring her home after Christmas break, but it was looking more and more like she wouldn't come home until after Spring Break, when she would have to be in town for AP tests.

No one would suggest compromising her academic future. If they took away her promise for Oxford, or even college in general, Alyx would rebel.

Peter was engaged in a delicate balance of pros and cons, and he would find the best solution as soon as possible, because he needed Alyx home with him just as much as she wanted to be home.

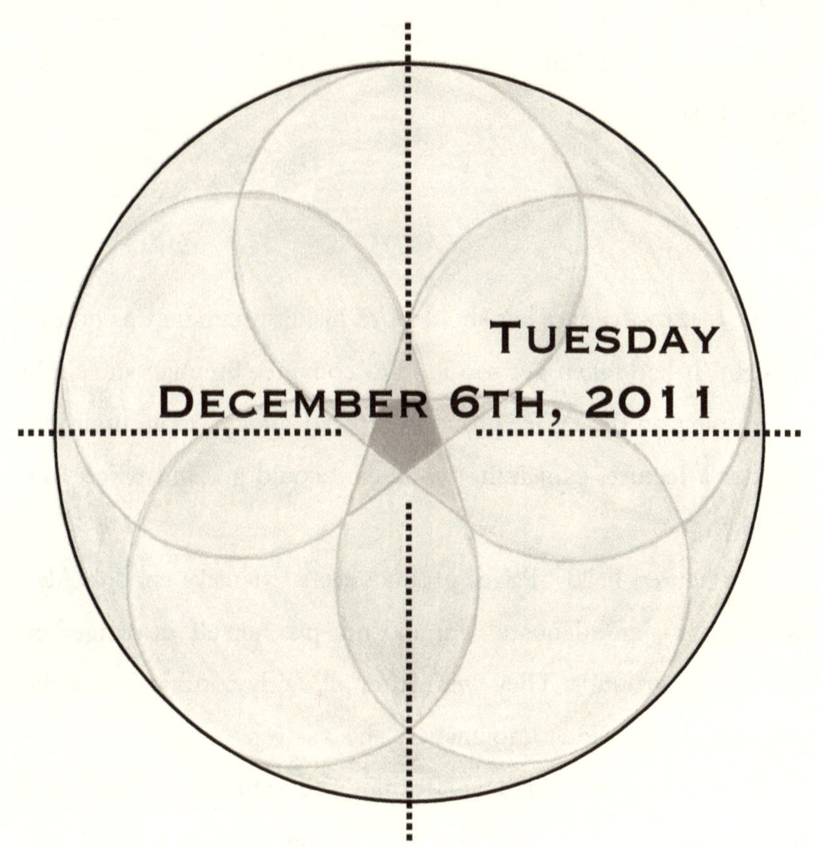
TUESDAY
DECEMBER 6TH, 2011

17:34 GMT

Twickenham, London

Feilds Palace

ALYX CHECKED over her shoulder to make sure there was no one in sight. It had taken her too long to convince Stephan she could go running on the Palace grounds. He had spent over an hour giving her a lecture, explaining where she could go, and where she couldn't.

He figured Feilds' Palace grounds were extensive enough Alyx could go for an adequate run, and not put herself in danger by leaving the grounds. They were, after all, fairly confident that the Circle of Fifths didn't know where she was yet.

Alyx felt suffocated. The last thing she wanted to do was stick to Stephan's very safe, but also very boring, running route. Once she was certain she could get away with it, Alyx climbed the wall separating Feilds Palace grounds from Orleans road. The wall was old, built of uneven stones, which made it easy for her to climb, and once she had thrown a leg over the top, even easier to climb back down on the other side.

Free from the confines of the palace, Alyx took a deep breath, taking a look up and down the road she had taken several times. In the many years she had stayed here, she had taken the small, quiet road for granted. She always thought it annoying how narrow it was, but now, she welcomed the narrow road, because it was the road to freedom.

As much as part of her wanted to run North toward the stores, she ran towards the river. She may have been mad at everyone else for handling her with kid gloves, and doing way too much in the name of protection, but the idea of returning to Tracy, or any sort of city for that matter, brought the image of Jackson's sniper on the roof, saluting as she registered a burning pain across her left arm.

Alyx sprinted down Orleans Road, jumping over the barrier that prevented cars from entering the riverside trail like a hurdle, rather than going around it like most people did. She followed the bend of the paved trail, not slowing her pace. It had been months since she had run a track-event distance at a full sprint, but she didn't slow down. She ran four, six, eight hundred meters at her full speed sprint. Every muscle in her legs was burning. She couldn't breath fast enough. Each inhale through her nose was interrupted by the jarring impact her feet made with the ground. Each exhale through her mouth was a huff broken in two. *In, in, out, out. In, in, out, out.* She concentrated on the consistent rhythm her body moved at, pushing through the pain, and using it to distract her from the pain she still felt in her arm. If she ran fast enough and far enough, maybe she could leave her fear behind.

She wasn't afraid of anything. Nothing scared her.

She stumbled. She had pushed herself too far, and her muscles started to give out. She collapsed to the ground, the momentum of the speed she'd been running not dying with her. She skid across the ground, rolling forward. She put her arm up to stop her from hitting her face, and ended up rolling over her shoulder onto her back.

Alyx stayed on the ground, laying on her back, gasping for air. She closed her eyes, focusing on how nice it felt to feel something other than the tightness in her left arm.

Now everything hurt.

She smiled, hearing the sounds of ducks on the river just feet from her. She envied those ducks. They could contently swim along one of the most iconic rivers in the world all day. And if they ever got tired of swimming, all they had to do was shake off their wings and take flight. They were free. They were safe.

Alyx rolled up, walking off to the side of the trail to watch the ducks sitting on the river. There was a pair of them, one female, one male. The colorful male bird circled the female, protecting her from any perceived dangers, but didn't restrict where she could go. He followed her, occasionally getting close enough he could nuzzle her with his beak.

Alyx missed Peter.

She looked at her watch and the stopwatch she had started when she left the Palace. Stephan had allowed her a half hour to run. She had been gone for twenty minutes. She needed to get back.

She ran back the way she'd come, this time not as fast. Her muscles still weren't happy with her, but she pushed her body to keep moving, because if she didn't, Stephan would come looking for her. She liked the idea of being able to sneak out again. He wouldn't let her so much as leave her room if he found out she had ignored his carefully laid out route around the grounds.

Alyx got back to Orleans road, and the section of the wall she had climbed to get out, and attempted to climb back over.

It was much harder now that she had fallen and scraped more of her exposed skin than she had realized.

Somehow, she made it over, finding herself back on the trail Stephan had deemed safe enough for her to run without supervision. She checked her watch. She was cutting it close. Even though she didn't think she had it in her, she started running, pushing herself harder and harder. It wasn't quite a full sprint, but she ran as fast as she could back towards the house, opting to use a side entrance, rather than any of the main entrances. She was covered in blood and didn't need anyone asking questions.

As was her luck, she ran into Stephan. He looked her up and down, giving her a questioning glance.

"What the…" He shook his head. "What happened to you?

You are a bloody mess."

Alyx tried to take a deep breath, but it was hard to do with her panting. "I was," breath "taking out," breath "my frustrations" breath "by sprinting," breath "and I pushed myself," breath "too far." She explained, still trying to catch her breath from her sprint back. "I fell."

"How fast were you running?" Stephan asked, as he escorted her to the bathroom on the first floor he had often taken her to mend her wounds. She had a bad habit of pushing herself too far and hurting herself in the process. Stephan had made it his habit to take care of her wounds when she had.

"I don't know." Alyx admitted. "Full sprint."

Stephan shook his head, pulling out the first aid kit he kept in the bathroom. "You need to be more careful." He chastised. "Sit."

Alyx did as she was told. Stephan didn't know she had snuck out, so he wasn't as mad as he could be, but he was still mad, which meant it wasn't going to be the most pleasant experience having him clean her road rash.

Then again, it would probably be more pleasant than when her mom had cleaned the graze on her arm.

9:31 PST
Tracy, California
John C. Kimball High School

KALEN KEPT his eyes peeled for Carlie on his walk to Psychology. Once he had decided to use her to infiltrate Alyx' friend group, he had tried to get as much information about her as possible. Yesterday, he had finally seen what direction she came from heading to class. Today he wanted to catch her before class to talk to her. Five days might be too soon for his uncle's timeline, but he knew if he let it go for too much longer, it might portray disinterest, and that was the last thing he wanted to do, his uncle's orders be damned. Fortunately, he caught sight of her before she was too close to the classroom.

Kalen started to jog to catch up with her, wanting as much time as possible to talk to her. "Carlie!" He called.

She turned around. When she saw him, her face lit up with a contagious smile that quickly spread to Kalen's face. "Hi Kalen!" She greeted. "Are you excited for the guided meditation today?"

Kalen shrugged. "I guess," he said. "What I'm more excited

about is the fact that I'm finally caught up, so if the offer still stands, I'd like to join you for lunch."

Somehow, Carlie's smile grew. "It does. With Alyx still gone and not replying to my texts, it would cheer me up to have you eat with us."

"One of your friends is avoiding you?" Kalen asked. He knew she was gone, and Banthup had learned enough to know she was hiding out in some safehouse, but the fact that she wasn't texting her friends was information that would be useful to his uncle. They didn't know anything about the location of the safe house, so the more they could piece together, the better they would be able to extrapolate likely locations of where she was hiding out.

He was also curious to know if Carlie knew much about what was happening.

Carlie sighed, her smile fading, making Kalen regret asking his question. "Yeah. Something happened when she came back from Thanksgiving break, and she hasn't been to school since. I only know something happened because I talked to Peter, and he told me she wasn't going to be at school for a bit. It just hurts because clearly it's something big, and she cared enough to tell her boyfriend, but she can't even reply to a single one of my texts asking if she is ok. I've known her for years, and she's only dated Peter for a couple months, but she's actively choosing him over the friends who had supported her for years, you know?"

Kalen nodded. "It sounds tough."

"It is," Carlie huffed. "I mean I know she is probably just not processing whatever happened very well. She seems to be in full on avoidance mode, and our friends can be…intense, but I miss her. You know?"

"Yeah." Kalen affirmed. "So what happened?"

Carlie shook her head. "I don't know. From the little Peter did say before telling me to talk to Alyx, it seems that whatever it was broke her, which is saying something because she is the strongest person I know. She's moved like twenty times and taken it like a champ. Her boyfriend was kidnapped a couple months ago, and she still had the presence of mind to make a plan and find him before her dad did, which is saying something since her dad is FBI, and had been on the case for a month." Carlie paused as they walked into the classroom. "I just wish she would talk to me."

Kalen watched Carlie silently as they sat down. It was hard to believe that all it had taken was two little bullets to break McLean, especially considering how close he'd been to capturing her in the Alps the summer before. He knew the game his uncle was trying to play, and he knew that Kalen shooting her in her home would shake her, but for the people close to her to say she was broken…

Maybe Alyx McLean wasn't the unbreakable super spy so many made her out to be.

"Is she in town?"

Carlie shook her head. "No. I stopped by her house on my way home last night, and her parents told me she was out of town. There is a construction crew out front, so I'm guessing whatever happened happened there."

"If she is out of town, how do you know she is getting your texts? Maybe she is somewhere she can't get service." Kalen suggested, while also trying to prod for more information. He couldn't imagine anyone could ignore a text from someone as nice and caring as Carlie. It seemed more than morally wrong. Kalen had broken more than a few laws in his short life, and even he could never ignore a text from Carlie.

Carlie turned to Kalen, "She left her read receipts on." She told him, the look on her face making it clear she was extremely annoyed with her friend. "She has read every single one of my texts." Carlie sighed. "I'm telling you, she has to be broken."

Kalen considered what Carlie had said as he sat down at his desk and pulled out his homework. He was having a hard time lining up the girl he had met in the Alps with the girl who was Carlie's friend.

11:46 PST
Tracy, California
John C. Kimball High School

THE WEATHER was starting to turn cold enough, the grassy hills in the quad of the school were nearly empty, as was the covered seating area just outside of the cafeteria. The students heading to lunch converged on the cafeteria, telling Thane it was going to be louder and more crowded than usual. All he could hope was that one of his friends had gotten there fast enough to claim their booth in the back.

As he watched the crowds heading to lunch, a stray figure broke away from the swarm descending on the cafeteria. He was hunched up in his letterman jacket, his hood up to protect him from a rain that wasn't falling, but Thane recognized him.

The Virginia key chain on his backpack gave him away.

Thane was starting to be concerned about Peter. He had been more withdrawn than usual at their Generation Meetings, and Thane hadn't seen him at Lunch since he had taken Alyx to the airport. Everyone was talking about how Alyx was handling the shooting, her mental state, how vulnerable she was to the Circle of Fifths and their offers to join them, and how the graze on her shoulder was healing, but no one had talked about how Peter was doing.

He had heard Peter talk about not joining the CIA when he graduated from the Promising Generation. If he didn't, it would be a great loss, but watching Peter at the moment, he couldn't help but wonder if they had put too much on him. Even if he did join the CIA, if something didn't change soon, he would be burned-out and not of much help in no time.

Alyx had brought balance to Peter's life, and having her life be in danger had skewed any sort of balance he'd found.

Thane sighed, walking into the cafeteria, looking for his friends in their usual booth. The problem was he didn't know who to talk to about Peter. His parents weren't in the picture, and it was unlikely they would care enough to try to do something if Thane told them. Even if they did, Peter hated them enough, he wouldn't listen. Thane couldn't tell his own dad. All he could see was someone who was doing everything he could to protect Alyx. It was a valiant effort, sure, but the cost was too high, and his dad couldn't see that. Nathan might be able to do something about it, but Thane could already see how that conversation would go, and it wasn't pretty.

Thane hadn't spent much time with Alyx, Peter, and her parents, but from the small interactions he had seen, talking to Sarah, Neil, or Emily about his concerns would probably yield the best results. Emily seemed to encourage the relationship, and Sarah seemed to have taken on a motherly role with Peter. He supposed Peter being close to her parents was inevitable, since Alyx was an only child. They were a close knit family, and Alyx was serious about Peter.

Then there was the fact that Sarah and Neil had been quick to adopt most of the friends Alyx brought over. It probably had something to do with losing two of their children. They started seeing their missing children in the faces of visitors. They filled the hole in their heart with love for any teenager that needed refuge.

Thane arrived at their booth, thankful to see that Carlie had arrived to claim it before someone else did. Next to her sat the new kid from his weight training class.

"Look! Thane is here!" She announced. "Kalen, this is Thane. He is one of the friends I eat lunch with."

Kalen stuck his hand out. "I believe we have weight training together."

"We do." Thane confirmed, accepting the outstretched hand with a shake.

"Kalen and I have Psychology together, and since he is new, I offered to let him eat lunch with us." Carlie told Thane.

Thane smiled. Sarah and Neil may have adopted everyone in the friend group, but Carlie was definitely the reason why all of the friends ate lunch together. If she saw someone who needed a friend, she couldn't help but befriend them, and ask them to join their group. Alyx had introduced Kaden and Savannah to Carlie at a church activity, and when Carlie had found out they attended the same high school, she had insisted they come eat lunch with her and Thane. When Alyx started high school the following year, Carlie hadn't given her much of a choice to eat lunch with them.

If Chelsi and Lynn had first lunch, Carlie would insist they eat with them as well, even though the booth they claimed was way too small for all of them.

Thane slipped into his spot in the booth. "Kalen, where did you move from?"

"Virginia." He replied.

Savannah slipped into the booth next to Thane. "I heard you had come from Virginia. What brought you here?"

Carlie rolled her eyes. "This would be Savannah. She hears all of the school gossip."

Savannah waved Carlie off. "We have art together. He sits next to me."

Carlie shook her head. Thane couldn't help but notice the way Kalen watched Carlie, smiling at her.

"Back to my question, what brought you to California?"

Kaden slid into the booth next to Savannah, causing Savannah to have to scooch closer to Thane, squishing him against the wall—not that he minded. They weren't sitting in their usual seats, not just because the new addition had misplaced them. It looked and felt a little like an interrogation of the new kid.

Knowing Savannah and Kaden, that was exactly what this lunch was going to be.

"My uncle took a new job here." Kalen answered.

Kaden put his elbow on the table, forming a fist to rest his chin on. "Do you live with your uncle? What happened to your parents?"

"They died when I was young. My uncle has raised me." Kalen told the group, his answer silencing the questions for a moment.

"I'm so sorry." Carlie commented, softly placing her hand on his arm.

Savannah, Thane, and Kaden all hid small smiles. Carlie liked this new boy.

Kalen turned to Carlie, giving her a sad smile. "It was hard at first, but it was a long time ago."

And the new boy liked Carlie.

15:55 PST
Tracy, California
Circle of Fifths Safehouse

KALEN WALKED in the front door of the house he was starting to call home, despite the many Circle of Fifths agents he shared it with. He headed to the stairs, immediately starting the climb to the room he had claimed before anyone else had shown up. Given his current assignment, he had convinced his uncle to allow him to have the room to himself. He kept a regular sleep schedule, and used the room as a refuge so he could do his homework, and maintain his cover.

He had only climbed a few stairs when he heard his uncle call for him from the closed off living room that had been set up as an office.

"Kalen, I need a report." Jackson hollered.

Kalen closed his eyes, dropping his backpack on the landing he had made it to. He turned around, walking back down the stairs he had already climbed to make an appearance in his uncle's office in accordance with his rude summons.

"Yes uncle?"

Jackson gave Kalen a stern look.

"I mean yes, sir?"

"Better. You have been at the school for a week. What progress have you made?"

Kalen took a deep breath. "I received an invitation to eat lunch with Carlie and her group of friends. With Alyx still gone for the moment, I figured now would be a good time to start building friendships with them, and imbedding myself with them. I ate with them today."

Jackson nodded. "Good job. Continue to build those friendships. Once Banthup gains some insight on where she is, and when she will return, I will be sure to pass that onto you so you can plan ahead. I believe you said stealing Carlie as a friend would be the most devastating blow to McLean, how hard do you think that will be?"

"Alyx is unknowingly helping me. I have established myself as enough of a friend that she confided in me today. Alyx hasn't been texting her. After a little bit of prodding, I did learn from her that wherever they have Alyx hiding, she has cell service. She has her read receipts on, so Carlie's messages are being delivered, and Alyx is reading them."

Jackson made a note. "That is very useful information."

"I thought so." Kalen nodded. "Is there anything else?"

Jackson looked up at Kalen, a hint of suspicion marring his

features. "Is there something else you need to share?"

"No, sir."

Jackson watched Kalen carefully for any signs he was lying. One of the benefits of teaching his nephew everything he knew, he knew all of his tells. Kalen didn't even appear nervous, as he sometimes did when talking to him, eager to please him.

Satisfied Kalen was telling the truth, Jackson nodded. "I will be leaving in a couple of days. The Nexus has asked that I join Bernard on the campaign trail. They are hoping my military background will help him get more of the vote." Jackson stood up. "Banthup has been given an assignment. Help him gather more information on where McLean is hiding, and win Carlie's loyalties. I need you certain that she will choose you over McLean. Banthup isn't sure when she will return, but we are getting closer to Christmas. If she returns after the break, I need you to have her loyalty before school lets out for Christmas."

"Yes, sir." Kalen replied. He watched as his uncle pushed papers into a file, picking up it, and the folder under it. The muscles in his arm tensed as he read the name on the folder: *McKenzie, Kalen*. His uncle had a file on him.

What was in that file?

Kalen knew that his uncle kept a file on most of the agents he recruited to keep track of their progress in the Circle of Fifths, and he definitely had a file on everyone on his team. It was a manipulation technique. He would even let the members of his team catch a glimpse of the file before he locked it away to let them know it existed. The files for the members of the team that failed and paid the ultimate price were often made accessible to the team so they could learn from their mistakes, and make sure their own file didn't start to look like their failed teammate.

Kalen had never considered that his uncle might be manipulating him too.

"Sir?" Kalen asked.

"Yes." Jackson replied, not stopping what he was doing.

Kalen paused for a moment, trying to think about how he wanted to ask his question. "One of the classes I am currently enrolled in for the assignment is Psychology. As you are engaged in psychological warfare to get McLean to join you, I was interested to see if you have a plan that you are following to do that."

Jackson smiled, pausing what he was doing. "You know that I was once a black-ops interrogator for the CIA?"

"Yes sir." Kalen replied.

"While working as an interrogator, I discovered I could use the same techniques in recruiting agents for the Circle of Fifths. Breaking someone is simply changing their concept of themself. If you are skilled enough at it, you can make even the most devoted individual turn against their cause."

"How did me shooting McLean through her window change her concept of self?" Kalen asked.

Jackson shook his head with a smile. "It didn't. Those bullets were simply the catalyst."

"How so?"

"The bullets created fear. Fear is a great way to manipulate your enemy into doing exactly what you want them to. When you took those shots, you instilled fear in McLean, yes, but more importantly, you instilled fear in her parents, boyfriend, and uncle. Now that we have planted that seed of fear, we can make other threats McLean won't see, but the effect will be felt, and she will become angry at her parents, until she starts hating them. The bullets should have also drawn attention to the fact that her parents have not prepared her for the attacks she will face because of who she is. She will want to prepare so she isn't caught off guard again. But our threats to her parents will mean that they won't allow her to prepare. If I can offer her the training she wants, but she can't get elsewhere, she will be more willing to join us."

"Is that all it takes?"

Jackson shook his head. "No. The most important thing I need to leverage her into joining us is guilt."

"Guilt for what?" Kalen asked.

Jackson walked around his desk, stopping next to Kalen on his way out to place a hand on his shoulder. "That's the beauty of it. It could be anything. Survivor's guilt is one of my favorites to leverage. The guilt is already there. A slight tweak of the narrative, and you have them believing they are a horrible person, and it is all their fault. Next thing you know, they are willing to do just about anything for you. The beautiful thing about humanity is anyone with a conscious has *something* they feel guilty about. All you have to do is find it. Then you can manipulate them to do what ever you want."

Kalen was quiet for a moment, turning to follow his uncle out of the office. "Since you know how to manipulate people, do you just hide the things you are guilty about so someone else can't manipulate you?"

Jackson laughed. "Oh no. No one can manipulate me because I don't have a conscious that makes me feel guilt. The Circle of Fifths gave me purpose." Jackson turned to look at Kalen. "And they let me do whatever I want. Breaking McLean—one of those pesky, self-righteous Halls—will be the highlight of my career. Sure, she might have her use for the Circle of Fifths, but her real usefulness is showing the Nexus I can turn anyone."

Kalen stopped at the stairs, watching as his uncle continued his journey out of the house. There was just one thing Kalen felt guilt for in his life, and that was killing his parents. What scared him was that he would be easy to manipulate into turning against his uncle if someone found out and knew what they were doing.

Maybe his file would identify his vulnerabilities so he could prevent himself from being manipulated.

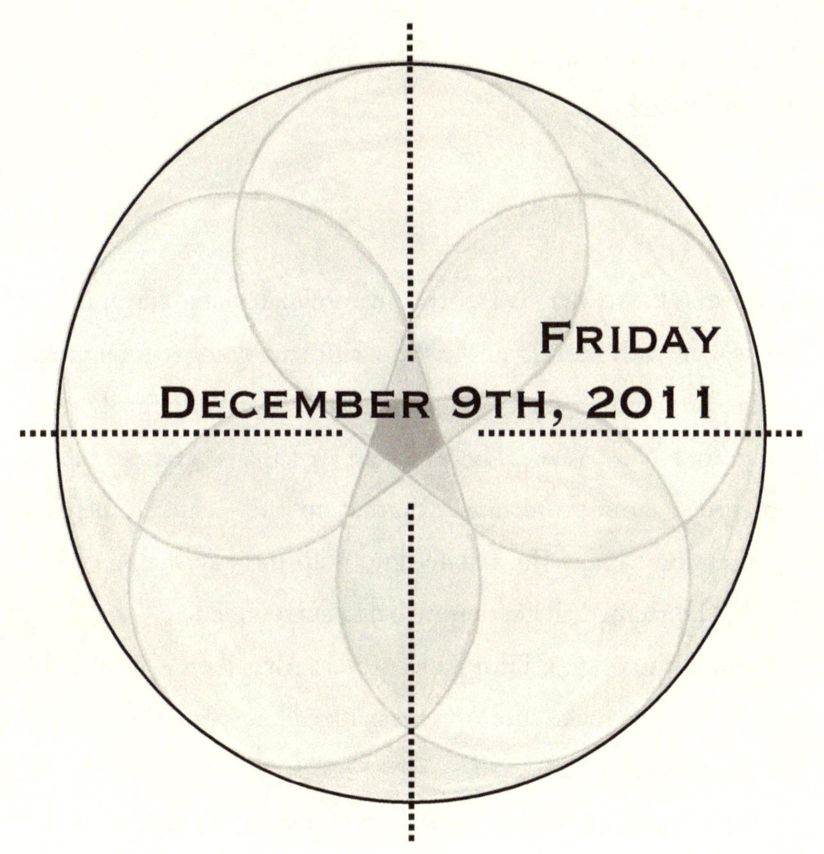
FRIDAY
DECEMBER 9TH, 2011

12:09 GMT
Twickenham, London
Feilds Palace

KATE ENTERED her dad's office carefully, making sure no one else was in with him. Lynn was in California doing a foreign exchange program so she could protect Alyx when she finally went home after New Years. The problem was that everyone was so con-cerned about protecting Alyx, that no one seemed to be paying attention to how she was feeling. With the way she had withdrawn, she seemed alone, despite being surrounded.

If Lynn got to go to California to protect Alyx, then Kate should be able to go to make sure Alyx wasn't so alone. Kate should go to protect Alyx from herself.

Kate knew it wouldn't be easy to convince her dad to let her go, but she had her list of reason, and if those didn't work, she had information she could question him about. She wasn't sure if she wanted the answers, but she knew she didn't want anyone else to know. She had intentionally waited until Stephan had left for Russia. He was spending Christmas with Lyshiria and her family.

Lynn wouldn't be back for Christmas with Sarah, and Neil for another week, and Dylan and his family would be coming in the following day. She wasn't sure if Emily was going to come, but if she was, it would be in the same time frame.

"Dad," Kate said from the doorway, "do you have a moment to talk with me?"

Michael looked up from the briefings he was reading. "Of course." Michael acknowledged, setting down the papers, closing the folder they belonged in, and moving it to the side.

He studied his daughter in front of him. He was mostly sure which twin was in front of him, but if it hadn't been hard enough to tell the sisters apart when Lynn had first showed up the summer before, it was harder now. The more time the two girls spent together, the harder it got to tell them apart, and he always felt like an awful father when he mixed them up. After all, he had married a twin, and had almost immediately been able to tell her apart from her identical twin. Why was he struggling to tell his own daughters apart now?

"The briefings can wait." Michael smiled. "The words won't get up and walk away if I don't read them right now." He said, an inside joke that he and Kate had shared since she was little. He had always identified Ally with confidence, and tried to do the same now. If he stopped second guessing himself, maybe his fatherly intuition would help him know which daughter was which.

Kate didn't laugh. Nor did she smile. Or acknowledge their

inside joke in any way. With the lack of reaction, Michael's stomach clenched with the fear that he had misidentified his daughter. If he couldn't tell them apart, how was he supposed to be secure in knowing he sent the right daughter to California. He knew whichever twin he had sent had put herself in danger posing as Alyx that first day. What if he had misidentified his daughters, and sent his sheltered daughter to pose as her spy sister?

Fortunately, he knew Kate's mannerisms. Lynn hadn't picked those up yet. As he watched Kate look at the ground, running her right thumb down the bone of her left, any uncertainty about which twin was in front of him evaporated.

Michael got up, walking over to his daughter. He put his hands on her shoulders. "Kate, what's wrong?"

Kate looked up at her father. "I want to go to California." Kate told him. "After Christmas. Alyx is supposed to go back, and Lynn is already there. I want to join them."

Michael shook his head. "Absolutely not." He said, dropping his hands from her shoulders. "It's too dangerous."

"For who?" Kate asked. "Me? How is it any less dangerous for Lynn to go?"

Michael sighed. "I can't exactly tell your sister she can't go. Your mother hid her away at MI:6. If I tried to tell her she's not going, she throws the protocols your mother wrote for her into my face. Her entire life has been dedicated to protecting our family, and I can't do anything to stop that."

"Protecting Alyx mentally is just as important as protecting her physically." Kate pointed to herself. "I can do that. While all of you are focused on protecting her physically, I can be there to protect her mentally and emotionally."

Michael shook his head. "There are plenty of people there to make sure she is doing ok. You don't need to go as well."

"There is the added benefit of me being able to learn more about another country. It will help me broaden my perspective, and open up career opportunities for me in the future." Kate added.

"All of those are things that you receive from your school now, as well as your interactions with Alyx. I believe you once threw a *Fourth of July* party and invited the children of American expatriates." Michael argued.

"If I were to go to California, and stay with Sarah and Neil like Lynn is, I will also be able to spend quality time with Sarah, and in my own way, get to know who my mother was a bit better, both from the stories only Sarah could tell me of my mother, but also by seeing how she, my mum's twin, is."

"It's not safe for you to go," Michael sighed. "My answer is no, and it is not going to change."

Kate rolled her eyes, picking up a folder she had set on the chair in front of her dad's desk before he had looked up. She handed it to him.

"What is this?" He asked.

"A risk evaluation." Kate answered. She had anticipated that her father would insist it wasn't safe for her to go to California, so she had preemptively asked Stephan to create a report that objectively evaluated the danger she would be exposed to if she went to California. "With my position to inherit the family titles after you and grandfather, as well as the added concern of Rafael, you have long insisted that I need a security detail at school. Truth is, after discovering Rafael posed no threat, I am in no more danger than most of my classmates, many of whom are in line for titles equal to, or higher than am I.

"With the decreasing risk for me here, it might be reasonable to assume I would be in more danger in California, where I would be in close proximity to someone who is being targeted. However, the risk to me in California because of my status is absolutely minuscule. Our titles are far enough down the peerage system that we are unknown to the main populous of the United States. My proximity to Alyx ends up not playing a role in the danger I would be in. In fact, the risk evaluation postulates I would be safer in California than here in the UK by a margin of twenty percent." Kate reported.

Michael looked up from the folder his daughter had handed him. "I don't care what the file says. If they shot Alyx in her bedroom…"

Kate pulled a second folder off the chair. "If you insist on forcing me to stay here, then you will answer some questions I have about mum's death, mainly why you lied to me about when mum died."

Michael took a slow breath, walking back around his desk to sit in his chair. He tossed the folder with the risk evaluation she had given him on his desk in front of him. Kate was definitely Ally's daughter. Part of him wanted to be proud of her for developing her talents, but the fact that she was using them against him was unfortunate. "I didn't lie to you about your mother's death."

Kate rolled her eyes. "You know I dug out mom's medical records and grandfather's reports on Rafael for my investigations last summer. My goal was to prove Rafael was in London when mum was poisoned in Russia, and I did that. At first I didn't take my research much deeper than dates and times. Yet something seemed off. I will admit, it took me longer to notice what it was, especially since I *am* mum's daughter." Kate paused, taking a deep breath. "You told me mum died shortly after I was born."

Michael was desperate, hoping to clasp onto any last shred of doubt Kate possessed to deny the truths she was giving him. If he could convince her to drop it… "That is correct." He answered her statement the same way he would when answering questions at a press conference. He had been trained. Be vague; don't elaborate. Confirm, deny, classified. No need for any more than that. He was the political face of an organization of secrets. Obfuscation was his job. He had perfected hiding the truth. He knew how to lie without letting anyone know what he was doing.

Only this time, instead of standing in front of a room of

reporters, his audience was his daughter. She had watched her dad give performances for as long as she could remember, and it looked like the one he was giving her now. And as the political figure she planned to grow up to be, she had some practice in the art of obfuscation herself.

If that wasn't enough, like a reporter with an inside source, Kate knew Michael was lying, and was armed with the facts to prove it.

"Then you shouldn't mind if I clarify some of the dates surrounding mum's death." Kate didn't wait for Michael to answer before continuing. The point was to catch him in a lie, so she was going to talk things through, whether her father wanted to or not. She opened the folder she had picked up off the chair. "According to Rafael, mum was barely three months pregnant when she showed up on his doorstep, poisoned. Assuming she was pregnant with Lynn and I, as she would be if she died when you claim she died, then the records should show she was poisoned in November of 1996."

"Sounds right," Michael replied, the sharp clipped tone becoming more evident the longer Kate questioned him.

Kate skimmed the file with, stopping as she found the date she was looking for. "This says she was poisoned in October."

"The file is wrong." Michael argued, not even looking at it.

Kate skimmed down the file a little more. "Her death certificate says she died November 15th, 2000." Kate stated, not letting any of the emotion she was feeling slip into her voice. "The medical reports suggest she was lucky to have lived as long as she did with the poison coursing through her system. It was a slow acting poison, but she should have died the week after administration of the poison without treatment, not three weeks. The baby died immediately, no chance for survival." Kate took a measured breath. It took everything to keep from bawling, and as a result, her voice started cracking. "Mum was pregnant with my baby brother."

"Kate—" Michael began.

"What would you gain from lying to me? Why did you tell me she had died just after I was born? I got *three years* with my mum, and while I don't remember those three years, I get flashes of memories—memories I have always written off as bonkers, as dodgy. Why would you let me think I didn't know my mum?" Kate demanded.

"Because that was what was easier for me to accept!" Michael snapped. He took a deep breath, rubbing his face before he continued. "Your mum was a spy. I knew that. I accepted it. Truthfully, I think I fell in love with her partially because of her life as a spy. She saw and understood me in a way no one else did. But sometimes…" Michael shook his head as he trailed off. "She had such a sense of altruism, and sometimes, because of it, it felt like she was choosing others over our own family. She died because of her altruism. She died because the Circle of Fifths attacked her sister's children. Sarah and Neil lost two children, and they were mourning. They were struggling to do everything they could to keep Alyx safe, that they couldn't look for the people who attacked her in the first place."

Kate sat down in the chair that had held her folders, hoping it would encourage her dad to continue. It wasn't easy to hear about her mum's death, just like she was sure it wasn't easy for her dad to tell her the story. But she needed the truth.

"When Stephan came to us, Ally enrolled him in the MI:6 orphans program, and took the information he brought with him to help her find who had attacked Alyx. The worst part is she asked Emily for her help. She was with your mum when the Circle of Fifths got her. I think she blames herself for what happened. She blames herself for her sister's death…" He took a deep breath. "After she was found, the doctors knew she wouldn't make it, but we at least got to say our good byes. You were too young. You didn't understand. And at the funeral, I saw how Alyx stood there, supporting you. The two of you were already so close, how could I tell you that the reason your mum was dead, was because she had given up a life with you to save Alyx? I didn't want to make you despise Alyx."

Kate shook her head. "So you've known that Alyx was in danger since 2000, and you didn't think that was important enough to reveal last summer when you sent her traipsing across Europe after the very people searching for her?" Kate demanded.

Michael threw his hands up in the air. If it wasn't one thing, it was an other. “To be honest, I thought they had been obliterated. After they killed your mum, the Circle of Fifths were hyperactive. Not a week went by that one of these briefings on my desk wasn't about the newest escapade on which the Circle of Fifths had embarked. Then the World Trade Centers in New York were attacked on September 11th, and they disappeared completely. It was the opinion of many intelligence officers that they had been killed by the surge of patriotism after the attacks. Only when they came out of the framework to kidnap Lynn did we realize we were wrong.”

Kate stayed silent, wiping the tears that were dangerously close to falling from her eyelashes. She didn't agree with what her dad had done, but she understood a little better why he had done it.

“I'm sorry Kate, but I thought I was doing what was best for you.” Michael apologized.

Kate shrugged. “I'm still narked that you lied, but I think I know how you can appease me.” Kate said, a smile growing on her face.

“What?” Michael asked, weary of the answer. He knew where this conversation had started, and had a guess of what she was going to ask, and considering the answers she had prodded from him, he would have a much harder time declining her proposal.

“Let me go to California. Alyx and I are close. She was there when I lost mum, I want to be there for her now. I think mum would want me to be there for her.”

Michael sighed. She had asked for exactly what he was afraid she would. He picked up his phone. "I will make the arrangements for you to do the foreign exchange with Lynn." He conceded.

Kate got up from the chair, a smug smile on her face. She ran around the desk. "Thank you." She said, giving her dad a kiss on the cheek.

As the phone rang, Michael watched Kate skip out the door. She was becoming more like her mother the older she got. Lynn and Alyx were teaching her how to get her way, and Michael wasn't sure how to not fall prey to it. Alyx and Lynn rarely tried to use their talents to manipulate. Kate had no qualms about it.

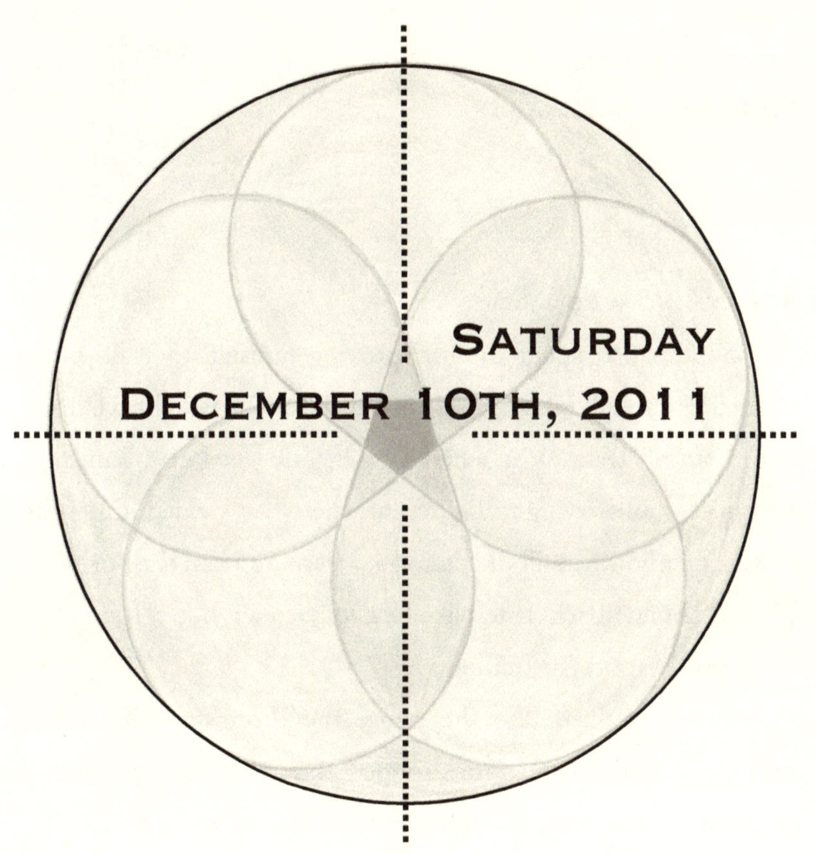

Saturday

December 10th, 2011

8:46 PST
Tracy, California
Promgen Headquarters

SOMETHING WAS wrong.

Banthup had spent months proving himself to Hall, but it seemed as though all of his work had been for naught. Hall was in and out of Tracy. Where he was going, no one knew. Banthup's efforts of subtly trying to figure out where had yielded no results. Not to mention he still didn't know where McLean was, or when she was coming back. It felt like he had been cut out.

It was beyond frustrating.

Banthup walked into the house the Promising Generation used as a headquarters. He dropped the Statistics textbook—a textbook he had because McLean was supposed to be in the class—on the table, startling Peter awake. Peter sat up, rubbing his eyes before waking his computer up. Banthup shook his head.

Pathetic.

"I know this girl is important to you because you love her or something, but I'm going to need some explanation as to why some terrorists are so interested in a teenage girl, and why it means I have to deal with this…" Banthup gestured at his textbook. "This… pile of absolute nonsense."

"You are taking her classes so we have someone in her classes when she gets back. I need her alive. Her parents need her alive. So she needs a security detail." Peter explained tiredly.

"Why me?"

"The school won't let me switch into her classes. They think I'm asking to switch because we're dating. And I can't tell them otherwise. One, they wouldn't believe me. Two, the CIA would have to admit that they've been training teenagers. You on the other hand, have been claimed by the FBI, at least as far as the school knows. By pulling just a couple of strings, we could put you undercover in her classes."

Banthup pointed at the textbook. "So I don't have to actually do the homework?"

"No you do. That's the definition of undercover. You have to do the homework, and do your best to pass." Peter corrected.

"What happens if I don't?" Banthup challenged.

Peter looked up from his computer, giving him a dirty look. "You don't pass, the school won't let you remain undercover. I can't imagine that bodes well for your position on Hall's team."

"Fine." Banthup huffed, sitting down at the table. "When does she come back?"

Peter returned his attention to his computer. "I don't know."

"Where is she."

"Somewhere safe."

"Is she coming back this school year?" Banthup prodded.

Peter sighed. "I hope so."

Banthup crossed his arms. "I'm going to need help with the math classes."

"So find a tutor."

"You're a tutor." Banthup shot back.

Peter's eyes flicked up to look at Banthup. *He did not just casually bring up his role in helping with his kidnapping.* Peter tilted his head up, making eye contact, and plastering a customer service smile on his face. "Unfortunately, none of our math tutors are currently accepting new clients, as their schedules are full. If it is urgent, I can suggest you visit our website pgtutoring.org. We have lots of videos that out tutors have uploaded to help as many students as possible." With the scripted line Peter had used when Hall's team had called him recited, Peter threw one more fake smile at Banthup, then returned to whatever he was working on.

Banthup ground his teeth, beyond frustrated with Peter. "What is so important? What is keeping you so busy you can't help me with the homework for the classes *you* put me in to keep *your* girlfriend safe?"

"I'm trying to find a safe place to bring my girlfriend home to." Peter snapped. "She won't reply to any of my texts, voicemails, or phone calls, and I miss her. She has some really big goals for her future, and she needs to be here in order to achieve them, and because I love her, I want to make sure I'm not preventing her from achieving her dreams."

Banthup shook his head. "Seriously, *who* is this girl, and why does *everyone* care what she does?"

"You really want to know what makes Alyx so special?" Peter asked annoyed.

"Dying to know." Banthup snarked.

"Why the Circle of Fifths is hellbent on recruiting her."

"Yes, please."

"And if I tell you, you will leave me alone?"

Banthup looked at Peter, considering the bargain he was about to strike. "Yes."

Peter nodded, standing up. He walked out of the room.

Banthup sat waiting at the table for what felt like an eternity. Well, it was worth a try. He picked up his textbook, getting ready to leave when Peter walked back into the room carrying a Manila file folder. He handed it to Banthup, before walking back around to his computer.

"What is this?" Banthup asked.

Peter nodded to the file he'd handed to Banthup. "She was five. That file explains how the Circle of Fifths knows about her, and it explains why they want her."

Banthup looked down at the folder, taking note of the name on the folder. "When do I need to have it back to you?"

Peter shrugged.

Banthup stacked the folder on top of his textbook, sticking both under his arm. He turned and started walking out of the house. Once he was through the front door, he allowed himself to smile.

He had *Icarus.*

9:21 PST
Tracy, California
Circle of Fifths Safehouse

THE SOUND of paper hitting the desk made Jackson look up from his meticulous notes on Kalen's performance. He looked at the file in front of him, then up at the man who had dropped it.

"What is this?" Jackson asked Banthup.

"Icarus."

Jackson picked it up, glancing at Banthup in disbelief before his eyes became glued on the file. "I wasn't expecting it so soon."

Banthup shrugged. "My annoyance with McLean is well known. I was vocal about my annoyance with my new assignment as well. Over the last few weeks, I made sure to ask the question as to why McLean was so important to the Circle of Fifths. I figured if it was a file you wanted, it would be a file relating to her and why you know about her. It worked. I annoyed Carlyle enough he handed it over this morning." He reported. "By the way, I know your plan was to break McLean, but Carlyle is also breaking. I don't think he has spent much time in his bed recently."

Jackson nodded. "Thank you for the update." He replied, flipping through the file. He smiled as he pulled out a paper sleeve with a disk in it.

"What is that?" Banthup asked.

Jackson closed the file, focusing all of his attention on the disk in his hand. He removed it from the paper sleeve, sliding it into the CD drive on his computer. "This is the key to breaking McLean."

"How is that?" Banthup asked.

"Come see for yourself." Jackson said, beckoning him to come to the other side of the desk.

Jackson opened a file that popped up once the computer read the disk. A video player opened, beginning to play the low-quality, early 2000s video footage:

Alyx held her dad's hand as they walked into a room with colorful chairs. There was a camera set up in the corner of the room. As they walked in, two adults looked at her. The woman with long hair and kind eyes smiled at her.

"Hello Alyx. My name is Renee Sanchez. I am a psychologist. And this is Lee Thompson. He is a Police Detective." The woman said, introducing herself and the other guy in the room.

Alyx just stared at the two strangers, clutching her dad's hand like a lifeline in one hand, while the other hugged a creme colored puppy stuffed animal, tightly into her chest. Despite her tight hold on her dad's hand, she didn't look up at him. Instead she just blinked at the woman who had spoken to her.

"I need to ask you some questions about today. If you would like, your

dad can sit with you, or he can sit in a corner, or he can wait outside. Which would you prefer?" Renee *asked.*

"Outside." Alyx said softly.

Renee *looked to* Neil, *who nodded, squatting down to look his daughter in the eyes. "I won't go far, so I will be right here if you need me, ok?"* Neil *told his daughter.*

Alyx just gave him a soft nod.

Neil *gave Alyx a kiss on top of her head, then let go of her hand, and left the room, closing the door behind him.*

Alyx stood frozen in the spot she'd been left in, the hand that was now free from her dad's hand reaching up to play with the face of her stuffed puppy.

"Will you come sit with me?" Renee *asked Alyx, pointing to one of the chairs set up in a triangle.*

Alyx nodded, letting herself go and sit down in the chair, continuing to play with the puppy in her arms.

"While I ask you some questions, Lee *is going to be taking notes for me, so I don't forget."* Renee *told Alyx. "When I ask you the questions, if you don't understand what I am asking, it is my fault. If you just tell me you don't understand, I can try to ask you another way. If you don't remember something, that is ok, just tell me you don't remember. And if you would like a break, let me know. Do you understand?"*

Alyx nodded, telling Renee *she understood.*

Renee *smiled at Alyx. "Ok. I need to start with some formalities. First, the date is July 12th, 2000, and it is 5:27 PM."* Renee *paused for a moment. "Can you tell me what your full name is?"*

Alyx nodded. "It's Alyxandrie Madelyn McLean. I was named after both my grandmas. A-l-y-x-a-n-d-r-i-e." She responded while she fiddled with her puppy.

Renee smiled at Alyx again. "It's a beautiful name. Do you prefer to go by Alyx, or Alyxandrie?"

Alyx scrunched up her face. "I don't know. My parents and—my parents call me Alyx, but my aunt Emily calls me Vee. I like her name for me, but I like Alyx. I like Alyxandrie too, but it's really long."

"Is it ok if I just keep calling you Alyx then?" Renee asked.

Alyx nodded.

"Thank you. Now Alyx, can you tell me how old you are?"

"I'm five." Alyx replied.

"Do you know when your birthday is?"

"Um. It's in June, cuz we just celebrated it last month." Alyx said.

Renee smiled at Alyx. "That must have been fun." Renee watched carefully as Alyx nodded. "Now Alyx, Do you know the difference between telling the truth and telling a lie?" She asked.

"Yes."

"Ok. Let me give you an example. If I were to say my hair is red, is that the truth or a lie?" Renee asked.

"Lie."

Renee nodded. "Ok, and if I were to say my hair is black, is that the truth or a lie?"

"The truth." Alyx replied.

Renee smiled at Alyx. "When I ask you questions, I need you to tell me the truth. Can you do that for me."

"Yes." Alyx said quietly. Her hand flew off the puppy she had been playing with, before quickly returning it to the stuffed animal's soft fur.

"Good. Alyx, can you tell me what happened today?"

"I killed my siblings."

Renee glanced at Detective Thompson. "What do you mean by that?"

"I don't understand. I killed my siblings."

Renee took a deep breath, looking up to think of another way to ask the question. "Can you explain to me everything you remember happening?"

Alyx nodded. "I guess. Mom put baby Cassie down for a nap, and I was being loud, so she asked us to play outside. Cole told mom we could go for a bike ride. I like bike rides. So we went. We just ride around the neighborhood. We rode past a house with bad men. I wanted to stop the bad men, so I rang the doorbell. I told them I knew they were bad, and I was there to stop them. They pulled me into the house. Cole and Annie had to sneak inside to save me. I wasn't strong enough. And then the fire started. And, and then… and then… I don't remember."

Renee nodded. "That's ok, Alyx. Do you remember who started the fire?"

"Yeah. One of the bad men. They tied me up in the room. They lit some papers on fire." Alyx replied, playing with her dog.

"Ok. So you were tied up in the room where they started the fire?" Renee confirmed.

"Yes."

"Firefighters saw you run out the front of the house. Do you remember

how you got untied and to the front of the house?" Renee asked.

"Cole untied me, and I ran."

"Ok. Now Alyx, you said you killed your siblings. Do you know what the work kill means?" Renee asked.

Alyx nodded. "Yeah. To kill someone is to be the reason they die."

"Almost." Renee corrected. "To kill someone is to cause their death. You have to take an action that stops their life. Did you do something to cause your sibling's death?"

Alyx nodded. "Yes."

"What did you do?" Renee asked.

"I ran into the house."

Renee crinkled her forehead. "Let me try to explain this another way. You said Cole untied you and you ran. Where was Cole when you ran?"

"He was in the room with me. Fire fell from the roof and he couldn't follow me."

"And where was Annie?" Renee asked.

"I—" Alyx paused, scrunching her forehead. "I don't know. I didn't see her in the house."

Renee nodded. "Thank you Alyx. Now we're almost done. I just have a few more questions for you. Is there anything else you remember that you want to share with me?"

Alyx shook her head. "No."

"Ok." Renee replied. *"And did you tell me any lies today?"*

Alyx shook her head. "No."

"Thank you. I'm going to check with Lee to see if I forgot anything, ok?"

"Ok." Alyx replied.

Renee looked over at Lee who just shook his head. "Ok Alyx. If you would like, I can get your dad now, and you can go home. Would you like that?"

Alyx nodded, so Renee stood up, offered Alyx her hand, which she grabbed.

The video ended and Jackson stood up. "You did well." Jackson complemented. "This video is exactly what I needed to push McLean towards her breaking point."

10:17 PST
Tracy, California
Promgen Headquarters

PETER WIPED the sleep from his eyes as he opened the door, finding both Hall and Special Agent McLean at the front door.

"He took it." Peter reported as the two men walked into the house. "Why would he want that file?

"Did you read the file?" Hall asked.

Peter shook his head. "I placed the tracker you asked me to, but didn't look at it more than that. I've been busy trying to find a safe way to bring Alyx back home."

McLean looked at Peter. "And when was the last time you ate, or slept in your own bed."

Peter glanced at Neil like a kid caught with his hand in the cookie jar.

Neil nodded. "That's what I thought. Did you know Thane is concerned about you? He came to talk to Sarah and I last night."

"I'm fine." Peter lied. "So anyway, what does the file have that Jackson might want, assuming Banthup retrieved the file for him."

"*Icarus* is a full report of the events leading up to the deaths of Cole and Annie McLean." Hall told him.

Peter shook his head. "No, I read that report. It was attached to Alyx' file. There wasn't a name associated with the file."

Neil scratched his head. "Dylan should have been more specific. *Icarus* is the investigation into how Alyx was involved in everything. The incident file that we put onto CIA servers was…" Neil trailed off trying to think of the correct word. "Truncated?"

"Truncated. You mean edited. As in it doesn't tell the entire story."

"As far as the CIA, FBI, or anyone else is concerned, the file you read that was attached to her file does tell the entire story. It doesn't do anyone any good to read the rest of that file." Hall told Peter.

"What is in that file? And if no one at the CIA needs to know what is in it, why did you have me give it to Banthup?" Peter asked. He paused for a minute. "Wait, do you not want the CIA to know what is in that file, or do you not want Alyx to know what is in that file?"

"Where did he go after you gave him the file?" Hall asked.

Peter looked back and forth between Neil and Hall. He knew they weren't telling him everything. He should have been more suspicious of a report that wasn't on any of the servers. Having only a single hard copy, and no digital back-up went against everything Peter had learned. Now they had given their only copy to

Banthup, who they assumed wanted to take it to Jackson, and Peter was beginning to be concerned that it contained something that would hurt Alyx if she found out.

Then again, it would probably hurt more to know her parents had kept another secret from her.

Peter gave up on trying to get any answers from the two men in front of him. Keeping secrets seemed to be something this family did *extremely well.* "He drove around for a bit. Probably trying to make sure he didn't have a tail, but it hasn't moved in a while. I'm guessing it arrived at its final destination." He reported.

Peter led the two men back to his computer, where he had a map pulled up, with a small red blinking dot on it.

Hall looked at the location of the dot, before turning to Neil. "Was the plan to bring Alyx back after Christmas?"

"It was."

"The plan has to change." He told Neil, turning to computer to him.

Neil looked at the blinking dot right behind the school his daughter attended, and his heart sunk. How was he supposed to protect his daughter from an enemy that had the resources to imbed itself anywhere they wanted to?

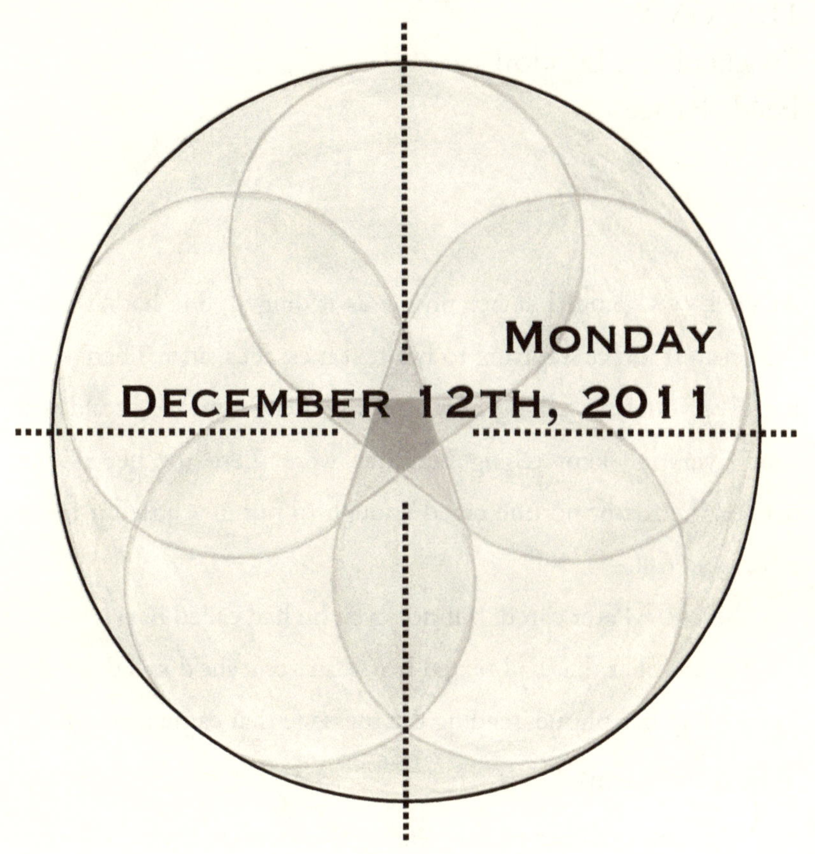

Monday December 12th, 2011

11:11 GMT
Twickenham, London
Feilds Palace

ALYX EYES glanced at her phone as it dinged. She hadn't done the greatest job of replying to her text messages since Thanksgiving. Everyone was asking how she was doing, and it got old real fast. Everyone kept telling her they were there for her if she needed them, but no one cared enough to put in a little bit more effort and call.

She knew Peter cared, but not even he had called her.

The number that had texted her wasn't one she'd saved, so she picked up her phone, reading the message that came through.

How is your arm?

Alyx unlocked her phone, reading the message again. Not very many people knew that she had been shot at, never mind the fact that one of the bullets had grazed her.

While she was staring at the message, trying to figure out who would know, but wouldn't have their number programmed in her phone, a second message came through:

It's too bad about your teddy bear. I had to make a point.

Alyx knew exactly who was texting her. She wished there were some way she could block the sociopath.

The nerve.

For the first time since she'd arrived in London, she actually replied to one of the text messages she'd received.

What point is that? That you hate teddy bears?

Alyx threw her phone onto her bed, returning to her open Statistics textbook so she could do the problems she was supposed to for the week. She was most of the way done, and it was still early. When she finished, she wouldn't have anything else to do for this class until the proctor her uncle had hired was sent her finals in a few of days. But she couldn't leave Feilds Palace, so she did her homework.

Only her phone buzzed again, and she couldn't help but pick it up to see what Jackson had sent in reply to her message.

Have you given my offer any more thought?

You killed my teddy bear.

And my aunt.

And tried to kill my cousin.

Not to mention you killed your own guard because I beat him.

Your point?

You're a sociopath. Joining you would be a death sentence.

If I wanted you dead, you would be. You are useful to me.

And when you decide I am no longer useful?

Alyx watched the conversation, waiting for his reply. She *was not* considering joining Jackson. Not again.

She locked her phone, shoving it under her leg when someone knocked on the door. Kate poked her head in the door just as Alyx picked her pencil back up, to make it appear she had been doing homework, not texting the man who had ordered a sniper to shoot at her. "You busy?" Kate asked.

Alyx ignored the vibration of her phone. "Kind—"

"Good," Kate replied, pushing into the room, and throwing herself on the bed beside Alyx and her textbooks. "I have some news. I am going to California with you after New Years. I convinced dad to send me, and everything has been arranged now."

"Is that really a good idea?" Alyx asked, overly conscious of the phone under her leg. Jackson wanted to recruit her. He had already showed that he could get to her easily. He knew where she lived, and by now he had to know where she went to school as well. She knew that Jackson would get sick of her sarcasm soon.

He had a short temper if his dead guard was any indication. How long did she have before he decided to escalate from shooting her stuffed animals, to shooting the people she loved.

She and Kate were safe here, but if Kate went to California, Jackson would have one more person to go after when he got sick of playing games with Alyx.

It was bad enough that Lynn was in Tracy. Kate couldn't be there too.

Kate just rolled her eyes. "Everyone is so concerned about keeping you safe, and ensuring your arm is healing," Kate said, tapping the bandage Alyx still had on her arm, "but I'm the only one that is actively asking you how you are doing here." Kate tapped Alyx on the forehead.

Alyx swatted away Kate's hand. She found her cousin annoying in much the same way she imagined she would have found her sisters annoying. Yet Kate's teasing still worked. Kate always had a way of making Alyx smile when she didn't want to.

Kate pointed at the small smile she had caused. "See. You need me." Kate closed the textbook Alyx had been working out of. "Besides, I need to meet your boyfriend. Lynn has given her stamp of approval, but I've known you longer, so mine means more."

Alyx smacked Kate with one of her pillows. "I don't need your approval. I am perfectly capable of judging if my boyfriend is good for me."

"I don't know. I mean I haven't met him yet, so maybe his

looks more than make up for it, but so far, I am not impressed with him." Kate said, scratching her chin thoughtfully.

"What has he done to earn your ire?" Alyx asked. "He's loving, and caring, and sweet, and thoughtful, and romantic—"

"And he hasn't called once." Kate interrupted. "Don't think I didn't notice."

"He has probably just been busy."

Kate scoffed. "With what? What could be more important than checking on your girlfriend, who was just shot at?" She got up, walking toward the door. "Just saying, calling seems like something a good boyfriend would do."

Alyx pulled her phone out, tapping it on her leg once Kate had left the room. If she called right now, Peter would pick up. There was no doubt in her mind he would. He was giving her space. She would call just to prove her point, but she didn't feel like discussing how she was feeling. She didn't want to add to his burdens. She looked at the notification on her Lock Screen. If she called him, she would have to let him know that Jackson had been in touch again. She couldn't add that to his plate.

She could deal with Jackson, his lies, and manipulations on her own.

I can show you how to always be useful.

Saturday
December 17th, 2011

9:48 GMT
Twickenham, London
Feilds Palace

IT HAD been a long time since Sarah had stepped foot in Feilds Palace. After her sister had died, coming to visit hadn't been the same. Everywhere she went reminded her of her sister. She remembered attending her first Feilds Ball. She remembered convincing her grandfather to help them, then pretending to be her mom. She remembered *looking* for her ticket in her clutch to distract the guard while Ally snuck in. She remembered working the crowd with Ally, trying to figure out who the Circle of Fifths agent was. She remembered watching as Michael approached Ally, and flirted. She remembered watching as Ally tried to stay on mission, but couldn't help but flirt back—at least a little bit.

Feilds Palace also brought back memories of many joyful moments over the years. It reminded her of helping Ally get ready for her wedding to Michael. She remembered a four-year-old Cole running around with Analyn, while she worried about how her baby bump looked in the brides maid dress, and Ally reassured her that she looked perfect. She remembered making the trip every year to attend Feilds Ball, watching as all their kids ran around together. She remembered coming to support Ally at the end of her pregnancy with Kate and Lynn. She remembered helping her sister while she antagonized over her decision to separate them to make sure they were safe.

But all the happy memories were overshadowed as Sarah stepped foot into the palace for the first time since she'd left after the funeral. Now, every happy memory morphed into watching Ally on her deathbed, asking Sarah to promise to keep their girls safe. All the good memories ended with Ally having a hard time breathing, and asking Sarah to protect Alyx, but also to protect Kate and Lynn. She remembered Ally crying as she asked Sarah to make sure Lynn knew she was loved, and to make sure she was welcomed into the family when it came time for her to return.

It didn't matter that it was Christmas, and the palace was decorated in joyful colors. Sarah walked in, and remembered her last moments with her sister. To her, the Palace might as well be decorated in black. Her sister was gone, and Sarah had failed. The people who had killed Ally were after Alyx, and Sarah had no idea how to keep her safe anymore.

Neil placed a comforting hand on her lower back, knowing how hard it was for his wife to return here. After Cole and Annie had died, they almost hadn't made it. Sarah blamed herself for their death, and had projected those feelings onto Neil. She pushed him away. Then they made the decision to quit the CIA. Neil had tried to make sure Sarah knew there were other options. She had trained her entire life to join the CIA, and he didn't want her to ever regret it, or blame him, or Alyx. She didn't take that very well. Neil tried to convince Sarah to be the one to join the FBI. In-stead, she applied to nursing school, and submitted Neil's application to the FBI for him. She insisted that their time apart would be good for them.

When Ally had died, it had been one more blow that Sarah didn't need. Despite her self-deprecating and self-destructive actions, Neil was there, comforting her. Watching as Neil cared for their daughter, made sure she was dealing with the losses she'd experienced, while also supporting and comforting her, and even Emily, Sarah couldn't help but fall more in love with him. He paid attention to everyone around him who was struggling, and gave them the love, support, and help they needed. Sarah hadn't been doing a good job of that. So she had recommitted herself to doing better.

As Sarah stood in the Grand Entry, memories swirling, and Neil made sure Sarah knew he was here if she needed him, Michael entered the room, greeting them. It had been a long time since he had seen his sister-in-law and her husband. It was strange to think he hadn't seen Sarah since Ally's funeral. He did, after all, see her daughter every summer.

Michael embraced Sarah in a long overdue hug. "I am overjoyed you have decided to join us for Christmas." He told her, ending the hug before embracing Neil as well. "It has been too long since we were all together."

Sarah nodded. "I'm sorry I couldn't bring myself to come back and visit sooner." She apologized.

Michael waved her off. "Bygones." He turned his attention to Lynn, who walked in the doors behind Sarah and Neil. He reached for his daughter with a smile. "I missed you, peanut." He greeted her, embracing her in a hug as well. "Are you sure you want to continue your studies in California? I miss you greatly."

"I'm sure." Lynn replied.

Alyx watched the scene from the side. There was really only one person she wanted to see, and he had yet to walk through the door. "Where's Peter?" She asked.

Her parents turned to look at her. Sarah tried to hide the hurt she was feeling. She missed her daughter more than Alyx could understand until she had kids of her own, and she looked like she was annoyed by her parents presence. "He couldn't come." Sarah told her daughter. "His dad has his passport, and wouldn't give it to him for the trip."

Alyx nodded, accepting the disappointment. Nothing in her life was working the way she wanted it to at the moment. Why would she be able to spend Christmas with her boyfriend? "I'm coming back with you though, right?"

Neil shook his head. "No. It's too dangerous."

Lynn cautiously approached her cousin. "I brought you his pullover. He said you would want it back."

Alyx took the jacket, but disappeared back into the house.

"How has she been?" Sarah asked Michael.

Michael shook his head. "She doesn't talk to very many people. Kate has tried to keep her company. The only other person she has even talked to is Stephan, and he left last week to spend the holiday with Lyshiria in Russia."

Sarah nodded, while Neil rubbed her back some more. They had been married for long enough, they almost knew one another's thoughts. Sarah was blaming herself for the way Alyx was reacting. Sarah didn't react very well to trauma, and clearly Alyx didn't either. Neil was trying to soothe her. It wasn't her fault. Alyx had to figure out how to deal with the trauma she had experienced herself. They could offer her all their love and support, but unless she accepted it, they couldn't do anything.

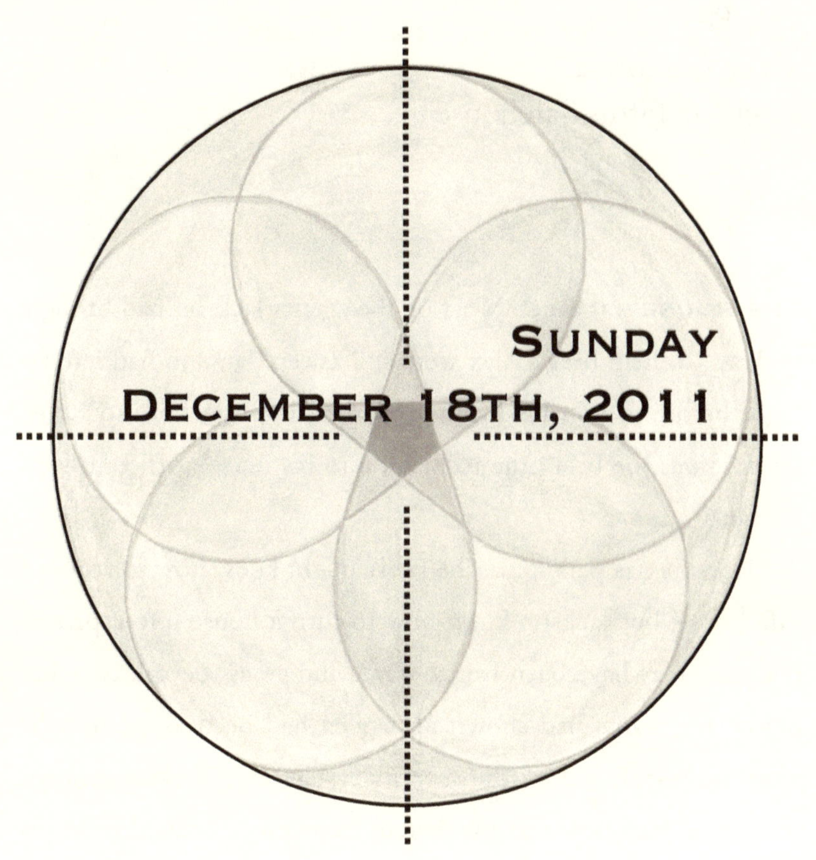
SUNDAY
DECEMBER 18TH, 2011

2:06 PST
Tracy, California
Circle of Fifths Safehouse

THE HOUSE was quiet. Most of the agents Jackson had brought to Tracy to help break Alyx were still asleep. Jackson had left the night before to join his brother on the campaign trail, so Kalen knew it was the best time to break into his uncle's office to steal his file.

Jackson was paranoid. The Hall's might know how to secure a safe house, but Jackson knew how to turn a house into a prison. His team may have been free to come and go as they pleased, but before the teams had shown up. Kalen had been asked to look after the installation of the security system after Jackson bought the house. He knew that the system included cameras that covered the house. It was impossible to get into Jackson's office without being caught by the cameras.

Kalen had been trained to evade cameras and surveillance for most of his life. He knew where all the blind spots in the system were, because he had been there when it was installed, and had spent more than enough time studying the footage before anyone else arrived. But Kalen's training taught him that sometimes evading cameras isn't necessary.

Sometimes you construct a narrative, and put on a show.

Kalen had used the blind spots he knew about to steal a uniform from one of his uncle's agents. Then at dinner he snuck laxatives in the food of the guard who was on-duty for the night shift.

He had been in and out of the bathroom all night.

Kalen watched the cameras from his uncle's remote account, waiting until he could see everyone accounted for but the guard he had drugged. With him in the bathroom again, Kalen started a timer on his watch, grabbed an empty black backpack he'd stolen from the guard's bunk, then snuck out of his room, down the hall to where the bathroom was before he stopped hiding. Dressed as a guard, when Jackson watched back the cameras, he wouldn't know it was Kalen who slipped into his office.

Kalen walked to the panel on the wall in the office, holding down the 9 key on the Scofield Security System panel that controlled the cameras in the house. Scofield Security Advisors was a recently emerging gold standard in security. Not only did they make security systems for homes, but they did systems for businesses, had multiple government contracts, secured any number of government buildings, had men that were hired for personal security, and had private contractors who were sent over seas. With a company growing so quickly, the Circle of Fifths had seen it fit to infiltrate and build themselves a back door into all their systems. It was something all Circle of Fifths agents were trained on. They all knew that holding down the nine key on the panel would force a system reboot.

Anyone in this house could have initiated that reboot, including the agent that would be missing from his post when the cameras went dark.

Kalen checked his watch to see how much time he had left. Just over seventeen minutes to find his file, copy it, find something to steal, hide it in the bunk of the agent in the bathroom, and get back to his room.

He had trained for this.

17:36 Kalen had been the one to set up this office before Jackson moved in. His uncle hadn't trusted him enough with the files—probably because he didn't want Kalen to know he had one on him—but Kalen had set up the filing cabinet, so he knew right where it was. He went straight to it, not wasting any time.

17:30 He pulled his lock picking kit out of one of his cargo pockets in his pants, using the skills his uncle had taught him to unlock his uncle's locks. He inserted the tension wrench, then used the pick to start moving the four pins of the lock into place. When the last pin clicked into place, he turned the lock, and slid the drawer out.

16:55 He flipped through the files in the drawer. He reached the *S* names before realizing he passed the M's, where his file would be, so he went back to the beginning and tried again. While his uncle had all of his files in alphabetical order by last name, Kalen couldn't find his folder. He searched through all of them to see if he was missing something. His file wasn't with the rest of the personnel files.

15:45 Behind a metal divider in the drawer, there were several large green folders labeled with the names of family members. He pulled his out, heading over to the commercial copier his uncle had brought in. He opened the first Manila folder, stacked the papers to be copied in the tray, selected the option to staple the packet, and hit the green start button.

15:10 With the copier reading the pages and spitting them out the copies like an automatic weapon spits out bullets, Kalen went back to the filing cabinet. He had seen a file that he thought would be useful to him. He pulled out the green file with the name Jackson, Kyrie on it. His uncle was always telling him that he was becoming more and more like his mother. She had been a traitor that was weak enough to let her own son kill her. If he wanted to make sure he didn't meet the same fate as his mother, he needed to study her and her mistakes.

14:50 The copier finished copying the papers in the first Manila folder. Kalen set the second green file down next to the printer, picked the originals out of the copied paper slot, put them back in the folder, opened the next one, and repeated the process.

Fortunately his green file only had two folders in it, so despite feeling the pressure of the clock, he was quickly done with his. He started copying the first of the folders in his mom's file, then took his file back to the filing cabinet, sliding it back into place so his uncle wouldn't know that it had been moved.

The first of his mother's folders finished copying, so he switched it over to copy the next one, then began to glance around his uncle's office. He had to find something that his uncle might not miss right away. He needed something valuable, but not too valuable. He needed something worth stealing, but something that wouldn't make his uncle furious when he discovered it was missing. If he stole information, his uncle would suspect a double agent. He didn't want to create an incident that escalated to the Nexus. He needed something mundane enough that his uncle wouldn't continue to look into things, but not something so mundane he became suspicious.

Kalen switched the folders over. His mother had three folders, but the third one was quite substantial. He started copying the third folder, using the otherwise wasted seconds coming up with a plan of what he could steal. Finally his eyes fell on something that could work. His uncle loved his books. He particularly liked to collect the first editions of some of his favorite authors. He had many books on psychology, criminal law, United States history, and even political theory. Among his collection of books, he had first editions of Sigmund Freud, and Machiavelli. Not only were they extremely valuable, but they would be easy to conceal, and their theft would appear monetary in nature. No one would notice that Kalen had copied some files.

10:50 With the unwavering knowledge that time was ticking away, he hurried over to his uncle's book shelf, shoving some of the most valuable first editions from the shelf in the backpack he had brought with him. Once the copier was finished printing his mother's file, he returned to the copier. He placed the books he was stealing next to the open folder, grabbed the papers that had just been copied, placed them back in the folders, and returned the file to the cabinet. He closed the drawer, and made sure the drawer locked. He pulled all of the papers from the copier, shoving them in the backpack as well. He pulled a rag out of his pocket, wiping down the handle of the filing cabinet and the copier.

9:53 With the back pack slung over his shoulder, Kalen left his uncle's office.

9:06 He snuck into his room, pulling the files out of his bag, and shoving them in his school bag to hide them among his school papers.

8:22 He left his room, walking down the hall to get to the bunk room for the guards. He found the bed that the missing guard slept in, and replaced the backpack he had stolen earlier. Now when Jackson went looking for the guard who broke into his office and stole his books, he would find it in the bunk of the guard who was the only one unaccounted for when the cameras blacked out.

6:51 Kalen found his way back to his room, quickly removing his things from the pockets of his pants, and stripping out of the guard uniform he had stolen. He couldn't get caught with the uniform, unless he wanted all of his hard made plans to go to waste. He threw on a pair of shorts he usually wore to bed, and left on the white shirt he had been wearing under the uniform.

5:43 He crumpled the clothes he had just changed out of, leaving his room to hurry back down to the bunk room. There was a hamper in the corner for them to place their soiled uniforms so they could be washed. If he could return the uniform to the hamper, it would no longer be in his possession for him to get caught with it, and it would be washed in a few hours with the other uniforms, getting rid of any DNA evidence that might reside on them from his dead skin cells that rubbed off onto the fabric.

5:27 He listened at the door of the bunk room, making sure the room was still sleeping, then slipped back in. He made his way over to the corner of the room where the hamper was kept, and opened the lid. He was immediately struck by the stench of dirty laundry. As much as he hated to do it, he knew what he had to do.

4:58 He lifted out half of the hamper of clothes, shoving the uniform he had stolen in the middle before replacing the clothes. Now they would smell like the rest of the clothes despite only being worn for a few minutes. It would also reduce the chance that they were picked out as the uniform the guard was wearing, and even if it was, they would be contaminated with who knows how many other DNA samples.

4:01 Kalen left the room, making his way back to his room for the final time, closing the door. He stood, back to the door, staring at his backpack which held the copied files. As much as he wanted to read them, now wasn't the time. He needed to leave his light off to ensure it appeared he was still asleep. He couldn't let any suspicion fall on him.

3:58 He made his way across the room to his bed, climbing in his bed and laying down. As he laid in his bed, he felt the carefully executed plan fighting against his curiosity for answers. Fortunately, his plan won.

3:07 He looked back over at the backpack one more time. Reading the files in the house was not a good idea. Here, he was under constant observation, and using the blindspots to hide was as much an admission of guilt as reading the stolen files in full view of the cameras. He could read the files at school. The students were as observant as blind mice. The school was his best option.

2:24 With a plan to read the files, so he could study the areas his uncle had noted as weaknesses, and improve on them, as well as make sure not to make his mother's mistakes, Kalen turned over in bed, turning away from the backpack and it's promises of answers.

1:30 Kalen closed his eyes, trying to fall asleep. His decision to stay up so late to break into his uncle's office had eaten up much of the time he should have been sleeping. It may have been winter break, but he always kept to a routine. He had to get up early in the morning to do his workout like he always did, or it would draw suspicion. It would be painful. He needed every precious moment of sleep to be on the top of his game. He had to convince Carlie to betray Alyx, figure out when she was coming home, not to mention pass his classes, and figure out how he could improve, so he wasn't giving his uncle anything negative to add to his file. He had only done it because he believed the files would be worth the sacrificed sleep. He could only hope they would be once he got back to school and found time to read them.

0:00 By the time Kalen's watch gave its gentle beep, and the security system came back up, he was sound asleep, dreaming about a girl and her infectious smile. A few minutes later, the unfortunate guard who was on duty left the bathroom, entirely unaware of the events that had occurred, nor the fact that he had been framed for them.

10:13 EST
Washington, D.C.
International Spy Museum

"**My complaint** remains. We need to find a new place to meet." George Carlyle said as he approached Phillip Jackson in the International Spy Museum.

Jackson shrugged. "Why change something that is working for us." He glanced at the man next to him. "You said you had information about McLean for me."

Carlyle sighed. "You are still trying to locate her, correct?"

"I wouldn't be talking to you if I wasn't." Jackson said annoyed.

"I discovered over Thanksgiving my son is dating her, going against everything I've trained him for."

"Old news. You better start giving me useful information, or this meeting is over. I am in town on Nexus business, and I have events to attend." Jackson snapped.

Carlyle bristled at Jackson's comments, but calmed himself down to deliver the information he had acquired. "He asked me for his passport so he could travel out of country for Christmas."

"How does that help me?"

"My son showed up on my doorstep no more than five days after McLean arrived to visit her grandfather. He never visits, but suddenly spends Thanksgiving with me the same week she is here?" Carlyle pointed out. "Those two can't spend more than a few days apart. But, as I understand it, she left home after you shot her, and hasn't been home since. It has been two weeks. Peter must be over eager to see her, and is likely planning on spending Christmas with her."

"I will look up his flight information, and see if I can't narrow down where she is at." Jackson commented.

"It won't do you much good." Carlyle said. "I told him he couldn't go."

Jackson flexed his right hand into fist, then back out a couple of times. "Then your information is useless."

"Is it?" He asked. "Because if my son was planning on making the trip to spend Christmas with her, it stands to reason her parents would as well."

Jackson stared at the exhibit they were in front of, not acknowledging the creativeness of Carlyle's suggestion. "Why did you tell him he couldn't go?"

"I don't approve of their relationship."

Jackson turned to Carlyle. "Well start to at least *appear* to like it, for the time being. I need their relationship to continue if I am going to break her."

"I thought the Nexus wanted you to *kill* her."

Jackson turned away so he was once again facing the exhibit. "I see an opportunity. She is moldable. I'm going to recruit her." Jackson glanced at Carlyle. "Your son doesn't seem keen to join us at the moment either, so this relationship that you don't *approve* of just might be the best way to make sure both of them join us."

9:23 PST
Tracy, California
Circle of Fifths Safehouse

KALEN SUBCONSCIOUSLY smiled as he received another text from Carlie. It had been a constant back and forth since they left school, and he would be a lying if he tried to say it was all just part of his mission.

He was lying to everyone. Including himself.

The two of them had plans to go to Winterfest at Great America on Tuesday. Just the two of them. It had been his idea. He had built a pretty good relationship with her before they left school for break, but if his uncle asked, he would explain his actions by telling him it was the best way to ensure the relationship was strong enough to withstand a McLean-sized battering-ram. Dating Carlie was the next step.

Kalen scowled as Banthup came into the room. "Jackson just gave me an assignment, and you are supposed to help me."

"What do you need me to do now?" Kalen complained. "I have my own mission, you know."

"Jackson believes that the Halls might be going to McLean for Christmas. We are supposed to figure out where they are going." Banthup explained.

"What's the point if she is just coming back after Christmas?" Kalen asked annoyed. He was really tired of doing a bunch of work for his uncle, just for it to be negated later. If there was a reason for it, and it made an actual impact, fine. But watching flights for two weeks just to figure out where Alyx was for a couple of days before she was back at home in her bed… It would be a better use of his time if he continued to develop his relationship with Carlie.

"I just do as I'm told. An order is an order." Banthup replied as he handed Kalen his laptop. "My orders were to have you help me. So help me and stop asking questions."

Kalen fumed as he put his phone down and opened his laptop. His uncle seemed to surround himself with people that never tried to think for themselves, and it was really starting to grate on his nerves.

14:56 PST
Tracy, California
Promgen Headquarters

Dylan Hall threw a suitcase in front of Peter, distracting him from the map he had in front of him. Since he had found out his dad wouldn't let him go to London, and it wasn't safe to bring Alyx home, he had thrown himself into finding a plan for stopping Jackson. He knew where the Circle of Fifths was hiding. Neil was working on a finding evidence of their crimes to arrest them. Once he had enough, and he had gotten the proper arrest warrants, Peter wanted to have a plan to catch them.

"What is this?" Peter asked.

Hall smiled. "You're coming to Hall Christmas 2011."

Peter straightened up, looking at Hall confused. "My dad has my passport and won't let me go."

"You need a break."

"Doesn't change the fact that I don't have my passport."

Hall nodded toward the bag. "Just pack your stuff. I will solve the passport problem."

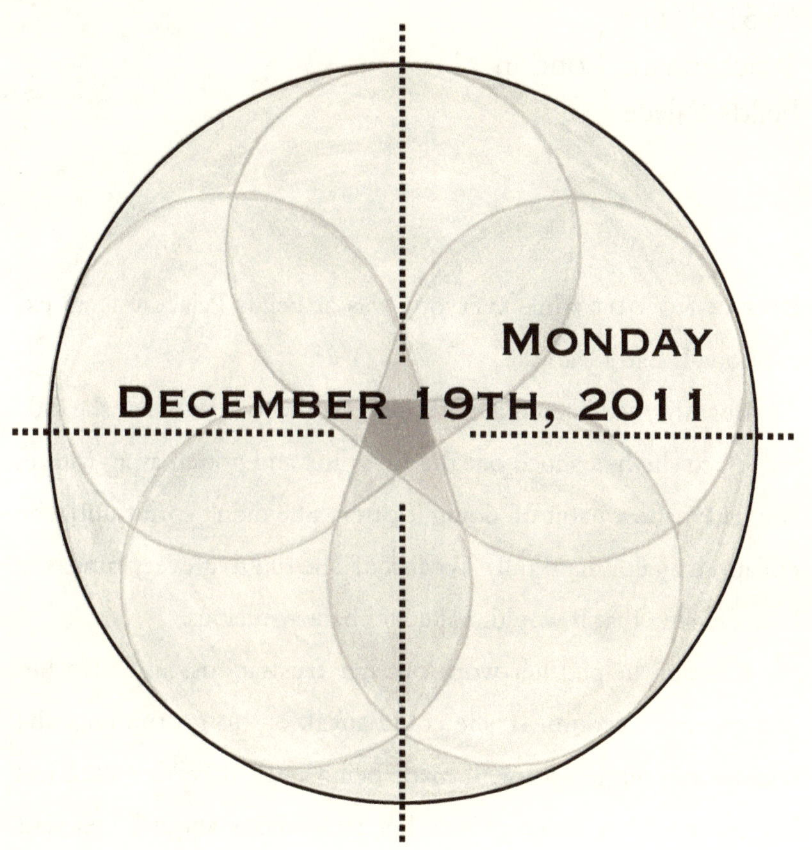

Monday
December 19th, 2011

15:51 GMT
Twickenham, London
Feilds Palace

SNEAKING OUT while everyone was at Feilds Palace was an exceptionally bad idea.

But Alyx had been full of those recently, so that's what she did.

Once she had snuck out the first time and gotten away with it, she had made a habit of doing it often. She didn't sprint until she collapsed again, thankfully, because if she did that every time, she had a feeling that it would make Stephan suspicious.

Running helped her work out her frustrations, and gave her just enough freedom. If she could sneak out to go running, she could sneak out to escape. It made being stuck at Feilds Palace feel like more of her choice. Once her frustrations about being sent somewhere against her will had faded, she was able to start looking into herself. If she was being completely honest, she didn't feel safe in California. Part of her was relieved she didn't have to go back with her parents. She had been dreading that moment for the entire two weeks she was gone, but she couldn't admit that without admitting that her parents were right, so she had been miserable to be around. Now that she knew she wasn't going back after Christmas, she could actually enjoy the holiday. Almost. One thing was missing: Peter.

She could be mad at him for not calling—like Kate was—but she knew why he hadn't. He had very clearly told her he would answer any time she called. He was being respectful and putting the ball in her court. When she was ready, she could call. She didn't know if she was ready to discuss how the shooting had made her feel, but she knew that if she could talk to anyone, it would be Peter. He wouldn't push her to do anything she wasn't comfortable with. He would listen, and offer her comfort. He would let her know she was loved, and remind her who she was.

That was why she so desperately wanted to see him for Christmas. Finding out that her parents had kept secrets from her had hurt. She wasn't sure if they would decide to lie to her again, or keep more secrets in the name of her safety. In one day, she had lost both of her closest confidantes. And the secrets they kept meant that she couldn't trust Emily either, which hurt more than her parents. She knew parents filter some of their struggles. But Emily had been a sister to her. Come to find out she was just another adult that didn't think she could handle the dark things she had experienced in life.

She was a little over a year away from eighteen. She was making plans for her future. They couldn't continue to keep things from her. Hopefully they learned their lesson.

Alyx stopped by the water, looking out across the Thames. She pulled her phone out of the zipper pocket on her nondescript track jacket. As she opened the phone app, she selected the contact at the top of her favorites: Peter.

It was time she reach out. If anyone knew how disappointed she was not to see him, it would be him, because he felt it too.

She watched the beauty of the Thames at dusk, as the lights of the city slowly turned on while waiting for him to answer his phone. Instead of connecting, and hearing his voice as he answered, asking how she was, she heard his voice reciting his mailbox message.

She had forgotten how nice it was to hear his voice.

"Hey Peter, I'm sorry I haven't called, I just..." She trailed off as she started leaving a message. "I miss you, and I was really hoping I'd see you when you came for Christmas, but I guess your dad is making that impossible. How are you doing with that?" Alyx paused. It was hard talking to a voice that couldn't respond. "Anyway, give me a call back when you get this? I'm not sleeping well, so anytime will be fine. I love you." Alyx hung up.

With one more look at the Thames as she put her phone back, Alyx decided it was time to go home.

She shook her head as she started jogging back. Since when had Feilds Palace become home?

16:12 GMT
Twickenham, London
Feilds Palace

"ARE YOU sure you don't want to come with us?" Michael asked his dad. Since the Circle of Fifths had killed his mom, his dad had withdrawn, and rarely interacted with the public. While he was still alive, he maintained all his titles, but Michael had taken on most of his duties. The only thing that had kept Michael from doing the same when Ally died was knowing he had a daughter that was counting on him.

Kate had been both his and his father's salvation.

Thomas Feilds may have withdrawn from the public eye, moved downstairs to one of the guest suites, and given Michael the Master's suite when he married Ally, but he maintained a role in both his son's and granddaughter's life. Since Ally's death, he had yet to miss a birthday or a Christmas. Their holidays were small, but they were meaningful. When they had discussed having Christmas somewhere other than Feilds' Palace, Michael had immediately worried about his father.

"I am certain. I think it's past time for me to spend time with your brother and his family for Christmas." Thomas answered.

Michael shook his head. "We could invite Rafael, Nika, Lyshiria, and Stephan to come with us."

"I don't think that boy is ready to face the family. That's why he ran away to spend time with Lyshiria in Moscow." Thomas commented. "Besides, you have jumped from one extreme to the other. I have not spent the holiday with more that just a couple people in many years. I think I've found I rather prefer it that way."

Michael sighed. "As long as you are ok with it," he conceded.

"Of course. I'm glad you can spend time with Ally's family. Kate and Lynn need to have someway to connect with their mother. Maybe I will be up to a big family Christmas next year or the year after." Thomas told his son.

Michael nodded. "Alyx and I will be back just after New Years."

"I will come back with Stephan." Thomas mocked his son.

They both turned to look as the entrance at the side of the house opened, and Alyx walked into the house, still panting from her run.

"Where have you been?" Michael asked.

"I went for a run. And before you ask, it was a Stephan-approved route, entirely within Feilds Palace grounds." Alyx lied.

Michael checked his watch. "Well you better hurry and pack. We are leaving for the airport in an hour." He nodded to his father. "Which reminds me, I need to make sure the drivers MI-6 sent are on their way." Michael walked away, most likely heading to his office.

"Airport?" Alyx asked Thomas.

Thomas smiled at Alyx, putting a kind hand on her shoulder. "I believe they decided you have been locked up in this stuffy place far too long. You are all heading to a place that I've never been, but I hear it is quite beautiful. After the year we've had, we all need a white Christmas." Thomas pushed Alyx towards the stairs that would lead to her bedroom suite. "Now hurry. You won't find out what this wonderful surprise is unless you get packed."

Alyx walked towards the stairs, glancing back at Thomas. Despite not being related to him, he had always treated Alyx like another granddaughter. He was the reason she hadn't gotten in more trouble than she had. More than once, he had caught her at the beginning of a boredom-induced stunt, and had redirected her energies. He had been the one to encourage her to search for the hidden passageways and rooms in the palace, which had led her to finding one of the rooms that Ally had taken her to as a little girl. That alone was enough for her to do as Thomas said.

He had also teased a surprise. She would do anything to figure out the surprise.

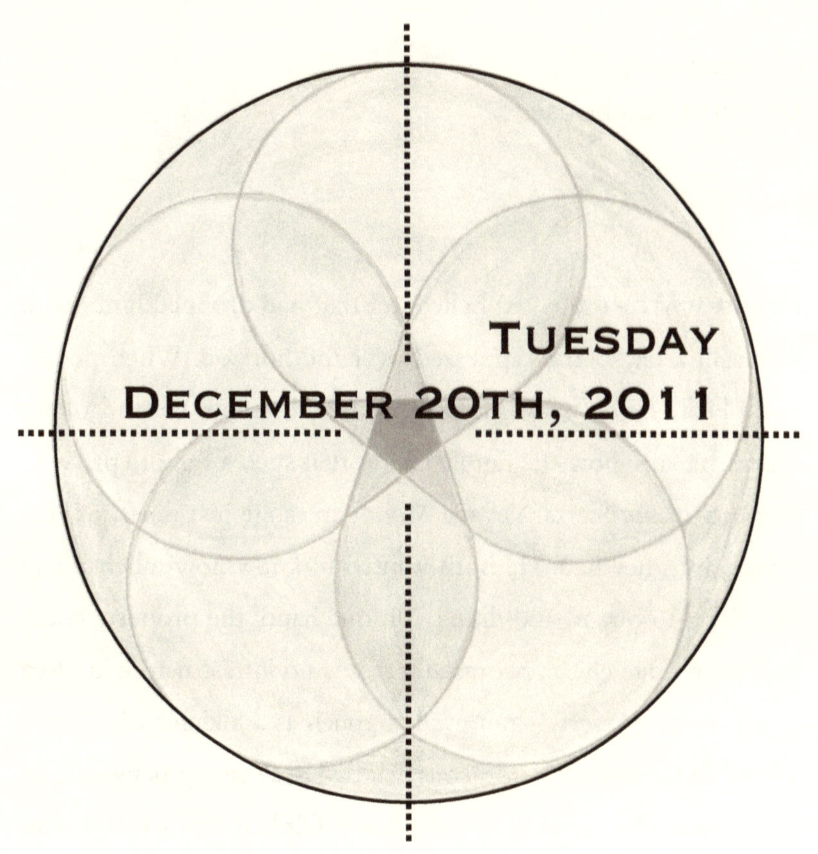

Tuesday
December 20th, 2011

12:16 PST
California
Waterfall Safehouse

Peter watched as the helicopter that had dropped him off at Waterfall a day before appeared over the horizon. When people said a Hall safe house was impossible to get to, they weren't joking. He wasn't sure how the family had gotten such a remote piece of property in the Sierra Nevada Mountain range just north of Yosemite, but they had. He both wanted to know how much it had cost them to buy it, and didn't. On one hand, the property could have been quite cheap, because there was no infrastructure in place to get to the property—not even so much as a hiking trail. On the other hand, it was on a gorgeous wooded peak sitting between two small lakes. The views were such that it felt like they were in a resort in Yosemite, not a private residence north of the well known national park.

The remote nature of the property, however, and the fact that the massive cabin was hidden among the trees, meant that the only way to get to the safe house was by helicopter, and know *exactly* where to land. When Hall had flown in with his wife, children, and Peter the day before, he had landed the helicopter in a small clearing separate from the house, and led them on an unmarked trail to the hidden paradise. Hall had made several trips back and forth since then, bringing in supplies, such as gasoline for the generators, and enough food to feed the sixteen people for the week and a half they would be staying. Addy had gone with him, insisting they needed food for a Christmas Eve and Christmas dinner, as well as stuff to celebrate the new year.

Before Hall left with his wife for supplies, Hall had given Thane and Chelsi a list of things they needed to do. They had spent the day collecting fire wood to burn in the cabin's many fireplaces in order to heat the living spaces. Addy had also given them the task of finding a Christmas tree. While they were waiting for Addy and Dylan to return, the three of them had chopped wood until they were exhausted. Fortunately, they had enough to last a couple of days.

When Addy came back, she had enlisted their help with putting groceries away while Dylan started the generators, preparing it for the rest of the guests. Even though they were all exhausted, she then insisted they decorate the Christmas tree. It was the first time in eleven years that they were going to have a big family Christmas. She was going to make sure it was perfect, despite it being a fairly last minute plan.

They needed this.

Watching as Hall guided the helicopter onto the unmarked landing pad, Peter couldn't help but think about how many people were coming together for Alyx. Fifteen people making last minute changes to their Christmas and New Years plans to fly to a remote cabin spoke volumes to how much she was loved.

Considering the plan had been for all of those people to meet them in London until Peter couldn't get his passport to travel with them, he felt as though they were making the change just as much for him as they were for him. In reality, it was likely because they knew it would make Alyx happy, but he hadn't been doing too well himself.

As soon as the helicopter touched down, Peter ran to the door to open it and help the passengers out. The person closest to the door was an older woman. Her white-blonde hair fell in soft waves down her back in a way that reminded him of Alyx. As she turned to him, her blue eyes filled with confusion.

"Il n'est pas un de mes petits-enfants." The woman commented. She looked at Dylan who was climbing out of the pilot's seat to help remove the luggage from the back of the helicopter. "Il est qui?"

"Je m'appelle Peter. Je suis le petit ami de votre petite-fille Alyx." Peter explained. He guessed the woman was Alyxandrie Hall, the mother of Sarah, Dylan, and Emily, making her his girlfriend's grandmother, and based on the way she lit up when he not only understood her questions to be able to respond, but did so in French, she was.

"I can see why my granddaughter is smitten with you." She replied with a smile. "She might complain about the small grammatical mistakes you make, but even your accent is quite good." She complemented Peter. She turned back to look at her daughter as she climbed out of the helicopter ahead of her boyfriend, who Peter had yet to meet. "Now if only my daughters had the good sense to marry men like Peter."

Emily rolled her eyes. "This is California, mom. Most everyone learns Spanish as a second language, not French. It's more useful." Emily nodded at Peter, giving him a hug. "I'm glad you could come." She snatched her boyfriend's arm. "Peter, this is my fiancé Bryan Ryneholt. Bryan, this is Vee's boyfriend Peter."

"Je n'ai jamais aimé ce surnommer que tu lui as donné. Ses parents ont donné un prénom très beau. Pourquoi dois-tu remplacer quelque chose de… de—"

"What would you have me call her? Alyxandrie. Too weird." Emily replied to her mother's complaint.

"You could call her Alyx like everyone else."

"Or, I could call her something that is meaningful to me."

Bryan extended his hand to Peter, shaking it with a chuckle. "It's not too late to bail. This family doesn't get any better. It's the sane thing to do."

Peter gave Bryan a small smile. "What does that make you, since you bought a ring instead of backing out."

"Fair enough." Bryan conceded. "But what can I say? I love Em, crazy family and all."

Alyxandrie shook her head and started muttering under her breath as she started the trek up to the cabin. "Il est un vrai beauf. Fou, pas de bonne andouille. Il va t'assassiner dans ton sommeil."

"Maman!" Emily protested, chasing after her mom.

Bryan leaned in close to Peter. "Hey, you speak French. Would you mind translating?"

"It's nothing worth repeating." Emily hollered back, making sure to send Peter a look that told him not to even think about translating what her mother had said.

Peter gave Bryan a sympathetic look. "Sorry."

Bryan shrugged, following Emily. "It was worth a try." Dylan just chuckled.

Peter loaded himself up on bags and turned to the last two passengers from the helicopter. Looking at the two of them, it was clear they were Neil's parents.

"Director McLean, Mrs. McLean." Peter greeted.

"Please. You are dating my granddaughter. Call me Madelyn." Neil's mother told him. Peter just nodded in response.

Neil's father placed a firm hand on Peter's shoulder. "Let's you and I have a chat on the way up to the cabin, shall we?"

"Yes sir." Peter replied, making his voice as steady as he could.

Dylan had to swallow another laugh. "I have to go pick up the rest of the group, otherwise I'd have fun watching this."

Dylan gave Peter a half-comforting pat on his shoulder before turning and getting back into the helicopter, leaving Peter alone with the Director of the CIA, who just happened to also be his girlfriend's grandfather.

What could possibly go wrong?

14:01 PST
California
Waterfall Safehouse

"IT'S BEEN too long since I last visited Waterfall." Michael commented through the headsets as Dylan landed the helicopter in a clearing of trees in the Sierra Nevada mountain range.

Alyx snapped her attention away from the window and the scenery beyond, but before she could voice the question that immediately appeared with Michael's comment, Kate did.

"You've been here before?" Kate asked.

Michael nodded, turning back to look at his daughter. "Just after I met your mother. Rafael and I were in danger, so my father asked Sarah and Ally to take the two of us somewhere we would be safe while we waited for the threat to be taken care of. Ally brought us here to hide out. It's actually when the two of us started to get so close."

"I didn't know that." Kate commented. "I don't think you have ever told me how the two of you met."

"It's a story I have a hard time telling considering how it

ended." Michael admitted. "But this place was a very important place for us. We came back a few times over the years. She actually told me she was pregnant with you here."

Alyx turned back to the window. This stupid family and their stupid secrets that they couldn't help but keep.

The helicopter landed, and the engines slowly started whirring down as Hall started switching stuff off. Michael, Sarah, and Neil didn't wait for the blades to stop spinning. They removed their headsets, opened the door, and Neil and Michael climbed out. They turned around, ducked down under the slowing, but still fast moving blades, and held out their hands to take the bags that Sarah started handing them. They looked like a well oiled machine that did this sort of thing all the time.

For all Alyx knew, they did.

Neil and Michael started carrying most of the bags to the tree line where they disappeared on some non-existent trail. Sarah looked at the three girls still in the helicopter as she got out expectantly.

"Are you girls coming?" Sarah asked, prompting the three of them to climb out of the helicopter. Sarah picked up the two remaining bags, and led the girls to the tree line where Michael and Neil had disappeared. Kate and Lynn followed, their bodies shaking with the eager anticipation of a big family Christmas they had never had before.

Alyx brought up the rear. She was not looking forward to

spending the next week and a half in close quarters with all of her family.

She wasn't looking forward to spending a week and a half with the people who had lied to her for the last eleven years of her life.

There wasn't a clear path to the cabin, but it was clear that Sarah knew exactly where she was going. She wove in and around the trees until they came to another clearing. Alyx looked around, admiring the effort that had been put into keeping the large cabin hidden. Despite there being a clearing large enough for the cabin, the trees were left to grow taller than it, their branches and leaves stretching far beyond their trunks, so the canopy hid the cabin, so it was extremely difficult to spot from the sky. The cabin itself was made from wood from the very trees that had been cleared from the area to build the house, giving it a natural camouflage. The roof was then painted so it too was camouflaged from the sky.

Despite the efforts to ensure the cabin couldn't be discovered from the sky, it was beautifully designed. Alyx didn't know how old the cabin was, but based on Michael's comments as they were landing, she knew it had to be at least a couple decades old. She couldn't tell. The design was timeless. It could have been 20, 30, 40 years old, maybe older, but it could have just as easily been designed and built last year.

"Why is this cabin called Waterfall?" Kate asked as she followed Sarah up the stairs to the giant wrap around porch.

Sarah reached for the door knob, opening the door. "It's a

code name. All of our safe houses have one. It's a way for us to identify where we are going, without our enemies finding out. This one got the name *Waterfall* because it is close to Yosemite. It's vague enough someone who hasn't been here can't figure out where it is, but it's something we can easily remember." She explained, letting the girls into the house.

Kate asked another question, but Alyx didn't hear it. She definitely didn't pay attention to her mom's answer. In the middle of the rustic great room, she saw Peter.

Everything else disappeared.

Alyx stood, stuck in the doorway as she waited to see if Peter would notice her, and what he would do when he saw her. He had said he would answer any time she called, but when she was finally ready to call, he hadn't answered. Now that she was here, and he was too, her brain came up with a multitude of logical explanations. They were so far from civilization, she doubted there was any cell service. If he had been here when she called, he couldn't have answered. If he was flying in the helicopter here, he also couldn't have answered.

Instead of any of the reasonable explanations, however, her brain decided to fixate on all the worst, and most unrealistic ones.

He didn't love her anymore.

The time apart made him realize it was just a relationship of convenience.

She had taken too long to call. He thought she hated him.

Peter looked over as the door opened again. Since he had walked back with Director McLean and his wife, he had been anxiously awaiting Alyx' arrival. When the door had opened to let Michael and Neil in, Peter had felt his hopes rise and fall faster than a pendulum. This time, as it opened, he watched as Sarah, Kate, and Lynn came in. Every person who walked in the door, but wasn't Alyx, increased the pressure he felt in his chest.

He was desperate to see her again.

As she stopped in the doorway, his eyes locked with hers. Under her winter coat, she was wearing the sweatshirt he'd given her, and in her hand, she was fiddling with the keychain he had given her the last time he'd seen her.

He had missed her so *much.*

Peter crossed the space between them with long strides, pulling Alyx into a hug, and the cabin. She relaxed into the hug, the anxious thoughts that had been spiraling in her head quieting the longer she stood in his arms.

Reason started to slip back in. She no longer needed the explanations for him not answering, because she no longer needed to combat the negative thoughts.

"I thought I wasn't going to see you for Christmas." Alyx finally admitted. Her voice was mumbled by Peter's shoulder, but her words still reached his ears.

"Your family decided to move Christmas here, so I could come." He explained. "They all love you a lot." He kissed the top of her head, running his hand down her hair. “I do too.”

Emily folded her arms, watching Alyx and Peter. “I see how it is. You start dating the boy you’ve been telling me about for years, and asked me for advise to talk to, and now I come second.”

Alyx didn’t move her head from Peter’s shoulder. She didn’t make any sort of movement that would indicate she heard Emily at all.

Sarah gave her sister a hug. “She hasn’t so much as acknowledged Neil or I while we were in London.” She told her sister. “She’s still mad we lied. Added to the trauma…”

“I’m right here.” Alyx replied, finally bringing her head out of Peter’s shoulder. “Please stop talking about me as if I’m not right here. Stop talking about me like I’m some sort of fragile doll that will break at any moment. Stop keeping secrets from me because you think I can’t handle it. Just stop.”

Alyx broke away from Peter, walking back out the door.

Without another look at everyone else in the room, Peter grabbed his coat, and ran out after her.

14:25 PST

Tracy, California

Circle of Fifths Safehouse

KALEN TURNED another page in his mother's file as Banthup threw down another passenger list from a flight leaving from Oakland International Airport. Banthup was insufferable, so any small amount of rebellion Kalen could get away with, he was going to take it. When Banthup had used his CIA clearance to request access to all of the passenger lists from the three surrounding airports servicing international flights, then demanded that Kalen print them all out, Kalen obliged. He printed out the lists from all the flights that had left San Francisco, Oakland, and Sacramento in the last few days, or were going to leave before Christmas. Kalen had then slid the passenger lists from Sacramento in a Manila folder with his mother's file. When Alyx had flown home after last summer, she had flown into Oakland, but the San Francisco airport was just across the bay, so he gave Banthup those two airports.

Banthup was given the illusion of help, while still being forced to find the McLeans by himself. And while he was at it,

Kalen got to read his mother's file. Two birds. One stone.

So far, his mother's file had been pretty boring. His uncle hadn't approved of her marrying Kalen's father, but when that marriage resulted in Kalen, he had taken the opportunity to send his sister undercover. Sarah Hall had formed a group of female agents who were also mothers, with the intent to normalize it, and offer the mothers support in a male-dominated and cutthroat field. From what he could tell, she was undercover with another agent, who had been recruited to the Circle of Fifths when one of its mem-bers got her pregnant. The two of them were close. Where he was at in his mother's history, her friendship with the other double-agent was starting the cause problems.

June 25th, 1999

Kyrie came to me with concerns about the methods the Nexus uses for recruitment and retention of agents. She has been talking with Elisabeth Stevens. Stevens told her she was blackmailed in order to join the Circle of Fifths, and that her son's father has threatened to take her son away if she doesn't do as the Circle of Fifths say. Kyrie is concerned what that means for her. Kalen is her world, and she would rather die than let anything happen to him.

Two notes from the conversation:

1. *I need to report this to George Carlyle. If Peter is going to be the asset we need him to be, his mother is an issue. She seems to be too soft, and not devoted to our cause. She is a liability, especially in Peter's life.*
2. *Kyrie might not be suited to this undercover mission. She is starting to lose faith in the Circle of Fifths. She is easily susceptible to per-*

suasion, especially when it comes to the children of the Promising Generation. She is not willing to do what is needed for our cause if it involves harming children. She might need to die if Kalen is going to be a loyal and useful asset to the Circle of Fifths.

Kalen reread the last sentence a couple of times. Was that his mom's fault? Was it her motherly instinct to protect children that led to her betrayal of the Circle of Fifths? But if that was the case, that brought so many other questions to mind. Why did Kalen kill her if she was trying to protect him, and make sure he wasn't taken away from her to make her comply with the Circle of Fifths?

"This makes no sense." Banthup complained.

Kalen looked up at Banthup startled, thinking Banthup was talking about the file Kalen had been reading, and the doubts it was causing. It took him a minute to realize Banthup was still very focused on finding Alyx. "What makes no sense."

"Because Hall has been holding all information even tangentially related to McLean very close to his vest, I don't know when her parents may have left, but I do know exactly when he left for vacation. Hall left with his family and Peter two days ago, but I can't find any flights in their names." Banthup complained.

"Maybe the safe house they took Alyx to is within driving distance." Kalen commented, turning the page. He had so many unanswered questions, like if Elisabeth Steven's son, who was mentioned, was Peter Carlyle. He seemed familiar, and if their mother's had been close, they may have played together. Of course, since he wanted answers, he found one of the passenger lists on the next page. He knew he would regret randomly inserting the pages.

"Except Jackson found proof that they used the private airport to fly her someplace." Banthup argued. "And Jackson's intel suggested Carlyle needed his passport."

"Mexico." Kalen suggested, searching through the list of names on his passenger list. "They could drive to Mexico. It might be a bit of a long drive, but if they didn't want where they were going recorded, they might think it's worth it."

"Anytime they go through customs, it would be recorded." Banthup argued.

"Then maybe they are using aliases." Kalen replied. "If you think that the Hall family doesn't have their fair share of aliases to use, you are sadly mistaken. Why do you think we haven't found Alyx yet?"

Banthup shot Kalen a dangerous look. "Maybe you have found something in your passenger lists."

"No Halls, Hayes, or Carlyles." Kalen answered. He finished reading through his list, turning to the next page to continue reading his mom's file. He checked his phone for the time. He had plans with Carlie he didn't want to be late for. "Well, this is great, but my mission calls. Good luck with the names."

Banthup scowled at Kalen as he left, picking up his next packet of names. This was going to take forever.

14:30 PST
California
Waterfall Safehouse

PETER SEARCHED through the trees to try and find where Alyx went, finally finding her on the bank of one of the lakes the cabin sat in between. He walked up behind her, taking note of the fact that she wasn't wearing gloves. What was even worse, was the fact that Peter knew how her parents were, and how they had been since the shooting especially. They may not have even told her where they were taking her, so she may not have brought gloves for the trip at all.

They thought they were keeping her safe, but it was putting her in danger instead. What she didn't know *could* hurt her.

And it was. More than they cared to notice.

Peter took his left glove off, handing it to Alyx as he joined her on the bank.

Alyx turned to look at him, a question in her eyes. "Thanks, but don't you need this?"

Peter smiled at her. "See, I was hoping I could share this with you." Peter showed her the hot hands packet he had taken out of his pocket after handing her his glove. It was sitting in his ungloved left hand. All she had to do was lock her fingers with his.

She put the glove on her left hand, then gave her right hand to Peter. With fingers locked, he pulled her hand into his coat pocket. Between the hot hand packet, the shared warmth of their intertwined hands, and his pocket, he was pretty confident in his ability to prevent frost-bite for their ungloved hands.

"I don't want to talk." Alyx told him.

"That's ok." Peter replied.

"And I don't want to hear you defend them. It's not going to work." She added.

"Wasn't planning on it." Peter reassured her.

Alyx sighed. "I feel so petty running away from my family. I mean, I know they love me, in their own weird, *extremely* overprotective way. They have made a huge effort to make sure we are all together for Christmas, and they even brought you, because they know you make me happy and they want to make sure I'm happy. I'm allowed to be mad at them for lying to me. I was mad at you for lying to me."

"Why did you forgive me so quickly?" Peter asked.

Alyx shrugged. "Did you actually lie to me?"

"I withheld," Peter admitted.

"I know," Alyx sighed. "I think I forgave you because I could tell you felt bad, and you've done what you could to not do it again. Every time I turn around, I discover something else they have hidden from me," she complained. "Case in point, Michael mentioned in the helicopter that he and Ally came here all the time. Apparently this is where their story started."

"Do you know how your parents met?" Peter asked.

"I think they told me once. I wasn't doing the best job of listening," she admitted.

"Does anyone in your family talk about Ally very often? I don't know that I've heard them tell very many stories about her."

"It's hard to talk about her. I was really little, but I remember her funeral."

"So how do you know that Michael hasn't told you about being here because he's keeping secrets, and not because it's hard for him to talk about his dead wife?" Peter questioned, forcing Alyx to address her doubts with reason.

Alyx smacked the arm that was holding her hand in his pocket with her gloved hand. "I thought I told you not to defend them."

"I'm just asking the questions you would be asking yourself if you weren't so blinded with anger." Peter turned to look at her, smiling at the frown on her face. "You are the one that said you didn't want to talk."

"You're right. Talking about my current dilemma will only make me even more angry, and blinded by anger, as you put it. Let's talk about your family drama."

"I'd rather not. My parents aren't worth mentioning."

"What a pair we make. Two kids who would rather not talk to their parents. We're not that different—"

"Your parents love you." Peter interrupted. "And even though they do things you hate, at the end of the day, you still recognize that. My parents don't love me. My mother left me with my father —who never acknowledged me—when I was maybe seven. I tried to call her *every* day, and she never called back. My father didn't do anything for me. I had to feed myself, find my own way to school, you name it. Then he left. Wraith stepped in as a *father figure* but all he cared about was himself and his position in the CIA. He saw me as a way to get there." Peter explained. "Hall might be a bit cold, but even he *cares*. You have been in London. They have no need to be nice to me, or invite me over for dinner. Yet they do. Your family has adopted me because I love you, you love me, and they want to love and support the things you love. Our families are nothing a like."

As Peter finished his rant, the echo of his words returned them to silence. He had been doing his best not to take sides in this fight Alyx had going on with her parents. He could see the argument from both sides, and he cared enough about both sides to stay neutral, but he couldn't do it anymore.

That was one way to ruin a relationship. Take sides against your significant other with her family. He really didn't want to ruin this.

"I'm sorry." He apologized. "I just…" He sighed. "Clearly I have a lot of issues with my family, and I know that you aren't happy with yours right now. I just want you to know that no matter how much you hate what they are doing, they are good people who love you and want the best for you. But if you need to be mad at them and give them the silent treatment, I can't judge. I've been giving my mom the silent treatment for ten years."

Alyx considered what Peter had said as she stared at the frozen lake. This was a gorgeous view. She knew that part of her was just mad that this was the first chance she had to see it. The other part of her had to acknowledge that her parents had done a good job of keeping her safe, because this *was* the first time she was seeing it. She hated that she didn't trust her parents. She hated that *they* didn't trust *her* with their secrets. It made her doubt herself. What had she done or not done that had broken their trust of her?

"Did they really invite you over for dinners while I was in London?" She asked.

Peter nodded. "Almost every night. I declined a lot of them, because I was working on finding a way to bring you home, and then they started showing up with dinner. I guess they figured if I wasn't coming over, I wasn't eating."

If Alyx had been paying closer attention to what Peter was saying, she may have asked if he was eating. Instead, all she could hear as he was talking was the little voice at the back of her head that told her that her parents trusted Peter more than they trusted her.

She fought to tune it out. The problem was it sounded a lot like Jackson.

18:05 PST
Santa Clara, California
California's Great America

CARLIE SMACKED Kalen's arm as they waited in line for the Vortex ride at Great America. He may have been trained to be his uncle's ruthless assassin, but he wasn't fearless. He was afraid of more things than he cared to admit. Some of the fears on his annoying list was a fear of failing, and a fear of not being in control. In all of his training, he had never been to an amusement park. When they had arrived at the park, Carlie had immediately taken him to the closest roller coaster, where he had discovered his fear of not being in control made him afraid of roller coasters. Carlie was not afraid. She loved all of them. She had grown up in the state, had been to the park every year, and had ridden every ride dozens of times. She was insane. After taking him on some of the easier roller coasters as a *warm-up*, she had finally dragged Kalen to her favorite one.

Kalen had been reluctant to agree to the ride. They had walked past the ride several times, and every time he had, he had seen the loops and corkscrews. Of all the rides he had seen, Vortex and Demon were the rides he least wanted to go on. Yet here he stood, going on a ride because Carlie wanted to.

"It's not too late to back out." Carlie told Kalen.

Kalen couldn't help but think about how wrong she was. It was a matter of pride at this point. How would he look if he backed out? He had made her a promise. If they could find the entrance to the ride, and the line wasn't too long, he would go on it. As someone who had been trained to manipulate people, he should have seen the signs that she was playing him. She knew exactly where the entrance to the ride was. She'd known the entire time. The moment he had made that promise, he'd sealed his fate. Now to keep his pride, he had to keep his promise.

And he had a desperate desire to impress her. The way her face had lit up when he had agreed to go on the ride was worth any fear he had to face. He just had to get a grip on his fear so he wasn't letting it control him.

"It's fine." Kalen said. "I promised I would go, and I'm not someone who likes to break his promises." He turned to look at her. He could get some shameless flirting in while he was at it. "Besides, I saw how much you wanted to go on this ride, and I want to make sure you're happy."

His comment gave him the reward of her smile. "Ok. What if we make conversation to distract you from the anticipation of your fear?" She suggested, showing just how smart she was. It was appropriate that he was in her psychology class, because she clearly understood the subject better than she let on. "This is supposed to be a date, so let's get to know each other. I'll ask a question, you answer, then you ask me a question and so on."

"What kind of questions?" Kalen asked.

"Well, I know you live with your uncle, and you told us why, and if you are willing to go that deep, we can, but let's start with the basics. What's your favorite color? Mine's yellow."

"Black." He answered. "You know that I am scared of roller coasters, apparently. What are you afraid of?"

Carlie shrugged. "I don't know. I don't like to dwell on my fears," she admitted, "but if I have to think of one, I think I'd have to say spiders." She shivered a little bit, thinking about the evil little creatures with their eight hairy legs.

Kalen laughed at her reaction. "Really? They're that bad?"

Carlie nodded. "Yes. They are evil." She paused for a moment. "What's another question I could ask you?" They stepped forward as the line moved, giving Carlie a little to come up with the next thing she wanted to ask Kalen. She smiled as she finally came up with a "What's your favorite song?"

"Song?" He asked, confirming he'd heard her right.

"Or band, or genre, if you can't choose just one song."

"I can do band." Kalen told her. "I really like Fall Out Boy."

"I don't think I've heard of them." She admitted.

"I kinda figured you hadn't. You don't seem to be someone

who would listen to their music."

"What is that supposed to mean?" She asked, mock outrage slipping into her voice.

He shrugged. "Well, I mean they are a punk rock band. You seem more like a One Direction kind of girl."

Carlie backhanded Kalen's chest.

"Ow," he complained. "Am I wrong?"

She narrowed her eyes at him. "I do like some of One Direction's stuff, and Taylor Swift, and most of the songs that are on the radio right now, but pop is not the end of my music tastes. I listen to quite a few early 2000s songs that fit into the punk category." She turned away from him. "What's your next question?"

Kalen sighed, "What is your biggest pet peeve?"

"Besides being prematurely judged by my date?" Carlie teased, turning to watch as Kalen scratched the back of his head in guilt. "I don't know. I don't like being lied to. Or when someone I consider a close friend and confidant doesn't trust me enough to tell me what's going on."

"Like what you told me is happening with your friend who isn't going to school right now?" Kalen asked.

She nodded. "Yeah. When she started dating her boyfriend, she didn't tell me either, so it just makes me feel like I've done something to lose her trust, even though I know I haven't. I don't know. Maybe it's more a fear of losing someone I see as important from my life."

“Makes sense.” Kalen acknowledged.

“My turn.” Carlie announced as they moved forward again. “What is your favorite childhood memory?”

Kalen went silent. When he didn’t answer after a few seconds, Carlie turned to look at him, noting the stoic look he had on his face. After the laughs and jokes, it was weird to see him not smiling. He wasn’t exactly easy to read, but Carlie could tell that her question had hit a nerve.

“I’m sorry,” she apologized. “I know you said your parents died when you were young, I just figured you would have some sort of happy memory…” Carlie took a deep breath. “I’ll come up with another question.”

“No, it’s fine.” Kalen said. “I’ve never really talked about it, but if I’ve learned anything in psychology, it’s that talking after a tragedy is…”

“Important.” Carlie finished.

“Yeah.”

Carlie shook her head. “Your uncle never took you to see someone after your parents’ death?”

Kalen shook his head. “My uncle doesn’t believe in therapy, and he definitely doesn’t believe in talking. I think he draws on trauma to make people do what he wants them to,” he sighed. “Something happened before my parents died. They had a falling-out with my uncle. For so long, I’ve believed that he was the one in the right. He took me in when no one else would. The more I learn about psychology, the more I realize that he manipulated me. I found— I found some old journals, explaining what happened. All she wanted was to protect me… how did that make her a bad person? But she has to be a bad person, because if she isn't, that means my uncle is in the wrong…"

Carlie grabbed his hand. "I don't believe that anyone is entirely bad. I'm sure they both had their reasons for what they were doing, but I think getting to know your mom through her journals is a great idea."

Kalen looked down at the girl next to him as they reached the front of the line, and stepped into the metal gates that separated people into lines for the cars they would ride in. This girl was a treasure. She was smart, and simultaneously helped him feel better about what he'd learned about his mom, and made him relax while waiting to face his fears. As the next train pulled up, and the passengers who had just been on the ride disembarked, Kalen felt some of the nervousness she'd helped him forget return, but it was too late to change his mind, and he was glad for that.

The gate they were standing behind opened. Carlie gently grabbed his hand, leading him towards the train. "This ride will be worth it. I promise." She whispered as they climbed into their seats.

The ride was a standing ride, which only made his fears worse, but somehow the girl next to him helped him cope with them. Her presence helped. But it wasn't just her presence that took his fear away. She knew enough about psychology, to help him figure out how to cope with it himself. As they waited for the ride operator to make her way through and check that they were all securely buckled, Kalen thought about the files that he had read. In his uncle's descriptions of his mom, she came across as a kind, caring woman.

If he asked Jackson to describe Carlie, he would probably say a lot of the same things about her as he had said about Kalen's mom. Carlie thought that no one was entirely bad. That meant that she was entirely good, or so close to it that anyone who tried to paint her as a bad person was just trying to justify something evil.

The ride attendant tugged on the huge metal, plastic, and vinyl safety bar that was holding him in the ride to make sure it was securely in place. He looked over at Carlie, who gave him a reassuring smile.

Carlie didn't deserve to die.

The speakers in the station made some announcements for the ride, and what they needed to do to insure their safety, then it started moving. They went down a little, around a corner until Kalen was looking at the massive chain lift hill they needed to go over before the ride would start. He had been on enough rides today that he knew this would be the worst part. Watching them slowly climb this steep hill, gaining height that would be lost as soon as they crested the hill was agonizing.

They reached the top, and the train plummeted into a loopy-loo. The entire ride lasted less than a minute, and before Kalen knew it, the train had returned to the start, and instead of hating it because he didn't have control of where the train went, he felt energized, and ready to go again.

The restraints released, letting the passengers remove them to disembark. Carlie and Kalen laughed as they ran off, leaving the ride. As they got out and collected their things, Kalen grabbed Carlie's hand, pulling her towards him.

"Thank you." Kalen whispered, much closer to Carlie than a friend might be.

Carlie gave a small nod, not trusting her voice for once.

Kalen leaned in, giving Carlie a short kiss.

23:40 PST
Tracy, California
Circle of Fifth Safehouse

KALEN THREW his keys down onto his bed, stripping his coat off to join them. He couldn't help the smile on his face. Today was good for his mission. It was better for him and his relationship with Carlie. Since he was starting to question his uncle and his true motivations, he cared more about his relationship than his mission at the moment.

"How was your *date*?" Banthup asked, leaning on the doorframe of Kalen's room.

Kalen rolled his eyes, then took a deep breath to school his features. Even if he wasn't planning on sitting up, Banthup was a good spy. He could hear the minute changes in facial expression in his voice. "My cover is well established, so when Alyx returns, my mission won't be compromised."

"Have you noticed that the more time you spend around her friend, you've gradually started referring to McLean by her first name, instead of her last name?" Banthup commented.

Kalen sat up to face Banthup. "What do you want?"

Banthup smiled. He had gotten a rise out of Kalen, just like he wanted to. "I made my way through all of the passenger lists you pulled for San Francisco and Oakland, and I didn't find anything. Since you decided to take off before you went through all of the Sacramento lists…"

"I'll give them to you if that's what you want." Kalen said before standing up to start looking for where he put the Sacramento airport passenger lists.

"No, I'll let you do that. I'm starting to think you are right, and they used aliases to fly, and I don't know what they are. Director McLean on the other hand had travel plans, and as a public servant for the Federal Government, his flight plans had to be filed."

"So where is the spy family hiding *McLean*?"

"Director McLean flew into Sacramento. I was hoping you could tell me."

Kalen sighed. "She is out of the country. We know that for sure. And she is somewhere she has cell service."

"How sure are you about that? It was her friend, after all that gave us that little tidbit of information. How do you know you're not being played?" Banthup asked.

"Carlie wouldn't lie to me," Kalen insisted. "No reason to."

"Unless she was trying to protect her best friend."

"I'll find the flight information for you." Kalen promised, turning around to face Banthup. "But I promise you, I am good at my job. Carlie doesn't know who I am, that I shot her best friend, or that I am trying to find her so my uncle can recruit her to an organization her family has classified as terrorists. If I asked her to find out where Alyx is spending her time, she would do it, and without any suspicion of my ill intent."

"So why don't you?" Banthup asked.

Kalen smiled. "Because she wouldn't suspect anything, but that doesn't mean those she asks questions of don't start to suspect something."

SATURDAY
DECEMBER 24TH, 2011

19:24 PST
California
Waterfall Safehouse

"THAT WAS a wonderful dinner, Addy." Alyxandrie complemented her daughter-in-law. "I really should make my way to California more often. I nearly forgot how wonderful it is to be with my children, their spouses, and grandchildren." She turned to look at William and Madelyn. "As well as dear friends" She smiled at Peter, "and new ones."

Emily rolled her eyes at her mom's not so inconspicuous snub of her fiancé, grabbing Bryan's hand in retaliation.

"I had help." Addy admitted, smiling at Emily and Bryan. "Bryan is quite skilled in the kitchen. I only wish he would have made it to one of our family dinners sooner."

"Peut-être s'il était moins égocentrique." Alyx whispered under her breath.

"Je crois que tu voulais dire s'il n'était pas un tueur en série." Her grandmother replied.

Peter looked back and forth between his girlfriend and the

grandmother she got her first name from. He had heard Alyx tell Emily she preferred her to come over without Bryan, and then he had heard Alyxandrie's comments about Bryan when they'd arrived. Hearing both of them speak in French, with each other, critiquing Emily's fiancé was weird.

Alyx was much more like her namesake than she realized.

"Maman!" Emily chastised her mother.

"Vous ne l'aimez pas?" Alyx asked her namesake.

Alyxandrie shook her head. "No. I'm glad to see someone else has some good sense around here." She leaned in closer to her granddaughter. "Tu as toujours été mon préféré. Maintenant, nous savons pourquoi."

"Don't you have more important things to worry about?" Emily snapped.

Alyx stared down the aunt that was like her sister. She stood up from the table. Her anger had mostly been focused on her parents, but Emily had slowly been earning more and more of her ire.

"Alyx, dear, we still have one more thing to do tonight." Madelyn told her granddaughter. "We have a tradition of reading the Christmas story on Christmas Eve before we turn in for the night. I don't know if the Halls have the same tradition, but I would like you all to join William and I."

Sarah nodded. "Neil and I have made that a tradition in our home as well, and it would be wonderful to share it will all of you."

Alyxandrie smiled. "One of the traditions Marler and I had

while you all were growing up was letting you open one present on Christmas Eve night." She smiled at her three remaining children. "Do you all remember that?"

Sarah, Dylan, and Emily all nodded.

Addy smiled. "Growing up, one of my family traditions was that we got Christmas pajamas the night before. Dylan and I have combined those tradition for our family. In fact…" Addy got up and walked to the other room, leaving them all waiting for her to finish her statement. She walked back in with a stack of presents. She walked around the table, handing them out, matching the name tag on the present with the person sitting at the table. "Maybe we can open these, change into the pajamas, then read the Christmas story before we all head to bed."

Madelyn beamed up at Addy as she handed her a present. "I think that is a lovely idea Addy. It's a great way to combine all of our family traditions."

Alyx looked at the present she'd been handed, then watched as the people around the table started opening their gifts. She had never pictured Dylan as the matching Christmas PJs type, yet he was eagerly opening the present his wife had handed him.

This family had way too many secrets.

She sat back down, staring at the present she had been handed. She flipped the wrapped box over and reached for the knife she had been keeping in her pocket since she was shot in her own house. Her hand paused, inches away from the knife. Normally, she would use her knife to quickly cut the tape on the wrapping paper before carefully unfolding the paper from the box to remove it. It would make sense if she did it to reuse it. But she never did. It was just super satisfying.

Right now, it would be super satisfying to just stab the box and slice the stupid matching pajamas to shreds.

Alyx glanced over at Peter, who had gotten his box open, and was smiling at the red pajamas he was pulling out of the box. Then again, Peter had never had a real Christmas. She may have been mad at her family, but she wasn't mad at him, and she wouldn't ruin his first Christmas with her family.

With the way this Christmas was going, if she pissed off her family, he would be at the next Christmas, and she wouldn't.

She moved her hand away from her knife. If she pulled it out to open presents the way she usually did, the temptation to stab it would be too much for her to resist. She tried to carefully remove the tape with her fingers, but it started to tear, so she gave up, frustrated, and just started shredding the paper, drawing the attention of all of her family. Her dad reached across the table, offering her his knife. She glared at him, crumpling the paper she had torn from the box. She opened the garment box, looking at the carefully folded pajamas in the box, with a fabric *made with love* tag where the store bought tag should be. Addy hadn't just gone out and bought matching pajamas for the family. She had bought the fabric, found patterns, gotten measurements—*somehow*, then made sixteen pairs of pajamas. As Alyx looked around the table, she saw sixteen different styles of pajamas, each one matching the style of the person it had been given to.

The present was *made with love* indeed.

Alyx had always loved how thoughtful Addy was. She was beyond busy, yet she had found time to sew *sixteen* different pairs of pajamas. Alyx couldn't help but think about how kind, and pure that was. Then she remembered that Addy was her aunt, and she had lied to Alyx for years by letting her think she was just the mother of two of her friends.

She was pretty sure that the only person at this table who hadn't lied to her was Kate.

The room was filled with echos of thanks to Addy, but Alyx just sat there, quietly looking at the Hall Christmas pajamas she had heard of for so long. A few months ago, she would have been thrilled to be included in this family tradition. Now it was hard to look at the people and the gifts and not see traitorous liars.

20:12 PST
Tracy, California
Circle of Fifths Safehouse

"**SO WHAT** are you doing tomorrow?" Carlie's voice asked through the phone sitting on Kalen's desk. He felt bad for splitting his attention between his conversation with Carlie, and the passenger lists from Sacramento. Unfortunately, he needed to at least appear to be helping Banthup and his uncle in their mission.

"I don't know," Kalen admitted. "Did you want to do something? I promised we could go to the mall and we haven't yet."

"The mall is closed tomorrow." Carlie replied.

Kalen put his pen down, focusing all of his attention on the phone call. "I thought the mall was open on Sundays."

"No, but tomorrow is Christmas." Carlie said. "Do you really not have any plans tomorrow?"

"No, my uncle is out of town, and we've never really celebrated Christmas anyway," he admitted. "So what are your Christmas plans."

"It's been a while since Christmas fell on a Sunday. We are going to go to Church first, then I think my mom is going to make brunch, and we are going to open presents. I'm looking forward to Church. It's just going to be an hour long, but from what I know about the program, it's going to be a very special hour."

"Sounds like a very nice day."

"Yeah." Carlie said. Kalen heard the smile in her voice. "Christmas is my favorite holiday, you know. Most of my favorite childhood memories happened around Christmas, and no, it's not the gifts. I remember the dinners with my grandparents. I remember my grandpa teasing my mom about the number of apple pies she owes him. I remember the year we got bikes, and went out to ride them, even though it was kind of cold. I remember the year we decided to give Christmas to another family. We got a description of the family, their clothing sizes, and some of their likes, and we spent our Christmas budget that year buying gifts for them. I remember helping my mom shop for gifts for this little baby. I don't think I have a single bad memory from Christmas time."

Kalen smiled through the phone. Carlie radiated goodness. He couldn't relate to anything she had said. He didn't have a single memory from Christmas, and he definitely didn't have any good ones. Yet as she explained why she loved Christmas, he couldn't help but feel her happiness as if he too had the memories she did.

"Hey, would you hang on for a second? I need to go talk to my mom." Carlie asked after a pause.

Just like that Kalen fell. "Sure. I can call you later."

"No. I'll be right back. I just have to ask her a question real quick. Just wait a minute for me to hop back on the phone?"

"I can do that." Kalen conceded.

The phone went silent, so Kalen returned his attention to the passenger records he was going through. He may have been losing his motivation to help his uncle, but since Banthup told him Director McLean flew into Sacramento, Kalen started thinking that it was likely others flew into the same airport. If he was taking a less traceable method of transportation to get to his final destination, the CIA would probably insist he flew someplace pretty close to his final destination. After all, the longer he was in a car, the more exposed and at risk he was.

If Kalen was right and the Halls were spending their Christmas in California, not out of the country like they had been led to believe, Director McLean wasn't the only family member that had to fly into town. If they were celebrating in California, it suddenly made sense why Dylan Hall and his family weren't on any of the passenger lists.

Kalen stopped, staring at the name on one of the incoming passenger lists. *Alyxandrie Hall.* That was odd. The first name on the passenger list was Alyx' full legal name, which was what was on her ID, and was the name she had to fly with. It was a rare name. It stood out. Yet if this was her alias, it was a really sad excuse of an alias. Why on earth would she use a fake ID and alias, but then use her legal first name, and her mother's maiden name?

"Kalen are you still there?" Carlie asked through the phone.

"Yeah, I'm here." He replied, pulling his eyes away from the name on the list.

"Cool." Carlie paused, her silence making Kalen's anxiety grow. Finding the name had sparked excitement, but that couldn't cover how nervous this girl made him. "How would you feel about joining my family for Christmas tomorrow?" She finally asked.

Kalen felt like his heart stopped. She did not just ask him that. She barely knew him. "Are you sure?"

"Yeah." Carlie laughed. "That's what I had to go ask my mom. Look, I know we're still getting to know each other, and this whole *spend-a-holiday-with-my-family* thing is probably weird, but I don't think anyone should be alone for Christmas. Fortunately, my parents like adopting strangers. We don't have any gifts for you or anything, but we can offer good food and company. And if you would like to join us for church too, I will just warn you that we're maybe not the best singers either."

Kalen stared at the phone on his desk. The perfect soldier his uncle had trained was yelling at him about what kind of opportunity this was. How it was perfect, and not to be wasted. The teenage boy was torn between guilt, and desperation. He would love to see what a normal family Christmas looked like. He wanted to see the faces of people as they lit up watching loved ones open gifts. He wanted to be surrounded in Carlie's infectious optimism.

"I would love to come. What time is church? And what do I have to wear?"

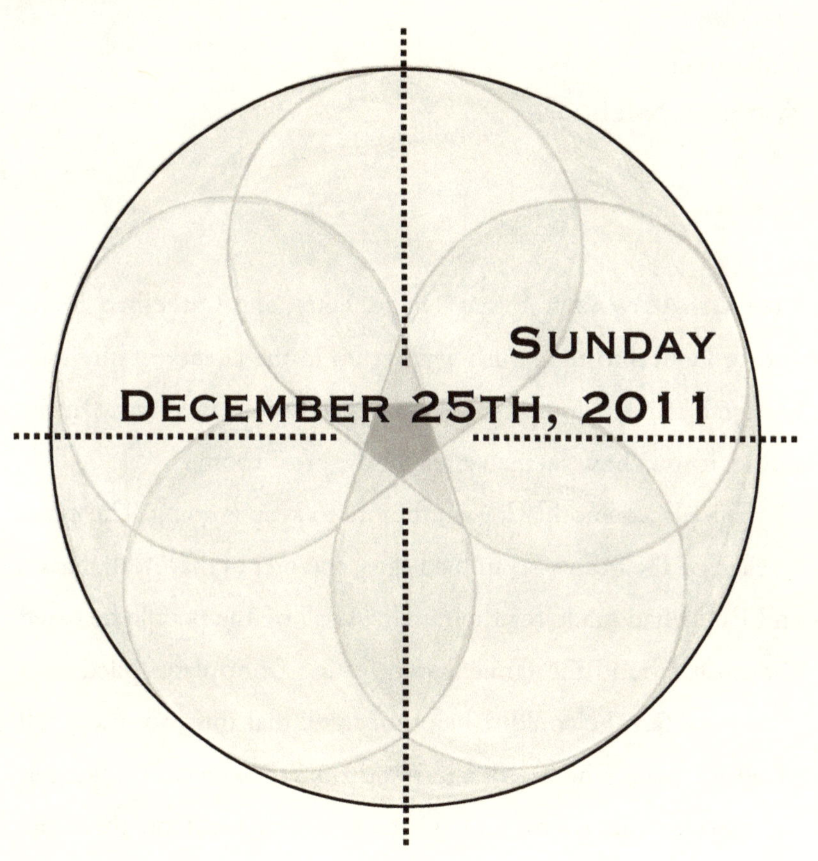
SUNDAY
DECEMBER 25TH, 2011

8:10 PST
California
Waterfall Safehouse

THE CHRISTMAS tree that Thane, Peter, and Carlie had found and brought into the house was set up in the corner of the two-story tall family room. Outside, the tree had seemed *large.* In the house, it somehow seemed small in the great room.

Hall placed another log on the fire to keep it going. The cabin smelled of the bacon, scrambled eggs, and crepes that Addy, Sarah, and Emily had made for the family. As all of the people he cared about sat around the family room, eating from plates piled with their breakfast, he couldn't help but think that this room was full of all the people he loved, and the people they loved. Looking at the faces in this room, and the happiness evident on them, he could see them doing this for many years to come.

If this was a new family tradition, he welcomed it. Even if his wife went over board on the matching pajamas.

Since their kids were little, he and Addy had agreed to combine their traditions. He had always been allowed to open one present on Christmas Eve, and Addy had always received a handmade pair of pajamas from her mom. It had taken quite a few years to get the hang of it, but Addy eventually perfected the art of sewing, and altering patterns to fit their kids. The happiness that she and the kids got from the pajamas was too much for him to deny, so he had conceded. It was the only day a year that he wore the matching pajamas his wife made. The bottoms sometimes survived, but the shirt usually found itself in a donation pile by February. But Christmas Eve and Christmas, he would appease his wife and kids and match them.

This year, with the promise of spending the year with their extended family, Addy had gone overboard. Not only had she somehow found time to make all of the extra pairs of pajamas, but she also decided to get some iron transfer sheets and design a logo. Not only were all sixteen people in this cabin wearing pajamas with matching red fabric, but the all had a large logo that had been ironed onto the front, boasting *Hall Family Christmas 2011*.

Fortunately, everyone had been good sports about the pajamas. In fact, everyone seemed to love them. Everyone but Alyx.

Hall could tell she was trying really hard to hide it, but she hated everything about being here. Unless it was Peter. Even then, he could tell that the young relationship was strained. Alyx had found herself a corner in the family room, as far away from the tree that everyone was gravitating towards. She was intentionally separating herself from her loved ones. Peter was being more supportive than Hall would have guessed he might be. As she separated herself, Peter found the spot on the couch, right next to the spot she had taken on the floor, and he was watching her eat her food more than he actually touched his own.

Thane was right. When they returned to Tracy, Dylan would be doing a much better job of keeping an eye on Peter. He couldn't protect Alyx if he couldn't take care of himself.

Addy brought Dylan his plate of breakfast, giving him a look that only a wife could. After so many years of marriage, he knew without words that Addy was making him eat, so he wouldn't let his worries distract him from the things he had to do to just maintain life. He had also been married long enough that he knew it would be much easier if he just cooperated with his wife's silent request, so he sat down and started eating the breakfast his wife had handed him.

Everyone made quiet conversation as they ate, and as Dylan played the roll he often did as the quiet observer, he couldn't help but notice half of the conversations happening were in French.

As a French emigrant, his mother had always been more comfortable speaking French than English, even though she spoke both. She and their father had wanted to pass that along to their children, so he had grown up speaking both languages. Sometimes it was a weird combination of the two. Despite being more comfortable with French, now that her children were grown, and most of her grand children had also been taught French, she would often speak English when she was in an English-speaking country, and French when she was not, so the fact that she had taken to speaking French for this trip spoke volumes about the distrust she felt for Emily's fiancé. Alyx had shown distrust for him for a while now, but she always seemed a little paranoid. Having his mother not trust him…

Sarah stood up in front of the fireplace everyone was eating around. "Ok, the plan for today is fairly simple. Neil and I found a ward we can go to for anyone who wants to attend church today. Their meeting starts at thirteen hundred."

"I thought we had a chapel here." Alyxandrie said. "The point of this safehouse is that it has everything you need to hide out for a while, besides the occasional supply runs. No one in the nearby cities know anyone is out here."

Sarah smiled. "That is the other option. We can have a small Christmas program here. We should all have clothes for church. After breakfast, we can get dressed for church, and go to the chapel on the property. Chelsi has a Christmas talk prepared, and Lynn has been preparing a Christmas number. Alyx can play piano for us, we can sing our favorite Christmas songs, and have a lovely Christmas program here."

Madelyn smiled. "That sounds like a lovely idea."

Sarah looked at her daughter. "What do you say? Would you be willing to accompany us for some Christmas songs?"

"Do I have a choice?" Alyx asked.

"Of course you do." Alyxandrie commented.

"You play piano?" Peter leaned down and whispered to Alyx.

Alyx gave a small nod. She was torn. She loved playing hymns, and Christmas songs were some of her favorite. Angels We Have Heard on High was especially beautiful. She would love to play the Christmas songs. But the other part of her was really tired of being around only family members, and would love to get out and see other people.

Unfortunately, she knew her grandma had a point. They were here to hide out. She hated it, but she was also scared being back in California. She really didn't want to leave this refuge.

"I will play the piano." Alyx conceded.

Sarah smiled bigger than she had in a month. "Perfect." She looked at her watch. "Let's meet in the chapel at ten hundred. That should give us all enough time to eat and get ready."

Alyx finished the crepe she had on her plate and stood up. "Once I'm ready, can someone show me where the chapel is? I'd like some extra time to practice."

"I'll take you." Alyxandrie smiled at her granddaughter.

8:32 PST
Tracy, California
Udall Home

KALEN FIDGETED with his tie in the mirror in the sun visor of his car. When Carlie told him he needed a dress shirt and slacks for church, he had spent the minutes following the phone call looking for clothes to wear. He didn't have many places he went that required a shirt and tie, and the stores were already closed.

He got out of his car, walking up to the house he knew Carlie lived in. She had sent him her address so he could pick her up for Great America the other day, but he'd already known where she lived. He was good at his job.

Usually, he'd also know what the inside looked like, which room was hers, and the best entry points. If his uncle knew that he hadn't broken into her house yet, he would be disappointed.

Kalen didn't really care what his uncle thought anymore.

A woman who looked a lot like Carlie opened the door. She smiled at him. "You must be Kalen."

"Yes ma'am." He replied.

The woman opened the door wider, and invited him to come in. "Please, call me Mariana. I'm Carlie's mom."

"Thank you for allowing her to invite me today." He said, turning to look at Mariana once he was in the house. She had a kind smile that was just as infectious as her daughter's. She had the same olive complexion as Carlie, just a couple of shades darker.

"Of course." Mariana replied. "I'm not sure if Carlie talked to you about your options for coming with us to church."

"She didn't" Kalen admitted.

"We have a free seat in our van, so you can ride to the church with us, or you can follow us over. Which would you prefer?"

"I can ride with you, if that's ok."

Mariana smiled. "That's perfect. We should be leaving soon. I'll go let Carlie know you are here. Have you eaten yet?"

Kalen shook his head.

Mariana beckoned for him to follow her. "We have breakfast in here." She led him deeper into the house until they reached the kitchen. Sitting at the breakfast nook table were three boys. One looked younger than Carlie, but he couldn't tell for sure, and the other two were definitely younger. They still looked very boyish, and had the energy to match, since the two of them were rough-housing from their chairs. "Max! Eli! Stop playing around and eat. We need to leave in ten minutes."

Kalen watched as the two boys quickly obeyed, glancing at him and his mother before sitting themselves back down.

Mariana handed Kalen a plate from the cupboard. "Here's a plate. Please help yourself."

"Thank you." He said again.

Mariana smiled and left, going to talk to Carlie as she had said. Kalen walked to the stove to get himself some scrambled eggs, then found a free chair at the table to sit down.

"You the guy Carlie went out with?" The older boy said.

Kalen nodded. "I'm Kalen." He offered the boy his hand.

"Ty," the boy offered, accepting his hand. Kalen was surprised by how firm the hand shake was. It was the kind of hand shake he was used to getting from the agents his uncle hired. It carried with it a confidence unusual for a young man in the midst of adolescence.

"So are you Carlie's younger brother?" Kalen asked.

Ty nodded. "Yes. I might be younger, but that doesn't mean that I can't be protective of her."

"It's always good to be protective of your siblings. I'm sure Carlie is protective of you." Kalen replied. He was pretty sure Ty was trying to threaten him, and it wasn't going to work on him, so it was best to derail the conversation before it got to that point.

Ty rolled his eyes. "Tries to be, maybe. I passed her up in height this last summer, and she's still in denial."

Kalen laughed. He looked up as movement caught his eye, seeing Carlie walk into the kitchen. She was gorgeous, wearing a beautiful red dress with long sleeves, and a skirt that flared at her waist and fell in loose pleats to her ankles.

"What's so funny?" She asked him.

"The fact that you think you will be taller than me again." Ty told his sister.

Carlie sent her brother a death glare. "I see you met Ty." She commented to Kalen. She walked to the table, sitting in the empty chair next to Kalen. "His entire goal in life is to make my life miserable, so that's mine as well."

Kalen finished chewing his bite of food before pointing at the table in front of Carlie. "Are you not eating?"

"I ate already." She smiled. "I didn't want to get my Christmas dress dirty before church."

Kalen nodded. Carlie had put on very minimal make-up, but the little bit she did have on accentuated her natural coloring and features. If they weren't sitting at her parent's kitchen table, he might have tried to kiss her. Again.

Her dad walked into the room, fiddling with the cuffs of his shirt. "Is everyone ready to go?"

"Just about." Mariana told him as she walked into the room behind him with his suit jacket. Carlie's dad took the jacket, putting it on as he looked at Kalen.

"You're Kalen?" He asked.

Kalen stood up, offering his hand to Carlie's dad. "Yes sir." He replied.

Carlie's dad took the hand, and held it firmly. "You and I

need to have a chat, but that can wait until after church."

"Dad? Really?" Carlie whined. "I finally find a guy that I like, and he likes me, and you are going to try and scare him off?"

Kalen maintained eye contact with her dad. He still hadn't let go of his hand yet. He could easily take her dad, but the point of this stare down wasn't to intimidate him. It was to show he couldn't be intimidated, but he could be respectful about it. If her dad knew that he had nothing but respect for Carlie, Kalen could gain her dad's respect.

It wasn't essential for his mission, but it was essential if he wanted a relationship past his mission.

"I look forward to getting to know you better, Mr. Udall." Kalen told her dad.

Her dad let the smallest smile crack his steely facade. He released Kalen's hand, turning his attention to his children. "Well, shall we go before we are late for church?"

Mariana nodded, fussing over their boys as she pushed them towards the door.

Mr. Udall placed a hand on Kalen's shoulder as he followed the family to the garage where their van was kept. "You don't mind sitting in the back with Max and Eli, do you?"

"Of course not, sir." Kalen replied.

He definitely would have preferred to sit with Carlie, but if he wanted to show he respected her and her family, he wouldn't fight about that.

9:16 PST
California
Waterfall Safehouse

THE KEYS of the piano moved with a dance of fingers as Alyx played the eighth notes of Angels We Have Heard on High. Long before she had discovered cycling, or running, or driving, she had spent many hours on the piano bench, using music to distract her mind from her problems. When she had turned twelve, and entered Young Women's, her leaders asked her if she would share her talent for playing piano, and accompany the girls when they sang. She was descent at sight reading music, but practice always made it better, so she started using church hymns to play when she needed a distraction.

Of all the hymns she had played over the years, she had come to list a few as her favorites. One of those was Angels We Have Heard on High, specifically because of the feeling of accomplishment she got from playing the eighth notes of the chorus.

She hadn't realized how much she missed playing piano.

"It sounds beautiful." Peter complemented. Alyx glanced up

at him, the muscle memory in her fingers meaning that the distraction didn't interrupt her fingers from playing the song.

"Thanks." She said.

"I didn't know you played piano."

"Piano was the original way I coped with things. I don't know how, but I somehow convinced my grandparents to let me take lessons when we lived with them in kindergarten. I went to a private school, so it may have actually been associated with the school." Alyx explained. "I used to play all the time. Now I usually go for a ride, run, or drive."

"Do you even have a piano in your house?" Peter asked, sitting on the bench next to her, looking at the foreign markings on the paper Alyx was reading, and somehow translating into the beautiful sounds filling the room. All things considered, he shouldn't have been that surprised that she could read music, because she was gifted in speaking many languages, and music was basically another language. When he was in fourth grade, he had been taught how to play recorder, and he learned some of the basics of reading music. He could at least identify quarter and eighth notes. He really hadn't done well with much beyond that. He could only play Hot Cross Buns because he memorized it. If someone placed a sheet of music for Hot Cross Buns in front of him, he probably wouldn't even know it.

He watched as Alyx flipped to a new page in the green book that sat on the ledge of the piano, and started playing a new song with a melody that Peter recognized, but not until he heard her start playing the notes. Music was definitely another language, and it was one that Alyx spoke fluently.

"We have a piano on the wall between the formal living room and dining room. We usually go the other way into the kitchen, so you probably haven't seen it. Honestly I haven't played it in a while, and I haven't played at all since they sent me to London. I would play in various church meetings fairly often, even if I didn't practice at home."

"In other words, we took away all of your coping mechanisms by sending you to London. I get it." Peter sighed. He just sat there for a minute, listening as Alyx practiced the music. "I wish I could listen to you play all the time," he admitted after a while. "Is it weird that listening to you play seems to just freeze time, and all of my problems seem to just drift away?"

Alyx shook her head as the final notes of Away in a Manger rang through the chapel, and she turned the page to practice another Christmas song. "Why do you think I like playing?"

Peter turned to look at Alyx, watching her eyes flick between the notes on the page in front of her, and the black and white keys her fingers were dancing over. Most of the time, her eyes stayed glued on the page. It reminded him of watching someone type on a keyboard. She knew where her fingers were, and just needed to glance at them occasionally to make sure they were still where she wanted them to be. She made it look so effortless.

If only she could cope with her trauma as easily.

When she had convinced her grandparents to let her take lessons, she was mad that her parents were always gone. She was mad that Ally had promised to take her exploring Feilds Palace some more, and she had died before she had made good on her promise.

She was mad at herself too, but she didn't remember why.

The music gave her something to focus her anger on. It was something she could control. It was something she could improve on. Eventually, she learned that if she could identify the cause of her anger, and do something about it, she could prevent future melt downs. It had been so long since she had felt the kind of anger she felt for her family right now, that she had forgotten how she had gotten over her anger as a child. She had been angry about things she couldn't control then. She felt like she didn't have control again, and her feelings of anger were reappearing. She didn't know how to deal with it, and Peter was right, her go-to coping mechanisms had been taken away from her when she was sent to London, which was probably why the first time she had a chance to run, she had pushed herself too far, and ended up hurt.

Piano always felt safe to her. If she was feeling angry, she could go to the keys, find a piece of music from her practice books (usually one of the classical ones) and play the song as aggressively as she wanted. As hard as she banged on the keys, they didn't hit back. As loud as she played the notes from the classical song, she wouldn't collapse and fall. She had particularly enjoyed

Mozart's Eine Kleine Nachtmusik, and had found arrangements with increasing difficulty over the years.

It had probably been funny to watch 7-year-old Alyx with a beginner's arrangement of Mozart bang on the keys. The melody had been so slow it was barely recognizable. As she got better at playing it, she played it faster, so it was more recognizable. By the time she was 10, she had gotten an intermediate arrangement.

Alyx glanced at Peter, smiling as she saw him watching her. "What?"

"Just admiring you and your talent." He commented, brushing some of her hair behind her ear.

"This is nothing." Alyx said. "I mean I have the music in front of me, and these are pretty easy songs to play. I mean, these don't have anything faster than eighth notes." She smiled at Peter as the final notes of the song she'd been practicing faded. "I think I have played enough of the Christmas songs. I can show you something else."

"Ok." Peter agreed.

Alyx closed the hymn book, then took a deep breath, lining her hands up on the keys surrounding middle C. The thumb of her left hand rested on the G just below middle C, while her pinky rested on the G an octave lower. Her right hand mirrored her left, her thumb and pinky resting on the two Gs up the octave, with her pointer finger resting on the B in between them.

"Do you not need music?" Peter asked, watching her.

"I've kind of played this song enough that I have it memorized." She looked at Peter. "It's been a while, so I might be a little rusty."

Peter held his hands up. "Hey, I'm already impressed."

Alyx gave him a sad smile, looked at her hands one last time, then closed her eyes, preparing herself to play. With a deep breath, she opened her eyes again, then started playing Eine Kleine Nachtmusik.

"Ok, now I'm definitely impressed." Peter commented as she moved from the aggressive eighth notes of the intro, into the faster, lighter notes of the main melody.

Alyx couldn't help but smile as her fingers flew across the keys, playing the sixteenth notes and trills that she had spent hours playing when she was angry. Maybe she had preferred this piece, because it allowed her to play certain sections as aggressively as she liked, but then asked her to pull herself back, and play other sections with a delicacy that was hard when she desperately just wanted to bang on something. The song had an ebb and flow to it that she loved, and helped her express what she was feeling.

"What does it say about me that I memorized the song I like to play when I'm angry?" Alyx whispered to Peter as her fingers danced across the keys, the muscles remembering where to go next, despite not playing the song in quite some time.

"I think the better question, is what does it say about you that your go to song when you're angry is Mozart?" Peter teased. "I think most people our age go to Punk music when they're angry. Maybe Rock. You know, something with electric guitars, and maybe some screaming."

Alyx shook her head. "I don't like to listen to, or even sing through my anger. Singing turns to yelling, and then my throat hurts. Playing piano though…" The soft, airy tones she had been playing transitioned back into the louder tones she had started with. With every aggressive note, her finger slammed the key, delivering the note with a percussive tone. "You choose the right song, and you can bang on the keys, and make something beautiful out of it, without hurting it, or yourself."

Peter smiled, watching Alyx play a song that he could tell meant a lot to her. He could see what Alyx meant about being able to take her aggression out on something in a way that created something beautiful. He was a little jealous that he wasn't better with music, and didn't have the opportunity for the same outlet. If he needed to hit something, he typically took to a punching bag. Nothing beautiful came of that. Sure, he had a white bag, and when he forgot to wrap his hands, and the blood from his knuckles painted his bag, the vibrant red against the white looked intriguing. But the blood dried, and it just looked…gross.

"So Mozart, Christmas music, and church hymns." He teased.

"Sometimes, when I am really angry, I'll play the opening chords of Beethoven's Fifth Symphony."

"What? Not the whole thing like—" Peter paused. "What are

you playing?"

"Eine Kleine Nachtmusik." Alyx replied.

Peter shook his head. "This isn't why you speak German is it?"

"You'll never know." She mocked. "And no, because Beethoven's Fifth Symphony is a bit beyond my skill level, and I never had enough motivation to practice it. I had Nachtmusik, and if that didn't help, I would bang out the opening chords, and not make it much further, before I felt better. I just needed a short burst of frustration, and usually I was good. If I went too much further, it was counterproductive."

Peter leaned in close, his lips brushing against her ear as he whispered, "And here I thought you were perfect at everything you did."

"Not by a long shot," she admitted. "Piano taught me some patience, but not much."

"So do you only play classical music and hymns?" Peter asked.

"Yes and no. I only play what I have sheet music for."

Peter pointed at the closed book. "You are playing Mozart without sheet music."

Alyx smiled. "I memorized it, but I have sheet music at home, and I played from it several times. If you were to ask me to play a random pop song by ear, I couldn't do it."

"Since when has there been something Alyx McLean *couldn't* do. I thought telling you that you couldn't do something was like issuing a challenge."

"It's more like I don't have the patience for it. I would rather find the sheet music someone else composed based on their trial and error attempts, and pay for it, than try to figure it out myself." Alyx explained.

"Says the girl who solves mysteries for fun." Peter teased.

Alyx bumped Peter with her shoulder. "Did you miss the part where I don't really sit down and play the piano much at home any more? I'm too busy solving actual mysteries to spend time trying to solve the mystery that is modern pop music."

"Fair enough." Peter conceded.

The two of them returned to silence, appreciating the way the chapel echoed with the sounds of the song Alyx was playing.

After a few minutes, Peter looked up as the first of the family entered the doors at the back of the chapel, and started making their way to the front. Alyx also noticed her family arriving, and promptly stopped playing, reopening the green hymnal, and flipping through the pages to return to the Christmas songs she had been practicing when Peter had arrived.

Peter was tempted to stay on the piano bench with Alyx, but when he glanced at Director McLean, he could tell he wasn't thrilled with the idea. Sarah waved at him, a non-verbal invitation for him to sit with her and Neil. Peter turned back to Alyx, placing a gentle kiss on her cheek before leaving to join her parents on the pews.

12:25 PST
California
Waterfall Safehouse

THE LIVING room of Waterfall could only be described as chaos. The discarded carcasses of the boxes that had once contained presents were scattered around the room. It looked like a bomb had gone off and had exploded red and green wrapping paper around teenagers who still sat on the floor opening presents. Most of the adults had already opened the few presents they had under the tree.

The ten adults may have spoiled the children present. Even Peter had opened his fair share of presents. He glanced over at Alyx. This was supposed to be the best day of the year. It was supposed to bring all sorts of joy. If ever there was a perfect example that things don't bring joy, it was watching Alyx open her presents. The tokens of love her family had given her weren't going to make her forget all the lies she'd been told.

When Kate had seen the presents under the tree, she had been shocked. She had never seen so many presents in one place, and when she'd admitted as much, there had been more than a little teasing. Alyx hadn't said anything, apparently unwilling to break the silent treatment she'd been giving the family to banter with Kate like she usually did. Instead, the taunt about a palace Kate expected from Alyx had come from Chelsi, which made her like her, but also made her jealous of her. Kate spent her summers with Alyx, but she had always wished she could go to school with her. It was clear that Chelsi had been friends with Alyx, if she reacted with the same taunt Alyx would have.

Once they had decided that they wouldn't take turns opening presents, since it would take too long, the pile had quickly begun to shrink. Chelsi climbed under the tree, reaching for some of the presents hiding at the back.

She handed a medium-sized box to Kate; "Another one."

Kate smiled at Chelsi, who gave a small smile back, then gave her brother, Lynn, and Alyx the other presents she'd pulled from under the tree. Kate read the label on the present. Her grandfather had always insisted she write Thank You notes for her presents, as a proper young lady of London society should. She appreciated the many hours she'd spent writing the notes over the years, because she paid attention to who gave it to her, and it made her think about that person every time she used the item.

To: Kate

From: Sarah and Neil

We look forward getting to know you better while you stay with us this year.

Kate smiled at her aunt and uncle, watching her from the couch. With the note read, she allowed herself to begin unwrapping the present. She wasn't as neat as Alyx was opening her presents. Alyx had a pocket knife at the ready, quickly slicing the tape holding the wrapping paper closed, then unfolding the wrapping paper. Kate used her finger to neatly tear the paper at the tape joints, then unfolded the paper from around the box, finding an Asics shoe box.

With furrowed eyebrows, Kate opened the shoe box, finding a sparkly white and blue pair of shoes, a planner with John C. Kimball High School's logo on the front, and a wide orange lanyard, with the royal blue letters declaring the school name. Kate pulled the lanyard out of the box, finding an ID already on it. She had sent Sarah a picture she believed the school would find acceptable for her ID, and clearly they had, because she saw that picture smiling at her, surrounded by the orange and blue ribbons with grade level, year, and more.

Kate looked up at Sarah excited. "Is this what I think it is?"

"You are registered for school. Your schedule is in the planner, and Lynn picked up the necessary forms for you to do Track as well, since you said you wanted to. We also figured you would need a pair of Track spikes, so we got you a pair." Sarah explained.

Kate jumped up, running to Sarah to throw her hands around her neck. "Thank you thank you!"

"Of course." Sarah told her. "We want you to feel at home

while you are staying with us."

Kate ran back to the box, pulling out the shoes to try them on. She inspected the shoes she had only seen in pictures before, noting the absence of the spikes in the toe of the shoe before seeing them in the bottom of the box with the wrench that she could use to tighten them in. She smiled, sliding the shoes onto her feet, and tying the laces.

She stood up, seeing how they felt. "Alyx, are you excited? You didn't have to bribe me. I'm going to do track with you," she gushed, staring at her shoes.

The room went deafeningly quiet. Alyx just closed her eyes, willing herself not to cry. It wasn't her senior year, but she was graduating, so this was supposed to be her last year of Track. It was supposed to be her glory year. She was supposed to take freshmen like Chelsi, Kate, and Lynn under her wings, and help coach them. She was supposed to work as hard as she could so she could make it to State Finals, and maybe even Nationals.

Kate looked up when Alyx didn't say anything. She knew her cousin pretty well, so she could see the struggle not to cry. She could see that something was very wrong. She looked around the room, at the adults with their eyes overtly averted from both Kate and Alyx.

There was something they hadn't told Kate. For once, it looked like they had actually told Alyx.

Alyx wasn't doing Track. Just last week, after Kate had told

Alyx that she was joining her in California, they had discussed the possibility of Kate doing Track. Kate had prodded, but she had gotten Alyx to talk about what she was excited for entering her final semester, and competing in Track was one of them.

"The threat to Alyx was worse than we thought it was. She's not returning to California yet." Michael answered the question he knew his daughter would ask.

"When is she returning?" Kate asked. "You can't keep her from school forever. She needs to live her life. She can't hide forever. Besides, she needs this. She has been looking forward to this Track season since she started high school."

"It's not safe." Hall said. "Her life is more important than her participation in a High School sport."

Kate shook her head. "You are all bloody fools."

"Kate!" Michael chastised.

"No. Clearly you imbeciles need to hear it. What you are doing is pointless. If Alyx can't do the things she enjoys, she won't be happy. When someone is unhappy, they will do everything they can to find happiness. If you think Alyx will just sit there, angry at you—for good reason, may I add—you are bloody insane. If anyone can find a way to escape from your prisons, it is her. And she will, too. You are so concerned about what physical attacks this psychopath after her might make, you are blind to the psychological torture *your security detail* is inflicting. She is miserable, and no one cares to try and fix it." Kate turned to look at Bryan, who she could tell hadn't been given the best welcome either. "Bryan, welcome to the Hall family. Be prepared for the secrets, lies, and manipulations. I don't know that they really love anyone, because they clearly don't show it very well."

Kate slipped the shoes off, slamming them into the box before storming off up the stairs to the room she had been sharing with Lynn. She had no idea how Alyx had lasted so long before having an outburst. Even then, she had just told them to stop, and stormed off.

Kate wasn't going to be so quiet about it.

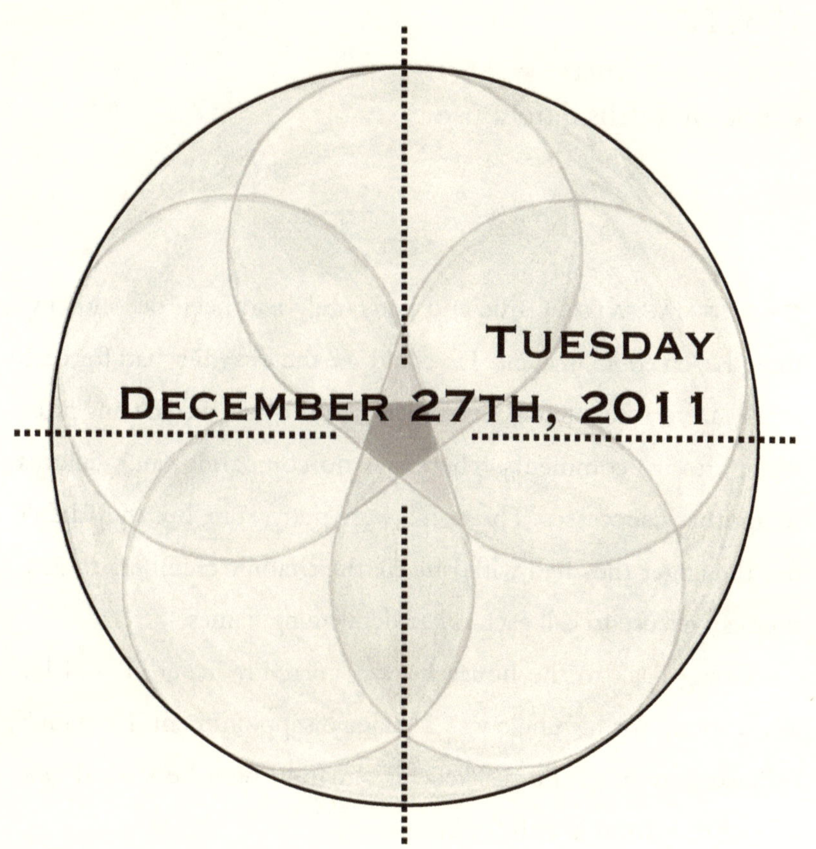

Tuesday
December 27th, 2011

17:34 PST
Tracy, California
Circle of Fifths Safehouse

CHRISTMAS WITH Carlie and her family had been beyond anything Kalen could imagine. He could see the love they had for each other in every interaction, even their fights. There weren't any passive aggressive comments. There was no comparing one's failures to another's successes. The fights were petty, sure, but they didn't use the anger they had with one of their family members to give them an excuse to call each other demeaning names.

Going back to the house he was currently living in, and his job working for his uncle was a major disappointment. He hadn't realized how much he disliked his situation until he started getting a break from it with Carlie.

It didn't matter how much he hated his job. It didn't matter how much he was starting to question his uncle. It didn't matter that he was starting to think his uncle was evil. Until he knew what he was going to do with what he was learning from his mom's file, he needed to play the part of the perfect soldier. If that meant finding Alyx, he would do it.

He had been distracted when he had noticed the Alyxandrie Hall that had flown into Sacramento, but with Christmas over, he had reapplied himself. He hoped if he found out where Alyx was, he could have the rest of his break from school to spend how he wanted—with Carlie. He knew it wasn't a coincidence that someone else with the same first name as Alyx had flown into the same airport as her grandfather, the current Director of the CIA. So he had looked up Alyxandrie Hall.

What he had discovered was extremely helpful, and gave him more insight into Alyx. Alyxandrie Hall was born in France as Alyxandrie Devereux, and was the daughter of a DGSE agent who later rose to a position of authority in French Intelligence. It was her father's role in French Intelligence, and her mother's role as a diplomat, that led her to meet Marler Hall, who she moved to US for, and married. Marler and Alyxandrie Hall then had four children: Ally, Sarah, Dylan, and Emily. Alyx was named after her grandmother. Both of them, technically.

And Kalen had wondered why she was such an annoying, overachieving twit. She had even more to live up to than Kalen, and he had come from a long line of Circle of Fifths agents. Alyx came from three legendary families in espionage, in two countries.

Kalen had dug into Alyxandrie's travel history more once he knew that she too was related to Alyx. It wasn't a coincidence that three of McLean's grandparents had flown into the same airport on the same day. Alyxandrie rarely made her way to California, despite all three of her remaining children calling the state home. It had to be something very serious for her to make a trip to California.

The last time she had been in California was for Emily's college graduation. Before that, she attended the funerals of Cole, Analyn, and Cassandra McLean.

The problem Kalen was having, was pinpointing exactly where they were all going. Emily worked for the Santa Cruz Police Department, and likely lived somewhere in the area. He knew that both Sarah and Dylan's families lived in the Tracy area, and the Sacramento airport was a plausible option to fly into visit Tracy. But he knew Alyx wasn't in Tracy. If she was, she would have been going to school, and they could have found her by now. It was possible that they had brought her back from wherever they'd been hiding her, but none of the Halls were home.

The one work related thing he had done while he was spending time with Carlie and her family was peek at Carlie's phone when she texted Alyx. The message never showed up as delivered, which meant she was out of cell service. Alyx had definitely moved from where they *had* been hiding her. This time, she was somewhere off the grid.

Somewhere in California.

Kalen took the passenger list with Alyxandrie's name on it with him to find Banthup, who was annoyingly in the garage, working out with the punching bag, instead of trying to track down

Alyx like he was supposed to.

Kalen was sick of doing everyone's jobs.

"I found something for you." Kalen told Banthup.

"About time." Banthup commented, throwing more punches at the defenseless bag, rather than turning his attention to Kalen.

"Director McLean and his wife weren't the only of Alyx's family members to fly into Sacramento. Her grandmother Alyxandrie Hall flew into Sacramento the same day." Kalen told Banthup, holding up the paper.

"How does that help?" Banthup complained.

Kalen waited a moment before replying, trying to calm himself down. "It helps because I believe they moved Alyx. We have been operating on the assumption that she was out of the country, and within range of cell service. But when Carlie texted her *Merry Christmas*, her message was never delivered, meaning she is now out of range."

"Still not hearing the helpful part." Banthup threw more punches at the bag.

"Maybe if you stopped for a minute, and used your brain, instead of your fists, and let me talk, you would understand what I'm telling you." Kalen snapped.

Banthup spun to face Kalen, his face suggesting he wasn't done punching things, but wanted to punch something breathing —something with Kalen's face.

"Good. I have your attention." Kalen said, throwing the

paper he had brought with him in Banthup's fists. "The Circle of Fifths at one point found intel suggesting that the Halls have a safehouse hidden off the grid somewhere in California. Unfortunately the state is massive, and we have never been able to narrow it down. Given what you gave me about Director McLean, and another Hall flying into the same airport," Kalen said as he pointed at the paper he had given Banthup, "I believe we have a chance to not only find Alyx, but burn their illusive California safehouse."

"How long has Jackson been looking for this safehouse?" Banthup asked.

Kalen shook his head. "The search for the safehouse predates my uncle. In '88, Sarah Hall and Neil McLean captured one of our agents who had been sent after Rafael and Michael Feilds. While Sarah and Neil interrogated our agent, Rafael and Michael disappeared from the public eye, and the fact that Ally wasn't with her twin led the Circle of Fifths to suspect that she was protecting the Feilds. That theory was reinforced when Lord Feilds later announced his son's engagement to Ally. They looked at passenger lists like we have been, and discovered Ally's passport entering the US through LAX."

"So if we find this safehouse, it will impress even your uncle's bosses?" Banthup prodded. Kalen shrugged. "What do you need to figure it out?"

Kalen rolled his eyes. "First, I want more proof that Alyx is back in California, and she is with her family. If you could try to get ahold of Dylan Hall, and see if he is in service, that would be step one. I will also need any records you can get for private flights entering Sacramento and surrounding areas. If they have been hiding her out of country, my bet is that they used a private charter."

"Done." Banthup replied. He handed the paper back to Kalen, then stripped his gloves off. He clapped a hand on Kalen's shoulder. "Glad to see you're ready to help out again."

Wednesday
December 28th, 2011

13:07 PST
California
Waterfall Safehouse

APPARENTLY THERE were downsides to spending two weeks in the middle of nowhere, completely off the grid.

With Christmas over with, and most of the planned festivities over, the days had been crawling. The lack of entertainment options had created a divide in the house. Most of the adults were well equipped at finding some way to pass the time. Neil and his father had grabbed the fishing rods they kept in the basement, and invited others to join them at the larger of the two lakes near the house. Bryan and Michael joined them, but the kids left the invitation unanswered. Michael only spent a couple of hours with them, before he returned to the house, spending his time on the porch, writing letters to Ally in his journal. Journaling had been something Ally had shared with him his first time at Waterfall, and it had been a way for him to still feel close to her despite her absence, which felt especially fitting now.

Sarah, Addy, Emily, Madelyn, and Alyxandrie had gone for a

hike in the woods, the day after Christmas, and found a nice clearing to practice shooting. When the guys disappeared to go fishing, Emily grabbed her rifle, Addy grabbed her hand guns, and the rest of the women grabbed ammo and the empty bottles from the sparkling cider they'd drunk for Christmas Eve dinner.

While they all knew the safe house and the surrounding areas were secure, Alyx was for the most part confined to the house, which meant that while everyone else took to the woods for their entertainment, Alyx and the other kids stayed in. Chelsi had explored the house her first night at Waterfall, and had found a collection of old board games in the basement, which she had brought up when Thane complained about being bored. She had annoyed her cousins to find people to play Monopoly with her. She convinced most everyone to join in. Alyx had secluded herself to her room, claiming she had homework to do. No one was sure whether or not they should believe her, since that seemed to be her go-to excuse. Unfortunately it was a good excuse. They could try and call her bluff and still make her play, but if she really did have homework, her grades would suffer. She was already missing enough school. If she was going to use homework as an excuse, there was little they could do to stop her. Kate also opted to sit out, her anger from Christmas not yet dead. She sat on one of the couches in the living room, where Thane, Chelsi, Lynn, and Peter sat around the coffee table playing Monopoly, reading one of the books Alyx had been given for Christmas.

She was mad at everyone, but her extroverted personality demanded she be somewhere she had company, which was annoying. It was even more annoying than growing up as the only child in a large palace.

Hall walked into the room, looking at the kids that were actually getting along. He had spent more time in this cabin than any kid wanted to be locked up with their siblings, and the same board game his kids were now playing had seen many fights between him and his siblings.

At least they hadn't gotten the chess set out yet. He didn't want to hear Sarah explain why one of the light bishops had a dark stain. It wasn't long after a rather unfortunate game of chess that their parents decided it was time to go home. If they stayed, they wouldn't have to worry about the Circle of Fifths coming after them, because their kids would have killed each other.

"I need to head into town to pick up some more supplies. Is there anyone who would care to join me?"

"I'll come." Thane volunteered. "Can I fly?"

"Don't see why not. You need to get your hours in."

"Can I join?" Peter asked. "I need to check in with Nathan."

"Of course." Hall replied. "I'm going to go get Neil. I know he needs to check in with his team as well." He looked at his son. "Will you head down and get the helicopter ready? We should be ready to leave in about thirty minutes."

Thane jumped up from the coffee table. "Yes sir."

Hall nodded, leaving the cabin, presumably to get Neil like he said he would. Thane went to follow, turning back when Peter didn't join him. "You coming?"

"I'll be down in a minute." Peter told him, standing up from their game. "I'm going to go check on Alyx."

Thane nodded, while Peter disappeared upstairs.

14:10 PST
El Dorado County, California
Waterfall Safehouse Staging House

THANE LANDED the helicopter in the field of the property the Halls owned as a way point for Waterfall. It was their way of ensuring Waterfall wouldn't be found, as it was close enough that they could easily fly down when they needed to make a supply run, but far enough away, none of the neighbors could pinpoint where the helicopter came from, or where it went.

Hall jumped out of the helicopter, ducking under the still spinning rotors as he ran towards a large barn. While the barn was disguised to look like an decrepit structure, if someone knew where to push, a hidden panel opened up, revealing a new, high tech lock, that was part of a Scofield 2012 Security system, which required both a biometric key, and a six-digit code. The advertisement for the system had claimed it was spy-proof. Peter had tested it. It wasn't inaccurate.

Once Thane had lined the helicopter up, and it was where they could push it into the barn, he shut off the engines. As soon as the helicopter engines started spinning down, Peter hopped out, and was checking his phone.

Kate had yelled at all of them, acting like it was only hurting Alyx by sending her back to London after Christmas break. What she couldn't see was how much it was hurting Peter too. After getting used to seeing Alyx everyday, the last few weeks had been torturous. It wasn't just that he couldn't see her. She was suffering. She was in danger. He wanted to be there for her. He wanted to give her a hug and let her know she wasn't alone. He wanted to loan her his strength when hers didn't take her to the finish line. And he wanted to see her smile when he needed something good in his life after a bad day.

He was trying to enjoy the time he had to spend with her before they had to return to the real world. This safehouse, and its refuge was a much greater gift than anything he had unwrapped on Christmas. But he was having a hard time pretending like their time together wasn't limited. He was painfully aware of each moment that passed, knowing it brought their imminent and indefinite separation closer.

He needed someone to have a solution for him.

Everyone scattered, performing the tasks necessary to make this trip as painless and efficient as possible. Neil headed for the house that could be used as a safehouse itself, checking messages as he walked. Thane and his dad would push the helicopter into the barn and close the doors. Once the helicopter was safely stored away, they too would head for the house to get the nondescript black SUV from the garage. Hall had rented it before leaving town. He didn't even bother trying to hide the rental with an alias, or a credit card registered to an alias. They had already put so many miles on the car, bussing people from the airport to the house, not to mention the many supply runs he and Addy had made. If someone found the reservation, and got ahold of the milage they put on the SUV, they would have a circle half the size of California to search. There was no way they'd find this house.

Peter followed Neil towards the house to check his messages, and see if there was any important progress on getting Jackson and the hired sniper so they could bring Alyx home. He got excited as he saw a message from Derek Stevens:

Call me ASAP.

He wasn't sure what could be so important that Stevens needed to relay it through a call, instead of a text, but Peter was hopeful it had something to do with Banthup.

Before Thane had even climbed out of the helicopter, Peter had dialed Steven's phone number, and was holding the phone up to his ear.

Peter held his breath as the line connected, and he heard his old teammate's voice through the phone answering, "Stevens."

"You asked me to call ASAP." Peter replied.

"Thank the heavens you got my message." Stevens breathed.

Peter's anxiety rose.

"Banthup is up to something."

And just like that, Peter's hopes to bring Alyx home after Christmas or soon after crashed. "What happened?"

"Your call to spy on his computer paid off, but not in a good way. After you left with the Halls, he used his clearance to pull the passenger lists from San Francisco, Oakland, and Sacramento International Airports. Clearly he was trying to figure out where you guys were going. The concerning part is what he's been up to since then. Yesterday, he began rooting around private flight manifests heading into Sacramento. I don't know what he found, but today he said Hall asked him to check on the plane we have waiting for McLean."

"He's driving up to Sacramento?" Peter asked. They had taken plenty of precautions to ensure the passenger manifest for Michael Feilds' private jet was inaccessible to anyone besides the people they wanted to have it. It was hidden behind layers of bureaucratic tape from two countries, and if someone got through all of that, they were classified: For CIA Director's eyes only. Even if they somehow hacked it, they would find a file so redacted, you couldn't actually get any useful information from it. Not that any of that mattered. They had made sure to use one of the backstopped cover identities they had created for Alyx. All of that effort would be wasted though, if the plane was compromised, and they couldn't get Alyx back to London.

"Yes." Stevens confirmed.

Zut. Peter turned around, looking at Hall. "Banthup is headed to Sacramento," he called.

Hall's eyes started to burn with fury. "When did he leave?"

Peter put his phone on speaker, then relayed the question to Stevens, who didn't hesitate in his reply. "40 minutes ago."

It didn't take them long to do the math. It was about an hour drive from Tracy to Sacramento. They didn't have enough time to get to Sacramento and intercept Banthup.

"Thanks for the update. Call me if something changes." Peter said, hanging up.

Neil had turned around, the situation unfolding with Peter more important than any of the leads he was going to follow up on. "I'll call the pilots and have them move the plane," he commented, while dialing a number.

Hall nodded. "I'll call the airport and get them access to take off." He looked at his son. "I need you to head back up to the cabin. Bring anyone you can down here, but not Alyx. We'll say whoever you leave up there is on a hike."

"And tell Michael that he is going home sooner than we planned." Neil added, the phone up to his ear. "We can't risk Alyx being in the country."

Thane climbed into the helicopter, and restarted the engines.

"But she's at a safe house they can't find." Peter insisted.

"If he found the plane, chances are, he's figured out that we brought her back for Christmas." Hall explained. "They're not just looking for her, they are looking for the safe house. The Circle of Fifths have been trying to find it for years."

"Clearly this is the best place for her to be." Peter argued.

Hall shook his head. "No. I know the rumors. That the best way to protect someone is to give them to a Hall. Do you know why that is? Do you know why none of the people we've been assigned to protect have been killed?"

"Halls know how to secure a house." Peter replied.

"No." Hall replied. "Our security measures for a house are the last line of defense, but they are far from impenetrable. Case in point is the how Alyx was shot after Thanksgiving. The reason none of our charges have been killed is because no one could *find* them to kill them. That doesn't mean no one's ever come close. But the second they get close, you give them bread crumbs leading another direction. You manipulate them and misdirect, then you move your protectee as far away from the threat is possible. That's the reason why we have so many safe houses, and that is the reason why *no one* has ever found one. If it ever even comes close to being found, we cut our losses, sell it and buy a new one." Hall explained. "Clearly, the technique works, because Sarah has been hiding Alyx from these people for twelve years. She was shot because I made a mistake. I should have told Sarah in June that it was time to move again."

"If she would have moved, she wouldn't be close to the Generation. You couldn't use us to protect her." Peter commented.

"If she would have moved, she wouldn't be in danger. Not like she is now. She wouldn't have been shot, that's for sure."

Hall walked off, effectively ending the conversation with Peter. Neil was up by the house, making arrangements with the airport, leaving Peter alone with his thoughts. If they would have moved Alyx in June, she wouldn't have been at Kimball in August. She wouldn't have asked Mr. Martin for help studying for the AP French test. Mr. Martin wouldn't have paired them together. Peter wouldn't have flirted with her. Alyx wouldn't have enacted her French only rule. They wouldn't have admitted their feelings to each other. They wouldn't have started dating.

But she wouldn't have been shot.

As much as Peter hated himself for it, if he had a time machine, Peter honestly didn't know if he would use it to go back and convince her parents to move. He would do anything to protect Alyx, and take away the pain the shooting had caused, but was he selfless enough to sacrifice his own happiness while he was at it?

Peter looked at the helicopter that Thane was taking off in. Based on how things were at the moment, he probably wouldn't see Alyx again for a while. It was pointless to focus on changing the past. All he knew was that right now, he would sacrifice his own happiness to keep her safe, and he would do it over and over again if necessary. He just hoped Alyx wouldn't hate him for it when all was said and done.

He just hoped Alyx would understand.

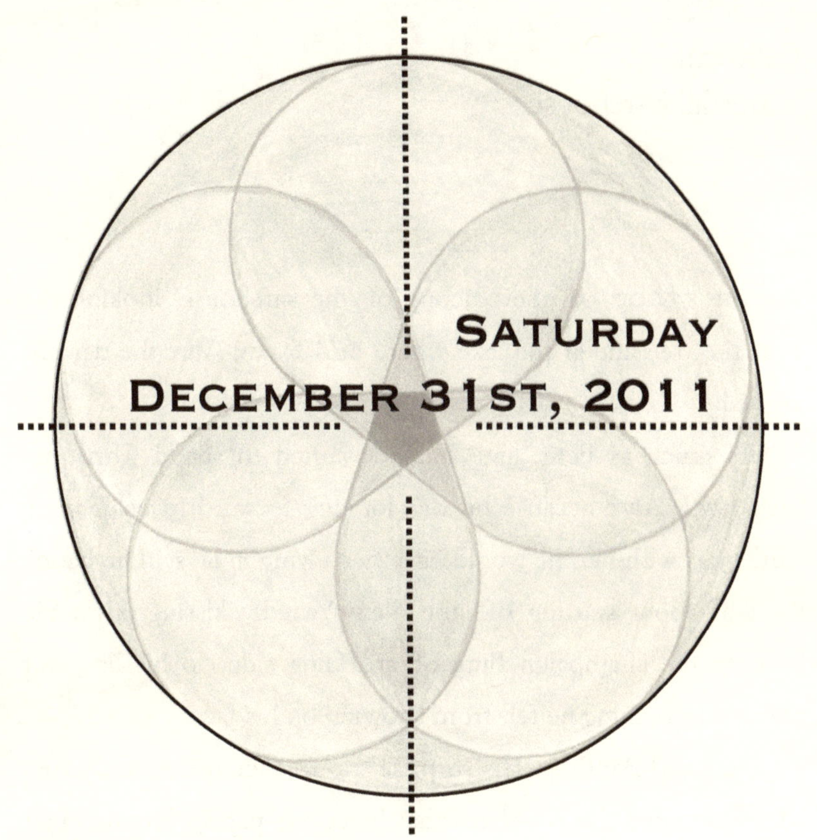

Saturday December 31st, 2011

23:15 PST
California
Waterfall Safehouse

PETER STOOD on the balcony of the safehouse, looking out over the tree line at the lake where he'd found Alyx the day she arrived.

As much as Peter had said he wanted to spend Christmas break with Alyx because he was looking forward to celebrating Christmas with her, he would have been lying if he said he hadn't thought about starting off the New Year by kissing Alyx. He brought the champaign flute of sparkling cider to his lips, not hiding the loathing he felt from showing on his face.

He hated Banthup. His surprise trip to Sacramento had caused nothing but chaos—chaos that Peter was paying for. Neil had given the airport a script to read about them moving the airplane. They weren't sure if he bought it, but Banthup hadn't found the house they used as a staging ground for the safehouse (which—Sarah had explained—was the situation Dylan had been preparing for by arranging for most of their party to come down). After spending a couple of nights in the house, waiting for Banthup to arrive, they had deemed that it was safe to return to the cabin. Only Alyx was already gone. She and Michael had left for London as soon as it was safe to meet the plane in a small private airport the Circle of Fifths would have a hard time locating.

Kate joined him on the balcony, looking out at the view, before turning to him. "You know the party is inside right?"

Peter shook his head. "I don't really feel like celebrating."

"I'm glad to see you are just as miserable as she is." Kate commented.

"What?" Peter asked.

Kate shook her head. "I was there with Alyx in London. I saw her moping everyday. She had been talking about you for years, so when she told me you started dating, I was excited for her. Then, I watched as she struggled with the aftermath of the shooting. She feels alone, and you didn't call her. Not even once."

"I was waiting for her to call. I texted her every day, and made sure she knew I would answer anytime." Peter defended.

"Have you met Alyx?" Kate asked rhetorically. "She will *never* admit that she needs someone, or if she needs help. If you really love her, my advise: call her. Don't wait for her. You will be waiting forever."

Kate didn't wait to hear Peter's response. If he was going to isolate himself, she would give him something to think about.

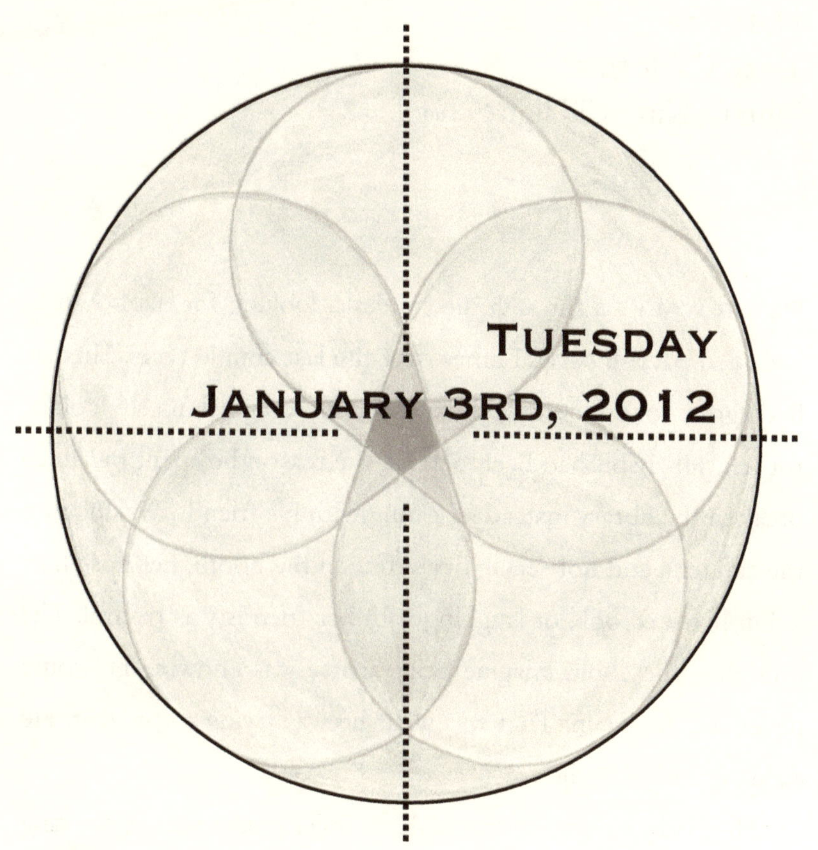
Tuesday
January 3rd, 2012

11:47 PST
Tracy, California
John C. Kimball High School

PETER WALKED through the cafeteria, looking for the booth he had seen Alyx in several times over the last couple years. She had been gone for over a month, and her still caught himself looking for her. His habit had been part of the reason he spent his lunch break in the library instead of eating with his friends. Waking into the cafeteria and not seeing her sitting in the booth, her nose buried in her textbook, or laughing with her friends was painful. The only thing he could imagine being worse was knowing he would never see her again. That was what he was trying to prevent. He didn't want her to die.

He made his way to the table as quickly as possible, wanting to get out as soon as he could. He didn't want to run into any more people than he had to. The last thing he wanted was to lie about his break one more time. When they asked how his Christmas and New Years was, they didn't really want to hear about how it had started off perfect. He got his first normal family

Christmas. He felt loved and wanted for the first time in his life. The problem was it was over shadowed by the threat on his girlfriend's life, and that very threat meant he didn't get the New Years he wanted. No one would listen if he tried to tell them. So he lied. He told them it was good.

He was losing his will to do so.

The only way he would get through this was by remaining mission oriented. He put on the blinders his father had taught him to, ignoring all unnecessary distractions. He had one lie he needed to tell today. One lie that was worth the risk of ending up in unwanted situations with his friends.

He arrived at the booth, a wrapped gift in his hand. He handed it to Carlie, who looked up at him as the gift appeared in front of her. "This is from Alyx." He said, getting ready to walk away.

"You saw her?" Savannah asked.

"How is she?" Carlie asked.

Peter shook her head. "I didn't see her. She bought the gift one of the times we were hanging out before…" Peter paused, not sure how to describe what had happened. "I knew it was for you, and she would want you to have it, even if she isn't talking to anyone right now."

Peter decided to make a break for it, before he got stuck talking to her friends. They knew her better than anyone, and if he told them the wrong lie, they would catch on. He didn't need to get them caught up in the dangerous game the Circle of Fifths was playing with her. At the moment, she wasn't acting like she cared about her friends very much, but Peter knew better. She did care. A lot. If something happened to her friends because of her, it would devastate her. He just needed to make sure she didn't destroy her friendships while trying to keep them safe.

"Hey Peter, wait up!" A guy called. Peter kept walking, not caring enough to turn around. "The girlfriend you told me about my first day, that was Alyx, Carlie's friend?" The voice persisted, matching Peter's strides.

Peter glanced at the person next to him, finding the kid that sat next to him in AP Gov. Kalen, if he remembered right. "How do you know Alyx? She hasn't been to school since you started."

"I don't." Kalen lied. "I just know that she is Carlie's friend, and her not texting Carlie back is really hurting her."

"What do you care if Alyx is pushing away her friends? She suffered a trauma, ok? She is pushing everyone she cares about away, me included." Peter admitted. "It's absolute torture having to watch from the outside as someone you love suffers, knowing you can't do anything about that."

"I know." Kalen admitted. "And I care, because we started dating. I care about Carlie, and it's hard to watch Alyx hurt her by ignoring her."

Peter gave Kalen a sad nod. "I'm sorry. Honestly, Carlie is lucky she doesn't have a front row seat to her friend's self-destructive spiral. It would hurt more if she did." Peter started to walk away before turning back. "Alyx cares. I know that, and for reasons too complicated to explain, she is pushing everyone away, probably because she thinks she is protecting them." Peter nodded toward the table. "Hopefully the gift will remind Carlie that Alyx cares. It's not apathy that is keeping her from her friends."

Kalen watched as Peter walked away. When Banthup or Jackson asked what the conversation was about, he would tell them he was hoping he would be able to get information out of Peter about Alyx. He couldn't let them know that he was starting to question the Circle of Fifths, their goals, and their methods for achieving the goals. As much as he didn't like Alyx, he couldn't stand by and watch as his uncle's plan to convince her to join him indiscriminately hurt everyone close to Alyx.

Carlie didn't deserve to suffer.

15:57 PST
Tracy, California
Circle of Fifths Safehouse

BANTHUP THREW his keys across the garage as he walked in, the fob bouncing off of the punching bag before clattering to the ground. He instantly regretted it, walking over to the fob on the ground, hoping that it wasn't broken. They were way too expensive to replace. He just felt like throwing something, and his key fob was what was in his hand.

The Hall family was really starting to grate his nerves. They had way too much power, and they used it to frustrate his plans. He had found a private plane that had flown into a small Sacramento airfield with a manifest that was hidden behind more layers of red tape than any normal flight should have. Even with his clearance, and Kalen's computer skills, he hadn't even come close to uncovering who was on the plane. Then again, all the layers of protection told him that Alyx had been on that plane.

Unfortunately, he had no idea where it had come from. All the important information was redacted.

The only clue he had was that some of the bureaucratic red tape he had tried to cut through was from the United Kingdom. When he had told Jackson that, he acted as if that was important information. He didn't know why. The United Kingdom wasn't as big as the United States, but it was still a fairly large place. There were so many places Alyx could be.

That was another reason he was angry. All of their intel had suggested that Alyx would be back at school after Winter Break. Banthup had sat through her classes for yet another day, and hadn't seen even the slightest indication that she was back. If she had been in California like he and Kalen suspected—despite never finding the safehouse—she had been scurried back to wherever they'd been hiding her before.

He didn't want to consider the possibility of them taking her somewhere else entirely.

"Bad day?" Kalen asked, much too chipper for everything that had been going wrong with his uncle's plan recently.

"McLean is still not back." Banthup complained. "We don't know where she was hiding. We don't know where she went. And we didn't find the safehouse."

"Did Jackson not like the update you gave him?" Kalen asked, wrapping his hands to start a session with the punching bag.

Banthup shook his head. "I don't understand. I expected anger. *I* was angry. Be he was *happy*. He's never happy. He sounded like the bit about red tape from the UK was actually helpful."

Kalen shrugged. "She has an uncle who lives in London. That was something that really bugged me about the entire situation. If they are being protective of her, why did they send her somewhere alone. She has to be somewhere with security they would trust. It would make sense if she was living with her uncle in London. Feilds Palace is basically a fortress. It took Jackson years to get an invite to Feilds Ball, and once he did, security was so tight, it was pointless."

"If she is at Feilds Palace, isn't that a bad thing?" Banthup asked. "Jackson can't get to her to make her feel unsafe."

Kalen shook his head. "That's not his plan. Besides, even if it was, all we would have to do was watch, and wait for Alyx to leave. She isn't great at staying in one place for long. If she hasn't figured out how to sneak out yet, she will soon."

Banthup narrowed his eyes at Kalen. "Ok, Mister Positivity. How are you going to spin us not finding the safe house into a good thing."

Kalen rolled his eyes as he lined up with the punching bag. "Finding the safe house was always a bonus. The Circle of Fifths has been trying to find *one* of the Hall safehouses for much longer than either of us have been alive. I will admit that the Halls are better at hiding their assets than I am at finding them. But Jackson hasn't found one yet either, so honestly, if he wants to get mad at us, he will have to get mad at himself first."

Banthup crossed his arms, watching as Kalen bounced

around the punching bag. Something had changed with Kalen. He wasn't sure what that something was, but he had an idea that it was related to Carlie.

Add it to the list of things Jackson would like to know.

17:38 PST
Tracy, California
John C. Kimball High School

KATE PANTED, trying to catch her breath while laying on the astroturf of the John C. Kimball High School football field where she had collapsed. Since Lynn had shown up last summer, she had taken exercise a bit more seriously, but she was woefully underprepared for Track.

She missed Alyx.

Not that Alyx being here would make it any easier to run. It wouldn't even make the coach any less crazy. But if Alyx had been here, she would have had someone who would support her, even if it was with a taunt or two thrown in for fun.

When Alyx had told her that she preferred to run sprints and hurdles, Kate had developed a very skewed vision of what it meant to be a sprinter. She envisioned running the straight portion of the track a few times, and maybe some drills. She hadn't anticipated being asked to do a light jog around the astroturf of the football field *six* times as a warm-up. The stretches had been a bit odd, but not unwelcome. What had killed her was the 600 meter sprint they had done once the sprinters broke away from the others.

She had burned herself out after the first 100 meters.

Not only did she have to finish one 600 meter sprint, but then they did a few more for good measure.

Kate's only consolation was that Lynn, Peter, Chelsi, and Thane were all struggling too. Not nearly as bad as Kate was. They had remained standing. But their breathing was labored, and she had heard Peter threaten the coach under his breath.

"Everybody up!" The coach hollered once the last group of students finished their last 600 meter run. "Two laps around the field as a cool down, then meet me to do some stretches."

Lynn offered Kate a hand for help getting up, which Kate unceremoniously swatted away, before proceeding to get up on her own. Lynn may have been her twin sister, but Alyx had been there for Kate for a lot longer. There was no way Kate was going to replace Alyx with someone who thought lying to her family was the best way to *protect* them. She definitely wasn't going to accept help from someone who thought Alyx should stay in London, taking away her ability to participate in her last year of Track, while she shamelessly participated in the very same sport. It was cruel and sadistic.

In Kate's opinion, it wasn't any better than what the Circle of Fifths was trying to do to Alyx.

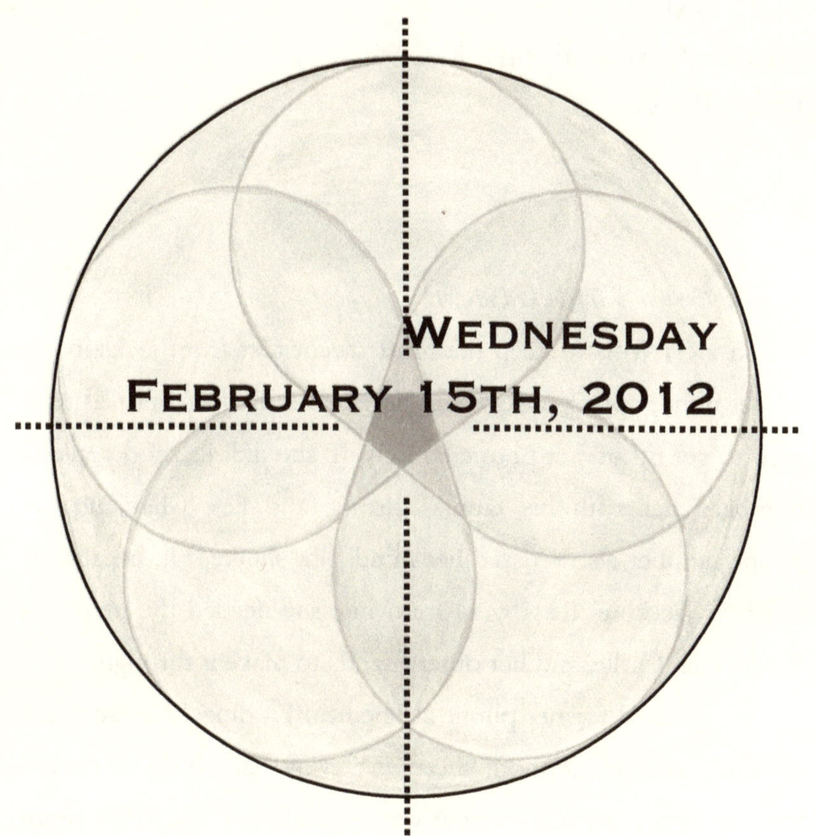

Wednesday
February 15th, 2012

14:41 GMT
Twickenham, London
Feilds Palace

Are you tired of being locked up yet?

ALYX TRIED to keep the most recent text from Jackson out of her mind, opting to focus on homework. Part of her was tempted to get rid of her phone entirely. If she did, Jackson couldn't bombard her with his taunts, threats, and lies. Changing her phone number also crossed her mind. But she kept it, because as much as Jackson's texts were annoying, she needed the messages from Peter, Carlie, and her other friends to make it through.

She jumped for her phone as she heard it ding. She had spent so much time in London, she didn't even really have to do the math to figure out what time it was in California. She felt it more than anything. It was just about seven in the morning Pacific Standard Time. Her friends were either already awake and at Seminary, or they were waking up and getting ready for school. It was their favorite time of day to check in on her.

Even if she never replied.

Peter should be calling soon. She wasn't sure if it was the voicemail she'd left him before she flew back for Christmas, or what, but he no longer waited for her to call. Every morning when he got up, he called her to check in for the day. It was really sweet of him, and she lived for those phone calls. She knew he probably wouldn't admit it, but she was pretty sure he lived for their phone calls too. That's why, when she could, she called him before she went to bed. She'd caught him during Track practice once. She heard Coach White yell at him for answering his phone. Then he took the phone, saw her name, and made Peter run laps while he told Alyx how much he wished she could be there. When Peter got done with his punishment, Coach had given back his phone, so Alyx could say good night.

After break they had been making long distance work better than she could have hoped for. She had actually felt herself returning to normal—whatever that was for her.

Instead of finding a text from one of her friends, however, she saw yet another text from Jackson.

> **Sociopath** Now
> You know that's why they sent you to Feilds Palace. They aren't concerned about me getting to you. They are concerned about what you will do once you realize they are lying to you.

Alyx would give Jackson one thing: he knew how to illicit a response from her. She was usually good at keeping her cool and not giving in to his taunts. As she clicked on the text message, opening the conversation with the contact she'd named *Sociopath*, she saw the evidence of her control. She had to scroll through several received messages before she found the last reply she'd sent to Jackson. But every once in a while, she couldn't help but give in and respond.

It frustrated her that Jackson knew that she was angry at her parents for keeping secrets. It aggravated her that he was capitalizing on her anger and their secrets to try and manipulate her.

She wouldn't fall for his pathetic attempts to convince her that her parents were evil people. They made mistakes, but they loved her, and only wanted the best for her. She may not like their methods, but she trusted they wouldn't do anything to intentionally hurt her or others. Unintentionally was another story.

Jackson, on the other hand, had already admitted to killing her aunt and torturing her cousin.

My parents might be many things, but they don't lie to me.

Jackson's response was near instantaneous.

So they told you who is responsible for your siblings death? They told you why you survived when they didn't?

Alyx jumped up off the bed, threw the phone down onto her

bed, and backed away. Jackson knew all the buttons to push, and she hated that.

How did he know so much?

Alyx ran her hands through her hair. Jackson knew too much about her. He knew where she was. He knew that she thought this was her prison. He knew that she was having issues with her family. He knew that many of the issues with her parents derived from them not telling her about her siblings. He knew that she wanted answers about their death, and not the vague, *the Circle of Fifths is responsible for their death*, answer her parents had given her.

How many freedoms do they have to take from you before you recognize that they don't trust you. I trust you enough to tell you the truth.

The unwanted text message appeared on the screen. Alyx hat-ed herself for reading it. She hated herself more for thinking about what he said. She walked away from her phone, leaving the taunting text message on the unlocked screen, not trusting herself to touch the phone even to lock it. It would time out, and the phone would lock itself.

She stormed off into the closet. She needed a run now more than anything. She needed to sneak out, and remind herself that she was free. She needed to pound her frustrations into the pavement with every stride she took.

She needed a run. And a swim. Maybe a drive. She definitely needed to play some tennis, and she was likely to hit the ball a little too hard, and lose more than one over a fence. And maybe after all of that, she would be calm enough that she could find the piano Michael had installed in the palace by the time they'd returned. Apparently Peter had said something. Once she had calmed down, she could work out the rest of her anger on the keys, and not break the piano. She would start with the beginning of Beethoven's 5th Symphony, get out any remaining need to hit stuff. Then she should be able to play her favorite piece.

Hopefully.

15:11 GMT
Twickenham, London
Feilds Palace

ALYX PULLED herself up over the fence, the same way she had several times before. She had run Stephan's route through the palace grounds, and it was definitely long enough for her, but she loved the excitement she got from sneaking out. There was something about the thrill of getting away with something she wasn't supposed to do that was addictive.

She also loved the freedom she felt from doing it.

She hadn't realized how free she was, and how much she had grown to love and rely on her freedom. Her parents had never stopped her from taking her bike out to go for a ride around her neighborhood. When she was younger, they had insisted on supervising, and limiting where she could go. The older she got, the farther she could go from home, and they cared less about supervising until she just had to make sure it was ok to go out front, and she was given a vague, *be home before dark*. Her parents were cautious, but trusted her to stay safe and follow their rules. Since

November, all of the freedoms she had enjoyed for the last few years had been revoked, and she saw no light at the end of the tunnel. If she had to take those freedoms back through sneaking out she would.

She dropped down on the other side of the fence, turning her vision towards the palace she was returning to, easing back into a jog.

"How was the Thames?" A voice asked from behind her.

Alyx' stomach dropped. She turned her head, looking at the origin of the voice. The moment she saw Stephan's face, she knew she'd been caught. Instead of defending herself, she just turned around and continued running back to the house.

"Really? You have nothing to say to me?" Stephan asked, keeping pace beside her.

"What is there to say?" Alyx asked. "Nothing I say will convince you to let me leave the house again."

"How long have you been sneaking out?" Stephan asked.

"You're supposed to be smart. Guess."

"So when you came back scraped up the first time—"

Alyx responded to the unfinished question with silence.

"Why?"

Alyx spun on Stephan. "Because I'm being treated like a bloody child. No, worse. Like some fragile little flower that will break if I'm allowed to do anything I like. I can take care of myself. I don't need to be coddled. I need to do the things I like doing. I need to do the things that make me feel like I'm normal."

"So we're just supposed to let you run along the Thames, where any Circle of Fifths member can find you, and shoot you again. Maybe this time they will kill you." Stephan yelled. "I'm not going to be the reason you end up dead."

"Well I'm not living. Maybe I'd rather be dead." Alyx yelled.

It seemed as if everything in the world fell silent with her admission. Stephan stared at the girl he had watched grow up; her words hurt him more than any physical attack could. She was his baby sister. How could he have missed how miserable she was?

"You have taken more from me than Jackson ever could." Alyx admitted, tears pooling in her eyes. But she was stronger than the tears. She wouldn't let them fall. "Go ahead. Tell me I'm never leaving Feilds Palace again. Maybe I'll just text Jackson. At least he'll let me go for a run along one of the most beautiful rivers in the world. I'm sure he'd let me choose the river."

Alyx spun, storming off back into her prison.

Stephan knew it was pointless trying to follow. She would disappear into one of the secret rooms she had found, and as hard as he had tried, he'd never found her. Instead, he pulled out his phone, typing a message before hitting send.

15:49 GMT
Twickenham, London
Feilds Palace

MICHAEL WATCHED from his study window as Alyx practiced serves on the tennis court below. When he had noticed her out there practicing, he had gone out and offered to call in one of the coaches she had studied under for years, but she'd declined.

Watching how hard she was hitting the tennis balls, he was glad. He hadn't heard of anyone being killed with a tennis ball, but if anyone was capable of turning the fragile things into weapons, it would be the girl on the court. He swore he had seen some of the poor things explode when she hit them, or when they hit the ground. The lucky ones escaped over the fences.

The only time he had seen her even close to how she was now was the first summer after Ally died. She was still trying to cope with the death of her siblings when she had also lost Ally. Sarah and Neil had been having problems. They thought Alyx hadn't noticed, but she had. She had gone out to the tennis court, found one of the small rackets he kept for the girls if they ever wanted to use them, and started hitting tennis balls…or trying at least. He went out to see what was going on when he heard yelling. She had tears running down her face, but an angry scowl on her face. She wouldn't tell him what drove her out to the court in the first place, but when he found her, she was yelling about not being able to hit the ball.

Tennis was one of the things Ally had done with the girls.

Michael was not great at tennis. He barely understood enough to play for the dreaded matches against political allies, and professional partners. He hated the sport. He had only tolerated it for so long because Ally would play with him when he was required to, and that made it 1000% better. After her death, it was just a painful reminder of her. So he had hired all of the best coaches to teach Alyx. He was pretty sure it had been a good way for her to cope with Ally's loss. It kept her grounded, gave her something to remind her of Ally, and allowed her to feel connected to Ally and her memory.

He had noticed that she tended to find herself on the tennis court, practicing her serves when she was angry about something.

"Do you know what set her off this time?" Michael asked Stephan when he heard him enter the office.

"No idea." Stephan replied from the doorway.

Michael turned away from the window. "You said you caught her sneaking back in. What was she doing?"

"Running." Stephan replied. "I gave her a route to run within palace grounds, and I don't think she has used it a single time. She used some strong language telling me off, and admitted she's been sneaking out since the first time I allowed her to leave."

"So is she mad at you." Michael asked.

Stephan grimaced. "I don't think so. I mean, yes, she was mad that I caught her, but something set her off to begin with."

Michael shook his head. "Is she really so mad at us that she had to go for a run, and she still has enough anger left to be on the tennis courts?"

"I don't know." Stephan admitted. "I thought she was going to disappear into the secret rooms, like she usually does. Instead, I saw her swimming laps, and one of the guards caught her trying to steal one of the cars."

"Did Peter—"

"No." Stephan answered before Michael finished asking his question. "Peter called me when she didn't answer for their daily call. She was already on her run. Whatever set her off happened before that."

Michael nodded, turning back to the window watch Alyx. "Her parents want us to jump on a call. They are concerned that she is sneaking out."

Stephan nodded, watching Michael watch Alyx. She had to know how many people were there for her. She had to know that they were all concerned about her.

16:04 GMT
Twickenham, London
Feilds Palace

NEIL PAUSED mid sentence as he heard the opening chords of Beethoven's Fifth Symphony filter through the video connection with Feilds Palace. "Is that…?"

Stephan looked toward the closed door of Michael's office, where he and Michael had joined the conference call. "Alyx just moved to piano." He confirmed. He had no idea how hard she was banging on the keys if the sound carried so far that not only could he and Michael heard it in the moderately soundproofed office, but it also carried through the audio connection to Tracy.

Neil exchanged a look with Sarah.

"What's wrong?" Dylan asked

"The only time Alyx attempts Beethoven's Fifth Symphony is when she is *extremely* mad." Sarah shared with everyone. "If she is going to use piano to calm down, she usually plays Mozart. She'll start with Beethoven if she is too angry to make it through the calm sections of Eine Klein Nachmusik."

"Have you been alerted about anyone trying to gain access to Feilds Palace?" Neil asked.

"No." Stephan reported. "Besides Alyx sneaking out to go for a run, we haven't had any perimeter breaches."

"What are you thinking?" Michael asked Neil.

"I think the Circle of Fifths knows where Alyx is, and they have started pushing buttons." Neil replied. "The alternative is that we have done something to make her that mad at us…"

"What would make her this angry?" Stephan asked. "Because I have been an older brother figure to her for years. I have pushed every button I could find, and I have *never* made her *this* angry. I've made her *I-need-to-go-for-a-run* angry, *I-need-to-go-for-a-swim* angry, *I-need-to-play-tennis* angry, but never all *three* angry, and this piano thing is new to me."

Sarah turned her head to the side as if she were trying to hear better. "I'm sorry, did you just say she has done *all* of her anger coping mechanisms?"

"Afraid so." Stephan reported.

"There's no way this was something done accidentally. Whoever made her angry did so intentionally." Neil commented.

"If this is Circle of Fifths as we all suspect, we have one very important question to answer." Dylan paused, for dramatic effect that was completely unnecessary. "What does the Circle of Fifths gain by making her angry?"

"The first thing Alyx did was sneak out to run along the

Thames, correct?" Peter finally piped in.

"Correct." Stephan confirmed.

"What if they have known where she is? They may have already seen her out running along the Thames." Peter suggested.

"So making her angry was their attempt to draw her outside the palace grounds, where she is protected?" Stephan asked. "How did they know what to do to make her angry? What did they say? How did they contact her?"

Peter shook his head. "None of that matters. What matters is that they did. They know where she is. They know how to manipulate her. They just showed us that she isn't safe in London, at least not any more than she was here in Tracy. So why don't we make Alyx happy and bring her home? Give her back some semblance of control in her life."

The people in both rooms exploded into a cacophony of arguments, most of them explaining all the reasons why bringing Alyx back to California was a bad idea.

Peter was tired of being the one trying to think about what was best for Alyx, not just the best way to protect her. He walked away, picking up his backpack so he could leave for school.

As he walked out the door, he couldn't help but recognize the irony of him enjoying freedoms that Alyx wasn't being allowed to. He could just leave when her family started getting on his nerves with their overprotective, and hypocritical arguments.

16:45 GMT
Twickenham, London
Feilds Palace

ALYX RETURNED to her room, feeling a little better. Not much, but a little.

She rolled her eyes at her phone, still sitting on her bed where she left it. Clearly, she hadn't worked out all of her anger, because she felt the nearly uncontrollable urge to just chuck the phone out the window.

Alyx picked up her phone, finding her phone overwhelmed with notifications. She had several missed calls from Peter. She had been so annoyed with Jackson that she had just left, completely forgetting that Peter would be calling her soon. Based on the calls, and the many *many* text messages he'd sent, Peter had panicked when she didn't answer.

So it was his fault that Stephan found her. Peter was constantly telling her that he didn't agree with what her parents were doing. He told her that it was just as hard for him to be away from her, but instead of helping her escape the clutches of her family's insane protection, he helped *them.*

At this rate, they wouldn't let her come home to take her AP tests, never mind walk for graduation. If they didn't trust that she would be safe at Feilds Palace, where no one knew she was, they would never trust that she would be safe sitting in the high school's small gym, where they always set up the AP test. If they didn't trust she would be safe in a gym that could be guarded, they wouldn't trust she would be safe sitting on the football field with the rest of the class of 2012, out in the open, while she waited to walk across the stage and receive her diploma.

She would be stuck living in Feilds Palace, or moving from safehouse to safehouse for the rest of her life. Forget the future Peter wanted with her. Forget the future *she* wanted. Forget Oxford, and a life with Peter. They were all so concerned about her being alive, about being helpless against Jackson. But instead of training her so she could face Jackson, she was being hidden. And they were failing, because Jackson knew where she was anyway.

Alyx unlocked her phone, the text from Jackson reappearing. If no one was going to *actually* protect her from Jackson, she would take things into her own hands. She typed two words into the message bar. She paused, taking a moment to think about what she was about to do. She couldn't undo it. If she took things into her own hands, it didn't guarantee her safety. Sending this message might just seal her early grave.

But she wouldn't know unless she took the risk. Her future depended on it.

She took a deep breath, hit send, then locked her phone and dropped it back on her bed before her message could mock her.

Prove it.

10:44 PST
Tracy, California
John C. Kimball High School

KALEN HAD been manipulated.

When he had gotten to school this morning, he had finished reading his mom's file. He wasn't sure what he was expecting for a final entry, but it wasn't what he read.

> *Kyrie has become a liability. The Nexus ordered her house to be bugged, and at 21:08 tonight, she let Ally Hall into the house. Based on their conversation, neither of them can be allowed to live. I know what I must do.*

Kalen had immediately turned to his file after reading the final entry. He had always been told that he killed his parents, but based on his mother's file, it seemed as though she betrayed the Circle of Fifths, and his uncle killed her for the Nexus. His entry didn't even show any trepidation or remorse.

When Kalen had started to read his file, it confirmed what he had read in his mother's.

> *Kalen woke up and made his way down stairs before I had a chance*

to order someone to clean up the bodies, ruining my original plan to convince him that his parents didn't love him, and abandoned him. I found him covered in her blood, sobbing. He is too young to understand what happened, and too delirious and tired to remember much from the night. He thinks he was the only one in the house with them, and believes he killed them.

His belief gives me a much better opportunity. If he believes he killed them, and feels guilt for doing so, I have an opportunity to use that guilt to my advantage. I called in Circle of Fifths agents to make sure the bodies were taken care of, and the investigation didn't lead back to me. I told Kalen they would make sure it wouldn't lead back to him. Now, I can make him feel indebted to me. If I use that, paired with his guilt, I can make him into the perfect soldier his mother was supposed to be.

Jackson had told him exactly how he would manipulate Alyx into becoming his perfect soldier. He had done it several times before. Including on his own nephew.

Kalen wandered into class seconds before the late bell, sitting down and pulling out his notebook on autopilot. He had been operating on autopilot all morning—since he read the files. He couldn't remember much from his previous class. Classes? What class period was this?

Carlie watched him, concern written on her features. Kalen wasn't acting like his normal self. He was distracted. He seemed sad, maybe even a bit angry. He was in class, but he wasn't present. His eyes were glued to the blank page of his notebook, but they were glazed over. He had yet to look at her, or the board, or the teacher, or anything other than the empty lines of the paper in front of him.

With a glance at the teacher, to make sure she was still sitting at her desk, checking email, and not looking at the class as they did their warm-up, Carlie reached out, gently touching Kalen's shoulder. It was hard to see her boyfriend sad about something, but trying so hard to deal with it himself. She knew from the little they talked about his home life that he didn't have the best support system. He was used to having to process things by himself. He hadn't had anyone he could talk to. But that wasn't true any more. She wanted to make sure he knew that.

Kalen turned to Carlie as she touched his shoulder, and she could see the conflict and emotion in his eyes. He had been trained to hide his emotions. He had been trained how to keep anyone from seeing anything they might need to manipulate him, but what was the point in hiding them when his uncle had been the one manipulating him all along. Why should he try to hide how he was feeling from the one person who actually seemed to care about him?

What would she think when he finally told her the truth?

When had he decided it was a *when* he told her the truth, not an *if*?

Are you ok? Carlie mouthed.

Kalen smiled, something that only she could get him to do. He nodded: *I am now.*

Carlie gave him a disappointed look. He hated it when she did that. He had been trained to hide his emotions; he could have sworn Carlie had been trained how to use her disappointment as a weapon.

He turned his attention to the board, paying attention in class for the first time today. Leave it to the girl next to him to snap him out of the fog he had been in for over an hour.

11:02 PST
Tracy, California
John C. Kimball High School

JACKSON SMILED at his phone and the message he'd gotten from McLean. It had been easy to manipulate her parents. He had proven the summer before that as soon as McLean's life was threatened, every single one of her family members would move to protect her. Shooting her, while counterproductive to trying to convince her to trust him, was a *very* efficient way to manipulate her parents into taking away all of the freedoms they had given their daughter. It had taken more effort to manipulate McLean, but this text proved success.

She was stubborn. He would give that to the girl. He hadn't anticipated how much she would push back against his attempts to convince her to trust him. If he would have known, he would have started to message her before he received the Icarus file.

That would be the first thing he broke out of her. She wouldn't be a good soldier if she was too stubborn to take orders from him and the Nexus.

If McLean really wanted him to *prove it* as her message said, he just had to convince her to meet with him, which probably required more trust than he currently had of hers. Fortunately, despite knowing she was in London, he was still in the United States. He would have preferred to fly to London, and do some surveillance, but the Nexus had insisted he join his brother on the campaign trail, and he hadn't had a long enough break to get to London yet. That would likely help him build trust with McLean.

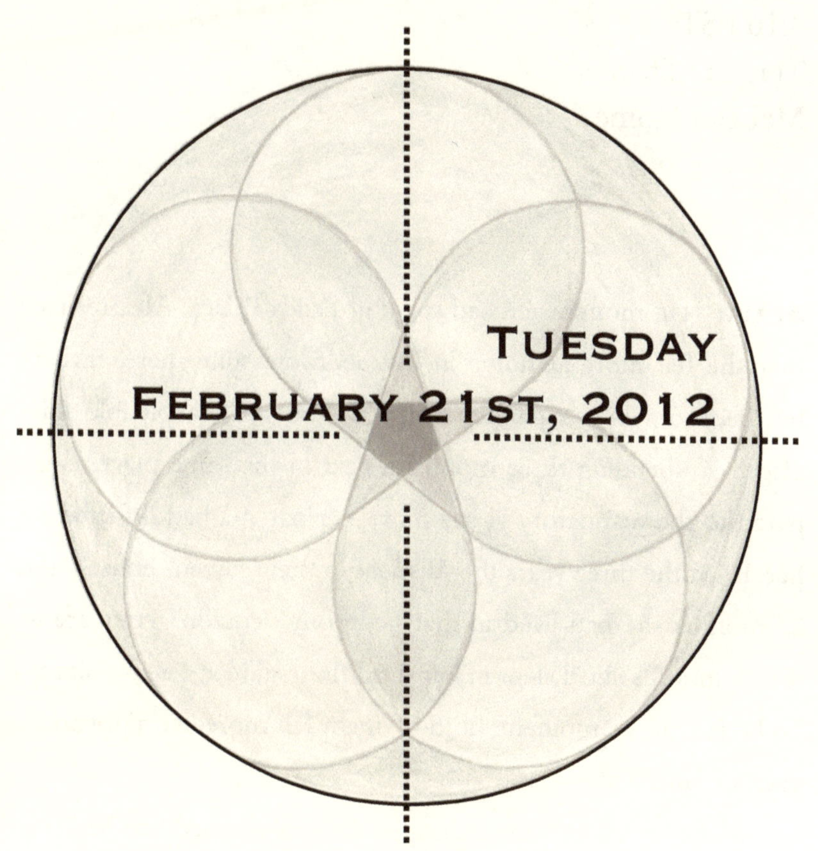

Tuesday February 21st, 2012

4:16 PST
Tracy, California
McLean Home

AFTER THE months she had spent at Feilds Palace, Alyx realized that she felt more at home in her bedroom-suite there, than in her bedroom in her parents house. It was an unavoidable side-effect of spending three months a year in the same place, compared to the mandatory yearly move her parents had inflicted on her. Even the three years they'd spent in their current house—the 27 months she had lived in that bedroom—couldn't compare to the 48 months she'd slept in her third floor suite at Feilds Palace. To be fair, at the moment, both of them felt more like a prison than a home.

As she lay on her side, staring at the wall her bed had been on for three years, it was easy to blame the math for the uneasiness she felt sleeping in her bed in California, and jet lag for her sleeplessness. Yes, the eight hour difference always took a bit to re-adjust, just like daylight savings time asked for a mandatory period to retrain her internal clock. But just like it was easier in the fall, with the extra hour gained being eaten up in sleep, making it easier, not harder, to get up in the mornings, it was supposed to be easier for her to adjust back to Pacific Time. She simply felt like she was being allowed to sleep in.

She sighed, giving up on feigning sleep until she succumbed to it, and turned to lay on her back, staring at her window. If it were up to her, it would have been open a crack to let the cool, crisp, morning air—full of the scent of the spring moisture—permeate the stuffiness of the air inside her room. The air carried the scent of Tracy: the smell of safety and freedom.

Then again, actually being safe was more important than a sense of false security. At least, that's what her parents had argued when she'd tried to open her window the night before. So the bulletproof glass in the newly replaced window stayed snuggled safely in its frame, latch locked. Her parents had also insisted that her blinds be closed, as if they would protect her if the sniper decided to use thermal scopes next time.

She knew just as well as anyone that if Jackson really wanted her dead, she would be. His text messages had made it clear he wanted her to work for him. He didn't want her dead. He had known that she was in London. She had snuck out of Feilds Palace so many times. It wouldn't have taken much for him to send his sniper to the Thames, and she would be dead before anyone knew what had happened. Even now, bulletproof glass wasn't going to stop the sniper if he wanted to kill her now. They just had to wait for her to leave the garage in a car, or use armor piercing rounds to penetrate the glass.

Alyx sighed, frustrated with herself and her brain that wouldn't shut off. She threw her blankets off as she spun and sat up, setting her feet on the floor next to her bed. She sat there, staring at her desk. She could use the time she had to do homework, but her eyes drifted to her phone, plugged in next to her laptop.

She stalked over to her phone, unplugging it from the charger, and opening her text messages. Jackson had the Icarus file, and he claimed it explained *exactly* what happened when her siblings died. He wanted to give it to her.

But she had to meet him.

She turned her head to look at the window that gave a clear view of her room to the rooftop next door. Maybe she should have stayed in London.

She threw her phone onto her bed, then opened her closet, grabbing her favorite pair of jeans from the hanging organizer, then found a light blue striped casual button-up blouse, pulling it off the hanger. She walked over to her bed, setting her clothes on the unmade bed before bending over to open the drawer in the bottom of her bed that was closest to the window where she retrieved an undershirt and sport's bra. With clothes in hand, she opened her door, and walked across the hallway to the bathroom. As she closed and locked the door, she leaned her head back against it, and took a deep breath. She looked up at herself in the mirror. She wished she didn't recognize the girl in the mirror.

She didn't know what was worse: the girl with fear staring back at her, or the anger glinting in her eyes, threatening to take over. She didn't want to let fear rule her life, but right now, that fear was the only thing stopping her anger from agreeing to meet Jackson. All rationality was quickly silenced by one of those two emotions; she had to decide which one.

She hurried and got dressed, then combed through her still damp waves. With one final deep breath, she composed herself, opened the bathroom door, walked across the hall with her back straight, and entered her room. She decided to not let the looming window and impending danger it represented rule her with fear as she made her bed and put her track bag together. When she finished making sure everything she needed for Track was in her duffel bag, she placed it on her bed, ready to grab when it was time to leave. Then she grabbed her MacBook, and walked downstairs to the garage.

5:45 PST
Tracy, California
McLean Home

LYNN CHUCKED a pillow across the room at Kate's sleeping figure in the bed. Since Kate joining her in California, this was their morning ritual. Lynn was usually up by the time the alarm went off, her years living with a couple of MI-6 agents having trained her sleeping schedule. At first, it had been hard to adjust to the time change, but she had been here long enough, she had long since adjusted to California time. Kate hadn't seemed to have a problem sleeping in to adjust to the new time zone. Lynn sometimes wondered how they were related. Kate could sleep through anything, and often did.

Lynn stumbled out of the room she was sharing with Kate, heading towards the bathroom. The benefit of Kate sleeping in every morning was that Lynn didn't have to fight her for the bathroom.

With face washed, Lynn wandered out of the bathroom, noticing that the door to Alyx' room was open. She knew for a fact that Alyx had shut it when she went to bed the night before, but hadn't been paying enough attention when she went into the bathroom to know if it was open before she went in. She walked over to the dark room, instead of the one she was sharing with Kate, peeking in the door. She saw Alyx' backpack sitting in the chair in front of her desk, and her duffle bag sitting on her bed, but Alyx was no where to be seen.

Lynn may have been pretty composed for a young teenager, but for a spy, she was not. Spies were supposed to be good at hiding their emotions, especially when they were feeling panic. But as Lynn went into the room she and Kate were sharing, she couldn't hide her panic with a façade of calm.

"Kate," Lynn hissed, shoving her to try and wake her up. "Get up. Alyx is gone."

Kate muttered something, rolling over as she pulled her blanket up over her head. Lynn had no idea what she had said to their father in order to convince him to let her come, but it seemed like a waste if she was just going to spend her time whining in bed. Lynn sighed, defeated by her sister's laziness, and left the room. She knew two more people in the house who would be more responsive. With caution, she padded through the hall toward the master bedroom, Lynn felt totally out of place in the doorway, looking at the two sleeping figures in the bed. She had been at Feilds Palace a few months, and not once had she just walked into her father's bedroom. She had been staying in this very house, living with the two people asleep just a few feet away, and she still felt like a stranger, despite being family.

Lynn didn't enter the room, opting for knocking on the open door, and hoping they were lighter sleepers than Kate because this was the better option.

Neil bolted upright, and when he saw Lynn, his panic didn't go away. It was the first night Alyx was back home, in her room, in the bed that had been shot at. Both he and Sarah had a very restless night. Every hour or so, one of them had gotten up and checked on Alyx and swept the house, their anxiety not letting them fall asleep until just a couple hours before.

Unfortunately, seeing Lynn standing in their doorway, his mind drifted to all of the things that could be wrong. Instead of letting his mind show him all the worst images it could come up with, he decided to just ask, "What's wrong?"

"Alyx isn't in her room," Lynn said. "Where might she go?"

Sarah was out of bed in what looked like a warm robe faster than Lynn could blink. "Have you called Peter yet?" She asked walking toward Lynn. "Is she in the Library? Is she in the kitchen?"

"I haven't checked the house yet. I don't know where she might go. That's why I asked you." Lynn admitted.

Sarah smoothed Lynn's hair the way a mother would. "That's ok. Neil and I will check the house. Why don't you get dressed and call Peter. If she's not here, he might know where she'd go."

Lynn nodded, trying to calm her racing mind. She didn't know how Sarah could comfort Lynn and be motherly to her, while her own daughter was missing. It had been one thing to experience Sarah's motherly love while Alyx was gone, and a completely different experience now, in a moment of panic. Lynn went into her room, not even trying to be quiet as she picked up her phone. With her phone call to Peter on speakerphone, sitting on her bed while it waited to connect, Lynn pulled clothes out of her suitcase and began to get dressed.

With the extra commotion, and the ringing phone, Kate finally stirred. "What's going?" She slurred tiredly.

Lynn just rolled her eyes, sliding a pullover on over a short sleeved shirt. As the thick sweater was over her head, she heard Peter's muffled voice through the phone. She quickly yanked it the rest of the way down. "Alyx isn't in her room. Her mom is checking the house, but I was wondering if you knew where she might go if she's not here."

Lynn could hear the same panic in Peter as she heard rustling, which she guessed meant he was getting out of bed. "Um, there's a park she told her mom we'd be studying at. I can check to see if she came here."

"Would she?" Lynn asked.

"I don't know." Peter admitted. "But she knows the alarm code. And it's not home."

"How does she know the alarm code?" Lynn asked.

“Figured it out. She yelled at me about it being easy to guess, and insisted I change it, but I haven’t had the heart to yet.” Peter admitted. “She’s not here.” Peter told Lynn, his check of his house complete.

“I didn’t find her either.” Sarah said from the door. Lynn looked at her aunt, defeat rising. Alyx had only been home for a few hours. How had they lost her already?

“I’ll be there in a couple of minutes.” Peter told them before hanging up.

6:03 PST
Tracy, California
McLean Home

ALYX SIGHED, closing her laptop when she saw the time. She needed to get breakfast and make sure her cousins were up before she left for Seminary, so she couldn't hide in her car any longer. It was a little chilly in her car, and with it being in the garage, it was irresponsible to turn it on to warm it up, but she had become oddly numb to it. She preferred the cold to the fear she felt sitting in her own room. But if anyone asked, she would tell them she simply missed her car while she was in London.

Alyx pulled her headphones out of her ears, pulling the jack out of her computer before rolling them up. With her headphones put away in her pocket, she slid across her backseat so she

was sitting behind the driver's seat, instead of stretched across the car like she had been, and opened the door. She folded her arms protectively across her MacBook, not so much to actually protect the computer, but to hold it to her, part of her brain thinking if someone took a shot at her, the computer might stop it before actually hitting her.

As she entered the house, she was surprised to hear voices in the kitchen. What surprised her even more than hearing that everyone in the house was awake, was the fact that she heard Peter's voice mingled with the others.

"Where would she feel safest?" Peter asked. "Because I would go where ever I felt safest."

Alyx furrowed her brow, walking from the laundry room where she'd been to the kitchen where she heard the voices. "Who's missing?" She asked, walking in to see her parents, Kate, Lynn, and Peter all huddled in the kitchen.

Sarah rushed to Alyx, enclosing her in her arms. "We were so worried. Where were you?"

Alyx stayed stiff, not returning the hug, and quickly pulled away. "Wait. You thought *I* was missing?"

"When I got up, your door was open, and you weren't in your room..." Lynn replied uncomfortably.

"I was in the garage." Alyx told the silent room. "You really didn't look very hard did you?"

Silence settled over the room. Alyx had known that she wasn't the only one that still had fears from the shooting. Their fear was the reason she had been stuck in London for months. Their fear was the reason that as soon as they discovered she was sneaking out to run in London, they brought her home. She thought that coming home to where the threat was meant they would watch her closer. She thought coming home meant someone would be awake, watching the house. She thought coming home meant they would receive an alert when she opened her window, her bedroom door, the garage door, the fridge. She thought coming home would mean greater safety, albeit at the cost of her freedom. After all, despite Jackson casually mentioning Feilds Palace in his texts to her, which meant he knew where she was, he had tried to insist he was still state-side. She didn't trust him. She didn't feel safe in London anymore either.

She had gone into the garage almost two hours ago, if they hadn't noticed, and were just in the starting phases of a search, she didn't feel any safer being home.

"I went out the the garage *two hours ago* and you are just barely starting your search *now*?" Alyx asked. "Two hours is a long time. If Jackson wanted me dead, I would be dead. If he wanted to kidnap me and coerce me into joining him, I would be so far gone, you might not ever find me." She chastised the room. "For a room full of people meant to be protecting me, you are doing a really lousy job. Clearly the last few months would have been better spent training me so I could protect myself, rather than hiding me from the psychopath."

"Training you wouldn't protect you from the Circle of Fifths." Sarah argued.

Alyx shook her head. "It's not the Circle of Fifths after me though. It's one man. Phillip Jackson. If you trained me, I could fight *one* man. I already fought his sniper and won once, *without* training."

"Jackson killed mum." Lynn said. "I couldn't fight him."

Alyx shook her head. "You were weak because Dylan is an idiot, and you are younger than me." She looked around the room. "I can stand my own."

"It's not a risk worth taking." Neil insisted quietly. "We've already lost two of our children to them, and can't see a third without risking her life too. We can't lose you to them."

Alyx shook her head, scoffing in disbelief. "I'm not asking you to train me and send me after him. I'm asking that you train me so I can defend myself if he breaks through your defenses, which he and I have proved are less than fool proof."

She stared at her parents expectantly, but neither of them seemed like they were ready to concede, and let her train. She nodded her head, their decision evident: they would rather take her freedoms away, than give her a fighting chance of survival by training her for the inevitable day Jackson decided to come after her again.

Alyx spun, leaving the room and the cause of her anger behind.

She stormed off up the stairs, pausing at the top, realizing that she had an opportunity to listen in, and find out what they would discuss while she was gone, so she plopped herself down at the top of the stairs.

Peter watched with despair as Alyx left. He was glad that she was back, but the second Lynn had told him that Alyx was missing, he was reminded why she had been in London.

"Is it even a good idea to send her to school? Jackson knows she goes there, and we know he has at least one agent in place to watch her." Sarah said.

"She needs this." Peter insisted. "She needs to go to school. She needs to be able to go to Track. She needs her life back."

"She doesn't need school if she's dead." Lynn commented.

Kate rolled her eyes. "Do everything you can to protect her life, and completely ignore her mental state, why don't you. Peter is right. She needs a little bit of normalcy in her life."

"Her mental state won't matter if her brain has a bullet in it." Lynn argued.

"Girls! Stop it." Neil interrupted their fighting before it got any worse. "Peter has been working on a security detail since he put Alyx on that plane. If anyone wants to protect her as much as us, it's him."

Peter nodded. "I will protect her."

"I'm still not sure sending her to school is a good idea." Sarah said. "Her teachers were fine letting her turn her assignments in remotely while she was in London. We can ask them to continue to do that, and…"

"And what, sweetheart?" Neil asked. "We have jobs we have to do. We can't be in the house with her 24/7, and we know that telling her to stay put would just be asking her to sneak out. Peter and Kate are right. She needs a little bit of normal back. Seminary, school, and track will do that."

"We also have an army of Promising Generation members at school with her." Peter added to reassure Sarah.

Neil pulled Sarah into a hug. "I've seen his plan. There will be more people watching her and keeping her safe if she goes to school than if we kept her here at home. There are a limited number of agents Dylan and I can assign to watch her." He turned his head to look at his nieces, without letting go of Sarah. "Girls, why don't you go finish getting ready for school. I need to go over a few things with Peter before he takes you to Seminary."

Alyx stood up from her seat, walking down the hall way back to her room. She hadn't learned anything *extremely* useful listening in, but she had learned who her allies were.

That was information that might prove useful later on.

6:08 PST
Tracy, California
McLean Home

ALYX WAS the first one back downstairs. Kate and Lynn had been bickering in the room next door as they finished getting ready. Alyx had already gotten ready for the day, and her bags were packed and ready for the day. The only thing she still needed was breakfast, and to grab the container of leftovers her mom had set aside for her last night, and put it in her insulated bag. So as much as she didn't want to face her parents at the moment, she needed to go to the room they were in to finish getting ready.

She couldn't avoid them. Not when she was living with them again.

Alyx walked in the kitchen, pulling out one of the open kitchen chairs to dump her bags on. She didn't care if she was interrupting their little *meeting.* It was about her, after all. And she needed to eat. They wouldn't have to worry about Jackson killing her if she died of starvation.

Alyx grabbed her lunch bag from its home in the cupboard,

then walked over to the fridge, pulling the container with her food out and placing it in her bag. She then grabbed a yogurt from the shelf, and turned around to get a spoon.

Peter was alone with her in the kitchen. She didn't know where her parents had gone, but Peter was standing awkwardly next to the table where he had been sitting before she turned her back to them.

Alyx was torn. Part of her wanted to take advantage of the moment she had alone with Peter. The other wanted to avoid whatever he had to tell her. The fact that her parents left her alone with him meant that she wouldn't like it.

Alyx opted for silence and avoidance. She opened her yogurt, stuck the spoon in it, then grabbed her bags off the chair she'd set them on, hooking them on her right shoulder before trying to leave the kitchen.

Peter caught her arm before she left. "Hey," he said softly.

"Hey back at you. I'm going to be late. I need to go." Alyx lied, trying to get out of the conversation.

Peter checked his watch. "Well, I'm your ride, and I figure we don't need to leave for at *least* another five minutes."

Alyx narrowed her eyes at Peter. She hated it when people lied to her, so she had been lying to them, trying to give them a taste of their own medicine. To have Peter so bluntly call her out on a lie made her wonder what else he knew she was lying about.

Then again, he was clearly one of the few people currently

on her side. Maybe she should use him, instead of push him away with lies.

"And you want to do what with those five minutes? Tell me what my security detail will look like? Explain all the ways you are helping my parents ruin my life?" Alyx retorted.

"Yes." Peter replied. "I do need to explain your security detail, and all the freedoms that are being taken away."

Alyx huffed.

Peter sighed, brushing her cheek with the back of his fingers. "But first, I wanted to check and make sure you were ok."

"I'm fine." Alyx lied, the words coming a little too quickly, and sounding a little too forced. She knew Peter wouldn't believe her, so she decided to add sarcasm to cover her mistake. "I'm thrilled to have parents that will handicap my ability to defend myself, and basically insure the man after me gets me."

Peter frowned. He gently pried the yogurt cup from her hand and set it on the table behind him, then grabbed the straps of the bags from her shoulder, and returned them to the chair Alyx had picked them up off of just moments before. Her hands clear, he grabbed both of them, making sure Alyx was facing him, and not turning to look at him over her shoulder like she had been. "You don't have to be ok." He sighed. "I'm guessing you didn't get up and hide in the garage for no reason."

Alyx pressed her lips together, frustrated that Peter had caught her lie, and her attempts to use sarcasm didn't hide her real thoughts from him. Fortunately, she had already prepared an excuse for her early morning trip to the garage. "I needed a quiet place to work. And I missed my car."

Peter didn't believe that as the only reason that had driven Alyx to the garage. He had been in her room after they'd shot her. He saw the pain it caused her, and the precision with which the shooter had sent his bullet into the head of her teddy bear. He also knew she was smart enough to know what he had seen the moment he'd stepped into that room: Jackson didn't want her dead *yet*, but as soon as he did, there was nothing any of them could do to stop it. She had been right when she tried to convince her parents to let her train. She was the only one they could count on for being there the next time Jackson made a move. She was the one they needed to make sure was capable of facing him.

Peter just took a deep breath, kissing her forehead. He couldn't help but linger, his forehead resting on hers. He wanted nothing more than to pull her into him. He wanted to make assurances that neither of them believed, but they both wanted to. He wanted to carry her off someplace safe to hide her away. But he knew that didn't work. He knew that being hidden wasn't what she wanted.

She was Alyx McLean. She didn't hide from her problems. She ran at them.

So instead of carrying her away, to hide her from the Circle of Fifths, he whispered, "I'll train you."

Alyx pulled away from Peter, looking up into his eyes, trying to judge if she'd heard him right. "What about the *perfect* security detail that even my dad was ready to sign off on."

Peter couldn't help but look straight back into her eyes, seeing the fear that her blue eyes were betraying. "Training you isn't going to replace the security detail." He sighed, looking down at her hands in his, while savoring the feeling of her hands in his again. "You were right. Jackson is probably going to get through it anyway, so the best way to protect you will be by making sure you can defend yourself."

"Thank you." Alyx whispered.

Peter nodded, looking back up, his eyes lingering on her lips before making their way all the way up to her eyes. "Maybe while I'm training you, you can tell me what has you so afraid."

Alyx shook her head. "I'm not afraid of anything."

"I am." Peter whispered. "Being afraid isn't a weakness. How you handle the fear can be." He cupped her face in his hand. "I am terrified of losing you." He admitted. "And I'm sorry I haven't handled it the best. I haven't agreed with some of the things your parents have done out of fear, and I haven't told them that enough. But if training you is what you need to help you deal with your fear, I will help you."

Alyx placed her hand on his, interlocking her fingers with his. She leaned into his touch, considering his invitation to be vulnerable with him, but she was strong. She was fearless. Part of her refused to show her fear to anyone, and that part of her won. She pulled Peter's hand away from her face before she gave in. "Training is what I need to beat Jackson. He is trying to control my life with fear, but if I am stronger than him, and know about my past, then he has nothing to use to make me afraid."

Peter sighed, missing the feeling of her hands in his. "I better tell you about your security detail then. I knew you would hate having a security detail, so for the most part, I've asked members of the Generation who are already in your classes to make sure they keep an eye on you. That leaves Lunch, as well as before and after school. Maybe it's because I'm selfish, but I claimed those for me."

Alyx blinked at him. "You're going to start eating lunch with me and my friends? What will all those cheerleaders and football players say about that?" She teased.

"The only opinion I care about is yours. What do you think about it?"

"I think you are a spy with a reputation to uphold, and I hurt that reputation." Alyx replied.

"Hey, that's not true." Peter shifted even closer to her as he cupped her face in his hands again, hoping she wouldn't push him away again. "You make me a better person in so many ways, and everyone can see that."

"Then why did it take me needing a security detail for you to ask that we eat lunch together?" She asked. "And why not ask me to come eat lunch with the cheerleaders? Wait, you have made out with most of them." She pulled away from Peter, turning to leave.

Peter caught her arm, gently pulling her back to him, and into a hug. "I love you." He whispered. He backed out a little bit so he could look in her eyes. "I'm sorry you felt like I was trying to hide you from my friends. I'm sorry for waiting for you to call, and not calling you every morning like I wanted to." He sighed. "Truth is, you mean more to me than they ever have, or ever could, so I was trying to be considerate. You are closer to your friends than I am to mine, and I didn't want to drag you away from them. But if you want to eat lunch with my friends, you are more than welcome to."

"Why do you do that?"

"Do what?" Peter asked.

Alyx sighed. "Make me believe you."

Peter smiled. "You know I could never lie to you." He looked at his watch. "But let's get going, or you might be late."

Alyx nodded, going to grab her stuff from the chair, but Peter beat her to it, throwing her back pack onto her shoulder, then sliding her duffle bag up onto his shoulder next. He offered his hand to Alyx.

She looked at the hand for a moment before taking his hand and letting him lead her to the car.

7:54 PST
Tracy, California
Circle of Fifths Safehouse

KALEN THREW his bag across the car from his open drivers door. His uncle had been in and out of town since before Christmas. He had come back into town a couple days before, and was waiting to hear back from Alyx to see when he was going to go to London to meet her.

Being in the same house as his uncle, knowing what he had recently learned, was absolute hell. His uncle may have taught him how to control his emotions long enough to take orders, and accurately shoot his rifle, but he couldn't hide the betrayal he felt from his uncle, nor the anger he felt about being manipulated like just another game piece in his uncle's ploy to stay relevant to the Nexus. At least, hiding his emotions from his uncle long term were proving to be extremely difficult.

"Kalen." Jackson called, walking out of the house to talk to Kalen right before he got into his car.

Kalen tried to remove the annoyance he felt from his face

before turning to respond to his uncle. "Yeah?"

"You were going to use the girl, McLean's best friend, to get into her friend group. How is that going?"

Kalen fought the urge to sigh, or defend Carlie to his uncle. "Carlie. Yeah. She wasn't dating anyone, so I have cemented myself in that role. My cover is ready."

Jackson nodded. "Good. Can you use that relationship to try and dig for more information about McLean. I need to gain her trust. Since offering her the file about her siblings deaths, she hasn't replied. I need to get her that file."

Kalen shrugged. "I can see what I can do. McLean isn't talking to her friends at the moment though. It's what made worming my way into Carlie's life so easy."

Jackson placed his hand on Kalen's shoulder. "You will make it happen. You are my best soldier."

Jackson turned away, letting Kalen get into the car to head to school.

As Kalen started his car, he couldn't help but think that if his uncle wanted McLean's trust, that was the last thing Kalen should help him get.

8:25 PST
Tracy, California
John C. Kimball High School

ALYX AND Peter stopped in front of the open door of her AP Statistics class. Alyx looked into the classroom, but didn't move away from Peter to enter. He studied her as she watched students sneak in the door around them, moving to their seats, pulling out their assignments, and catching up with friends as they opened their notebooks.

He gave her hand a couple of squeezes. "Are you ok?" He asked quietly.

Alyx nodded. "Yeah. It's just weird to be back here after everything." She admitted. "I just need a second." She turned to look at Peter. "You can head to class if you need to. I don't want to make you late for class."

"It's fine. I can stay with you until you are ready." He told her. "You are important."

Alyx gave Peter a patronizing look. "More important than being on time to class? More important than learning?"

Peter grabbed Alyx' other hand, turning her to face him. "Right now, yes. My teacher will understand if I'm a little late because I was making sure you are ok."

"I'm not going to let you destroy your future for me," Alyx commented.

"Well, I'm the reason you're not going to Oxford in October." He threw back at her. He took a deep breath. "And you're deflecting. If you aren't ready to come back—"

"I want to be here." Alyx insisted. She watched as Banthup snuck past her into the classroom she was supposed to go into. He looked surprised Alyx was there, which he tried to cover up with an evil smirk. "What is he doing here?"

Peter glanced at Banthup, dread pooling in his stomach. They had decided to bring Alyx back so fast, he hadn't had a chance to figure out what to do about Banthup, and now it was too late. "He, um, his schedule was rearranged to fill in the gaps in your schedule where other members of the Generation weren't already in your classes." Peter told her.

Alyx narrowed her eyes at Peter. "Why does he look like he didn't know I was back, and why do you look like you forgot that he was part of my security detail?"

Peter shook his head. "I just made the plan months ago. I was trying not to disrupt your life."

"I don't like him." She told him. She looked into the classroom to see him talking to the teacher, pointing at her standing in the door. "And clearly, he didn't understand the *not disrupting my life* part of his assignment." She muttered, turning back to look at Peter again, who seemed more distracted than he had before Banthup walked up. "What aren't you telling me?"

"Nothing." Peter lied.

She shook her head. "Now I see why you told me this morning you could never lie to me. You suck at it."

Peter took a deep breath. "Screw the Halls and their secrets," he muttered, barely audible to Alyx. He locked eyes with Alyx, his voice low so only she could hear him. "You said you don't like him. You have good instincts. Trust them. I don't like him either, but unfortunately, I can't pull him from this assignment."

"And he is in three of my classes?"

Peter nodded. "This one, Calculus, and AP US History."

Alyx turned to look into the classroom. She was already working really hard to stay strong enough to come to school, but with the apparent secrets her parents were still keeping, and now Banthup in her classes, she started to feel some of the distress she had been pushing away. "I could always fight him again. I might not be ready to fight Jackson, but I already beat him once."

Peter brushed her chin, bringing her attention back to him. "It's his job to protect you, and he knows he better do it, and do it well. Otherwise, he will have a long list of people who will fight him, not just you." He paused for a moment, watching her face. It had been too long since he had seen her smile. "I would hate to see what Emily would do."

His effort was rewarded by the smallest little smile. She may have been mad at her family, but as mad as she was at Emily, even she could admit that pissing Emily off was a very bad idea. And despite many of Emily's current faults, hurting Alyx was one *very quick* way to make her angry.

The smile he had drawn from her didn't last long though, as the teacher came to the door, interrupting them. "Alyx, it's good to see you back. Why don't you come in and join us?" Alyx turned to her, giving the teacher a small nod. The smile Peter had taken effort to drag from her was gone, replaced by the mature, serious look he'd seen from her since the shooting. "And Peter," the teacher continued, drawing his attention away from Alyx, and to the person addressing him. "I believe you have your own class to get to. I will see you third period."

Peter nodded, gave Alyx a kiss on her forehead before stepping away, and jogging towards his class.

Alyx walked into the classroom with her teacher, watching over her shoulder as Peter disappeared. "Tim told me why he is here. I will sit him next to you."

Alyx sat down at her desk, taking out the assignment that was due today, as well as her notes. It felt like she had never been gone, except for the man sitting in the seat behind her. She could feel his smile. He was going to make her life miserable.

9:28 PST
Tracy, California
John C. Kimball High School

ALYX LET out a sigh she hadn't realized she was holding as the bell rang, marking the end of first period. She closed her notebook, half-hazardly dropping the pencil she had been using to take notes into her backpack. She would likely regret doing that later, but right now, she didn't care. She just wanted to be done.

She had hated sitting in Feilds Palace, doing her homework in her room, with no change of scenery as she did six classes worth of work. She thought she would love coming back to school, sitting in classes, and feeling like normal. But now that she was back, she remembered how much mediocrity she had to put up with by sitting in class.

She may have hated it at the time, but she missed being able to go her own pace, sitting in her suite at Feilds Palace. She could study something until she understood it, then move on, not waiting for a classroom of her peers to understand it as well. Boredom led to wondering about Jackson, and when he would strike next, or what he wanted to give her, and if it was worth it.

As she was putting her notebook in the main pocket of her backpack, Timothy Banthup walked up to her desk, a smirk on his face. "How was your first class back princess?"

"Don't call me princess," Alyx replied, not even looking up at him. Instead, she just continued what she was doing by zipping up her backpack.

His smirk grew. "That bad huh? I mean, I understand. This is only the first of three classes Jackson has me shadowing you for, and already my head wants to explode."

Alyx froze, looking up at Banthup. She didn't hear him right. It wasn't possible. There was a difference between not liking someone, not fully trusting them, and them being a traitor, working for a psychopath like Jackson.

"Did I say Jackson?" Banthup asked, acting like he had misspoke. "I meant Hall. Too many bosses to keep straight. You should probably keep that little slip between the two of us. You tell your boyfriend that I am working for Jackson, and he won't have anyone to guard you in these classes, and you'll have to go back to London."

Alyx tossed her backpack on her shoulder. "If you think stats is hard, you should give up. No one would judge you. I mean, Calculus is harder." If Banthup was going to threaten her, she would threaten him right back.

"Is that an insult?" Banthup asked.

"No." Alyx said, brushing past Banthup as she left. "It's a threat. Disrupt my life, and I will make your life a living hell." She paused, looking back at Banthup. "Then again, if you couldn't recognize that, you are denser than I thought."

"What do I get if I just fade into the background so you don't notice I'm there? Will you do my homework?" Banthup prodded, following her out the door.

Alyx spun on Banthup. "What do you get? You fade into the background, and I won't try to ditch you every chance I get. Fade into the background, and I won't do everything in my power to get you expelled. What happens to your job on Hall's team if you can't finish your assignment to protect me? And I am assuming that you are only useful to Jackson as along as you are on Hall's team. I mean clearly, you're not the greatest agent."

"You wouldn't dare."

"Try me." Alyx threatened. "In case you hadn't noticed, a group of terrorists are after me because they are afraid I'm resourceful enough to catch them. I have connections to the administration at this school, as well as in positions of leadership at the CIA. Oh, and don't forget that Jackson has been texting me on a daily basis. You don't want to piss me off." She spun back around, hurrying to her second period English class.

Banthup smiled, watching as she left. Only one class into the day, and she was already threatening to ditch her security detail. This was going to be easier than he thought.

10:41 PST
Tracy, California
John C. Kimball High School

Mr. K looked up from the email he was composing as a student walked up to his desk. He smiled as Alyx set her backpack under the desk at the side of the class for his TA.

"Alyx! You're back!" He greeted her. Alyx replied with a tight lipped smile and a small nod. "How was London?" He asked.

Alyx shrugged. "Not much different from the last time I was there. It has been a while since I've spent Christmas with my cousins, so that was nice. I also had the opportunity to tour Oxford."

"Do you still think you want to attend there?"

Alyx nodded. "Yeah. It's a really cool place. My uncle arranged for me to tour a few of the colleges there. I think St. Annes is my favorite. With everything going on, I'm glad I decided to take a gap year, but after that, I will really enjoy learning there. Plus I will be closer to my cousins. Then again, they came back with me, so I guess I will know at the end of the semester if that should be a pro or…" She trailed off as a student approached them.

Mr. K turned to look at the student walking up to him. "Can I help you with something Tim?"

"I was hoping with Alyx being back—" Banthup started.

"We already discussed this when you were first assigned to my class. I don't mind you sitting in on the class, but you must do the work like the rest of the class, and appear like just another student. Alyx is my TA. She will be grading tests and the like, so you can not sit with her. You will have to do your job from the seat you are already sitting in." Mr. K told Banthup.

Alyx smiled. Mr. K was one of her favorite teachers at Kimball. Not only was her great at making sure he taught students the concepts in such a way that he was understood, but he knew when to be fun and light hearted, but he also knew when he needed to be strict. "If you are supposed to be here to protect me, just remember that an intruder will have to walk past you to get to me."

Banthup rolled his eyes, giving Alyx an annoyed smirk as he made his way to his seat.

Mr. K started playing with the buttons on the wall for the projector to get the warm up on board for the class.

"Hey Mr. K, would you mind if I went to the library today?" Alyx asked. "I'm feeling a little bit overwhelmed being back after… if you have anything for me to grade, I can take it with me. And if not, that's ok, I can just deal with it—"

Mr. K looked over at Alyx. He didn't know exactly what had

happened last November, but he knew that whatever it had been had made her parents scared enough to pull her from school and send her to London, to stay with her uncle who had a lot more security that she could get here in Tracy. He could also see what happened to the happy, successful, promising young woman he had taught the year before. After absorbing everything she could learn in Calculus AB, she had asked to be his TA. It hadn't evaded him that when he didn't have tests for her to grade, she was doing practice problems. Sometimes she was doing the practice problems that he was having the students in class doing. Sometimes they were problems from the Calculus book the school used for their class, and based on where she was in the textbook, they were probably problems from Calculus II, or the second semester of Calculus BC. She knew she could use her time in his class to do homework for other classes, and occasionally she did, but she was always going above and beyond to learn.

Whatever happened to her had dimmed her smile. Her eyes had always betrayed a sense of observance, but the way her eyes had been flicking around the room since she walked in, it seemed to be exaggerated, and paranoid. Her hands were moving almost subconsciously, betraying the stress she felt.

He didn't think he'd seen even one indicator she was stressed the week before AP tests last year, even though he had identified several of the other students using various coping mechanisms while they prepared for the sole reason for taking the class.

"That's fine. I'll write you a pass." Mr. K told her.

"Thank you." Alyx sighed.

Mr. K nodded, handing her the pass. "The rest of the class might be relieved. You make Calculus look much easier than it is sometimes."

Alyx smiled as she took the pass and grabbed her backpack.

Mr. K returned to getting the warm-up on the board. As Alyx walked around to the back to leave, Banthup looked up, giving her a dirty look. Alyx returned the smirk he'd given her earlier, showing off her pass like a trophy. It was her way of saying *I told you I have connections.*

If she had to finally use them to gain her freedom, she would.

11:42 PST
Tracy, California
John C. Kimball High School

PETER THREW everything into his backpack, watching the clock. The second the bell rang, he zipped up his backpack, throwing it over his shoulder as he got up and ran out of the room. He wanted to catch Alyx as she left Mr. K's room so they could walk to lunch together.

He was really looking forward to eating lunch with Alyx, whether it was with her friends or his. Before they had started dating, he often found his attention almost inexplicably drawn to her in the cafeteria, and once they had started dating, albeit secretly, he found himself looking at her so often he was afraid he was going to betray the secret. Once Alyx spread the rumor, he found himself looking at her almost constantly. He had wanted nothing more than to spend his lunch with her, and had she not gone to London after Thanksgiving break, he likely would have started. Instead, the mere idea of looking at her group of friends, and having his hopes crushed time and time again when she wasn't there, he had started spending his lunches in the library.

He may have pitched the idea of him eating lunch with her as part of a security detail, but that was more out of fear she would say no if he didn't have an excuse.

Her reaction to him telling her the plan this morning had only shown him all the reasons he had been stupid and insecure to think she would say no.

He waited outside Mr. K's classroom as students rushed out, either heading to lunch, or their fourth period class if they had second lunch. As the students leaving turned to a trickle, and he saw Banthup leave, a sour look on his face, he panicked.

"Where is she?" Peter asked Banthup.

"Ask Mr. K. She walked out like a victor with a hall pass before class started, and never came back," Banthup grumbled.

Peter pushed his way into Mr. K's classroom. There was a group of students moving some desks and putting their backpacks under them. They all started walking toward the door with Mr. K. From what Peter understood, Mr. K let students eat with him in the classroom as they played various card games, or did other math related things.

"Hey Peter!" He greeted when he saw Peter coming in. "Are you going to join us? I was just going to run to the teacher's lounge and get my lunch, then Sophie is going to teach us a new game she learned from her aunt in Utah over the weekend."

"I was just looking for Alyx. I was hoping to walk with her

to lunch."

Mr. K nodded. "She asked if she could spend the class period in the Library. She said she was overwhelmed being back."

Peter took a deep breath. "Thanks." Three periods was all it took for Alyx to figure out how to ditch her security detail. He thought having something that was non-invasive and discreet would prevent her from wanting to ditch her detail, and even if that didn't work, he hoped it would be impossible for her to succeed in ditching them. While he always prepared to be wrong when it came to estimating Alyx' abilities, he really hated it when he was.

Peter started walking towards the library, not sure if she would still be there, or if she would have headed to the cafeteria by now. The students that had been in Mr. K's classroom loitered around his currently closed door, waiting to go back in until he came back with his lunch.

Since the library was in the same direction as the administration building, where the teacher's lounge was, Mr. K was not far behind Peter. "Hey Peter, can I talk to you for a moment?"

Peter turned around, facing his teacher. "Sure."

"I'm concerned about Alyx. Do you know what happened last November?" Mr. K started.

"Y-yeah," Peter stuttered, "but it's not my place to share." He finished cautiously.

Mr. K shook his head. "I'm not asking you to. I asked

because I wanted to make sure you knew what she went through. Like I said, I'm concerned about her. I only interacted with her a couple of minutes, but it was clear that whatever she went through has affected her, and I'm not sure she is mentally ok. If I were to ask her about it, she wouldn't respond well, and I'm sure it's the same for most of the adults in her life. She has always tried to portray herself as mature and put on an air of not needing very much of our help. But I think she would respond much better to you. You are a peer. Try to know what she is going through, and make sure she knows you are there to support her and help her through it. She is going to need a really good friend right now."

Peter nodded. "I'm doing my best."

Mr. K smiled. "Thank you. I will see you fifth period," he said, then he started to walk to the administration building again.

Peter watched him for a moment. He and Alyx hadn't told any of their teachers that the two of them were dating, but he knew the teachers heard at least some of the rumors the students spread, and Alyx had somehow ensured that the rumor that the two of them were secretly dating spread *exceptionally* well. When he had come back to school after being kidnapped, students that usually stayed out of the school rumor pool were whispering about their secret relationship.

As he looked out across the courtyard, he saw Alyx walking from the library to the cafeteria. Peter held his backpack on his shoulder as he ran to intercept her, dodging the various bodies that crossed his path to her. He slowed to a stop next to her, sliding his hand into hers.

"How was the library?" He asked her

Alyx turned to look at Peter, nearly hiding the guilt and disappointment she felt getting caught. "How did you know?" She asked.

"I can't reveal all my secrets," he teased. "Why did you ditch your detail?"

"I didn't ditch my detail, I ditched Banthup. There's a difference." Alyx corrected. "Did you know he is working for Jackson. After he made Statistics unbearable, he practically shouted it at me. Then he tried to make Calculus unbearable. That class is my sanctuary. I'm Mr. K's TA so I can have a respite from my intense classes, and do homework when Mr. K doesn't have tests for me to grade."

As she finished her rant, she turned to look at Peter. Ready for him to say something about Banthup working for Jackson. But instead of the shock she expected to see, he looked guilty.

Alyx narrowed her eyes at Peter. "And that was what you were trying to warn me about this morning. Banthup is a traitor. Got it. It's not something I should know."

Peter sighed. "I hate that they didn't want to tell you."

Alyx rolled her eyes. "They don't want to tell me *anything*. Don't you know that what I don't know can't hurt me?" She asked sarcastically. "It's like they don't trust me to not run at anything I perceive as evil." She looked at Peter, taking a deep breath. "How long have you known?"

"Since the morning we sent you to London. He followed Thane and Derek to Seminary, then school. He seemed pissed when he saw it wasn't you in the car." Peter admitted.

"So the jacket worked." Alyx commented. "I was wrong."

"I'm sorry they didn't tell you. We decided to let him think we didn't know, and try to use him to figure out where Jackson is, and what the plan was. I didn't think we would bring you back while he was still on your security detail." Peter apologized.

"Leave him." Alyx said. "It's not like he is as smart, or as talented as he thinks he is. He might still be useful."

Peter kissed the side of her head. "I told your parents you would take it better than they thought." He gave her a smile that told her he was proud that he seemed to know her better than her parents.

"Yeah, yeah." Alyx giggled. "Don't get too excited. Clearly they haven't trusted me enough in a very long time."

Peter shook his head, opening the door to the cafeteria for Alyx. "So if Calculus was overwhelming, would you prefer to eat with your friends today, or do you feel up to meeting mine?" He asked as he walked in behind Alyx, letting the door drop as his retook her hand.

Alyx looked across the cafeteria at his question, quickly

finding her group of friends, but also finding Peter's out of habit. As much as she wanted to see her friends for the first time since Thanksgiving, she wasn't sure if she could handle the bombardment of questions she would face. She had already done her best to avoid Carlie in English, using Thane as a shield as best as she could. If Peter ate lunch with her and her friends, she would have both Thane and Peter there to try and shield her from their incessant questions, but she had a feeling it would still be too much.

She glanced at the table that Peter usually sat at again. The sheer number of popular kids gathered around that table seemed daunting, but it seemed like a much better option compared to the interrogation that was waiting among her friends.

She knew she would have to face them eventually, but today was not that day.

"I want to meet yours." Alyx told Peter.

Peter gave her hand a squeeze, and gave the right side of head a kiss. "Ok. Just let me know if it's too much, and we can find someplace quiet."

Alyx nodded.

Peter couldn't help but glance at Alyx several times as they made their way through the cafeteria towards the table his friends were at. She was trying so hard to look like she was doing ok, but he could see conflicting emotions swirling in her eyes.

"Look who decided to join us!" Trevor announced as the two of them got close enough to the table. "Seriously Peter.

Where have you been? I know you've been in class, but it was like you disappeared after Thanksgiving break. I thought maybe you were too good to be seen eating lunch with us."

Peter could see Alyx' head snap to look at him out of the corner of his eye as he looked at Trevor. "Yeah, sorry. I had a project I've been working on. It took up all of my spare time."

Alyx looked around the table of Peter's friends. She recognized all of their faces. She had classes with some of them. Some were on the track team with her. Others she had just seen around school the last three years. Then there was Jacob, the one she knew best. Hearing that Peter hadn't eaten lunch with his friends since she went to London meant her eyes immediately went to him, silently asking her question of the one person who would know the real reason why. He just gave her a small smirk that told her *you know why.*

Trevor nodded, a smile that said his mind was in all the crude places on his face. "Yes, a project taking up all your spare time. It wouldn't be related to the other thing that took up your spare time during football season, making it so you didn't want to come to parties…"

Scarlett smacked Trevor, giving him a dirty look. "She hasn't been here, buffoon."

Trevor's smile disappeared. "Oh shhhh" he started in a whisper. Scarlett smacked him again, gesturing towards Alyx with her head. They all knew Alyx didn't swear, and out of respect for her choices, Scarlett would police her friends to make sure they didn't either when Alyx was around. It didn't matter that Alyx wouldn't say anything. "Shoot," he corrected. "I forgot."

Peter gave Alyx' hand another squeeze as the table went deafeningly silent. Alyx wasn't sure if anyone other than the teachers and her friends would notice she wasn't at school, and she definitely wasn't sure what they would know, or be told. Based on the looks of sympathy she was getting from the table of Peter's friends, they had at least heard enough to know it was tragic.

"If it were up to me, I would have left all of you *buffoons*, to use Scarlett's word, behind. But my girlfriend is much better than me, and wanted to meet you, so we're going to eat lunch here today, unless there are any objections." Peter told the group.

Of course Peter would divert conversation away from what happened to her. He assumed she didn't want to talk about it, and he was right. That was why she wasn't eating with her friends. But she really wanted to know what the cover story was. She felt like all she had to do was let Trevor talk a little bit more on the subject, and she could figure it out. Instead, Peter moved the conversation away from it, and everyone seemed grateful.

Maybe she should have gone to eat lunch with her friends. She knew how to manipulate them to get the answers she needed from them. Then again, maybe it wouldn't be so hard to learn how to manipulate a new group of people.

Being able to get answers out of this crowd might be useful.

"Alyx, this is Trevor, Scarlett, Jacob, Crissy, Jasmine, Nia, Mark, Brendon, and Seth." Peter pointed at his friends one by one to show Alyx which was which.

Alyx gave the group a small wave with her left hand, still holding onto Peter's hand with the other like it was her lifeline.

Trevor nodded to Alyx. "McLean," he greeted. "If you are back, does that mean you are going to join Carlyle at Track?"

Alyx looked over at Peter. "I didn't know he was doing Track." He was full of surprises today.

"Yep. Jacob and I have been trying to convince him to join us since Freshman year. If I knew that all I had to do was introduce you two, I would have made introductions last year."

Scarlett got up, walked around the table and hooked her arm through Alyx'. "I knew you two would make a cute couple." She whispered, pulling her away from Peter.

"Hey, I didn't bring my girlfriend here to have you steal her away." Peter complained.

Scarlett walked Alyx around the table to the empty seat next to her, ignoring Peter's complaints. "How *did* the two of you meet? Since, apparently, you two were already secretly dating when I gave you his phone number."

Alyx looked up from setting her backpack on the floor, finding Peter's eyes as he grudgingly took a seat across the table. "We took Algebra II together. He sat behind me, and we would occasionally talk to each other, but I didn't think he really noticed me. As it was, I spent most of the year trying to beat him for the top spot in the class, and I never succeeded."

"I noticed." Peter admitted with a smile.

"Wait, you were the girl that had him constantly studying for that class like his life depended on it?" Jacob asked.

"The one and only. I didn't know how else to impress her, and I wasn't sure it worked." Peter replied.

"It worked." Alyx admitted.

"So you've been dating for two years?" Scarlett asked, throwing Peter a dirty look.

Peter shook his head, his eyes not leaving Alyx. "No. I was too afraid to ask her out. I asked Mr. Martin for help studying for the AP French test, and apparently so did she. He assigned us to study together at the beginning of the year, so I finally got her number."

Alyx smirked. "Someone is a romantic and wouldn't stop flirting while we were trying to study. I had to enact a *no English* rule, which didn't actually stop the flirting. He just started flirting in French."

"Hey now," Peter complained. "I have a reputation to uphold."

Alyx just shrugged. The look on her face almost told him that it was payback for lying and keeping secrets with her parents.

The other girls at the table started snickering. "What reputation?" Scarlett asked. "You might have the guys fooled, but the rest of us know you are nothing but the perfect gentleman. I mean come on, taking a girl to dinner because you got dared to *kiss* her at a party?"

"Dinner huh?" Alyx asked. "How come you've never taken me to dinner?"

"We have dinner with your parents all the time." Peter replied.

Alyx shook her head. "I thought you said that was weird. Besides, if studying isn't a date, neither is dinner and games with my parents."

"Seriously? I knew McLean was your type, but I had no idea she would completely change you." Trevor commented.

Peter smiled at Alyx across the table. "She didn't change me. She just gave me what I didn't realize I was missing." He looked at Trevor. "Her dad might be this scary FBI agent, but you can tell he loves his wife and daughter more than anything. It was hard to convince him at first that I wouldn't hurt Alyx, but once I did, he's really cool, and everything I aspire to be," he looked at Alyx, "minus a few annoying habits." He looked back at Trevor. "Her mom is a real-life hero too. She works in the Trauma Center at Stanford, and when she gets home, all she wants to do is hug her husband and daughter. Alyx has an awesome family, and they have been quick to adopt me into theirs. I think everyone deserves that."

Alyx smiled at Peter, but it didn't reach her eyes. It was hard to accept that she had an awesome family when she was so angry at them. They had been lying to her for so much of her life, and clearly, they hadn't learned their lesson. It was easy for Peter to say she had an awesome family when he wasn't the one suffocating under their ridiculous restrictions in the name of *safety*.

He was the one they trusted with the truth. Not her.

12:03 PST
Tracy, California
John C. Kimball High School

CARLIE LOOKED across the cafeteria at where Alyx was sitting with Peter's friends. She and Peter were discussing something as they sat across the table from each other, and his friends thought it was funny, as evidenced by the smiles and laughs.

Carlie let out a defeated sigh, returning her eyes to her food. She wasn't sure why, but she always kind of assumed if Alyx started dating someone, her boyfriend would join them for lunch, the same way Kalen joined them for lunch. Maybe it was just selfish on her part. She didn't want to lose her friend.

Savannah rolled her eyes as she looked over at Alyx and Peter. "If I would have known she would ditch us as soon as she started dating Mr. Popular, I wouldn't have encouraged her. Or pointed him out when I saw him." Savannah commented.

"She was already dating him," Carlie said.

"Don't remind me," Savannah snarked bitterly. "Why did she tell you first anyway?"

"Probably because she was afraid of the rumors you would start." Carlie defended.

Thane snapped his fingers between Carlie and Savannah. "Chill. This isn't doing anyone any good. It seems you are both mad at her right now. Maybe you should talk about it."

"Like what? Tell her?" Carlie questioned. "She has to acknowledge us first."

"Who are you talking about?" Kalen asked. Carlie was almost never mad, so he wanted to know who had done something so bad that it pissed her off.

"Alyx." The table said in unison.

"We all know something happened during Thanksgiving break." Kaden said. "But she's been radio silent."

"What happened was…" Thane trailed off, trying to find the right word. "Traumatic."

"And who better to talk about what she's going through than her friends who understand her?" Carlie asked. "But it seems we've been replaced by her boyfriend and his friends." Carlie turned to Thane. "Although I'm sure you are still in her circle of secrets."

Thane threw his hands up. "Hey, I might be her cousin, but that doesn't mean she has talked to me any more than the rest of you. She barely talked to me the night it happened, and she did a great job of *not talking* over Christmas."

"So her boyfriend replaced all of us."

Thane shook his head. "Nope. Kate yelled at him on New Years because he had been waiting for her to call, and she never did. She never took him up on his invitation to call anytime while she was away."

"That's not healthy." Carlie whispered, looking across the cafeteria again, this time with sadness and pity, instead of anger. Watching Alyx, it was almost impossible to tell that she wasn't the same person she'd been before Thanksgiving Break. She was laughing and joking around with Peter's group of friends like nothing was wrong. She looked like she had been at school everyday, and she hadn't missed school for months for reasons they had been left to speculate about. All she knew was that someone her dad had been chasing killed their next door neighbor, then broke into their house, and was still there when they got home from Virginia. What actually happened to Alyx was a mystery no one would talk about.

Watching Alyx again, looking for signs she was different, and not ok, Carlie could see the signs she hadn't seen before. Alyx may have been sitting at a table of the school's most popular kids, but her eyes were on Peter, and she seemed to be addressing him, and no one else. If one of his friends asked for his attention, and it left Alyx, drawing his friends attention away from her, her façade dropped, if only for a second. Her attention sporadically searched the cafeteria for who knows what. If Carlie was closer, she wouldn't be surprised if she saw panic or fear in her expression. For just a second, Carlie received Alyx' attention. Alyx gave a small smile and wave, her façade back as she turned back to the table.

Alyx was struggling, and Peter was her anchor.

Kalen put a comforting hand on his girlfriend's back, drawing Carlie's attention back to the table of her friends. She could feel the tension of their unasked questions. She would be the first to admit that she had spammed Alyx with text messages asking what happened, why she left, and how she was while she was away. Watching Alyx again with Thane's new insights let her see how fragile her friend was, and how hard she was trying to hold herself together. That was why she was eating with Peter's friends, and not them. Peter's friends would ask her about their relationship. Their questions would invoke happy memories, and help her ignore what happened. Eating lunch with her friends would mean answering questions about her trauma, and clearly she was trying to avoid it.

Even if Carlie knew avoidance wasn't a healthy way to deal with whatever had happened, it wasn't her place to call Alyx out on it, and force her to sit down and talk.

But someone needed to.

12:18 PST
Tracy, California
John C. Kimball High School

THE BELL rung, indicating the end of lunch, and telling them they had six minutes to get to fourth period, pulling Kalen out of his thoughts. He had been surprised when the group had told him that Alyx was back at Kimball. Last he knew, Alyx was in London.

The part of him that had been trained to be his uncle's perfect soldier knew his uncle would find the information useful, and yearned to give it to him. But given what he had been learning recently about his uncle, he watched Alyx instead, trying to find anything evil in her. The part of him that loved Carlie didn't like Alyx hurting Carlie's feelings. He also felt guilty hearing her friends talk about the reason she had been gone, and the reason she hadn't talked to them. Thane had used the word *traumatic.*

Traumatic was as good of a word as any, he supposed. Having bullets shot into your bedroom was probably traumatic. Having one of those bullets graze your arm was traumatic.

Kalen was the one who inflicted the trauma.

He knew that he was only acting on his uncle's orders. He knew that his uncle was to blame for pulling all the strings in his game of manipulation to draw Alyx to him. But he also knew that he had to accept at least some of the guilt. He could have chosen not to pull the trigger. But he had chosen to blindly follow his uncle and his orders. He thought that his uncle was right. He though that Alyx was no different than them. After all, she had attacked the guards at the cabin in the Alps. She had injured them. And when she fought Kalen in the forest around the cabin, she had beaten him, and left him unconscious. The temperature could have killed him.

But she didn't kill him. She left him alive. Just like she left the guards alive.

Watching Alyx, he didn't see the same girl his uncle had coaxed him to see. The scar he had given her may have been hidden beneath her shirt sleeve, but he saw all the other scars she tried to hide behind her smiles and laughs. And he knew that his uncle was going to use those scars to make her change how she saw herself, until she saw the girl he had convinced Kalen to see.

Kalen couldn't let him succeed.

18:33 PST
Tracy, California
McLean Home

KATE LOOKED up from her textbook as she noticed Lynn putting on her shoes. "Where are you going?" She asked.

"For a run," Lynn said.

Kate rolled her eyes. "I'm not as dumb as you think I am. And neither is Alyx." She turned her attention back to her homework. "I hope you know that what you guys are doing will only piss Alyx off and drive her away."

"What are you talking about?"

Kate sighed, setting her pencil down. "I've been where Alyx is. Basically my entire life. I *always* know when you, dad, and Stephan are keeping things from me *supposedly* to keep me safe. But I know, and I know how to use it to get what I want." Kate gestured at herself sitting on he bed. "Case in point." She gave Kate a smug smile. "I used what I knew to manipulate dad into giving me what I wanted. What do you think Alyx will do?"

"I don't know if you've noticed, but she's not exactly at the top of her game right now." Lynn snarked.

Kate rolled her eyes. "If she's not at the top of her game, what are you going to do when she *is*?" Kate started counting the number of times Alyx had escaped their airtight security detail on her hand. "She has snuck out of Feilds Palace *we don't know how many times*. She got out of the house, and hid in the garage this morning, sending everyone into a panic. She ditched a class to get away from her security detail."

"And that's why I need to go for a run." Lynn replied.

Kate shook her head, picking her pencil back up. "If you don't want Alyx to catch you, maybe you should find another excuse. No one believes that you would honestly want to go for a run after the three hour Track practice we just had."

Lynn huffed annoyed, leaving the room.

If Kate was Alyx, she may have followed her twin sister. She would have spied on the meeting, and depending on what she heard, she would either interrupt them, then storm off, or stew in anger, eventually figuring out how to get out of the tighter security detail she was being subjected to.

Kate closed her eyes. It was only a matter of time before Alyx snuck her way into one of their security detail meetings. It was only a matter of time before Alyx felt suffocated and decided to do something about it.

It was only a matter of time before Alyx rebelled.

18:35 PST
Tracy, California
McLean Home

ALYX LISTENED to her cousins arguing in the next room. If she hadn't already figured out that most of her family was meeting to discuss her security detail, their conversation in the next room would definitely tell her they were.

She sighed, rolling her eyes as she plugged headphones into her phone, and put them in her ears, turning her music up until she couldn't hear the argument. Lynn may have been the one that trained with MI-6, but Kate was much smarter than she had ever let on before. She had just finally found something worth expending the effort for it.

As Alyx unlocked her phone to find a new song to listen to, she got distracted, opening her text messages. Since she had asked Jackson to prove that he trusted Alyx with the truth, he had been pestering her much less. He had asked her to meet. The ball was in her court. She just had to tell him when and where.

With Banthup working for Jackson, she was surprised he

hadn't texted her again, with some quippy remark. She felt in control of something for once, and it was a nice change from what her parents had been doing recently. Jackson definitely knew what he was doing, and Alyx didn't like it. He knew how to manipulate her. She didn't want to be manipulated.

Before she had a chance to think about it, she initiated a conversation with Jackson for the first time.

By now, you have to know I am back in town, so I have to ask: what gives?

I want you to know I trust you.

Alyx rolled her eyes at Jackson's instantaneous response. He had been waiting to hear from her.

If you are reaching out, does that mean you are ready to meet?

I don't think anyone is ever ready to see your ugly face.

Alyx smiled as she hit send on her message. If she couldn't insult Jackson, it wasn't worth texting him.

Why don't you save me the trip and the trouble, and send it with Banthup.

If you don't trust me enough to meet with me, you're not ready for the file.

What is that supposed to mean?

Alyx stared at the conversation, waiting for Jackson to reply. The time under her message told her Jackson had gotten the message, and he had read it, but the little dots at the bottom that told her that he was writing a message back never showed up.

That was a new one.

18:47 PST
Tracy, California
Circle of Fifths Safehouse

Kalen knocked on the door to his uncle's office, waiting for his response telling him to come in. Once he heard his uncle's gruff voice tell him to come in, he opened the door, watching as Jackson set his phone down on the desk while Kalen closed the door behind him.

"I thought you would like to know that McLean is back. She was at school today." Kalen told Jackson. He might have decided that he didn't want to help his uncle gain Alyx' trust, but he had to at least feign usefulness until he figured out how to get out.

"Banthup texted me before first period." Jackson replied. "Actually, she just told me herself," he said, picking up his phone to emphasize his point. "You are a bit late to that party."

Kalen took a deep breath. "Sorry. I thought it would be best to tell you in person."

"Did you get any information from Carlie about gaining McLean's trust?" Jackson asked.

Kalen shook his head. "As I suspected, they aren't on talking terms."

Jackson nodded. "Ok. Don't hide from McLean at school but don't do anything to make her feel threatened."

Kalen furrowed his brow. "Has the plan changed?"

"I need her trust." Jackson told him. "She knows Banthup is working for me. She will recognize you. I need her to see that I have you in place, but you are not there to harm her. Hopefully she will be ready to meet me soon so I can give her the file."

"Understood." Kalen said, taking that as his queue to leave.

19:01 PST
Tracy, California
Promgen Headquarters

HALL LOOKED up as Lynn came into the room, her face flushed from exercise. She dropped into the chair they had saved for her, and quickly grabbed the full glass of water that was waiting for her, chugging the contents.

"Were you followed?" Hall asked.

Lynn shook her head. "No. I took two laps to make sure. Alyx didn't follow me." She told the others.

Hall nodded. He looked around the table to make sure everyone else was accounted for. Peter sat at his table, his face buried in his phone, probably texting Alyx, not that he would get a reply. Banthup, Thane, and Jacob were also in attendance, to report how the security detail was going. Sarah and Neil, like Lynn, had also snuck out from the house to come to the meeting. With Emily hiding in a corner, and Michael and Stephan joining them via phone, everyone who had anything to do with Alyx' safety was present for this meeting. "We can start. Peter," Hall started, "how is the security detail going?"

Peter looked up from his phone, and over to Banthup. "She seems to be responding well to most of her security detail."

"Most?" Neil asked.

"I thought the plan was simple. There are Promgen members in her classes, and if she's not in class, you are with her to keep her safe." Sarah commented.

Peter nodded. "That is exactly right."

"But she doesn't like her security detail?" Sarah prodded. Peter nodded in response. Sarah shook her head. "I don't think I will ever understand her. It's like whatever we do, she hates."

"She's a teenager." Emily commented from the corner. "And she is mad at us. She is being defiant."

"Technically there is just one part of her security detail she doesn't like." Peter clarified.

"Is she giving you a hard time for following her around all the time?" Neil asked.

Peter shook his head. "She hasn't said anything about not liking the extra time we spend together. She hasn't tried to give me the slip even once, which is saying something." He reported.

"She's been distant, and doesn't say much to me in our classes, but she hasn't tried to ditch me either." Thane reported. "She has actually been using my presence in her classes to guard her from the questions our friends are asking."

"Same here." Jacob echoed. "The only thing that has

changed, is I keep a closer eye on her in our class, and wonder how I never noticed her."

If they weren't discussing something so serious, Peter may have snickered. He knew that once the Generation members found out that the girl from the BOLO in August sat in classes with them, they would wonder how they missed it. It had taken *him* a while to notice her in Algebra II. But once he had , he couldn't help but wonder how he hadn't seen her before.

"What part of her detail does she not like?" Sarah asked.

Thane, Jacob, and Peter all turned to Banthup. "She's not a fan of Banthup, and moving him to her classes was more of a disruption than she wanted." Peter admitted.

"That shouldn't be a problem." Hall commented. "We made sure it was students in her classes for a reason, because she cares about her education. As long as she stays in class…" He trailed off as he looked at the faces of the four young men who were in charge of his niece's security detail. "She has already figured out how to ditch class without facing consequences, hasn't she?"

Hall's question was met with a chorus of nods before Peter explained, "When I went to find her after Calculus, she wasn't there. Mr. K told me she asked to go to the library because she was overwhelmed being back, so he gave her a hall pass."

Of course Alyx would be the one student who could figure out how to ditch class and get away with it. It made sense, given who her parents were, after all. Neil had done his fair share of ditching classes in high school and Sarah had started to help him so he either wasn't caught, or got away with it when he did.

Alyx was definitely her parent's daughter. In this case, she was the worst combination of them. The only reason they hadn't seen this problem before was because she had never had the drive to ditch class.

She was the walking epitome of *if there's a will, there's a way*.

As someone who had found himself on the losing side of a battle against Alyx, Hall almost pitied Banthup.

"How many times will that excuse work?" Hall asked.

"She told me she had lots of resources, and is more than willing to use them." Banthup told them. He would have preferred to not share the threat she'd made, given his assignment from Jackson. His orders were to give McLean a little bit of freedom in the otherwise stifling detail. If she had one person that she could get away with ditching, and Jackson was the reason she got away with it, Jackson hoped she would begin to trust him. Unfortunately, Peter had caught Alyx ditching him. In order to keep his cover on Hall's team, he had to give them something, so he was divulging something he had hoped to keep to himself.

"What resources?" Sarah asked. "Why is she so vague?"

Neil covered his mouth to hide the laugh that was trying to escape. He had heard his wife be *extremely* vague with some of the things she had done, especially in high school.

Dylan just smiled, watching the interaction. "If she is

anything like her mother, we will never be able to find and eliminate all of those resources." He commented. "So what do we need to do to stop her from *wanting* to use those resources?"

Banthup took a deep breath, a thought coming to mind. "She told me about the resources as a threat. She promised if I fade into the background so she doesn't notice I'm there, she won't try to ditch me. Today, she showed me how serious she was. Lesson learned. You don't mess with her and try to call her bluff when she makes a threat."

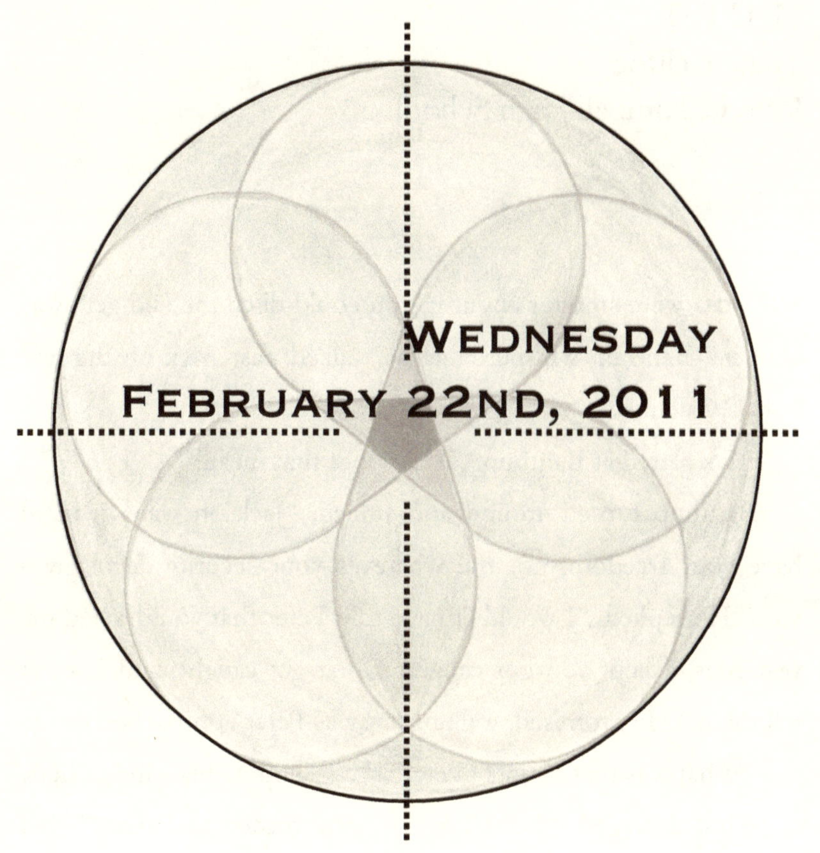
WEDNESDAY
FEBRUARY 22ND, 2011

11:43 PST
Tracy, California
John C. Kimball High School

"IF YOU were smarter about it, you could ditch me and get away with it." Banthup whispered as he walked past Alyx on the way out of Calculus.

Alyx glared at Banthup. "What does that mean?"

Banthup turned around and smiled. "Jackson wants you to have your freedom, not the whatever your security detail gives you." He replied. "I wouldn't have told Peter that you ditched me yesterday, except you got caught. Don't get caught, and I won't tell them." He promised, walking away as Peter approached them.

"What was that about?" Peter asked, slipping his hand in hers.

Alyx shrugged. "I don't know." She turned to Peter. "What did you guys say to him last night? It's like he did a complete 180 from yesterday to today."

"You threatened him, and made good on that threat."

Alyx rolled her eyes.

"Anyway, who did you want to eat lunch with today?" Peter

asked as they neared the cafeteria.

Alyx sighed. "I should probably stop avoiding my friends."

"I'll be with you the entire time." Peter promised, squeezing her hand.

She nodded, letting Peter open the cafeteria door for her. Once she was through the door, she stopped, waiting for Peter to retake her hand. He led her through the cafeteria, straight towards the booth she knew her friends would be it. She watched him as he cut through the tables. The fact that he knew where her friends would be, his eyes locked on where he was taking her, instead of searching the room for them, told her that she hadn't been the only one that had searched the other out. There was something satisfying knowing that he had looked for her everyday, just like she had long before they started dating.

Alyx tore her eyes off of Peter as she heard a squeal. They had reached the booths on the west wall of the cafeteria, behind all the food windows, and her friends had seen her coming to sit with them. She looked up to see her friends, but froze in place. Peter stopped as he noticed she wasn't moving forward any more, looking back at her to see what was wrong.

Sitting next to her best friend, Alyx saw the face from her nightmares. She was frozen, not reacting as Carlie's face lit up, patting Kalen as a way of telling him to slide out of the booth so she could get out. She ran up to Alyx, enveloping her in a hug. "I'm so glad you are finally back, and decided to eat lunch with us. I've missed you."

Peter had let go of Alyx' hand, giving her the opportunity to return the hug Carlie had thrown on Alyx, but she didn't. She stayed stiff as a board, eyes on Kalen. He didn't look at her like he recognized her, but he had a cover to keep. He didn't have the same murderous contempt in his eyes as the last two times she had seen him, but he was in the middle of a high school cafeteria.

She couldn't believe it when Kalen shook Peter's hand. "So I see the famous girlfriend is back," Kalen said, and Peter nodded, like they were friendly, and had talked about her before.

Carlie released Alyx from her hug, but still, Alyx didn't move, and her eyes didn't leave Kalen. Carlie turned to look over he shoulder to see what Alyx was staring at. She smiled. "Oh yeah, you haven't met Kalen yet." Carlie reached out her hand, which Kalen took, pulling Carlie close to plant a gentle kiss on her cheek. "This is my boyfriend, Kalen McKenzie. Kalen, this is my best friend, Alyx."

"Hey!" Savannah called. "I heard that! I thought we agreed that there were no *best* or *favorite* friends in this group."

"You're my best friend." Kaden told Savannah.

Savannah smacked his arm. "That's not helpful right now," she said with an eye roll.

As the friends bickered, Kalen stuck his hand out, a genuine smile on his face. "I'm glad to finally meet the famous Alyx Mc-Lean. I was beginning to think you didn't exist. After all, I've heard a lot of great things about you, and I didn't think any person could be that *good*."

Alyx' eyes never left Kalen's, but she also didn't make a move to shake his hand. Peter gently placed a hand on the small of her back. "Hey, are you ok?"

Alyx finally glanced away from Kalen. Her eyes scanned her friends faces. All of them were watching her, wondering why she wasn't shaking the hand of the newest member of the group. She could see their judgement. She had always been cautious when there was a new person. She urged the group to slow down, and make sure they were inviting the kind of person they could all get along with in, and not someone toxic they would come to regret. But her time away meant she had given up her right to make decisions on who they accepted into their group. She had spent too long missing from their lives, not replying to any of their texts or calls, or even emails. She couldn't waltz back in now, expecting everything to be the same, and for them to allow her objections on who they had invited in while she wasn't talking to them. She could make objections, but what was the point if they wouldn't accept it. And she knew she couldn't expect that of them, not when she had been an awful friend.

Kalen had won.

Alyx spun away from Peter's hand, and started walking away. She could hear footsteps following her. She expected it to be Peter, and to have his hand try to slip into hers, so she closed her hand into a tight fist. She could feel her nails digging into her palms, and she knew it would leave marks, but she was angry, and she didn't want Peter to grab her hand as a lifeline to her, only to drag him down with her. Instead of feeling Peter's hand grab her arm, though, the hand she felt was small and petite. As she turned around, she came face to face with a concerned looking Carlie. "What's wrong?"

"He's won." Alyx whispered.

"Who's won?" Carlie asked.

"Kalen. You have all accepted him into our friend group, and I'm too late to object. It wouldn't matter what I say; you would choose him over me." Alyx laughed, despite the tears on her cheeks. "But I can't just pretend like nothing is wrong. I can't…"

"What are you talking about? You just met him." Carlie argued.

Alyx shook her head, a mix between a scoff and a laugh coming from her mouth. She took a deep breath as she started nodding her head instead. "You just proved my point."

Carlie shook her head, gesturing back to the table. "Come eat lunch with us. Get to know him. He's really sweet. I think you'll like him." Carlie smiled. "I hoped you would be happy for me."

"I want you to be happy. I really do, but…" Alyx sighed. "None of your texts told me you were dating someone?"

"Yeah, well, it's still pretty new, and it's not like you told me the second you started dating Peter, and I saw you, in person, everyday." Carlie shot back.

Alyx nodded her head, turning to walk away.

Carlie reached for Alyx' arm again. "I'm sorry." She sighed. "I just…" Carlie paused, taking a deep breath. "I don't know exactly what happened, but I know it was a lot, and I didn't think it was a good time to bring up my happiness."

"Did you ever think that maybe sharing your happiness was exactly what I needed. My life has been pretty dark since Peter got kidnapped. I discovered way too many secrets. Then there was everything that happened after Thanksgiving… I read every single one of your text messages. All of them asking how I was. All I really wanted to hear, was that as awful as my life has been, yours was going pretty well."

Carlie just shook her head. "Do you even heard yourself right now?" She asked. "Friendship goes two ways. A phone works two ways. So you read my messages. Great. Did you ever think to reply? If you wanted to know that I was doing well, you should have picked up the stupid phone, and typed up a short message. All *I* wanted was to know that you were ok."

"No, what you wanted to know was what happened." Alyx sassed. "Because I know for a fact that Thane and Peter told you I was alive."

Carlie shook her head. "Alive and *ok* are two *very* different things."

"So did they tell you what happened?" Alyx asked her friend.

"No."

"I'll tell you what happened." Alyx said, a harshness entering her tone. "A sniper killed my neighbor, climbed onto his roof, and when his boss told him to, he sent two bullets into my room." Alyx took her jacket off, showing Carlie the horizontal scar that ran across her left arm. It had been easy to hide the scar with the weather maintaining its crisp coolness as it headed towards spring. She was one of many people wearing light jackets, and sweaters. No one had questioned it, so she had effectively hidden the physical reminder of Jackson's psychological game. "The first bullet gave me this. The second went straight through the head of the teddy bear you gave me the first Christmas we were friends."

"Alyx..." Carlie started, sadness in her voice.

"I saw the face of the sniper. I recognized him. He was the same assassin that chased me down in Austria last summer. My parents sent me away while they tried to find him. They still don't know his name. But you just introduced him as Kalen McKenzie. Who knows if it is his real name."

Carlie shook her head. "Alyx, I'm sorry that you had to go through that, but there is no way that it's Kalen. I know him, and there is no way he is who you think he is." Carlie laughed. "See, I was supportive of you and Peter. I was happy for you. But..." Carlie shook her head. "I was happy for you, but when I start dating someone I really like, you throw around accusations that are absurd. I just wanted you to be happy for me."

"I can't promise happiness." Alyx replied. "I won't be here."

Carlie turned and walked away, revealing Peter who was a short distance away, far enough to let Carlie and Alyx have a moment to talk, but not too far that he couldn't hear, or step in if Alyx needed help. From the look on his face, Alyx could see that Peter had heard everything she had said, and he didn't seem to believe her any more than Carlie had.

Carlie slid back into the booth, receiving curious looks from their friends. "What did she say?" Savannah asked. "She seemed spirited."

Carlie sighed. "We argued about what kind of friend she's been recently. She told me what happened to her, why her parents sent her away." Carlie took a deep breath, remembering the look on Alyx' face, recognizing the trauma in her body language from her psychology class. "She's not handling it well, and she's blaming anything she can't control."

Kalen glanced at Alyx, a solemn look on his face that didn't have to be faked. Carlie turned around to look at her friend who stood, a devastated look on her face as she stared at Peter. Carlie watched as Alyx turned away, trying to mask the pain she felt as she put her jacket back on to re-hide her scar. No one believed her. Carlie knew the feeling, but she couldn't help Alyx. As Peter ran after Alyx, Carlie watched, glad that someone could show Alyx the support she needed right now.

11:50 PST
Tracy, California
John C. Kimball High School

Peter pushed through the cafeteria doors, chasing Alyx as she walked into the courtyard. "Alyx," he called as he jogged after her. He hadn't known how to respond to her confession. He knew Kalen. He was starting to build a friendship with him. When he had met Kalen, he had been reminded of happy time in his childhood, before his mom left. Kalen reminded Peter of the little boy who was his mom's friend's son. Alyx had been the first person he'd let in since his mom left. Meeting Kalen let him think he could recapture a happy youth, and he let that hope cloud his thoughts while he should have supported Alyx.

She wouldn't lie about who had shot her. She had given a painstaking description of the man who had shot her. She had told everyone at the time that it was the same man she had fought in the Austrian Alps. When he had given himself a moment to think about it, he realized Kalen perfectly matched the description she had given that night. If he were to look at the sketch they had her do with the FBI sketch artist, he was sure it would match perfectly. He had let his guard down. Alyx had a security detail. Somewhere in his head, he had let himself believe she was safe here. He let himself believe that Banthup was the only agent Jackson would have undercover at the school. He hadn't let himself believe that Jackson would try to infiltrate her friend group.

But what else would someone trying to manipulate, and fight a psychological warfare try to do? She had separated herself from her friends the night she was shot, and when she was finally ready to face them, and rejoin them for a sense of normalcy, she was met with the face of the man who harmed her.

"Alyx." He called again, finally getting close enough to gently grab her arm, and turn her to him. "I believe you." He told her. "I believe you."

Alyx buried her face in Peter's chest, causing him to wrap his arms around her in a hug. She hadn't actively sought comfort after she had been shot. Not until now. Clearly, she really needed it, but she wouldn't verbally acknowledge it. She wouldn't cry. She would just hug Peter and take comfort in the fact that someone believed her, even if none of her other friends did.

"I still see his face when I close my eyes. I've been seeing him in crowds since I got back, and I thought I was crazy. But he's here. He's here and he's dating Carlie and I don't know what he wants from her and no one will believe me. He could hurt her and it would be my fault. He could hurt her..." Alyx rambled, her eyes squeezed tightly shut, while she was still hugging Peter.

"I believe you." Peter told her again. "And I won't let anything happen to you, or her." He promised. "We have a name now. We can tell your dad, and Emily, and even Hall. They've been looking for him. Your ID, and the sketch should be enough to arrest him, and even press charges."

Alyx took a deep breath. Peter's words were supposed to make her feel like finding him was a good thing. But they *knew* Banthup was working with Jackson, and he was still sitting in her classes, taunting her.

"What about Banthup?" She asked.

"They have evidence tying him to the crime scene at the neighbor's house. He was the one that killed the neighbor. That's what warned us that he might be working with Jackson." Peter smoothed her hair, kissing her head. If they could tie both Banthup and Kalen to Jackson, they would be able to arrest him too, and this would all be over. Alyx would be safe.

Alyx opened her eyes, staring off into nothing as she thought about what Peter had just admitted. If they had evidence that Banthup had killed her neighbor to get Kalen onto the roof to shoot at her, and no one had moved to arrest him, why would they do anything to arrest Kalen.

Jackson was winning.

"What about me? "What happens when we tell my parents that the man who shot me is part of my friend group?"

"What do you mean?" Peter asked, backing away from Alyx just enough he could look down at her, his eyebrows furrowed.

"Where am I sent while we wait for the FBI and the CIA and whoever else is involved to make all the connections to Jackson? Where am I sent when they get out on bail awaiting trial? Where am I when they discover that they don't have enough evidence, and the charges are dropped? Where am I sent? What do I miss? We are literally weeks away from AP tests I have paid to take, and then graduation."

Peter shook his head. "That is way too many what ifs." He argued. "You are assuming the worst."

Alyx pulled away. "Well forgive me for expecting the worst with everything that has happened recently. Forget Murphy's law. I'm pretty sure I'm living O'tool's law."

Peter sighed, taking Alyx' hand to stay by her side as she walked away towards an empty grass hill where she could eat her lunch. "What do you want me to do?" He asked. "I have to keep you safe…"

"Can Kalen make a move at school?" Alyx asked. "I mean, if I am safe sitting with Banthup in class, surely Kalen, who isn't in any of my classes isn't that big of a threat."

"Alyx…"

"If we don't tell them, we can investigate on our own. Find the evidence we need to convict them. Make sure it is all airtight. Then we tell them." Alyx suggested.

"And what if we never find this *airtight* evidence you are looking for?" Peter asked.

"If we don't find it, we tell them the day after graduation." Alyx bargained.

Peter opened his mouth, all of the reasons why her idea was dangerous and wouldn't work on the tip of his tongue. As he turned to look at her, and tell her all the reasons he wanted to, he saw the girl she had been the previous semester. Alyx almost looked back to normal, minus the pleading in her eyes.

He didn't want to ruin it.

"Fine." He agreed. "But if we don't find the evidence, we will tell them at *midnight* after graduation, and not a second later. And you won't complain about any precautions I take between now and then."

Alyx drew her right pointer finger over her heart in an x shape.

"And we are doubling your training sessions." Peter added. "After every track practice. Extra laps. Extra push-ups."

Alyx smiled, kissing Peter. "Thank you."

Peter shook his head, letting go of her hand with a smile as she sat down on the grass, pulling her lunch out of her bag.

Friday
May 4th, 2012

10:40 PDT
Tracy, California
John C. Kimball High School

KALEN FROWNED as he left AP Government, frustrated with how cold Peter had been towards him since Alyx had come back. He didn't know what Alyx had told Carlie the day she had come to eat lunch with them, but he knew Peter had overheard them, and based on Peter's sudden shift in attitude toward him, he could guess.

He hated that Carlie didn't believe her own friend. He hated that he had manipulated Carlie into being the mean girl she wasn't, and to someone that he could tell meant a lot to her.

He hated that Carlie was a casualty to his uncle's war.

As he walked into class, he saw Carlie look up and smile at him. Peter's attitude had changed after he found out who Kalen was, but Carlie was the same as always. He would have preferred her to at least tell him what Alyx had told her. He would have loved her more if she stood up for herself and confronted him about what Alyx told her. Instead, she smiled at him like her best friend had told her nothing about who was responsible for shooting her.

What surprised him more than Carlie being totally normal, was the fact that Thane had been as well. He assumed that if Peter found out, Thane would be told. Maybe Thane had been told, and he was really as good of a spy as the Halls were known for.

"Are you ok?" Carlie asked as Kalen sat in his seat.

Kalen shook his head. "Peter isn't talking to me."

Carlie rolled her eyes. "Alyx isn't talking to me, I bet it's related," she replied. "His loyalty belongs to Alyx and no one else. He probably believes what she told me about you."

Kalen closed his eyes. So he was right. Alyx told Carlie that he had been the one to shoot her. And instead of believing her friend, she sided with him. "What did she tell you?" He asked, his voice quiet. Even if he knew, he wanted to hear it from her.

Carlie's face morphed into one of disgust for a moment, before she caught herself, covering it up with a smile as she turned to look in Kalen's eyes. "Nothing true."

The bell rang, indicating the start of class. Kalen and Carlie looked to the front, expecting to see the warm-up like usual, but the projector screen was up, and the board was blank.

"Ok folks!" The teacher announced. "We're going to do something a little bit different today. As you may have noticed, we've gone through the textbook, so for the next few weeks, you will be working on your final project."

The class groaned.

"I know, I know, but I promise, the final project will be at least a little bit of fun." She grabbed a stack of papers from her desk, and started counting them out, and handing smaller stacks to the front person in every row, asking them to pass them back. "You will be working in pairs. You can choose your partner. And the best part: you can choose your topic."

Kalen and Carlie looked at each other, already knowing that they wanted to work together. Kalen looked away as he saw the project paper appear in front of him.

What is a practical use for Psychology?

Kalen looked up at the teacher as he finished reading the top. One thing came to mind when he heard about the practical use of psychology.

"You can choose something that we use psychology for in some aspect of life. The project will entail explaining *how* psychology is used, *why* it's important, useful, etcetera, and any harms of using psychology."

Kalen looked back down at his paper. His uncle had compared what he did to break people to Interrogation Techniques. He knew what he wanted to do his project on.

It practically wrote itself.

SATURDAY
MAY 5TH, 2012

9:47 PDT
Manteca, California
Sierra High School

Alyx glanced up into the packed bleachers and all the parents and friends that had come to watch their track runner compete against the best from the State of California. Alyx blew out a shaky breath as she turned around and did high kicks back to where she had just done high knees from. The 200 Meter event for Frosh/Soph boys was starting. The Varsity Girls ran the event last, which meant it was her turn to warm-up. It was one of her best events. She had a great chance for qualifying for CIF finals, and maybe even State.

Yet she was distracted.

When she had made her deal with Peter, she was certain he wasn't going to let her continue to run track. She had bargained for the AP tests that were starting next week, and graduation, not her final season of Track and Field. But for some reason, he didn't try to talk her out of participating in track. She wondered if it was because he was doing it with her, or if it would be hard to explain to her parents, Kate, and Lynn why it suddenly wasn't safe for her to do the sport he had fought hard to let her participate in not even a week before.

Peter had done everything in his power to make sure she could participate in her final track season, and do her best, and go as far as she could.

And she was about to risk it all.

Alyx glanced at the people next to her. Kate, Lynn, and Chelsi were on her left, following her lead for their warm-up, as was Peter and Thane, on her right. Her window of opportunity was limited. The 200 Meter Dash was the only event that all of them ran. While they were on the track, it would be her only time alone today. The window was small, and chances that she took too long, and missed her event were high.

Since she got back, and discovered that Jackson had Banthup and Kalen undercover at the school, she had watched them for anything they might be doing that would hurt her. They hadn't. Banthup had even covered for her when she snuck out of class to ditch him, so Peter, nor her parents found out.

Jackson was protecting her freedom.

The least she could do was meet Jackson and get whatever file he wanted to give her.

The starting pistol announcing the first of the Frosh/Soph boys 200 Meter heats was shot, the explosion of gunpowder in the blank round echoing around the track as the sound of cheers erupted from the crowd. Peter sighed, looking at Alyx as he finished his warm-up. "Are you ok?"

Alyx rolled her eyes, pointing at her parents, as well as Dylan and his wife, in the stands. "I'll be fine. Someone is always watching." She replied. "Before we know it, I will be running into your arms after setting my personal best 200 Meter time, and winning the event."

Peter leaned in, giving Alyx a quick peck on the lips. "I will hold you to that." He promised, then he and Thane took off to get to the Start line. The two of them had gone to check in for the race before they had gone to the warm-up field, but as they walked off, the announcer asked the participants for the Girls Frosh/Soph 200 Meter to come check in.

Chelsi jumped up off the ground, nervousness bubbling over into excitement for her first event of the track meet. "That's us."

Kate and Lynn finished their stretches, then followed her.

"Good Luck!" Alyx called after them, waving at them when they turned back to look at her, before she sat down on the ground to start stretching some more.

Once they were out of sight, she stood up, pulling her phone out of her warm-up pocket. Usually, she left her phone in her bag with the rest of the team when she went to warm-up, but she knew she didn't have time to run back to her bag, grab her phone, text Jackson, and meet him before her event.

Before she had the chance to send the message, a man

wearing Kimball colors, and an oversized floppy hat meant to protect one's face from the sun approached her. If she didn't know better, she would have thought he was one of her coaches. He looked the part to perfection, but under his floppy hat, Alyx saw the face of the man who she'd met at Feilds Ball.

Jackson.

He smiled at Alyx, showing her the CD he had in his jacket. "As promised."

"I thought I would have to find you." Alyx commented.

Jackson shrugged. "You said you had a tight window. You were so meticulous with your planning I was impressed."

Alyx rolled her eyes, extending her hand to take the CD. "What is this, anyway?"

"Have you ever heard of the *Icarus Incident*?" Jackson asked.

"Can't say I have." Alyx admitted.

"It's the name they gave the incident where your siblings died. That CD has the video files of a witness statement that was used to write the report. Banthup had to return the file to your boyfriend, but I was able to make a copy of the video." Jackson told Alyx.

"Peter has the file?" She asked.

Jackson nodded. "He gave it to Banthup when he asked what made you so important that we wanted to recruit you, and made the CIA hellbent on protecting you."

Alyx looked toward the check-in station when she heard the

call for Varsity Girls to check-in. She turned back to Jackson. "I can't make any promises about when I can watch this. AP tests start next week, so if I'm not exhausted after today's meet, I need to study."

Jackson shrugged, walking off. "You have the CD now. You can do whatever you want with it, but if I were you, I would want to watch it. I would want to know why my siblings died."

Alyx sighed, jogging over to the check-in station. She would just hide the CD in her warm-ups while she ran her event, but she didn't want it to get stepped on and broken. As much as part of her didn't want to see what was on it, simply because Jackson asked her to watch it, she couldn't deny the fact that she desperately wanted to know what was on it.

Once she checked in, and got her number to put on her uniform shorts, she ran back to the bleachers, and the spot in the stands where their school had a shade tent. She found her bag where she had left it, shoving the CD and her phone inside. She also decided to strip out of her warm-ups, shoving them inside.

If anyone asked, that was the reason for this trip.

She knew her event was dangerously close to starting, so she hurried down to the track.

Friday
May 11th, 2012

16:47 PDT
Tracy, California
Udall Home

CARLIE'S FOREHEAD crinkled as she read Kalen's research arguments. She had thought it would be fun, and a bit intriguing to do their project on Interrogation Techniques when Kalen had suggested the topic. She had spent quite a bit of time at the McLean's house over the years, being Alyx' friends, and she had always been quite curious about Mr. McLean's job. When she was little, she had wanted to be a cop, like the ones in the TV shows she watched with her parents, and here was her best friend's dad: a real life super-hero just like the main character of those shows. As she got older, and started watching shows like Criminal Minds and Bones, she realized that she was intrigued by the psychology of it all, and how it could be used to catch criminals.

Kalen's topic hadn't been exactly what she would have chosen for the topic of their project, but it was pretty close. She was glad Kalen had suggested it, because it was another way cops could use psychology that she hadn't thought of yet. She had asked their teacher if they were allowed to use first-person resources for their paper, and she had agreed they could once Carlie explained their topic, and that she wanted to interview Special Agent McLean for their paper. He was a trained interrogator, and his job overlapped with their topic, so she had thought that it would give Carlie and Kalen the perfect opportunity to see psychology at work in a way the paper never could.

Special Agent McLean had been a good sport about the project as well, telling her that he would talk to them for their paper, and even offered to do a mock interrogation with them so they could see what it was like from both sides. Carlie loved the idea.

The two of them had agreed that they would divide their paper in two. They would do the first half of their paper before they met with Agent McLean. They would do their research, and use that research to form a thesis about what it would feel like to be interrogated, and the long term effects of an interrogation. They would then record their interview with Agent McLean, and use the second half of their paper to talk about the actual experience, and whether it was similar, or dissimilar to what their research had told them it would be like.

While Carlie approached the paper from a law-enforcement lens, Kalen approached it from a criminal lens, and his arguments seemed extremely hostile towards the interrogation process.

"What's wrong?" Kalen asked Carlie as he finished reading what she had written for the first part of their paper. He could see her confusion on her face as she read what he had written.

"You just seem to be…" Carlie took a deep breath. They had done their research together, and had found an article that detailed what a good interrogator would try to do in an interview. Carlie had written the introduction, and used the research to detail what the interrogation would look like. Kalen was responsible for detailing the psychological effects of the interrogation, why it led to confessions, and make a hypothesis about recidivism rates following a confession. He had taken an extremely critical approach to his portion. "Your portion has a much more critical tone to it than I thought we were going for."

Kalen shrugged. "The research we've done suggests that in order to get a confession, most interrogators leverage guilt to force a change in how the suspect views themselves. If the interrogator changes how they perceive themselves, if they force a suspect to see themselves as a bad person, don't you think that their recidivism rate is going to be higher?"

Carlie shook her head. "No. I think it would be lower."

"Really?" Kalen asked.

"Really." Carlie said. "I mean we couldn't find any research that *actually* studied what we are talking about, but based on what I know about psychology, and guilt, and repentance, I know that acknowledging guilt is the first step to change."

"Repentance?" Kalen asked.

Carlie sighed. "Yeah, sorry, my religion is showing."

"No." Kalen shook his head. "Don't apologize. I'm curious."

Carlie bit her lip, staring at Kalen, and his eyes, which were eagerly staring at her, hungry for learning. "Repentance is something that we talk about a lot in church," She started, "but I think it's something that all of us practice on some level. Repentance is kind of just a fancy word for change. It's the idea that when we do something we know is wrong, we have a process to change, and be better next time." Carlie paused, getting up. "Actually, let me go get something and show it to you."

Kalen nodded, watching as Carlie left the room. Was it *really* possible to change? Could *he* change after everything his uncle had done to train him to be a perfect soldier and tool of death?

To be fair, when Kalen thought about it, his uncle probably hadn't been as successful as he had thought. Kalen's doubts proved that. And when Kalen looked back at the missions he had already executed for his uncle, he realized something. He had been ordered to kill Lynn. He hadn't. At the time, he blamed his failure on Alyx, but he'd hesitated, and he decided to make up for his *failure* by bringing in Alyx, instead of going after Lynn. He had failed to bring Alyx in too, because he hesitated, not wanting to kill her either.

His uncle had told him he was a killer. He had trained him to be killer, but every time he had been asked to prove that definition of himself, he had failed.

He wasn't a killer.

Carlie returned to the room with a small brown and white paperback book, flipping through the pages inside until she found *Repentance* in the alphabetical reference book. "Here it is. Yeah, I was right. The steps here are basically the same. I mean here is uses the word *sorrow for sin* or *godly sorrow* but the description is basically just a more pure version of guilt. Guilt means you feel sorrow for what you've done. This just specifies you don't feel that sorrow because of consequence. Once you acknowledge you have done something wrong, feel sorrow for it, the next step is to *confess* that sin. Usually, the small sins I'm guilty of are just confessed in prayer, but larger sins, or broken laws, or whatever, should be confessed to ecclesiastical leaders, and the proper authorities. Then you abandon the sin, aka don't do it again, and make restitution. In a way, it's kind of similar to what the criminal justice system tries to force people to do. The big problem is forcing people to repent *never* works. But those who allow the system to work for them…"

Kalen smiled at Carlie. He loved that she was so hopeful, but even though she preferred to see the best in the world, she could see the faults in the system too.

"So you have used this repentance process?" He asked.

Carlie nodded. "Everyday. Some days it's harder than others, and some things are harder to repent for than others. For example, how I treated Alyx. I'm still working on that one. I need to tell her that I was wrong, and ask her to forgive me, but I'm still struggling with feeling sorrow. Part of me is still really mad at the way she treated me, and I'm letting that pride, and anger stop me from apologizing, which are just two more things I need to repent for." Carlie sighed. "Like I said, it only works if you let it."

Kalen nodded. "Do you think I could read that?"

"Of course." Carlie smiled, handing it to him. "So does that mean you are going to change your arguments?"

Kalen laughed, stealing a kiss from Carlie as he took the book from her. "I'd like to try it myself before I change my opinion."

Carlie smirked. "Oh yeah?" She asked. "And what might my perfect boyfriend need to repent of?"

Kalen's smile disappeared. "I have plenty of skeletons in my closet." He admitted.

Carlie nodded, brushing her hand through the hair on the back of his head. "Take your time." She told him. "But if you feel bad about something, it's not a bad thing." She told him. "It's our brain's way of encouraging us to change and be better." She sighed. "Only sociopaths don't feel guilt."

Kalen looked at Carlie, seeing nothing but love and encouragement coming from her. How was it possible she looked at him with more love than his own uncle had in the eleven years he had lived with him? He was starting to think that Carlie was onto something with her sociopath comment. It wasn't that his uncle didn't feel just guilt.

He didn't feel *anything*.

18:22 PDT
Tracy, California
McLean Home

"IF YOU are going to test this training camp, I'm coming too." Kate complained, following Lynn into the kitchen.

"You're not a spy." Lynn argued.

"Who said?" Kate asked.

"Said mum, who sent me off to train with MI-6 from birth." Lynn replied, closing the fridge.

Kate rolled her eyes. "Oh, so because I just *happened* to be born first, and you were born second, I'm suddenly incapable of being a spy." She said. "I can't do *anything* spy related. It's not like I'm faster than you or anything."

Lynn spun on Kate, scoffing at her twin. "Are you ever going to let me live that down? You beat me by what, a hundredth of a second?"

"Four tenths." Alyx corrected from the dinner table, where she and Peter were sitting. They were going over the practice tests they had taken the day before. The AP French test was on

Tuesday. The results of their studying efforts for the year were about to be seen, but Alyx couldn't concentrate on the words in front of her, because her cousins were arguing. *Again.*

Lynn rolled her eyes, folding her arms across her chest. "I blame you for this. She wasn't doing well until you came home."

Alyx looked up at Lynn, raising her eye brows. "Would you have preferred I stayed in London, where Jackson knew I was? I thought you were supposed to be advocating for my safety."

Lynn shrugged. "That was before you started picking favorites."

"I don't have favorites!" Alyx complained. "Et si j'ai un favorite, ce n'est ni l'un ni l'autre d'entre vous."

"I knew it!" Lynn exclaimed. "She prefers Chelsi to both of us."

Alyx fake-smiled at Lynn. "Try Lyshiria."

"You're not even related to Lyshiria." Kate complained.

"Exactly." Alyx said, turning her attention back to the test in front of her.

Peter snickered, trying to keep his eyes on his practice test. The McLean house had definitely become much more lively since the first time he came here to study.

Sarah walked into the kitchen, snapping at the twins to get them to stop fighting. "Stop. Now. Or I am sending you both back to London."

Sarah's threat worked immediately, quickly silencing their

arguments. Before she had lost two of her children, she had learned the benefit of having a good threat to use to bribe good behavior. It was only useful if the kids knew that she would actually carry it out, and since the two girls had shown up, she had executed plenty of other threats, so this one was golden. Neither of them wanted to go home, and they knew if they became too much for Sarah to handle, she would send them back to their dad.

"Sarah, I want to go to the training camp that Lynn is going to after the school year. Can I?" Kate asked.

"Ask your dad." Sarah said, not looking away from the fridge where she was trying to figure out what she could make for dinner.

Alyx had to bite her lip to prevent herself from laughing. She had no idea how many times she had played that game with her parents. Sometimes she could have sworn it was their favorite game to play with their daughter. *How many times can we get Alyx to run back and forth before she gives up*?

"Dad says he doesn't care, as long as you are ok with it." Kate replied.

Sarah turned to look at Kate, disbelief in her eyes. "I will call him."

Kate shrugged. "Ok."

Sarah took a deep breath. "As long as your father doesn't have a problem with it, I don't see why you can't go with Lynn."

Lynn groaned. "Seriously, what do you have on dad that has

him letting you do whatever you want?"

Kate smiled. "That's for me to know." She taunted, skipping out of the kitchen, quickly followed by Lynn, who was being more than a little vocal about her desire to know what Kate was using to blackmail their father.

"Do you know very much about the training camp?" Alyx asked her mom.

"Yeah. An old friend of Dylan's called. He heard he and your father got control of Promgen. He asked Dylan to send a few of the members to test the camp." Sarah replied.

"I can't believe you got your parents calling it Promgen." Peter complained under his breath, loud enough that Alyx heard, and smiled.

"It's safe enough to send Kate to?" Alyx asked.

"It's so covert it wasn't on Dylan's radar, so yeah." Sarah commented.

"So it's safe enough that I can go." Alyx commented. "Maybe learn something to help me protect myself?"

"No." Sarah replied.

"Come on, mom."

"I already said no."

"Why not?" Alyx asked.

"Because you going puts everyone else at risk." Sarah answered. "And you have already committed to translate for Michael at the Conference. The training camp will still be going when you should be there."

Alyx huffed, pushing her chair out from the table before storming off, leaving the practice test open.

She was tired of only being good as a translator.

Saturday
May 26th, 2012

19:14 PDT
Tracy, California
Promgen Headquarters

PETER DUCKED the punch Alyx threw at his face, pivoting to throw his own, finding Alyx had already anticipated the move, and deflected his punch, before sneaking one in on him.

"Good move." Peter complemented, bouncing back and away from her to give himself a moment to recover.

He smiled as he watched Alyx bouncing on the balls of her feet, watching him to try and find an opening. She was getting tired, and he could see it on her face. She was determined to learn everything he was teaching her and more, and had done a decent job of absorbing everything he had taught her since she got home. Her form was better, she was getting better at predicting her opponent's moves so she could block them, and she had figured out how to conceal some of her moves, making it more difficult for her opponent to predict her next moves. When Peter let her practice with more than just the boxing he was teaching her, she could seamlessly stitch the multiple martial arts she knew together, along with hurdle kicks and gymnastics, and use a fighting style that no one else had seen, and was impossible to predict. The one problem she had wasn't strength, technique, speed, or even form. Her only weakness was endurance. If she found herself up against someone who wasn't thrown off by her unusual fighting style, and matched her pretty evenly, she couldn't last longer than about five minutes. Any longer than that, she started to get tired; she started having a hard time keeping her fists up to block her face, and she started slowing down enough that she slowly started taking more and more hits.

As if wanting to prove Peter's observation, Alyx threw another punch at Peter, but it was much slower than her previous punches had been, allowing Peter to step out of the way, catch her wrist, and use his grip on her to spin her into him, where he planted a kiss on her cheek. "Let's call it quits for today." He told her, letting her go.

She walked out of his hold taking a deep breath before turning around and raising her fists to block her face again. "I'm not ready yet."

"Alyx, you're exhausted. We've been training for hours."

She bounced on the balls of her feet. "And you keep beating me. I get tired, I mess up, and you knock me down, or put me in a hold. If I'm fighting Kalen, or Banthup, or Jackson, they're not going to just get me in a hold to kiss me. They will kidnap me, or kill me. Let's keep going. At least until I beat you once."

Peter shook his head, throwing his arms up in surrender. "Well I'm done for the day. You've made great improvement. Let's take the wins, and continue to work on it Monday."

"Fine," Alyx said.

Peter sighed, happy that she hadn't tried to fight him too much on it. Instead of walking over to her duffle bag to unwrap her fists and drink some water, though, she walked over to the punching bag that was hanging from the overhang over the back porch. He followed behind her, wrapping his arms around her waist from behind as she started punching the bag. "There is such a thing as training too hard."

"I'm not strong enough." Alyx complained softly. "We've been at this for months, and I'm still not good enough to defend myself against you for more than five minutes. How am I supposed to defend myself from Jackson, who has years and years of training."

"You don't have to fight them alone." Peter told her. He spun her around, so he could look into her eyes. "Besides, we are practicing worse case. You are smart. Smart enough that something has to have gone *very* wrong if you end up trading punches with Jackson."

"Well, then why haven't we been able to connect Jackson with Banthup or Kalen?" She asked. "If I am so smart, then why haven't I found the missing piece that ties the entire thing together?" She sighed. "Clearly, he's still smarter."

Peter shook his head, pulling Alyx into a hug. "He's just had more time to hide." He told her after a moment of silence. "We'll figure it out. I promise."

"You know he's trying really hard to recruit me." She admitted softly. "He's been texting me since Kalen shot me. Part of me is tempted to accept his offer. If I accept his offer, it might be easier to figure out his plan. Take down the Circle of Fifths from the inside."

Peter shook his head, subconsciously holding Alyx a little bit tighter. "Joining Jackson is a bad idea for *so* many reasons." He said. "Not to mention if he figures it out, he would have no problem killing you."

"What if it's the only way to beat him?" Alyx asked.

"We still have other options. Let's wait before we use the nuclear option, ok?" Peter waited until he felt Alyx nod in his chest. "We should celebrate though. You survived AP tests."

"You took some AP tests too." Alyx mumbled.

"So let's celebrate the fact that both of us survived AP tests." Peter conceded. "And we crushed the French AP test, so you are guaranteed a spot at Oxford."

Alyx pulled her arm out from awkwardly hanging at her side, where it got stuck when Peter hugged her to stop her from training, and smacked Peter's shoulder. "Can you wait until I actually apply, or get asked to interview, or get an acceptance letter before you try to jinx it?"

"I'm going to take you home so you can get a shower, then we'll find someway to celebrate." Peter continued.

"Fine." Alyx agreed, letting Peter take her hand as he released her from his hug.

20:02 PDT
Tracy, California
McLean Home

ALYX' EYES lit up as she opened the back door, seeing the decorations that had been strung up across her backyard. Someone had painstakingly crisscrossed Christmas lights from the house to some tall poles at the fence and back. Both the oleander and the walnut trees in the back corners were also wrapped in lights. Standing in the center of the concrete patio, dressed with a dark suit and a smile, was Peter.

Alyx smiled at Peter. "What is this?" She asked him.

"It wasn't safe enough to take you to Prom, but I convinced your parents to let me bring Prom to you." He said. He gestured to a table next to the house. "We have refreshments…" He gestured to the speakers plugged into the house. "We have music…" He pulled his phone out of his pocket. "And even better than Prom, we can control the music." He stuck his hand out to Alyx. "What do you say? Alyx McLean, will you be my Prom date?"

Alyx looked down at the fancy dress that Kate had insisted

she put on after shower. Suddenly it made sense. "I mean we are already dressed, so we might as well." She said, trying to play down how excited she was that Peter was doing this for her.

"Good." Peter said, grabbing her hand, pulling her in close, and starting to sway to the music he had playing.

This was exactly what he wanted to be doing right now. He would dance with her until she was tired and wanted to go to bed.

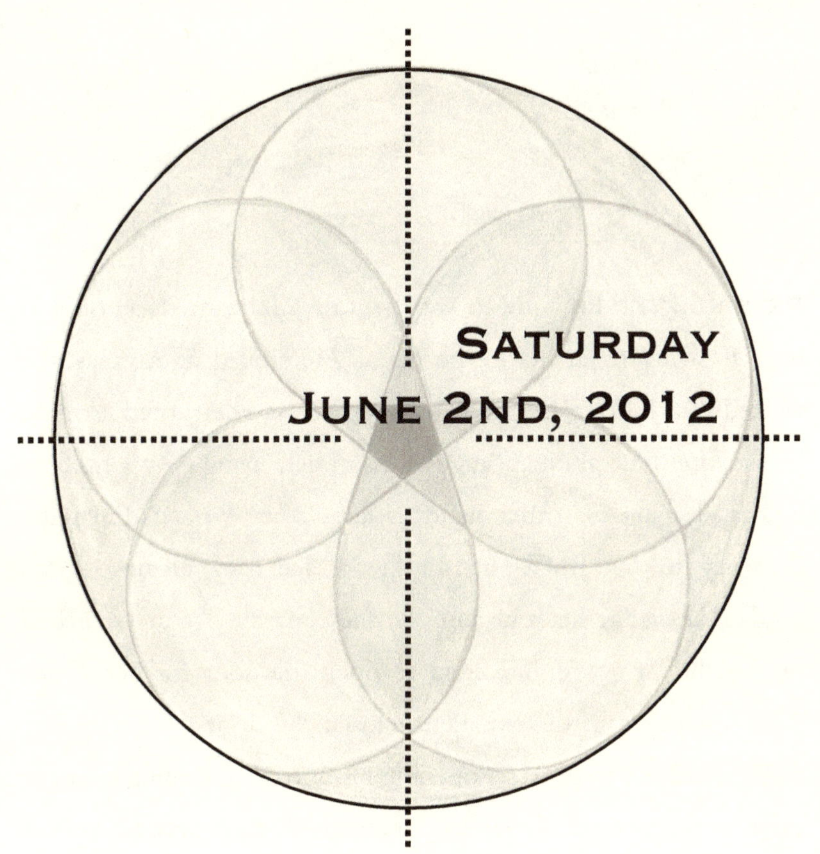
Saturday
June 2nd, 2012

7:32 PDT
Tracy, California
McLean Home

PETER LIFTED his hand to knock on the McLean's door, only to have it swing open before he could. He smiled at Alyx as she walked out, locking the door behind her. As she turned around, he took her blue graduation gown from her, laying it over his arm before slipping his other hand in hers. They walked down the driveway to his BMW hand-in-hand, her lacy cream-colored sandal-like wedge heels clicking on the concrete. As they reached his car, he let go of her hand to open the door for her. Once Alyx was safely in the car, Peter closed the door for her before walking around to his side, opening his door, and leaning over the drivers seat to carefully lay her graduation gown over his on his back seat. He climbed back out the door, looking over at Alyx as he slid into the car properly this time.

She was gorgeous. For the first time in weeks, she had the slightest smile. Even if it wasn't as big as the smiles he had seen from her at the beginning of the school year, this small smile was all he had wished for on his birthday. And here it was. That smile alone made it so he didn't notice that her cream colored knee length lace dress matched her shoes, or the fact that she had been up early making sure her natural waves had more definition than usual, with the front curls being pinned back on her head so they weren't falling into her face. All he cared about was that as she gracefully sat in the passenger seat of the car she had used to rescue him eight months before with her blue cap sitting in her lap, she seemed happy for the first time in too long.

"Are you excited for today?" Peter asked as he backed out of the driveway.

Alyx nodded, looking over at Peter. "Yeah. What about you?"

"You have no idea." He admitted. "I am so ready to leave high school behind."

"What? Mr. Popular doesn't like high school? But you had it all. You played football. You have a brand new BMW, which fulfills the cool car requirement. You had all the popular friends…"

"Don't forget the perfect girlfriend who loves me." Peter added.

Alyx pointed at Peter. "I'm not sure if I would use the word perfect, but you do have a girlfriend who loves you, so I guess that fulfills that requirement. You literally had everything that a not-cool kid like me wanted. Why would you want to leave?"

Peter laughed. "You and I aren't that much different. You have a brand new car, and you have a boyfriend who loves you."

"I wasn't a cheerleader. It's a must for my cool status." Alyx told Peter seriously.

"Tennis or track aren't acceptable alternatives to cheerleader?" Peter asked.

"Nope."

Peter rolled his eyes. "I want to leave because of the ridiculous societal standards." He glanced at Alyx. "Also, you are the only good thing I got from my entire high school experience."

Alyx' smile grew to be a legitimate one he hadn't seen since November. It was addictive. All he wanted to do was make her smile over and over until she couldn't remember all of the things that made her sad.

"So how does it feel to be 17?" Peter asked as they turned onto Lammers Road heading towards the high school.

Alyx back handed Peter's shoulder. "You should know. You're 17. It feels no different than 16."

"I'm 18." Peter corrected.

"What? Since when?" Alyx asked.

"Last Saturday."

"Why didn't you tell me? We could have done something. I mean, I could have tried to convince my parents to let me take you out somewhere."

Peter shook his head. "All I wanted was to spend my day with you, and that is what I got." He admitted. "It was perfect."

Alyx rolled her eyes. "We are doing something for your

birthday." Alyx insisted. "We have to go to the mall to get you a present, which mean we'll have to duck my parents, and the security detail you've set up, but I'll be with you, so that should be doable, especially if you let me drive…"

"It's your birthday." Peter laughed. "I'll do whatever you want today."

Alyx looked over at Peter as he parked the car in the school parking lot. There were several students walking through the parking lot to the large gym where they'd spent the day before rehearsing for today, but Alyx felt frozen in this car, staring at Peter. This graduation was supposed to symbolize the start of the rest of their lives. It was about celebrating their accomplishments and looking forward to the future.

Over the last few months, her idea of what her future looked like may have crumbled, but if Alyx still knew anything about what she wanted her future to look like, she knew that Peter belonged in it. Peter was her future.

"Should we go in?" Peter asked, drawing Alyx out of her thoughts. He was the only one who could. If she was with him, she never went spiraling out control with her thoughts becoming more and more dark and self deprecating. If she was with him, she believed she was worth his love. If she was with him, she remembered who she was.

Alyx nodded, giving him a small smile, which he returned even bigger. She loved his smile. It was warm and caring. He leaned across the car, giving her a kiss on her temple.

"I'll come open your door." He told her. It was his way of asking her to let him, which she gladly obliged. If getting her door for her made him happy, she would let him.

She wanted to see his smile over and over. It made her feel safe, and not much did anymore.

After helping her out of the car, he leaned her seat forward so he could more easily grab their blue gowns. He handed her the top one, which she unzipped then tossed over her shoulders with a flourish, sliding her hands into the flowing sleeves as Peter pulled his own from his back seat. Peter pulled his gown on, fiddling with the neckline until it sat decently over his dress shirt.

Alyx smiled at Peter's choice in tie for today, which she knew he had bought specifically for today, just like she had bought her dress. Alyx set her cap on the car, stepping in to help Peter straighten his orange tie. "You just had to wear our school colors one last time, didn't you?" She teased.

"What can I say?" Peter replied. "Forever orange and blue."

"Next thing I know, you'll be chanting."

"Let's go Jag-uars!" He yelled in reply.

"Let's go Jag-uars!" The other kids in the parking lot replied.

Alyx ducked her head into Peter's chest, hiding her snickers. "You are ridiculous."

Peter shook his head, lifting her chin. "Am I? Or did I only do that to get you to laugh?" He asked. He leaned down, giving her a soft kiss. "I love hearing you laugh."

He turned around, pulling their orange stoles from the car. He looped one around Alyx' shoulders as she zipped up her gown, looping the other around his own shoulders. He leaned back into his car to pull out his cap and a stack of cords, which he quickly looped around Alyx once more.

Alyx rolled her eyes, pulling away one of the three he had placed on her shoulders, looping it over Peter's instead. "I believe this one belongs to you."

Peter shook his head, but didn't remove it. "Maybe I thought someone else deserved another honors cord. I mean, apparently they don't give out a cord for graduating early, but I think they should."

Alyx rolled her eyes, grabbing her cap from the top of Peter's car to put it on. She used some Bobby pins she'd put on it to keep it on her head.

Peter closed the car door, sticking out his hand for Alyx to take. "You ready?" He asked.

Alyx nodded. She was ready to enter her future with Peter by her side.

10:56 PDT
Tracy, California
John C. Kimball High School

Kaden smiled as he stood up at the podium on the stage erected on the north end of the football field. "Class of 2012, please join me in standing." He waited until the sea of blue and orange was standing before continuing. "We have been presented to the school board and accepted. We have crossed this stage, and have been awarded our diplomas. I am now pleased to ask you to turn your tassels. Please join me in moving your tassel from right to left."

The stadium cheered as the graduating students moved their tassels in unison.

Kaden stood smiling at his friends and classmates waiting for the cheering to die down. "Congratulations! We are officially the Graduated class of 2012!"

Whoops went up among the students, as well as a few caps, even though they had been asked not to toss them.

Kaden stepped down off the stage as the sound system

began to play "Celebration" by Kool and the Gang. As much as they had practiced the processional to leave the stadium, the excitement of being free and the music made it so the processional devolved almost the second they left the football field.

What could the school do? They were free. They were no longer students. Peter found Alyx as they walked down the hill behind the football field. He wrapped his arm around the side of her waist, placing a kiss on her cheek. She giggled.

"We're free." He whispered.

Alyx nodded, turning to look at Peter with a giant smile plastered on her face.

The two of them walked hand-in-hand through the campus with the other students, trying to find Alyx' family. They were all meeting in the courtyard to take pictures with family, friends, and classmates.

Scarlett stopped them as they walked past, insisting she take a picture of the couple, then get a picture *with* the couple. Peter watched Scarlett and Alyx pose for one last picture. Scarlett came over to him after punching his arm. "Ow, what's that for?" He asked.

"You better take care of her." She told him, giving him a look that threatened what would happen if Alyx became just another one of the girls he'd kissed.

Peter laced his fingers through Alyx' as she returned to his side. "Trust me. I will."

Alyx laughed as Scarlett took two finger, pointing at her eyes, then at Peter. He pulled on Alyx' hand, pulling her further into the courtyard to find her friends and family. Kate found them first, running at Alyx and wrapping her arms around her.

"Congratulations!" Kate yelled as she squeezed Alyx. Her family came up to them smiling. Alyx was quickly surrounded, her parents and grandparents wanting to give her hugs, congratulations, and words of advice. Even Michael and his father were there—they may have been in town to celebrate Kate and Lynn's birthday the day before, but they didn't have to come today, so their attendance spoke volumes. Peter was happy to take a step back and allow Alyx to get the attention and love she deserved from her family.

When Sarah was done giving Alyx a hug and sharing her congratulations, she turned to Peter, surprising him by giving him a hug as well. "Congratulations!" Sarah told Peter. She glanced over at Neil as he gave Alyx a hug and whispered his own congratulations and advice to her. "Neil and I might not show it in the best way, but we are really glad that you are in Alyx life. You are really good for her. And not to get your hopes up, but Neil has commented that she looks at you the way I looked at him when we were your age."

"Thank you." Peter smiled.

Sarah nodded. "I know you don't have the best relationship with your parents, so we want you to know, no matter what happens, we will always be here for you. If you ever need advice, or a friendly ear you can always come to us."

Peter nodded. "I will." Peter looked at Neil as he clapped his shoulder the way he imagined a proud father would his son. "I have to thank you two for being so accepting of me. Being able to spend time with your family has made me realize that I really want what you guys have. I didn't know what I was missing, and I'm glad that you guys have welcomed me into your family."

Neil just gave a small nod with the smallest smile while Sarah beamed at him. "Let's take pictures!" Sarah told them. "First, we have to get pictures of the two of you."

Peter couldn't help but look at Alyx as she settled herself into position under his arm. She smiled looking at the camera, while Peter smiled looking at her. Sarah smiled herself as she snapped the picture before Peter turned to look at the camera, capturing the candid moment. She snapped a few more, then got pictures of Alyx with Kate and Lynn, and some with Peter as well. Kate offered to take some pictures of Alyx with her parents. After getting a few good ones, Sarah insisted Peter join them for a couple. Peter then took over, snapping a few pictures of Alyx, her parents, Kate and Lynn.

Thane came over with Chelsi, Emily, his parents, and his mom's parents, and the group pictures got bigger. Alyx' smile was genuine as her mom snapped a picture with all of her cousins. Peter took the picture as they crammed all of their family together for another picture. Emily insisted she get some pictures with just Alyx, since she had gotten some pictures with Thane.

Sarah was looking around for someone to take a picture with all of them, including Peter, when Peter froze. "I'll take some pictures for you," a middle-aged man offered, taking the phone from Sarah.

"George," she greeted. "I didn't know you were coming today."

"I wouldn't have missed it." He answered, shooing her towards the group that was already mostly lined up. Alyx and Peter were in the middle. Thane was next to Alyx with Chelsi by his side, while Kate stood next to Peter with Lynn next to her. Sarah, Neil, Dylan, Addy, Emily, Alyxandrie, Madelyn, William, Michael, Thomas, and Addy's parents filed in next to and behind the kids.

Peter forced a smile for the picture, but the happiness he'd been feeling all day was gone. The bubble popped. Each graduate was only given five tickets to the ceremony. He had very intentionally given all five of his tickets to Alyx and her family. He hadn't told his parents that he was graduating. He hadn't told them the time, the place, or anything. He didn't want them there. This was supposed to be a happy day for him. As soon as his dad showed up, it was anything but.

Once George had snapped a few pictures, he handed the phone back to Sarah, and approached Peter.

"It's time to go son." He told Peter.

"I'm not going anywhere with you." Peter told George, grabbing Alyx' hand and holding onto it like it was his lifeline.

George followed the movement with his eyes. He eyes flitted over to the girl whose hand his son was holding. "I don't believe we've met," he commented, extending his hand. "I'm George Carlyle, Peter's father."

Alyx accepted his outstretched hand, shaking it. "Alyx McLean."

George smiled. "I've heard a lot about you." He told Alyx. "You are a very promising young lady."

Alyx gave a tight smile, pulling her hand back.

George turned his attention back to his son. "You are needed in Langley. You need to train before you start your mission."

"You mean the mission Wraith arranged for me before he was fired from the Generation." Peter asked.

"The mission Wraith kindly recommended you for, yes. It will be a great way for you to start your career." George told him.

"I'm not so sure I want a career with the agency." Peter told his father.

"Nonsense." George laughed. "What else would you do?"

"Study to be an engineer." Peter replied.

George stopped laughing, eyeing with malice the way Peter still gripped Alyx' hand. "You have promised to take the mission, so you will. It's time to go." George insisted. "It seems you need more training than I thought."

"You gave up the right to control me a long time ago." Peter told his dad. "I'm not a child anymore. I'm 18. You couldn't control me anymore if you wanted to." He said. "I'm not leaving. I'm needed here much more than I am anywhere else."

George came in close, gripping Peter's shoulder. "As I understand it, she is more than capable of taking care of herself." He glanced at Alyx, whose hand Peter clung to. It was infuriating to see his son, who he had taken painstaking efforts to ensure was attachment free, dependent on a girl who couldn't even protect herself. "But maybe I'm wrong. If I am, wouldn't you like training to make sure you can *protect* your little *prize*."

Peter took a deep breath, trying not to let his dad see how much he was affected by his words, or how much his grip on his shoulder hurt. Looking past his dad, Peter could see Hall, as well as Neil, both of them watching the interaction carefully. Hall could do something about this situation, and with a small nod, he promised Peter he would.

But first, Peter would have to go with his dad.

"Can I at least finish celebrating today? It's a big day. For all of us." Peter asked. He could feel Alyx' grip on his hand tighten. Despair welled up inside Peter. He didn't want to leave Alyx. He couldn't. He had made her so many promises for today, and he intended to keep them. But more than that, he knew she needed him. And he needed her.

George shook his head. "Our flight leaves in 3 hours. You

need to get packed so we can head to the airport ASAP." Fortunately, he let go of his shoulder.

Peter turned to Alyx, gently lifting her chin. "I'll be back soon. Hall will figure this out for us." He whispered so his dad couldn't hear.

Alyx nodded, her face a passive, blank canvas.

After seeing her smile all day, seeing her face return to the emotionless façade she'd kept all semester was devastating, even more so than if she would have shown sadness or anger. He sighed, leaning in to give her a soft, sweet kiss. "I love you," he said, placing his forehead on hers with his eyes closed.

"Je t'aime, toujours et pour toujours." Alyx replied.

Peter gave her a sad smile, backing away to follow his dad. "I'm a phone call away." He promised, handing her his keys.

Alyx nodded, watching as he walked backwards for a bit, his eyes on her, almost as if he was memorizing her. He turned around, following his dad towards the parking lot. He glanced back a couple of times, his face screaming that he didn't want to leave her.

Alyx kept the keys Peter had handed her in the palm of her hand, hiding it from the others. She had a feeling if she let them know she had Peter's car, they would take it from her too, and she didn't want to lose another piece of him.

22:02 EDT
Dulles, Virginia
Dulles International Airport

FIRST STEP off the plane in Dulles, and Peter had his phone up to his ear, calling Alyx. As they walked through the boarding walk way towards the gate, George pulled the phone away from Peter.

"You are too dependent on her. It's a weakness. Some time apart will do you some good." George told his son, ending the call.

Peter snatched his phone back from his dad. "It's her birthday." Peter told him. "Not only did she just graduate from high school, and you took away the one thing that kept her sane enough to study and finish school while a group of terrorists chased her, but you took me on her birthday. I had convinced her parents I would take care of her today so we could celebrate, and give her some freedom from her security detail, which she feels suffocated by. And then you showed up and took *everything* she wanted today away."

Peter put some more distance between him and his dad, then

dialed Alyx again. As he waited for the phone to connect, he sighed. "I have to make sure she's ok," he mumbled.

Alyx didn't answer, and he sighed as he got her voice mail. He though about whether or not he should leave a voicemail, opting not to. He could always try to call her again later.

21:12 PDT
Tracy, California
McLean Home

THE HOUSE was dark, light coming from the few lights that had been left on that morning before the McLean's had left to go to the the graduation ceremony. Sarah and Neil had tried to keep Alyx out most of the day, taking her anywhere she wanted to go, both to celebrate her accomplishment and her birthday, as well as to keep her mind off of Peter's departure.

After spending the day surrounded by *all* of her family, Alyx needed to be alone for a bit. She headed upstairs to her room while her mom and dad carried in the to-go boxes with their left-overs from their dinner, and the party of people in town filed into their house. She walked through the doorway of her room, kicking off her heels as she threw her graduation gown and cap onto her bed. She looked around her room, taking a deep breath. She had finally become more comfortable being in her room. Still, she couldn't help but check the neighbor's roof to make sure Kalen wasn't there, waiting to take another shot at her.

Alyx sighed, looking around at the room that had become her prison. Now that she had graduated, she wasn't sure when she would next be allowed to escape the house. Her parents had slowly whittled down the things she was allowed to leave the house for, and the two survivors had been church and school. With Kalen attending church with Carlie, she hadn't gone to church or seminary in weeks. Worse, her parents had given up on trying to convince her to come with them. School had been the only thing she had left the house for in the last month, and now she was done. Until Michael went home, and took her back to London and the prison that they called Feilds Palace, she was stuck in this house.

The only thing she had to look forward to was the silence she would get when her family left her alone to go to church for three hours on Sunday.

She looked over at the book shelf that held her favorite books. When she'd been shot last November, she had yet to read most of those books. Between school, sports, translating, and church, she hadn't had very much time to read. Now she had read through all of those books, as well as quite a few from the Feilds Palace Library. If she was allowed to leave the house, she would just go to the book store and buy all of the books that she might even remotely like to read. It might have been a joke, but Peter had mentioned taking her to the book store today.

She heard Kate holler that she was going to go get the mail, then the door opened and closed. Alyx closed her eyes, feeling a heart stab. Kate, the girl who was usually the best protected in the family, was able to just casually leave the house to walk down the street and get the mail. She had convinced her dad that she was safe enough to come to the US and live here with her aunt and uncle. While Alyx had suffered through a security detail that got exponentially stricter, and a security perimeter that tightened like a noose until she couldn't breath, Kate got to experience the freedom that she had always longed for. Kate gained the privilege to walk down the street by herself and get the mail, while Alyx had the same privilege revoked from her.

Alyx sunk down to the floor, leaning against the drawers that were in her bed. She pulled her knees to her chest, wrapping her arms around them as she hid her face in her knees. She could only take so much of this. With her eyes closed, she began imagining all of the ways she could escape. She could wait until her parents went to church tomorrow. That was the easiest solution. Someone would be assigned to watch the front of the house, and her parents would get a notification if any of the windows or doors opened. But she had lured them into a sense of security. They had left her alone for several Sundays by now, and she hadn't made any attempts to escape. Why would this week be any different. By the time her dad could alert whoever was watching the house from across the street, Alyx could be over two fences and halfway to the school. They didn't know she had the keys to

Peter's car, or that his car was still sitting in the school parking lot. They wouldn't know to look there until she was already gone.

The real question was where would she go? As much as she felt trapped, this was where Peter would be coming back to find her.

"Hey Alyx?" Kate asked from the doorway. "Are you ok?"

Alyx looked up, giving Kate a small smile and nod.

Kate walked into the room, joining Alyx on the floor. "I know today didn't exactly go the way you wanted it to. I'm sorry."

Alyx shook her head. "I'm glad I was able to spend the day with you."

"Yes, but I'm not Peter," Kate giggled. She leaned over and bumped Alyx' shoulder. "Plus, I'm not blind. I can tell you don't exactly like spending time with your parents right now."

Alyx looked over at the cousin that for a long time had felt like a sister. They had both believed they were only children, and were the only two Hall children. The last year had showed them how much they had been lied to. Kate had a twin sister, and they had two more cousins from the Hall side of the family. The two of them had blinked and had more than doubled the cousins they had. Alyx had also discovered that she had a little sister hiding away somewhere away from Alyx, so she'd be safe. There were also the two siblings that were dead…

"I'm not sure what happened…" Kate started.

"Do you ever think about all the lies that our parents have

told us in the name of *keeping us safe*?" Alyx asked.

Kate sighed. "Why do you think I'm here? I had to convince dad somehow." She looked at Alyx. "I know the lies he told me aren't as big as the ones your parents let you believe, but..." She took a deep breath. "Did you know that dad told me mum died shortly after I was born? I thought she died when I was just an infant. When I did the research that proved that Rafael couldn't have killed her, I realized she died in 2000, which meant I was three." Kate shook her head, wiping a tear from the corner of her eye. "I took that research to dad and asked him about it. He gave me a decent response as to why he lied. I'm still not happy about it, but I understand why a bit better."

Alyx shook her head. "You were so little. I barely understood what was happening, but I can only imagine..." She looked at her cousin. "Why do they think lying to us about the trauma we've suffered will make it go away?"

"I don't know." Kate whispered. "But I still love my dad. I missed him, so I'm glad he came for my birthday. And I know that even when he drives me mad with his ridiculous demands for my *safety*, I know that he is only doing it because he thinks it is what will protect me."

"Yeah, well, my parents demands for my *safety* are suffocating me." Alyx admitted. "I just graduated from high school. If I hadn't decided to take a gap year, I would be heading off to college in a few months, but instead of slowly letting me have more freedoms as I enter adulthood, they have taken away the freedoms I did have." Alyx scoffed. "I mean how much longer can they really hide me away from Jackson. I have to live my life."

Kate shrugged. "Maybe you should talk to them about it." She stood up. She handed Alyx a small box with a bow on top of it and a card. "I found this on the porch when I went to get mail. It's addressed to you."

Alyx smiled at it, recognizing the writing on the card. "It's from Peter."

Kate nodded. "I figured as much." She gave Alyx a smile. "I'll leave you alone so you can open it." Kate watched Alyx stare at the writing on the card. She didn't so much as acknowledge Kate as she left, because her attention was entirely consumed by the card as she flipped it over and opened it. Kate turned and left the room, closing the door as she did. She didn't expect that anyone else would be coming up to talk to Alyx in the next little bit, and it seemed like even if they did, Alyx was so enraptured with the gift from Peter, she was unlikely to be disturbed, but Kate still figured she would like the privacy and moment alone.

She didn't get very many of those.

Alyx pulled the card out of the envelope, smiling at the silly birthday card he picked out.

Alyx,

I'm sorry I couldn't spend the day with you like we had planned to. My dad may have pushed me out of town faster than I like, but I had to make sure you got your birthday present. Today might not be toujours et pour toujours, but I want to make you a promise I will be back. You are my future, Alyx McLean.

I love you. Toujours et pour toujours.

Peter

Alyx ran her fingers over the ink on the card that had recorded Peter's words. It didn't matter that his handwriting was messy, and it was hard for her to read it. It was a message for her. Reading his letters on the page, she could hear his voice. She could imagine him placing a gentle kiss on her forehead as he whispered his declaration of adoration, and his promise of always and forever, just as she had promised him she loved him always and forever before he left with his dad.

This card brought her hope and happiness after an otherwise hard day.

Alyx picked up the box, pulling a knife from her headboard to cut the tape from the small brown box. Once she had it open, she turned the box sideways, letting a black velvet jewelry box land in her hand.

Her mind raced as she stared at the box. Jewelry was a serious gift. Her mind skipped from earrings to ring, to necklace. She glanced at the card again, frozen with the box in her hand. Once she opened it, she would know. Her hopes climbed and crashed over and over. *Toujours et pour toujours* could be represented by so many things.

With a deep breath, she opened the hinged box. Only Peter could make her smile while he was across the country.

Inside the box was a thin gold ring with a simple yet beautiful pattern carved into the top where it was plated with white gold. It was perfect.

Alyx grabbed her phone from her headboard, where she had left it this morning since she knew she couldn't take it with her into the graduation. Her smile fell when she saw that she had two missed calls from Peter. He had probably been trying to get in contact with her to ask how she liked her present. What if he thought she didn't like it. What if he thought she was going to refuse it.

What was the ring for?

Alyx hurried and called Peter back. That had been what she was planning on doing any way. The missed calls just increased her urgency to call him back and let him know that she liked the ring. She wasn't sure if she was ready for what the ring meant, but she also wasn't sure what it meant. The card had been vague. Was it just a ring, a promise ring, or something more?

The phone only rang a couple of times before Peter picked up. "Hey you. How was the rest of your day?"

Alyx shook her head a small smile on her lips. "My day was good. Not as good as it would have been with you, but it just got better."

"You got my present?" Peter asked.

"I did. It's beautiful. But I have to ask…" Alyx paused, staring at the ring. "It's not an engagement ring is it?"

Peter laughed. "No. Trust me. When I propose I will be there, on one knee. I will have talked to your parents, and one of your cousins will likely be in the bushes recording your reaction."

Alyx smiled into the phone before she caught herself. "Then what is the ring for?"

"Do I need a reason to buy you a ring?"

Alyx laughed. "I guess not." She thought about what Peter had said. "Wait. *When* you propose. Not *if*?"

"Every guy has a proposal plan. I didn't say when I proposed to *you*, did I?" Peter teased.

"Oh yeah?" Alyx asked. "So you've bought lots of girls rings for their birthdays then?"

"Nope." Peter told her. "This is my first ring purchase."

"And you bought it for no particular reason." Alyx prodded.

Peter smiled. "I bought it as a promise to eventually replace it with an engagement ring."

Alyx smiled at the ring, setting the box down so she could pull the ring out of the box with one hand and put it on. "I will wear it until then." She promised. "How was your flight?"

"It was good." Peter told her. She heard a door close. "I wish I was there." He sighed.

"Do you know when you start training?" Alyx asked.

"My dad is taking me in tomorrow." Peter told her.

Alyx stood up, moving her gown over on her bed, then sat down. "You aren't going to be able to talk to me while you are there, are you?"

"Not at first." Peter admitted quietly. "I hate this, Alyx. I want to be there with you. We should be celebrating our freedom. Celebrating our accomplishments before starting on our next journey. Instead—"

"You are starting the life you always planned to have." Alyx snuggled herself back on her bed, making sure her pillow was between her and the wall.

"Maybe the life I once thought I wanted to live." Peter told her. "I want a life with you."

"Who says we can't have a life together in espionage?" Alyx asked. "Isn't that how this started? Spies together?"

Alyx could almost hear Peter's smile through the silence on the phone.

"Your dad was right too. Shouldn't your training help keep me safe, whether you go on your mission or not?" Alyx asked.

"I still hate not being there." Peter whispered.

"I know." Alyx told him. "How long is training?"

"Too long." Peter sighed. "I should be able to call tomorrow to let you know I arrived, and give you a mailing address. At least, when the other Generation members came for training, they called their parents, and since mine… I will try to make sure you are my phone call," he promised. "After Basic, I will be living with my dad, so I can call every night, you know, as long as I can get away from him."

They both went silent for a minute, thinking about how different this was from the plans they had been making just the night before.

"Two weeks, Alyx. I promise you'll hear from me in two weeks."

"I'll hold you to that." Alyx whispered.

Peter sighed. "Alyx, I didn't just drop the present off at your house before leaving town today." He admitted. "I made a phone call to Thane, too. I swore him to secrecy until one of us tells him he can tell his dad, or your parents, but he knows about Kalen."

Alyx closed her eyes. "So he's going to tell his dad at midnight."

"No." Peter said. "I'm going to be gone, you're going back to London. You're right. We need more evidence. We can wait to tell them until we find it."

"Thank you." She said. "How did he take it?"

Peter laughed. "About to be expected."

Alyx chuckled, imagining the words her cousin had to say about their secret. "I love you, Peter."

"I love you too." He told her, the words still meaning quite a bit to her, despite hearing the distance between them in his disembodied voice. "Two weeks. I promise." He repeated, before signing off, the distant voice of his dad yelling at him to get off the phone.

As Alyx brought her phone down from her ear, she closed her eyes, trying to memorize the way his voice sounded as he told her he loved her. She wanted to hear those three words, in his voice, from her memories, every time she saw the ring he'd given her on her finger.

Thursday
June 7th, 2012

17:27 BST
Twickenham, London
Feilds Palace

AFTER HOW exciting the previous summer had been, Alyx *hated* how boring her summer had been so far.

Kate and Lynn had left to test the training camp in the early morning hours of the day after graduation. Michael and Thomas were heading back home that morning as well, so Alyx had been put on a plane before she had a chance to even decide if she wanted to go to church or not that day.

Without being able to talk to Kate, Lynn, or Peter, she was beyond bored. She was so bored she finally decided to watch the video Jackson gave her.

Now she wished she had watched it sooner so she could have asked Peter for the full file. She didn't want to believe what she saw.

She found the contact she had named *Sociopath*, and hit call.

As soon as the call connected, Alyx started speaking, not waiting to hear hello. "What the hell is this video?"

"You were the sole witness of what happened to your siblings, so you were interviewed. Your parents didn't like what you said in the interview, so they buried it." Jackson told her.

"Why did you decide to give it to me?" Alyx demanded.

"You think you are so high and mighty. You think you are better than me. This video proves you're not." Jackson said.

"My boyfriend would beg to differ with you." She argued, hanging up and throwing the phone back onto her bed before Jackson had a chance to reply.

If Jackson wanted to play games and try to manipulate her, he would have to try a lot harder.

21:15 EDT
McLean, Virginia
Langley

HALL READ the report on the desk in front of him for the fifth time. It didn't matter how many times he read the report. It wouldn't change what it said. Still, he read it hoping it would. If it didn't, he would have to have a conversation he didn't want to.

He closed his eyes, rubbing his face with his hand.

Just when he thought things couldn't get worse.

Hall lifted his head, picking up the phone from his desk. He wouldn't have come to Washington if he knew this was what was waiting for him. He dialed the number for Neil's work phone, which was quickly answered.

"I got the report," Neil said as he answered.

"What do we do? Alyx will be devastated." Hall asked.

Neil sighed. "Are we sure it was him?"

"DNA says yes." He shook his head to himself. The accident with the grenade meant what was left of his body wasn't even recognizable. But it was him. "Peter Carlyle is dead."

FRIDAY
JUNE 15TH, 2012

20:47 BST
Twickenham, London
Feilds Palace

ALYX EXCUSED herself from the conversation she'd found herself in, walking off to lose herself in the crowds. It didn't matter that she had attended every Feilds Ball since she was fourteen, she felt uncomfortable and out of place, and if that wasn't enough, she didn't even have Kate by her side this year. Translating for her uncle at the Intelligence Conference had been a welcome distraction and way to pass the antagonizing week leading up to when Peter said he could call her. Despite the vastly different demographic and music, Feilds Ball made her think of the Prom she had missed because of her parents' concern for her safety.

"Alyx!" A voice called, a hand brushing her arm as she walked by. She turned to face the voice, seeing none other than the young man the tabloids speculated she was dating last summer. He stuck his hand out.

"I believe I have yet to dance with you tonight," James said.

Alyx looked at the hand, then up at James. He had the

sweetest smile, but his eyes betrayed the questions he wanted to ask her, causing her to hesitate.

"You're not going to deny me my yearly dance, are you?" He prodded, his smile fading as he saw her hesitate.

Alyx took a deep breath, accepting his outstretched hand. "Do you always get everything you want?" She asked him.

"No." He replied, his smile back as he led her to where there were other dancing couples. "For instance, I would love to dance with Kate tonight, but she seems to be notably absent. You wouldn't, by chance, know why that is?"

Alyx rolled her eyes. "I do. It seems she has somehow managed to take my life of freedom in the States, while I have been corralled into hers," she answered as they started dancing.

"Corralled?" James asked. "That is an interesting choice of word."

"I don't want to talk about it." Alyx stated.

James nodded. "Noted. Do you want to talk about your new ring?" He asked, tapping the top of his middle finger against the gold ring on her right ring finger. "You were fidgeting with it while you were walking through the crowd."

Alyx glanced at the ring Peter had given her. She hadn't been wearing it for very long, and already she would subconsciously play with it when she thought of him.

She thought about him a lot.

She had contemplated taking the ring off for tonight. She had learned the hard way the year before that the press was here, and the last thing she needed was them deciding to fixate on her, and start speculating as to why she was wearing a ring on her wedding ring finger. She couldn't bring herself to do that, so she had moved it from her left hand to her right.

"It was a birthday present. A promise ring." She answered finally. "I play with it when I'm thinking about him, and I am supposed to hear from him either today or tomorrow, so being stuck here without my phone…"

"Is making you think of him more." James finished.

Alyx nodded. Dancing with James didn't help either. As he held her hand in his, leading her across the dance floor, she couldn't help but remember when Peter had done the same, twirling her through her backyard. When she blinked, she saw the twinkle lights he had strung in the trees around the yard. When she breathed, she smelled the flowers blooming on the oleander tree. If she tried hard enough, she could imagine it was Peter dancing with her at Feilds ball, not the prince the tabloids spent way too much effort trying to convince their readers she was dating.

James watched as she closed her eyes for a moment and smiled. "You're thinking about him now, aren't you?" He asked quietly.

Alyx opened her eyes, looking at James. "I was."

James gave her a tight smile. "I'm torn between being happy

for you, since I haven't seen you smile like that all night, and hating him because he has left you alone, which made you sad to begin with."

Alyx shook her head. "There are plenty of other things making me sad. I'm not exactly the same girl you danced with last year." She admitted quietly. "He didn't want to leave. And if he could have, he would have called me every day. I'm just terrified I will miss his call."

James nodded. "He wouldn't be where Kate is?"

Alyx shook her head softly, a knowing smile forming on her lips. "No. Have you been in communication with my cousin?" She teased.

"Our families are friends." James deflected. "I thought she might need some friendly messages while in the US."

Alyx' smile grew. "She is with her twin sister. She was staying with me. And my parents. Our cousins on our mother's side were just ten minutes away. She wasn't alone…" Alyx watched to see if James would respond. He didn't; his face slowly turned red. "What happened to her being too young to have a boyfriend?"

"She is. We're not…" James sighed. "I like her. You know that. I just want to—"

"I get it," Alyx told him.

"Do you?" James asked. "It looks like you jumped right into a serious relationship."

Alyx shook her head. "I liked him for a long time, and you

know that. There were also lots of things that drew us together." She smiled. "Does she like you?"

James shrugged as the song ended. "She told me she would like it if I messaged her. I think for now I just want to be her friend. If when she gets a little older she wants to date, I would love it, but I won't force it."

Alyx smiled. They had stopped dancing, but they still held the stiff ballroom dance position. "She is very lucky."

"You aren't?" He asked.

"Peter is amazing, yes, and I am lucky enough that he wants a future with me." Alyx told him.

"I'm glad." James said. He glanced around. Another song was starting up, and more couples were coming to dance while others were heading towards the refreshments, or their tables. He dropped his arms, and almost immediately, Alyx began rubbing her right shoulder. He noticed a few more eyes on her than usual, most of them rigid suits he would recognize anywhere. She had a large security detail. He offered her his arm, escorting her away from the middle of the floor where others were once again dancing. "Michael has spared no expense on security this year." He commented.

"He and Stephan insisted." Alyx said, irritation in her voice. She huffed as she saw Stephan walking towards them with Lyshiria on his arm. "Speak of the devil."

James moved his right arm, causing Alyx to retract the hand

that had been resting in his elbow as he escorted her off the dance floor. He extended his right hand to Stephan. "Officer Cross. I didn't realize you would be attending tonight as a guest."

Stephan nodded. "Your Highness. I always attend in an official capacity, but when Lyshiria asked me to escort her tonight, Michael and I decided it might be wise to have me attend undercover."

James nodded with a smile, turning to Lyshiria. "How do you feel about that?"

Lyshiria shrugged with a smile. "I am just glad to be able to have him by my side tonight."

James laughed. "I can see how that might be preferable."

"If you all wouldn't mind, I think I am going to excuse myself for the night." Alyx interrupted. She nodded to James. "Thank you for the dance." She turned to leave, heading towards one of the sets of double doors that led to the rest of the palace.

Stephan watched after her, twitching to follow, but Lyshiria just patted his arm, shaking her head discreetly. "I will walk with her." She kissed Stephan on the cheek. "I will be back in a moment."

Stephan sighed, letting Lyshiria go. "Let Derek know. He has insisted he be stationed outside her room, considering…"

Lyshiria nodded, telling Stephan that she would.

James watched the interaction with curiosity, maintaining his silence as Stephan watched Lyshiria leave after Alyx, one of the suits he had noticed watching Alyx earlier leaving as well.

"I apologize." Stephan told James as he turned back from watching them leave. "We can't be too careful with her protection at the moment."

"I noticed." James admitted. "If I may, why is it so important for her to be protected right now? She mentioned being corralled into Kate's life while we were dancing."

Stephan took a deep breath, looking at the prince who spent more time at Feilds Palace than was necessary for just his official duties. In many things, he had a security clearance higher than Stephan did. But Alyx wasn't a matter of national security. Michael's interest in protecting her was because of their familial connection, which didn't tie back to the United Kingdom in any significant way. "It's not my secret to tell."

"But she is in danger?" James guessed.

Stephan nodded. He looked around with a sigh. "Do you remember how she spent quite a bit of time here at the end of last year into the beginning of this one?" He asked as he continued to search and make sure no one was within ear shot.

James nodded.

"She was here because she was shot. Her parents thought it would be safer for her to stay here, and Michael agreed. She won't let anyone see, but she's scared." Stephan said quietly.

"Please let me know if there is anything I can do." James offered.

Stephan nodded. "We might take you up on that offer. We have to give her some bad news, and I don't think she will take it very well. She will be mad at Michael and I, so it might be worth it to have you here so she has a friendly face."

"Bad news? What might that be?" James asked.

Stephan sighed again, looking at the door Alyx had left through. "Her boyfriend died in a training accident. She doesn't know yet. No one wants to tell her because they know it will devastate her."

"But she is waiting for him to call her. She said he is supposed to call tonight." James said, urgency in his voice.

"We know. We just don't know how to tell her, but she will start wondering soon. We figured we could let her enjoy tonight, and maybe wait until tomorrow." Stephan shook his head. "She was only just starting to return to normal after..." Stephan's voice broke. "I don't know how she will survive this."

James turned to look where Stephan was. He knew quite a bit about her. He liked to think he was one of her best friends, at least in London. She had felt comfortable enough around him to confide in him about her crush on the boy in her Algebra II class, and he felt close enough to her to tell her about liking her cousin Kate. As much as he was torn seeing her sad earlier, he was happy that she was finally dating her crush. To find out that he was dead, especially so soon into their relationship, was tragic.

If anyone didn't deserve the tragedy, it was her.

21:14 BST
Twickenham, London
Feilds Palace

LYSHIRIA CLOSED the door behind her as Alyx ran to her nightstand, picking up her phone to check for any missed calls. Alyx visibly deflated, locking her phone before tapping it in her hand a couple of times.

"I don't know whether I should be relieved that I didn't miss his call, or anxious because he hasn't called yet." Alyx said.

Lyshiria gave her a sad smile. "Tough choices." She said quietly. "Were you going to return downstairs, or turn in for the night?"

Alyx held onto her phone with a vice-like grip. Lyshiria wouldn't have been able to pry the phone from her hand if she wanted to, and she knew Alyx would have to put the phone back on the night stand if she were to return to the party, so she had her answer, but still, she had to ask, hoping that Alyx might acknowledge the silliness of waiting for a phone call that probably wouldn't even come until the next day.

Instead Alyx shook her head.

"The ball is just reminding me of Peter. I had kind of hoped I might invite him to come with me this year, so not having him here…" Alyx told Lyshiria.

Lyshiria nodded. She could imagine what Alyx felt like. When she had told Stephan she wanted him to be her date to Feilds Ball, she had felt the pit in her stomach when she thought he would have to say no because of his job. Alyx' situation wasn't that much different than her own. She wanted to invite her boyfriend to accompany her to Feilds Ball, but she couldn't because his job got in the way. And now she was waiting for a phone call that wouldn't come.

"You should go back though. I'm just going to get changed, curl up in bed, and watch a movie to try to get my mind off of it." Alyx said.

"Are you sure you're ok?" Lyshiria asked.

Alyx nodded. "Yes. Of course. Go. Dance with Stephan."

Lyshiria gave Alyx a sad smile. "I will come back to check on you after it's over. I will come join you for movies if you haven't gone to bed yet."

Alyx smiled, waving as Lyshiria left the room. Her eyes flickered with annoyance as she noticed Derek Stevens standing outside her door. In Peter's absence, he had insisted to act as her personal guard, following her to London despite there being an entire force of guards at Stephan's disposal to assign to her security detail. There was no way the Circle of Fifths could get Kalen into a position to shoot her, and no way for them to get through their defenses to even make it to her room. If anything, Derek's post outside her door felt like an admission to her being a prisoner, not someone they needed to protect.

Once Lyshiria had latched the door closed behind her, Alyx made her way to her closet to change, reemerging with a pair of joggers and a t-shirt on. As she had promised Lyshiria, she grabbed her laptop, then climbed into her queen-sized bed, settling herself in the center with a pillow between her and the wood headboard. Once she was sufficiently snuggled into her blankets, she set her phone on top of the covers next to her, and opened her laptop.

She searched through her movies, trying to find one that she wanted to watch, which proved to be more difficult than she had anticipated. Her usual choice of movies tended to reside on the spy side of the action and adventure genre, but since she'd been shot, most of them felt too real to her. They reminded her of her current situation. If she was watching a movie, she was trying to escape reality, not relive it. She had been know to sometimes indulge in a romance, typically a romantic comedy, but watching one of those to take her mind off of the phone call she was waiting for wouldn't work.

She selected *The Adventures of Tintin.* It was still an adventure, but it was animated, and was based on a French comic. She hoped it would be light-hearted enough to be the distraction she wanted, while not being too realistic.

When she was about halfway through the movie, she felt her phone vibrate on the bed next to her. Suddenly, she couldn't convince her body to move fast enough. She hit the space bar on her computer with one hand while she snatched her phone up and answered it in one motion, not even looking at the caller ID. She was expecting a phone call from Peter. Who else would it be?

"Hello." She said, anxiously waiting to hear Peter's voice on the other end.

"Alyx, I am so sorry for your loss. I know how much the boy meant to you." A voice that she instantly recognized as Phillip Jackson answered her greeting through the phone.

"What are you talking about?" She asked.

"Peter Carlyle. I just saw the news report about his funeral happening this morning." Jackson told her.

Alyx scoffed. "Why would I believe you? If Peter was dead, someone would have told me. They wouldn't make it so I couldn't go to his funeral."

"If you don't believe me, you can look up the article yourself. I don't know what really happened. Since it's clear he was in Virginia when he died, I assume he was training, so I'm not privy to the incident report like your uncle. All I know is it must have been pretty bad. The obituary doesn't mention a viewing."

Alyx hit escape, making the full screen movie on her

computer smaller so she could open a search window. She typed *Peter Carlyle* into the google search bar and hit enter. She held her breath as her results appeared and she clicked on the top one. What she saw took away her desire to continue breathing. She felt her comfortably numb existence since November shatter and an overwhelming pain take over. She wouldn't believe it. She couldn't believe it. She hit the back button, clicking on the next result from another news site. The Circle of Fifths had far reach. She wouldn't trust just one article. It was on several local sites, and even on some national.

His death had made national headlines. That meant her parents had to know. Not just her uncle. *His death. His obituary. His funeral. His pictures.*

Tragedy.

Car accident.

Life taken too young.

He had his entire life ahead of him.

His parents are struggling with the loss and have asked to be left alone to mourn during this hard time.

Alyx felt like she was reeling. She ended the phone call that was still going, but had been silent since Jackson had given her the news. *Peter was dead, and no one had told her. His funeral had already been held. She had missed his funeral.*

Why didn't anyone tell her?

Alyx closed her laptop before disentangling herself from her covers and getting out of her bed. She slid her phone into a pocket in her joggers, part of her still holding out hope that Peter was alive and would call her any minute. She walked to her door, throwing it open. She needed to find someone, *anyone* to tell her it wasn't true.

Derek snapped to attention as her door flew open and she stormed out. "Alyx," he called, falling into step beside her. "What's wrong?"

Alyx turned to Peter's friend, tears forming in her eyes that she was having a hard time keeping in. "Please tell me it isn't true." She whispered.

Derek knew what she was talking about. He could see it written on her face. She knew. "I'm sorry." He replied.

Alyx covered her mouth, the tears that had been collecting on her bottom lid cascading down. "So it's true? He's dead."

Derek nodded. "Training accident. A live grenade during explosives training."

Alyx felt like she wanted to explode. No one had told her. It was true, and no one had told her. They hadn't just withheld information from her for her safety this time. They had lied to her. They had betrayed her. They had robbed her of her chance to attend his funeral and say goodbye.

Alyx turned and stormed away from Derek. She couldn't be here any more. She couldn't be under the same roof as people who knew her boyfriend died and didn't tell her.

The more chances she gave her family, the more they disappointed her. They withheld, and lied, and mislead her any chance they had.

Alyx found herself in the garage. She couldn't remember most of her journey down here, but she was too out of it to let it concern her. How could she when she had so many other things to think about? She wasn't sure where she was going, but she knew she couldn't stay, and she desperately needed to go for a drive. She grabbed the keys for the Audi, walked over to the right side of the car, opened the door, and climbed into the drivers seat. She had never driven a right hand drive car before, and with all of her uncle's cars being manual transmission, had she been in her right mind, she may have taken a moment to stop and think about what she was doing. It wasn't that she didn't know how to drive manual—she did; it was the fact that she would have to shift with her left hand, which she had never done before. Since she wasn't thinking clearly, she stuck the key in the ignition, turned the key, and pushed the button to open the garage.

As soon as the door was open enough for her to get out, her left foot lifted from the clutch as her right foot pressed the gas. She chirped the tires as she left the garage, and continued spinning tires as she drove across the gravel driveway. She maneuvered around the cars in the way from the Ball, clipping a couple of their bumpers, and causing several drivers waiting out front for their employers to dive out of the way, or risk being hit.

Derek ran out into the garage in time to watch Alyx leave, and witness the chaos she was leaving in her wake. He tried running after her, but he knew it was futile. He looked at the other cars in the garage he might be able to use, but as he looked in them, they were all manual, and he didn't know how to drive them.

He walked back out the garage door, terrified of the destruction Alyx was leaving behind her. They had been playing a delicate game for her sanity, and he feared that they had just lost. That had been why they had opted not to tell her, but somehow, he knew they had only made it worse.

Alyx wasn't afraid anymore. She may have been crying when he last saw her, but she wasn't sad either. No, she was angry. But not at the Circle of Fifths or Jackson.

She was angry at them.

As Stephan walked out the front door to evaluated for himself the situation he had been told they had by his employees, he saw Derek standing in front of the open garage, and he knew. When Derek met his stare, it was only confirmed. Stephan walked over to garage, grabbing the keys for the Jaguar from the wall. Derek didn't even have to be told. He got in the passenger seat. As Stephan went to climb into the Jag, he locked eyes with Lyshiria, who just gave him a small nod. He eased out of the garage, closing it behind them as they left.

They had to find Alyx before she lost herself.

22:03 BST
Twickenham, London
Feilds Palace

ALYX DUG her phone out of her sweat pants pocket, as she drove down the narrow lane leading away from Feilds Palace. She unlocked her phone by typing in her four-digit passcode, then hit the green app with a white phone shape she had pinned at the bottom of her screen. She glanced away from the road to see the screen, selecting Peter's contact from her favorites.

She listened to the endless ringing of her phone waiting to connect her to Peter while her eye sight blurred with tears. Her heart froze as she heard the ringing stop, then crashed.

Hey, you've reached the voicemail box of Peter Carlyle. Leave me a message and I will get back to you as soon as I can.

Alyx hit the red button on her phone, glancing down as she tried to call Peter again. She couldn't give up on him yet. She wouldn't. If she had to fly to Washington and fight her way into Camp Peary, she would.

Peter couldn't be dead.

Stephan accelerated a little more when he finally saw the tail lights for the Audi Alyx had taken up in front of him. He knew she was a good driver, but as he watched the car weave back and forth he shook his head. He would wonder what she was thinking, but he knew she wasn't. She was emotional and distracted. She was not in a state to drive, never mind try to drive a right-hand drive car when she had never driven one before.

When he was confident enough in her not wandering into the lane next to her for a moment, Stephan downshifted, turning the steering wheel to the right, pulling out from behind her, then accelerated to pass her.

As Stephan pulled even with Alyx, Derek looked over into the Audi, watching as she glanced down to her phone, with tears streaming down from her eyes. "She's going to kill herself, and hurt someone else while she's at it." Derek commented.

Stephan shook his head. "No she's not."

Alyx looked over at the two men in the Jaguar that pulled up next to her. Derek gestured for her to pull over. She glared at them. She wiped the tears from her eyes with her right hand. It was habit, with that being the hand that she usually had on the shifter at home. She had forgotten the shifter was on the left, so the car drifted for a moment before she panicked, and put her left hand on the wheel.

With her eyes clear of the tears that had been falling just seconds before, she stuck her foot to the floor, taking advantage of the turbocharged Audi engine that was faster than her car.

Stephan responded, staying next to her, but not quite able to pull ahead of her. He was glad that the road was deserted, and he hadn't been at risk of a head-on collision so far. But if he didn't get ahead of Alyx soon, he was afraid she would end up in the Thames. It was dark, there wasn't any warning for the corner, and they were driving much faster than was advisable. He was familiar with driving these roads. She was not.

Alyx glanced at the car that was alongside her as it started to fall back. She knew Stephan. He didn't give up that easily, and he could definitely make that car go faster. When her eyes returned to the front, she realized why he slowed down. She hit the breaks, trying to downshift, but it was on the wrong side, and it was backwards from what she was used to.

She turned the wheel, desperate to keep the car from going in the river. Her stomach dropped as the car started to slide, the river getting closer and closer. She heard a crunch. She finally got the car slowed to the stop, with just feet to spare. She glanced in her mirror, her brain registering how close she had almost come to ending up in the river, when she noticed the headlights of the Jaguar. The left front of the car was smashed, while the right front tire leaned into the river.

As much as she was mad at Derek and Stephan, they didn't deserve to die.

Alyx took the car out of gear, pulling the parking break, then climbed across the car to get out through the passenger side, away from the river. She walked over to the Jaguar, looking in at the two men she had been so mad at, she had decided accelerating away from them was a good idea.

It didn't look good.

Alyx ran a hand through her hair as the tears resumed their journey down her face. This was her fault. Jackson had told her she was no better than him, and at the moment, she had to agree with him. She hadn't cared who she hurt when she stole her uncle's car, and now two of the people who had risked their lives to protect her more times than she knew…

It had been her fault her siblings were killed when she was five. Now it looked like she had killed the man she had come to see as a brother too.

Lyshiria.

Alyx dropped to the ground, a hand covering her mouth as she started sobbing. Just a few minutes ago, she had discovered her boyfriend was dead. The emotional pain was awful. She wouldn't have wished that pain on her worst enemy. Now she would be the cause of Lyshiria's agony. Stephan had told her before he left for Christmas that he was going to wait a bit, but Lyshiria was his future, and he wanted to start planning his proposal. He was saving for a ring.

She was in pain, so she had caused others pain. Her future had been ripped away, so she had ripped away someone else's.

Life was easier when she didn't care.

Alyx wiped the tears from her eyes, locking her feelings away, where they belonged. She picked herself up off the ground and pulled out her phone. If she was going to act no better than Jackson, she should stop lying to herself. She had a useful skillset. Nothing was keeping her here. All of her loyalties were dead.

Peter had told her that going undercover with Jackson was the nuclear option.

It was time for the nuclear option. She had already destroyed everyone else. She had to redeem herself. If she destroyed herself while she was at it, she didn't care. Not anymore.

She had to at least hear out Jackson's offer.

It didn't take Jackson very long to answer the phone.

"I'm ready to hear out your offer." Alyx told him.

"Glad to hear it." He replied.

Alyx looked at the wrecked cars. "Where do I meet you?"

"I have business in Santa Cruz. Meet me there."

Alyx looked down at herself. She didn't have any money or form of identification. She would have to rectify that in order to get back to California. "I'm in London. It will take me a while to get back to the states."

"Call me when you do. I will give you a meeting place then." Jackson told her. "I look forward to working with you."

Alyx took her phone away from her ear as she ended the call. She had a lot of work to do.

22:36 BST
Twickenham, London
Feilds Palace

Feilds Palace was chaos. When Michael had gotten the call about his car being found at the end of the road, half way in the Thames, he had asked his staff to inform his guests' drivers that they would need to take another route when they left. He then diplomatically asked his guests to excuse him, letting them know he had an emergency to attend to.

With the guests gone, Michael had grabbed the keys to his personal driver, which he rarely used. Lyshiria suddenly found herself in charge of answering the staff's questions as they cleaned up from the ball—until Michael called her.

With Lyshiria now on her way to the hospital, and Michael still down the street with the police, trying to figure out what had happened, and most of their security staff with him, the chaos was perfect for what Alyx needed.

Alyx closed her bedroom door behind her, leaving the light off to not draw attention to the room. She was familiar with the room. She could find what she needed in the dark.

She made her way to her bed, opening up her laptop. She had two tabs open: the movie she never finished, and he news articles about Peter. She opened a third, where she bought a plane ticket to Cancun.

She then went to her suitcase, pulling out the French book she had thrown in before she left, a hairbrush, and a can of shaving cream. She unscrewed the false bottom of the shaving cream, pulling out a wad of cash she had hidden in there. She knew her parents would be less suspicious of her pulling out twenty, thirty, fifty, or even a hundred dollars here and there with the purchases she made, than her pulling out a lump sum when she decided to run, so that's what she'd done. She had gotten cash back with every purchase she'd made for months, slowly accumulating enough money that she felt safe to run.

She tossed the shaving cream can to the side, returning to her closet. She dug around at the back, behind her clothes until she found the backpack she had brought with her in November. She took it out to the main portion of her room, unzipping it to make sure the Maglite flashlight, batteries, atlas, burner phone and charger, paracord, blanket, and envelope of pounds and euros were all in the bag. She shoved the French book at the back with the atlas, and threw the brush in there.

She looked down at what she was wearing. She may have been comfortable, but she would stick out if she didn't change her clothes. She needed to be just another anonymous face in London if she was going to succeed.

Alyx went to her closet, changing into a pair of jeans with a pair of brown flat sole leather ankle boots, and a pastel colored blouse. She found a light grey hoodie, pulling that on over her blouse, shoved a white cardigan in her bag, then put on her brown leather jacket. It was enough layers she should stay warm tonight, and she could remove one as she got warmer while traveling, or ditch one if she needed to lose a tail.

There was one last thing she needed to do before she left. Alyx looked down at the hand where the ring Peter had given her sat. Everything else had been easy for her to do so far. Everything about her life the last few months had prepared her to cut all ties and disappear. With Peter dead, she had no one keeping her here. But still, taking off the ring he'd given her felt like a betrayal to him and his memory. She couldn't keep it. It was a mockingbird laughing at the life she thought she could have. It was also something that would help identify her. Leaving it behind would also send a clear message to those who would try to find her. She took it off, setting it on her nightstand.

She grabbed the keys she had brought in with her, threw her backpack over her shoulder, and took off before she could change her mind about the ring. If she knew what she was doing, no one would be able to find her.

Alyx McLean was dead.

23:17 BST
Twickenham, London
Feilds Palace

MICHAEL LOOKED around at the scene he had been called to. The first officers on the scene had called him when they had discovered the car was his, and that the driver worked for him. The car had been pulled back from the river so they could work on getting the passenger door open without fear of pushing the car into the river. That had also given them the space they needed to open the driver's door and get Stephan out.

When he had arrived, the ambulance with Stephan was leaving for the hospital. His first phone call was Lyshiria, so she could meet them at the hospital. Stephan didn't have any family left, but he deserved at least one person there. If Michael wasn't dealing with the police at the scene, he would have gone.

As they loaded the black body bag into the second ambulance, Michael sighed. As much as he would like to go to the hospital to be there for Stephan, like Stephan had been there to help Michael, and like Stephan had been there to support Kate and

Alyx, he had more pressing concerns to take care of.

He had to figure out where Alyx was.

The police were investigating the hit and run that had led to the car being almost in the river, but Michael knew why the car was on the road in the first place: they had left to chase down Alyx. He didn't know what Alyx knew. Derek did. But he was dead. Michael didn't know where Alyx might go. Stephan would. But he was in a coma in the hospital.

Michael had been entrusted with Alyx' safety. He had been warned she would likely try to run. Her parents had trusted him with her, and he had failed.

He wouldn't fail at finding her.

Michael pulled out his phone, calling Barnes. If anyone could help him, Barnes could.

Once he had Barnes looking for Alyx, he could give himself the time to call Dylan. He needed to inform him of Derek Stevens' death, so Dylan could notify his family in the US. He also had to let his sister-in-law and her husband know that her daughter was missing.

Tonight was going to be a long night.

23:48 BST
Isleworth, London
West Middlesex University Hospital

LYSHIRIA WALKED into the private room Stephan had been taken to after he was evaluated and treated. He was lucky. At least that was what all of the doctors, nurses, and first responders she had talked to had told her.

He was lucky the car didn't go further into the Thames.

He was lucky the car hadn't been hit on the other side.

He was lucky they had gotten him out of the car when they did.

He was lucky the airbag didn't deploy.

He was lucky he was wearing his seatbelt.

He was lucky he had someone to talk to him while he tried to wake from his coma.

As Lyshiria sat down in the chair next to Stephan's bedside, she couldn't help but think about all the people that weren't so lucky tonight, and feel guilty.

Peter was dead.

Alyx had lost her boyfriend.

Derek was dead.

When Stephan woke up, she would have to tell him that Alyx was missing. All he'd wanted to do since he heard she was shot last November, was do everything in his power to protect Alyx. He had threatened to quit his job so he would be free to go to California when Alyx did. If it had been up to him, he would have been everywhere she went. Instead, Lyshira and Michael had talked him out of it.

Now, Lyshiria doubted there was anything they could say to talk him out of going to the ends of the earth to find Alyx once he woke up.

For the moment, as much as she hated it, she was glad he was in a coma. His body needed time to heal before he chased Alyx down.

Hopefully Michael, and Alyx' other family members could find her before Stephan woke up so he would be able to take his time to heal. He wouldn't do anyone any good if he was constantly putting himself back in the hospital because he didn't let himself heal the first time. As much as Lyshiria cared for Alyx, she cared for Stephan more. Right now, he was her priority.

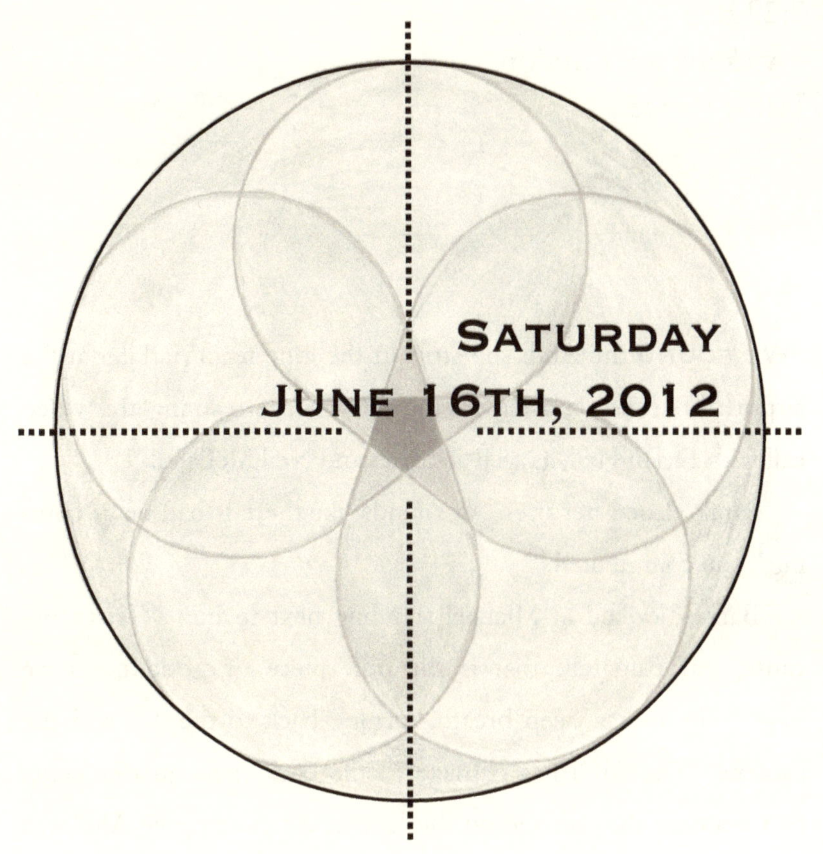
Saturday
June 16th, 2012

7:29 BST
Twickenham, London
Feilds Palace

"WE FOUND the Audi she stole in the long term parking at the airport," Barnes reported to the television streaming the video call with Dylan Hall, as well as Sarah and Neil McLean.

Sarah closed her eyes. "It sounds like there is bad news coming," she commented.

Barnes looked at Michael standing next to him. "That's because, unfortunately, that is the only piece of good news we have." He took a deep breath, turning back to the TV and the camera. "The Audi has damage to the back right quarter panel that matches the damage on the Jaguar. We can't prove Alyx was driving, but it looks as though she was. She is the one responsible for Derek's death, and Stephan's injuries. Whether or not that is the reason she is running has yet to be seen."

"We checked her laptop in her room here. She bought tickets to Cancun," Michael added. "But either she missed her flight, or she never intended to be on it."

"Has the airport been searched? When I pulled her location from her phone like you asked me to, it pinged in the airport." Dylan reported.

"We did." Barnes replied. "Her phone and passport had been turned into the lost and found. Alyx was not there."

"She left her passport?" Sarah asked.

"Yes." Barnes confirmed.

Sarah turned to look at her husband and brother on the other side of the camera, addressing them with her question, not the two in London. "If she left her passport, what is she planning to do?" She shook her head. "I mean, she doesn't have any aliases she can use, does she?"

Neil shrugged. "I don't know. I would guess not, but who knows with her. Especially with how she has been acting recently."

"Where would she get a fake identity?" Hall asked. "She doesn't exactly have the resources the rest of us do."

Sarah and Neil just shook their heads. They didn't know any more than the others on the call. Sarah hated that. She was Alyx' mother. She should know more about her daughter than some stranger, but she didn't. Alyx had become distant, so Sarah knew absolutely nothing about her daughter's life, and she hated herself for that. It had taken her too long to notice the ring Alyx had started wearing.

"Well, if we don't know what name she is using to travel, what do we do?" Michael asked.

"We start checking the pictures of travelers matching her description." Barnes said.

"We have to narrow down the pool of people we are checking though." Hall replied. "If we scour every passenger list, it could take us days, if not weeks or months to find her, and by that time, she could be absolutely anywhere."

Sarah nodded. "She's much smarter than we gave her credit for."

"So where would she go?" Barnes asked. His question was met by nothing but silence.

That was the problem: *no one knew.*

7:33 BST

ALYX WATCHED out the window as the the world blurred by. City turned to the brown and green of farm fields. Soon she would see the blue of the ocean.

At one point in time, she would have enjoyed the scenes she watched out her window.

Alyx turned her attention away from the window, pulling off the grey hoodie. Her leather jacket sat draped over the seat next to her, discouraging others from asking if they could sit there. With her hoodie removed, she put the white cardigan she brought with her on, and rolled up the hoodie to use it as a pillow. She then pulled out the blanket she had shoved in her backpack, and pulled it over her.

It was going to take her a long time to get to where she was to meet Jackson. She might as well settle in and get comfortable. At the very least, she could take a nap while the train she was on travelled to France.

Acknowledgements

While I was writing this book, I called it Trauma. That's not the actual name of the book (obviously), but the ending of Morning-star left Alyx traumatized, Peter traumatized, the readers traumatized (at least my niece), and it was trauma for me to write. Trying to do right by the characters and the readers was difficult, so if you have made it to this page: Thank You. Deciding to continue on the journey of the Promising Generation means a lot to me, and it's why I worked so hard to push through the writers block. There are many more Promgen Files to be written, so Thank You for coming along for the ride.

There are a few people in my life that deserve Thanks for supporting me while writing this. First is my roommate Ambri. Thank you for all the late night brainstorming sessions, and for being my body double so I'd actually write.

I would also like to Thank all of my friends in "The Gang." Thank you for not questioning me when I put in my head phones for my writing sprints at 10 PM, and for not saying anything during my dramatic keyboard smashes, or my Fiiz cup demolitions. I know it's abnormal, but this book was…frustrating.

Last but not least, I want to thank Emmie for being a very willing Beta Reader. I don't know when I'll give you this book (I don't want to traumatize you anymore), but Thank You for reading Morningstar twice before the release, and being so excited while you told me your favorite parts. Don't give up on me after reading the end of this one.

Finally, since the purpose of publishing these books is for the readers, Thank You for reading. But words are just one thing. Actions are another… So for those of you who know what this means, my favorite salad dressing is Caesar, and you will need my first and last initials from the front cover. Happy Deciphering.

www.ingramcontent.com/pod-product-compliance
Lightning Source LLC
Chambersburg PA
CBHW020242030826
48979CB00030B/2479/J